HER DAUGHTER

A NOVEL

Fran Hawthorne

Black Rose Writing | Texas

ISBN: 978-1-68513-699-4
LIBRARY OF CONGRESS CONTROL NUMBER: 2025942943
PUBLISHED BY BLACK ROSE WRITING
www.blackrosewriting.com

Printed in the United States of America
Suggested Retail Price (SRP) $23.95

Her Daughter is printed in Minion Pro

For every Alice and Esme

PRAISE FOR
HER DAUGHTER

"About parenthood, love, the mystery of estrangement and hope of reconciliation, this novel is a stunner."
–Caroline Leavitt, *New York Times* best-selling author of *Pictures of You* and *Days of Wonder*

"In the wake of an acrimonious divorce, Alice becomes estranged from her daughter, Esme, and grows increasingly desperate to reconnect, risking her career and friendships... Part mystery, part family drama, *Her Daughter* is a poignant, page-turning, emotional read."
–Jennifer Rosner, National Jewish Book Award finalist and author of *The Yellow Bird Sings* and *Once We Were Home*

"To read *Her Daughter* is to explore the relentless pain and self-doubt of a mother's estrangement from her only child, especially as the father's vengeful lies keep blocking every pathway to connection. In her poignant, honest depiction of what it takes to persevere, Fran Hawthorne takes us deep into the beauty and strength of human attachment."
–Mary Ann McGuigan, National Book Award finalist (1997) and author of *That Very Place*

"A true page-turner! I was captivated by the richly drawn characters and gripping story, and I'm looking forward to reading much more from Fran Hawthorne."
–David Heska Wanbli Weiden, award-winning author of *Winter Counts* and *Wisdom Corner*

"In this beautifully crafted family drama, unspooled in parallel timelines, a mother strives for answers, questions herself, and aches for a crumb of communication with her long-estranged daughter. Your compassion for both women will soar as you read this relatable and realistic story."
–S.M. Stevens, author of *Beautiful & Terrible Things* and winner of Indies Today's Best Literary Book of 2024

"Alice, a single mom, hasn't heard from her daughter, Esme, in years. But when she learns that Esme has been arrested, Alice begins a desperate journey to find her. Ultimately, Alice's realization of who she is and how she has related to the people around her will go straight to the reader's heart."
–Thaddeus Rutkowski, author of *Safe Colors: A Novel* and winner of the Asian American Writers' Workshop members' choice award

"*Her Daughter* takes us through Alice and Esme's complicated relationship, from Alice's longing for a child, through the unpredictable cruelty of a vengeful ex-husband, and into the mysterious, agonizing period of alienation between mother and daughter. With candor and compassion, Hawthorne highlights the heartbreaking reality of parent-child estrangement, a phenomenon which has grown to epidemic proportions in our time."
–Julie Castillo, author of *The Long Man's Pillow*

HER
DAUGHTER

CHAPTER ONE

The email came from Dan's professional account:

I'm only telling you in case the police contact you. Esme was arrested, but I'm handling everything, and she doesn't want to hear from you.

Alice's fingers couldn't move properly. They hit the wrong keys on her phone, the 7 instead of the 8, the pound sign, the 9; then the stupid phone fell on the tile floor. Finally, she managed the ten digits for Dan's veterinary office. But all she got was his recording. "The Wilson Animal Clinic is closed on Mondays. If your animal needs immediate medical care, please call the Animal Hospital of San Fernando Valley."

On Dan's home line in Calabasas, the phone rang and rang, just like when Alice had tried to talk to Esme six years ago.

CHAPTER TWO

It wasn't true. Her daughter couldn't have been arrested. For what?

Was Esme in a jail somewhere, that very minute? Terrified, shivering, in a bare cement cell with a hard bunk and a stinking, lidless, steel toilet in the corner, clutching her royal blue sorority T-shirt for a blanket?

"That fucking volcano in Iceland erupted again!" someone said sharply in the hallway outside Alice's office.

"Crap. We've been cutting our positions in the airlines, haven't we?" another male voice replied.

"Not enough."

The footsteps in the hallway were moving fast, and Alice shut her office door.

It wasn't true. Dan was playing mind-games with her, the same way he'd been doing in the nineteen years since their divorce. Since before their divorce. Esme wasn't the kind of person to commit a crime and be arrested.

Yeah, and how would Alice know what kind of person her own daughter was or wasn't, since Esme hadn't lived with her for nine years, hadn't spoken a word to her in six, and the sole clue Google had ever revealed was the picture of Esme with her sorority sisters at UC Santa Barbara, cleaning litter from El Capitan?

Dan's email was still blinking on Alice's computer monitor. What could a mother do, sitting in a financial advisory office a mile from Santa Monica Beach?

She could call Roz. Roz might see something Alice was missing. She'd been there for Alice when Alice first started thinking about having a baby, and when Esme needed a sleepover while Alice went to check the forests in Humboldt County, and when Esme had her ballet recital. When Dan went crazy. When Esme ran away to live with Dan. But Roz didn't answer her phone.

Okay, then—even better—Alice could call the police! Surely the police would tell a woman why her own daughter had been arrested. A traffic accident? A protest march that turned violent? Was she in jail? Which police? In Santa Barbara, the city where the detective had found an address for Esme last year? Or Calabasas, near Dan's big house in the hills? For that matter, the arrest might not have happened in California at all. Esme was almost twenty-four years old. Now that she was no longer a student reliably enrolled at Santa Barbara, and still opaque on Google and Facebook, she could be anything, anywhere.

Alice dialed.

"SantaBarbaraPoliceDepartmentCanyouhold?" a woman's voice answered, and then the line went silent.

Outside Alice's window, the sky was pale blue with cheerful clumps of white clouds.

The Esme that Alice knew was the one displayed all around her, in her sunny little office. The framed photo on her wooden desk showing seven-year-old Esme in the pink fairy costume from her ballet recital; one of the photos teenage Esme had dumped in the garbage. The uneven, grayish-brown bowl that six-year-old Esme had made in her pottery class, painted with delicate orange and white flowers. *This bowl is for your pencils at work, Mommy.* Four No. 2 pencils were propped inside it.

According to her computer clock, Alice had been on hold for more than a minute.

Calling the police was a ridiculous idea. The only way to get their attention was to show up in person. It might take two hours to reach downtown Santa Barbara even if Alice left her office in the next ten or fifteen minutes, well before rush hour. She would simply tell Fred that she needed to go…somewhere. With luck, he'd be too absorbed in the Iceland volcano's impact on air travel to notice.

In his corner office, Fred was wearing his wide red tie with a pattern of clowns tumbling downhill, rolling a pencil back and forth on his black desktop with a thin, manicured hand while he muttered to his computer screen.

"I have to go out for a while," Alice said from the doorway.

"No, you don't," Fred replied promptly, without moving his head.

"It's a family emergency."

"The Cordwainer officials will be here in three days."

"I'm sorry."

Fred's snappy voice grew louder and more staccato. "You can't be 'sorry.' It's a three hundred fucking million-dollar foundation, and they're coming to speak with you, specifically. You're the environmental guru of this firm. You're the expert who can explain when companies are doing legitimate environmental goody-goody shit and when it's greenwashing, and why your green portfolio is better than Bank of California's or any other money manager's."

"I'll finish the analysis tonight, after I get home. I promise."

"You know the world is just now pulling its asses out of the worst financial collapse since the Thirties? You know the stock market has barely halfway recovered?" Fred flipped his pencil high toward the track lights above him. "I doubt that carbon-neutral is at the top of these Cordwainer folks' agenda. We can't piss them off."

"I know. I'll get it done." Even if Alice had to write the whole analysis by hand, sitting in the police waiting room.

The pencil landed smack in the center of Fred's outstretched palm. "You sure will."

In Fred's vocabulary, that could be translated as authorization for Alice to leave.

It was hard to run in her Stuart Weitzman kitten heels, down the two flights of stairs from the Seshat Financial Advisors offices to the parking lot. Her left ankle wobbled. She grabbed the iron railing along the staircase, and her shoulder bag kept banging against her side, and the hair in the bun at her neck was shaking loose like Esme's wild hair in her French braids, and the Prius's damn door was stuck. When she finally got started, the traffic on Santa Monica Boulevard inched fitfully past the dusty sandwich shop, past the insurance office that was never open. Reaching Santa Barbara would take four hours at this rate, not two, with Esme maybe sitting in a bare cell while a guard yelled . . .

A little before the next red light, Alice pulled over to try Roz again. Voice mail. But a second later, Roz called back. "Oh, sweetie, I don't believe it." Her husky voice.

"I don't know what to think."

"What could she possibly be arrested for?"

"I don't know!"

"Do you suppose Dan bailed her out? Can you ask him?"

"Ask Dan anything? Are you crazy?"

A short noise came from Roz's end, as if she'd been about to say something else. "No, of course you can't. Where are you now?"

"Driving to the Santa Barbara police station. Trying to."

"I'll be done with my last client at five. I can meet you then."

"Oh thank you, Roz, but you don't have to. That would be such a hassle for you."

"I probably should tell you," Roz said slowly. "I got a call from her. About six months ago."

A thick, steady thrum of cars moved onward in the lanes next to Alice, blue sedans, gray SUVs, white hatchbacks, hybrids, gas-guzzlers, a line of colorful ants, all on their determined route to somewhere. A breath froze in her windpipe. "Esme called you?"

"Yes. Just—"

"And you never told me? What did she say?"

"She wasn't—It was mainly about Jenny. A question about Jenny."

About Jenny? Why would Esme be so interested in news about Roz's daughter? It was years since the two girls had made jewelry and pottery together, the flowered bowl for Alice's pencils, the chains of big fat beads for both mommies. They went on to different high schools, different colleges. "What did she ask about Jenny?"

"We only spoke for a few minutes."

"How many?" Why were Alice's fingers continuing to clutch the steering wheel as if she was still driving, pushing her way into the line of traffic? Alice let go and shifted her butt on the hard polyester seat.

"I don't know. A few."

"Five minutes?"

"Maybe. Four. Six. I don't know."

"Was she congratulating…?" But Jenny wouldn't have been pregnant yet, when Esme called Roz.

"No, no," Roz mumbled. "Nothing like that."

"What was it? What—what did she say?"

"Well, first there was the usual polite, hello kind of thing. 'How are you and Walt and everybody?' Then…" The silence from Roz's end was enough for the inhaling and exhaling of a normal breath. "She asked how long it took Jenny to get fully back to normal after the drugs and the anorexia in high school. If she had any, you know, permanent damage. Like kidney damage or stomach damage."

Alice's stomach was kicking her. The way Esme had kicked when Alice was pregnant. "Esme was on drugs?"

"I'm not saying that."

"But she asked you about drugs."

"Yes and no."

"That's why she was arrested, for being on drugs! Or selling drugs."

"Maybe not, sweetie." Roz's voice was calm and steady, probably the same way she spoke with her most hysterical clients. "The topics people seem to be talking about aren't always what they actually want to talk about. That's one of the basics we learn as social workers."

"Did she—did she say—did she mention specific drugs?"

"No."

"Did you get her phone number?"

"She wouldn't give it to me. And I forgot to do that star-six thing. I'm sorry."

"What else did she say to you? Where was she living? What was she doing? Did she have a job?" There were too many questions, too much missing information that Alice should have known about her own daughter.

"She didn't really say anything else."

"Nothing?"

"She just—She just asked me not to tell you that she called."

The May sunshine bored through the windshield. Alice pressed the phone tight against her cheekbone.

"That's why I didn't tell you about the conversation before today," Roz rushed on, no longer so calm and steady. "I was trying to keep the channel open with her, because I was afraid she'd cut me off. If she's still as stubborn as she used to be. Remember when she decided to copy Jenny, and she wouldn't eat any food unless it was orange?"

For months and months, when Esme was four years old, those meals that had consisted entirely of carrots, orange juice, and Kraft macaroni and cheese. Tricolor pasta, but only the orange noodles. Tortilla chips. Even her shampoo had to be orange-color, and Roz miraculously found a brand made from apricots.

"Look," Roz said, "if it was simply about drugs, she could have called any addiction clinic to ask those sorts of questions. She deliberately contacted me."

"Because of Jenny."

"Yes, but why would she go out of her way to phone her mother's best friend, to ask about the friend's daughter? You see?"

"See what? That Esme was worried about drugs? That she still hated me and wouldn't dream of calling me or emailing me directly?"

"No!" For that single word, Roz's voice jumped almost to a shout. "Subconsciously, I think she might have been reaching out to me as a substitute for contacting you. So I thought she would call again in a few weeks. And then eventually I'd ask her if I could tell you about our conversations. And that could be an opening."

Roz and her rose-colored glasses as red as her hair, always the social worker with her faith in God, even in college, trying to find the happiest possible explanation for bad news. *Esme wasn't on drugs. Esme had actually wanted to talk to Alice.* Roz meant well, but she was wrong. The likeliest explanation was the most straightforward. Esme had asked about Jenny's drug use because she herself was seriously on drugs, and she didn't want to speak to her own mother.

"I have to go, Roz. Before I get stuck in rush-hour traffic."

"Call me later?"

"Sure. Thank you."

"I'll pray for you, sweetie."

"Okay."

Sweat was trickling into the neck of Alice's silk blouse, and a mistyped text beeped from Fred: "Alterntvs to solar & wind?" "K," she typed back. "Light green ok" he immediately added. Solar energy. Carbon emissions. Drugs. Jenny. Santa Barbara police. "Yes," she typed. A gap opened up in the traffic stream one lane over, as the cars slowed for a red light at the corner, which was the only good luck so far in sight.

CHAPTER THREE

"Please move away from the window, ma'am," said the woman in the short-sleeved, navy-blue shirt on the other side of the bullet-proof glass. Her voice was curt, and her hair was blonde and straight, cut barely below her ears.

"Sorry." Alice released her elbows off the smooth countertop in front of the window.

Her blazer was too heavy for this warm, crowded lobby. Her butt hurt from three hours on a car seat. Her throat screamed with dryness. But to the blonde policewoman behind the bullet-proof glass, her appearance needed to declare: *I'm not a common criminal like other people who come in here. I wear designer shoes and a blazer. I help university endowments and nonprofit institutions and pension funds like yours in the police department invest billions of dollars in environmentally conscious companies every year!*

"Esme Wilson," Alice repeated, a little louder, from her new spot further away from the policewoman.

The woman typed on her computer keyboard. "No one of that name is in custody at this time," she said without glancing up.

In custody at this time. "In your jail?"

"In custody. That's what that means."

So, Esme wasn't sitting in a dark, dank basement cell underneath this police headquarters building, shivering desperately from drug withdrawal. She might be partying with friends this very minute.

Strolling along the beach. Dan might have bailed her out. There had, nevertheless, been an arrest. *At this time.* Alice grabbed the counter edge, although it meant she was pulling herself an inch closer to the forbidden glass. "Was she, before now? In custody?"

"I can't go searching through years of records." Finally, the policewoman was looking at Alice, her voice clearly exasperated.

"No, no, of course not. Not years."

"When was the arrest?"

Dan's email hadn't said when, but it must have been recent. Why would he delay telling Alice? "I'm not sure. Maybe yesterday?"

With a huge, obvious sigh, the woman slapped a few more keys. "Not yesterday."

"Or the day before?"

"Are you going to ask me to go through every day of the past week? The past six months? There are limits to the availability of public records."

"I'm sorry." Alice swallowed. "I thought you could find it, just based on her name."

"What were the charges?"

"I don't...." *Esme was arrested*

Esme Wilson, age twenty-four next month, five feet three inches, wild brown hair, browner eyes, thick eyebrows, heart-shaped face with a dimple and a lovely small chin, front lower teeth that crowded each other a little, last known address east Santa Barbara, California, had been arrested for something, on some date, at some place.

"I can't help you right this minute, ma'am. You'll have to wait." The policewoman was already waving to the teenager behind Alice. He might have been a surfer, the sunburn on his nose peeling from crepe-thin brown to baby pink.

Alice backtracked to the wall opposite the policewoman's counter, stumbling against one of the bright blue, molded chairs that were positioned against the bare wall like a lineup of suspects. An endless parade of people crossed over the brown tile floor between Alice and the desk officer with her all-important computer. The sturdy, black leather shoes were most likely police. The dirty sneakers would be from prisoners and visitors. What shoes would Esme have been wearing when she was arrested? She'd loved Ugg boots in junior high and high school, the same as every other teenager in America. When she was little, she had four pairs of jelly sandals—bright pink, orange, purple, and sparkly silver. She wore them to the Santa Monica Beach, where she dug fishing pools in the sand using her green plastic shovel with a frog's head at the top of the handle, and she dug and dug without ever getting deep enough until the shovel broke the summer when she was five years old, and they had to go to four different stores to find a replacement because the season was almost over and the stores were out of beach toys. "And the waves never stop, Mommy?" she asked. "No, honey. They never stop."

The surfer had left the counter, and a short, bald man in a tan golf shirt had taken his place. Alice's phone rang. Roz's number.

"No cellphones!" snapped a policeman passing straight in front of her, and he jabbed his forefinger toward a sign on the wall above her. *Please turn off all cellphones*, with a sketch of a red diagonal line slashed through a phone. But what if Esme called? What if she called now, in a panic, for the first time in six years?

The bald man in the golf shirt had disappeared, and the policewoman was waving. At Alice?

Through a narrow dip under the glass, the woman slid a computer printout. "I found the case you were looking for. April 25, 9:45 p.m."

April 25? A month ago?

"It's forty cents. Twenty cents per page," the officer added.

Briskly, like a normal person on perfectly normal business, in kitten heels and a professional blazer, not like a mother whose daughter had been arrested, Alice walked out the building's arched entryway and down one short tier of steps to a white stucco ledge where a normal person might sit. A cluster of rough shrubs brushed against her hip, and the ledge was gritty with a thin scrum of dirt. Feet in police shoes climbed the steps past her.

Two names, two pieces of paper.

Wilson, Esme, Calabasas CA, DOB 6/17/86

Corning, Robert, Cincinnati OH, DOB 9/25/85

Apprehended at 9:45 pm on April 25. Burglary, forcible entry, trespass, and vandalism, at an address in Santa Barbara

Esme Wilson had been released on her own recognizance to Dr. Daniel Wilson on April 26.

Robert Corning had been released on $30,000 bond on April 28, co-signed by Esme Wilson.

Why would Esme co-sign a $30,000 promise to a burglar? Because he was her drug dealer? Her boyfriend? Both?

CHAPTER FOUR

ALICE AND DAN

December 1984
Westwood, CA

Small gray-green Pacific waves dribbled onto the shore. The sand rolled unevenly past deserted lifeguard huts and concrete cubes of shuttered bathrooms and Greek-columned lamp posts, not yet lit for the evening. Across the highway, a few clumps of brush and trash clung to ledges on the steep cliffs up to Ocean Avenue. An orange-and-white sawhorse balanced, wedged at ninety degrees, against one outcropping.

"Is your heart set on Bali?" Dan asked, swinging Alice's hand.

The sand dipped, and they stumbled for a moment.

"Don't get me wrong. Bali looks amazing," he added. "Miles of blue waves and waterfalls. Exotic, fresh seafood. Ancient temples."

"Hiking trails overlooking the shore."

"A monkey sanctuary."

"Dirty beaches we can clean."

Dan's dimple flickered as he grinned. "You bet. We're not merely going on a decadent foreign vacation. We're saving the planet at the same time."

"Exactly." With her free hand, Alice tapped Dan on his perfect, straight nose.

"I'm only asking because I found a couple of other eco-cleanups in Thailand and Spain that are less expensive. They all have beautiful, dirty beaches and great food, so honestly, I'm fine with any of them."

A single white rectangle rested on the ocean's edge, against the horizon. A cruise ship, filled with lucky tourists headed to Bali? Or Thailand?

Dan tickled Alice's intertwined fingers, and she leaned over to kiss his cheek, which was smooth though chilly in the December air.

"Of course," she told him. "It doesn't have to be Bali."

"I promise, we'll go to an exotic beach somewhere that needs environmental volunteers."

"And if we can save money, like you said."

"And I'll make certain they have chardonnay."

"Thank you for handling all the research and organizing. You know, if you want me to take care of the plane tickets or something?"

"It's fine." Dan kissed her in return, a nice, warm, long one on the lips. "I enjoy organizing things."

A seagull streaked low over their heads, shrieking, and an instant later a shaggy, brown-and-white dog was racing along the sand after it.

With a short whistle, Dan squatted while the dog abandoned the seagull to trot over to him. He scratched the dog's head between its long, floppy ears. "Silly boy. You'll never catch that bird."

Bending slightly, Alice patted it once on the head.

"Try stroking a little more," Dan told her. "He won't bite you."

Two children were running along the sand from the direction the dog had come, bulky in their bright green winter jackets, their high-pitched shouts flying in the wind like the cheerful upper notes of a horn. A man and a woman followed more slowly, the man holding the woman's elbow. A faded Dodgers cap was clamped on top of the woman's head.

"Buffalo!" one of the kids called out, waving. "Come back here!"

The other child repeated, "Come back!"

They were little, the sizes of maybe a three-year-old and a six-year-old. The dog barked toward them, its tail swishing rapidly.

"That's a beautiful animal," Dan said, giving the dog a long pat before straightening up, as the man and woman arrived. The kids and dog started chasing each other in a circle. "Part English Springer Spaniel, right?"

"You got that." The man nodded.

Dan grinned at the dog. "Still a teenager."

"Oh yeah? You can call dogs teenagers? We figured he's just an overgrown puppy."

A shout came from the kids-and-dog circle. The bigger kid yelled and threw sand at the smaller one, who burst out crying.

"You boys, stop it!" the father shouted.

"Ricky hit me!"

"Noah was pushing Buffalo!"

"I was not!"

The mother started walking surprisingly fast through the lumpy sand toward the boys and dog, and the boys hurled themselves at her, hugging her around the waist and legs. One after the other, she worked magic, patting one head, kissing another, then tickling them both, and murmuring something to the dog, too, as it dashed to each of them, until her sons broke away, laughing, and chased the dog further down the sand.

●　　　●　　　●　　　●　　　●

"Did you have a chance to read the brochures from Spain?" Dan asked, slicing a meatball on his plate.

"You're changing the topic."

"What topic?"

"Jenny. Roz and Walt's new baby."

Across the kitchen table from Alice, Dan chewed for far too long. Heavy rain was punching the narrow window above the sink. "I thought we were done with that."

"You and Walt sure looked like you were having a good time yesterday, playing with your light sabers with her." The way Jenny had laughed, a trill of birdcalls, as she grabbed for the flashes of blue light zooming from Dan's saber and the red flashes from Walt's.

"Alice."

"What?"

"We both agreed, when we got engaged. No kids."

Alice stretched out her hand to stroke Dan's arm. Her fingers slipped, brushing against a mushy edge of his mashed sweet potatoes, so she pulled away. "You're right, we agreed. And I meant it when I said it, back then. But that was five years ago, Dan, and people change their minds. All the time." With her napkin, Alice wiped the potato mess off her hand. "You've established your clinic now. I got the promotion at Seshat. I'll be twenty-eight in a few months."

A series of thuds rumbled above their heads, along with muffled shouts. The twins in the apartment upstairs, no doubt stir-crazy after hours stuck indoors, must have been jumping and running across their floor. *Is this honestly what you want?* Dan was probably thinking. *This kind of noise and commotion that kids make?*

Yes.

"You know," Alice went on, speaking too fast, "seeing Walt and Roz with Jenny stirs a lot of feelings in me. The idea of cradling my own warm, tiny baby in my arms, the way Roz holds Jenny. Do I really want to spend the rest of my existence working and going on hikes and—what? Cleaning up a beach in Bali or Spain? Saving endangered owls? I mean, that's okay, but maybe I could have more. Not just a thing I do, but a different way of being a person, of loving—I can't describe it. Don't you think about those kinds of questions, too?"

Dan sliced another meatball in half. Did he honestly like the meatballs? Alice had overcooked them again.

"You've been saying you'd like to buy a house," she added. "A house with a yard and room for a new dog. That would be a major life-change, wouldn't it?"

"A house is not a baby, Alice."

"I know that. I'm just pointing out that people change about all kinds of things."

"You can't suddenly declare that you've changed your mind about having kids and expect me to go along."

"I'm not. I'm suggesting we could talk about it."

"I don't want to." Standing, Dan took his empty plate and gestured toward Alice's. "Are you done?"

She was handling this all wrong. Dan's focus was on getting his animal clinic on its feet, with only enough spare brain cells to plan the vacation he certainly needed. He was worried about attracting enough clients and repaying the loans from his mother, and of course still hurting from his old dog's death. He wasn't imagining a curly-haired little boy digging in the sand all the way to China with sunburned arms and a stubby plastic shovel. A little girl, with dark blue eyes like his and light brown hair like Alice's, pointing to each letter of the words in the picture book wide open in her lap. D-O-G

To be fair, too, it was easier for her to change her opinion about the kid thing than it was for Dan. He'd had a lousy childhood that he didn't want to duplicate as an adult, while Alice simply hadn't thought much about the topic. Marriage, baby carriage, maybe, maybe not. At that moment, when she was twenty-two years old, freshly graduated from UCLA, scared, insecure, scrounging for whatever kind of job she could get with a useless degree in environmental studies, when she and Dan were sitting on the picnic blanket on Santa Monica Beach and he uncorked the bottle of chardonnay and turned to hand her a wineglass, only instead of a glass it was a little velvet ring box, and her breath stopped in her throat, and he ran his fingers through her hair—being a mother was nowhere in her mind.

If she waited a couple of months, until Dan's clinic was more established and he was feeling more relaxed, that would be a better time to raise the topic.

"I'm saying we ought to consider it. Eventually. That's all." Alice smiled.

Dan leaned over until his face was close to hers. His blue eyes, unblinking, with their extravagant lashes; his black hair curling around his ears; his round chin; the tiny, jagged-oval scar on the left edge of his jaw that a person could see only if she was near enough to kiss him. He stroked her hair against her cheek. Then he kissed her, languidly, from the left side of her lips to the right.

"No, thanks," he said.

"We could get a dog, too, if you want."

Dan emitted a long sigh. "I am not bargaining with you, Alice."

A shout came from somewhere. It could have been a person on the sidewalk whose umbrella had turned inside-out. A driver, yelling at a cyclist. Nothing that Dan could blame on children.

He'd laid out two bowls of cat food on the linoleum, and the cats were already lapping noisily. He returned to the table. "We're a team. Dr. and Mrs. Daniel Wilson, cleaning up the beach in Spain. You and me against the world. We don't need anyone else." Wrapping his right hand around her left, Dan gently pushed apart Alice's fingers, one by one, until his thumb bumped into the hard gold of her wedding ring. He stroked a half-circle around the ring, then glided his thumbnail into her palm, along the skin, and down to her wrist. "That's the radial artery. The one people slice open when they kill themselves."

"Dan!" Alice tugged her hand away. "What're you doing?"

He kissed her again. "Simply changing the topic of conversation. Thank you for cooking dinner tonight."

CHAPTER FIVE

ALICE AND DAN

February to June 1985
Santa Monica, the San Fernando Valley, and nearby

The Northern Spotted Owl once ranged across the towering forests of the Northwest from British Columbia all the way to the edge of San Francisco. It relies on trees such as the wild Douglas fir and the Western hemlock that are at least three hundred and fifty years old. However, the survival of these majestic birds is increasingly at risk due to intensive logging, and the expansion to the Humboldt County acreage under consideration would

Seshat's pensions and foundation clients would scoff, of course, at phrases like "towering forests" and "majestic birds" when they read Alice's report. Fred would groan dramatically. "Green poetic bird shit," he would say.

So, it was a draft, twenty-seven pages paper-clipped in an orange folder on Alice's desk. She could easily revise it before handing the final version to Fred. Eliminate the poetry.

But in that case, if all she was going to discuss in her report was the same basic financials that any traditional analyst would include, she'd wasted her time fighting for her new title as Seshat's environmental impact specialist. If her title was to mean anything, she had to find the words that would make these investment clients envision the actual owls and the trees. Or, if that was asking too much, to envision the negative PR that would result from being seen as hurting those wise owls and majestic trees, if they continued to fight the environmental groups' lawsuits against clear-cutting in Humboldt County, Oregon, Washington, and Canada. To consider, for that matter, that the environmentalists might actually win their lawsuits. Did these officials in their nice leather loafers truly want to be seen as killing majestic, endangered owls?

Dammit, the poetry was staying! Fred might groan, but in the end he would give in.

The most recent photo from Roz, framed in heavy silver, was propped on Alice's desk near the orange folder. One-year-old Jenny sat on Roz's lap, sucking the second and third fingers of her left hand and wearing a forest-green dress with a wide white collar, her chubby legs in their white tights jutting straight out on top of Roz's thighs. Roz and Walt also wore green. They were grinning broadly, sitting side by side. Roz's hair cascaded below her shoulders like auburn ballroom drapes, and a necklace of big black beads dangled around her neck. Her tortoise shell-framed eyeglasses had been removed for the few minutes of picture-taking, though Walt had kept his rimless pair. Her hands were clasped over Jenny's belly, and Walt had one skinny arm wrapped around her, protecting Roz protecting Jenny, a beautiful spiral circling forever.

•   •   •   •   •

Silently, Alice gave Dan her list as he walked out of the bathroom.
Ten Reasons To Have a Baby

1. *You could take him/her to see all the future* Star Wars *movies I don't want to see.*
2. *And Dodgers games.*
3. *We can all go hiking in Joshua Tree, and you two can howl at the sky like coyotes.*

4. *He/she might want to be a vet and help you in the clinic.*
5. *He/she will be a playmate for the cats. And when you're ready to get another dog, think about how much fun it will be for the dog to have a kid to play with.*
6. *You can watch him/her grow up and see whether he/she has any of your physical characteristics. (your curly hair? your dimple?)*
7. *I will change all the diapers.*
8. *I will clean all the messes (like spilled food).*
9. *I will get up in the night when the baby cries. You will never have to.*
10. *I won't nag you anymore.* ☺

Dan spent a few seconds eying the words. He opened his mouth. Then, instead of saying anything, he brushed a kiss on the side of Alice's forehead, folded the paper, and slid it into a rear pocket of his jeans.

●   ●   ●   ●   ●

Inside the dark, concrete-walled basement club, Alice and Roz's tiny table wobbled as Roz picked out a chunk of ice from her glass of Tab. She crunched it energetically. "Thanks, Alice. Boy, I needed to get out of the house. Jenny was driving me crazy, climbing all over me and Walt."

"She was pretending to be a squirrel. It was sweet." Alice put down her glass of tasteless chardonnay. "Anyway, I told James I'd come to the open mic here to listen to his new songs, and he needed me to bring more bodies with me."

"I hope his band is on soon. I'm eating too many peanuts, waiting for him."

"I think you're about to get your wish."

Three figures climbed onto the stage, which was raised only a couple of inches above the floor. One of them pulled off several white cloths that had covered a drum set in the corner. Another, carrying an acoustic guitar, fiddled with the long arm of a mic stand. "Check," he intoned into the mic, his voice echoing too shrilly through the room. And "Check" again, a little less shrill. James took his guitar and a wooden chair to a different mic stand. Sitting down, he bent halfway over and began adjusting the tuning pegs, his head almost caressing the instrument's long neck. Behind the stage, a mural filled the entire back wall with muted sketches of people playing guitars, pianos, drums, violins, saxophones, even a harp.

As soon as it began, the music pulsed through Alice's blouse. *Da da DA da DA da da DA da da da DA* "*When I heard the rain, and the shouting was insane,*" James sang in his imitation-Dylan rasp, spread-legged in his seat. His sun-blond ponytail fell over one bony shoulder, smooth and long like it was in high school. The top three buttons of his white shirt were undone, and a hint of his right kneecap poked through a rip in his jeans, a glimpse of blond hairs and pale flesh shining in the spotlight.

He arrived at their table when his set was done, holding a bottle of Dos Equis, of course, along with his guitar. "Hey." He cocked his beer toward each of them. "Thanks for being here and boosting my attendance numbers." Maybe a dozen other people were sitting at the scattered round tables, plus two who were already moving toward the exit.

"I came because Alice promised me free peanuts," Roz said, plucking one more from the metal bowl on their table.

"Was that first song new? The one about driving away in the rainstorm?" Alice asked.

"You like it?"

"It's got a fantastic beat. I was practically jumping up and dancing right here at our seats."

"Yeah. Well, sorry. I wrote it two years ago." As he sat, James stretched out his long, lean legs, a sandaled foot almost touching the foot of Alice's chair. "My creativity's dried out. No one's interested in my style anymore. Sixties. Dylan. Pete Seeger."

Alice exhaled. "Every six months you go through this drill, James. Is your music any good? Should you give up and copy the Top Fifty instead?"

James grinned at her over the lip of his dark-green bottle.

"Dylan just had a gold album, by the way," Alice added.

"He's not the same Dylan."

"Stop it! Why do you think I asked you to play at Dan's and my wedding? Because people would hate your music? Come on, you know I love your songs. And that one you wrote for Dan and me, about dancing in the ocean, on top of the ocean?"

"That song was really beautiful," Roz agreed.

"And I love your oldies, too, okay?" Alice went on. "They make me feel as if we're both sixteen again, hanging out in your parents' basement, listening to Dylan on the stereo and drawing Earth Day posters."

"Trees with green peace signs." James tipped his bottle while he smiled.

"I tried to draw doves in a few of my trees, holding the peace signs in their beaks. But they looked like blotchy white leaves."

"They looked great, Allie. I was impressed. They were classic snow-covered trees, not blotches."

"Did you guys have a particular reason for making those posters?" Roz asked. "Were you planning to take them on protest marches?"

James frowned at Alice. "Do you remember why? It might've been for a contest."

People were bustling around the stage area now. With a screech, a musician dragged one of the mic stands to a new spot. The confined air in the room was growing warmer and crowded with the smells of beer, cigarettes, and sweat. James kicked languidly against Alice's chair. Quietly, he began singing the refrain from "Shelter from the Storm" while he strummed the side of his bottle.

Roz hummed along with him for a few bars, off-key as always. "If you want to try a different style, James, I could hire you for Jenny's next birthday party. Do you know 'The Wheels on the Bus'?"

"*How does it feel, to be a wheel, on a bus?*" James murmured. "I'll make you a playlist, Roz."

"That sounds great."

"I like singing with kids, because they get so into it."

"Yes!" Alice shoved her paper napkin toward James. "That's my point. That's who you are, in your soul. Music runs in your veins instead of blood. Isn't that what you told me ages ago? Since before I met you. Since you got your first calluses from your first guitar. You were twelve?"

"Nine."

"That proves my point even more."

On the stage, a guitarist was testing a few chords – more cheerful ones, no doubt, than what James would have chosen.

Alice's foot, in her black Birkenstock sandal, edged toward James's long, thin toes.

He ran his fingertips up and down the side of her glass.

Abruptly, Alice stood. "I need to leave. I'm sorry, I have an early meeting with an important group of investors tomorrow. James, I'm getting tired of re-boosting your ego every six months, but I'm telling you this: I went to every single dance when your band played in high school, even if I didn't have anyone to dance with, and I'm going to buy every single one of your albums someday, so you can't quit playing guitar." She tapped lightly against his stubbly jaw, brushed her lips on his cheek, and hefted her shoulder bag. "Roz? Are you ready to go? Could I give Jenny a goodnight kiss when we get back, without waking her?"

•   •   •   •   •

Sunday

"What did you think of my list?"

"I know you want a baby, Alice."

And?

Thursday:

"Dan, I realize that your parents weren't the warmest of people. We don't have to be the same as them. We'll just copy the best parts. Like when your father used to take you to Dodgers games, before they got divorced."

"I have plenty of friends to go to the games with."

Of course, but …

Saturday, a week later:

"Is this a bad time to talk? We can talk another time."

"I've told you, Alice. I'm happy with my life the way it is. I'm happy with you. That's enough for me."

Dan would never say yes. He wouldn't even discuss it. Not when she was twenty-eight, not when she was thirty, not when she was thirty-eight. There would never be a "right time," nor any magic words to change his mind. He was forcing her to choose, him or a baby.

To quit? To lock the door on having children, forever? Never to have an eight-year-old son who would race her into the waves, or a teenage daughter she would take shopping for her first pair of heels for her high school prom? A little girl who would pick up a smooth shard of sea glass and ask, *Mommy, is this a diamond?*

All right then, have a baby, and the hell with Dan! It was his fault for forcing this decision. She'd find someone else. The world was full of men who would love to be a father. For that matter, she could forget all about men and go to a sperm bank, or adopt.

But to throw away their marriage? His fingers tickling hers, dammit, and his dimple, his lips on her neck, and his firm, warm body spooning her in bed. Their trips to Joshua Tree; the time he stood on a boulder at the Wonderland of Rocks and howled like a coyote. When she was pricked by the cactus, how he patiently picked the spines out piece by piece and then kissed her arm until the chills overwhelmed the sting. The way he proposed to her, with a wine bottle and a diamond ring on the beach. For that matter, his loving patience with animals, didn't that prove he'd be a good father? And her half-raw roast chicken and burnt meatballs, only a person who truly loved her would tolerate that.

Divorce was so drastic.

She'd almost tried it already.

Right after Dan had proposed, and she'd said yes, and then she'd panicked. What was she doing? She was too young to tie herself down. She needed more experience, more options. Where would a person go in order to test whether she was ready for marriage? To a convenient bar. Order a glass of chardonnay. Pretend to chat with the bartender, who must have played out that same script every night of the week, until some guy in a dark suit rested an elbow on the counter next to her. *Mind if I sit here? What're you drinking?* She knew she wouldn't go to his place with him after these drinks and have sex, so did it make any difference?

You save trees? That's an unusual job description. How do you save them?

The guy was too old for her. His wavy hair was as gray as rain clouds, and he had kids in elementary and junior high school, a freckled boy and a gap-toothed girl, in the photos he pulled out of his wallet to show her. He was divorced, so he claimed. He bought her a second glass of wine. When he leaned over to open his wallet, his jacket brushed her sleeve, and he smelled of breath mints. He was—he laughed a little—a divorce lawyer. *Well, someone's got to do it.*

I'm sure you have other hobbies.

In fact, I'm training for my first marathon.

Really? How far do you run every day, to practice?

When he asked for her phone number, she gave him a fake one.

So nothing had happened.

But she'd been tempted. How could she marry Dan, if she'd been almost flirting with another man? Actually flirting.

She'd told him, the following evening, sitting in his Camaro. "Dan, I think it's a mistake. To, you know... do this. Too soon."

"This?"

"Get married."

He didn't say a word. He stared out the windshield, his fingers gripping the steering wheel.

"I mean," she mumbled, "we could keep dating. Or see other people, too. Or separate, for a while. Take a breather."

Still, Dan didn't speak.

"Dan? Don't you have any reactions, to what I'm telling you?"

His voice sounded almost robotic. "Please. Alice. I'm paralyzed."

"What do you mean?"

"I can't move."

"I don't understand. You're talking. Isn't that moving?"

The way his face was positioned, facing straight ahead. His dark blue eyes and rich black lashes. The scar on his jaw. His mouth, slightly open. He wasn't smiling or quizzical, nor serious or annoyed. None of his usual expressions. His face was naked. And it was true, he wasn't moving, not even blinking. His arms didn't twitch; his fingers didn't tap on the steering wheel or on his thighs. He didn't shift his weight. A foot didn't shuffle the floor mat.

"Dan?"

Was he truly paralyzed? At the thought of losing her? He was breathing, certainly.

The exposed skin of his wrist didn't jerk when she tapped it. Up the dark hairs of his forearm, to his shoulder, under the light cotton of his shirt. Touching him was like touching his mother's polished dining-room table. Nothing stirred. She kicked, gently, against his shin. Still no reaction.

Except for the shivers that shot through her own arm and spine.

He loved her. He loved her so deeply that his body itself was begging her to stay. How could she abandon a future with a man who loved her like that?

"Dan—Move! Please! Do something." She tried to pull him toward her, but his dead weight was too heavy. Burying her face against his curly hair, she tugged again and frantically kissed all around his head. Until, finally, his hand touched her shoulder.

•   •   •   •   •

A baby? Or Dan?

Why did she have to choose?

What if, instead …. If it was a done deal? A *fait accompli.* If Dan held his own baby in his arms and looked into eyes as blue as his own; if he rested his fingers against soft hair as black and curly as his. If the baby gazed back at him and clutched his finger with its fingers and let out the quietest wisp of a sigh. Wouldn't he change his mind then?

She could do it. "Forget" to use cream with her diaphragm. Put it in hours too early.

No. Not that way. Not by cheating. That would be so wrong. Tricking Dan.

•   •   •   •   •

Georgia Wilson brushed a sharp, bright-red fingernail against a couple of the orange and pink rose petals in the small cluster that Alice held out toward her, from across her kitchen island. "Thank you," Georgia said, without taking the bouquet. Instead, she picked up a packaged box of crumb cake from the granite counter and strode toward her dining room. Alice followed her mother-in-law, clutching the roses.

Two places were prepared at one end of the long, polished, dining room table, each with a bowl and plate of Georgia's gold-edged Lenox, a five-piece setting of her heavy silverware, and a white damask napkin folded in an isosceles triangle. Georgia sat at the head. Alice's spot, at her left, looked straight out the sliding-glass doors to the sloping garden and patio where Alice and Dan had been married. Pink hibiscus and orange-yellow marigolds huddled near the doors, while bougainvillea spread, gloriously purple, up the hill.

The dining room had a tall cabinet, a grandfather clock, and two extra chairs, but no vase or any other container appropriate for a set of roses with long, wet stems. Alice put the flowers in her lap. Then she moved them onto the tabletop.

"Apparently, we have some sort of indoor-outdoor infestation now." Tipping her dessert knife sideways, Georgia carved a thick slice off the cake, still in its flimsy box. "It's absurd. The entire neighborhood is bringing in, I don't know, fumigators. All the rooms in the house will need to be packed up, and I will actually be living out of suitcases in a hotel for a week."

"Really?"

"As for the garden?" Georgia waved curtly in the direction of the sliding-glass door. "Carlos and his men will protect what they can." At the same moment, an invisible hedge trimmer whirred somewhere outside.

"Oh dear, I hope nothing is ruined. Your flowers are always so gorgeous."

"Part of it will most certainly be ruined. The question is, how much?"

The ignored roses had dribbled a thin stream of water on the table. "Is there something I could put these in?" Alice held up the bouquet.

Wordlessly, Georgia headed back to the kitchen, returning with a pear-shaped Waterford crystal vase, about one-third filled with water. She set it next to Alice's plate.

"Did you have a garden when Dan was little?" Alice asked, as she lowered the flowers into the water. The vase was inches too short, but to ask for scissors to cut the stems, in addition to the vase, would be pushing her luck with Georgia.

"As soon as we settled into this house, yes."

"Did Dan help you with it?"

"I gave him and his sister a few basic responsibilities. Pruning, for instance, that was what Dan chose."

A tanned, compact, muscular Dan in a T-shirt and shorts, with a big set of clippers, crouching at a trail of bougainvillea vines. He would have been a teenager when they moved here. Before that, in the first years after the divorce, there had been the tiny, two-bedroom house in Studio City where Dan, his younger sister, and Georgia had squeezed in along with all sorts of expensive roll-top desks and delicate porcelain lamps, heavy beveled mirrors and high-backed rocking chairs, living on bologna and peanut butter, until Georgia could find an affordable storefront where she could launch her antiques business. Dan and his sister had shared a bedroom, which must have been awfully uncomfortable. They were confined to that bedroom, the kitchen, and the bathroom, and at all costs forbidden to even brush against the antiques.

Pets were out of the question. Not in the crowded house in Studio City, and not in the perfect house in Woodland Hills. Dan finally got Stingray as soon as he had his own apartment at UCLA, and then the cats. Stingray had been okay, for a dog, not too jumpy or insistent on crawling onto Alice's lap all the time, and she'd honestly meant it when she told Dan she'd be glad to get another dog after Stingray died, she really had.

With her fork, Alice maneuvered a small slice of the crumb cake to her plate. "My dad had two rosebushes and a tiny vegetable garden that I used to help him weed when I was a little girl, before he died. I think that's why I became interested in the environment."

"Now you prefer the big picture, rather than actual gardens."

"Well, sort of. Not exactly. My mother's planting lettuce this year."

"Is your mother all right?" Swallowing a bite of cake, Georgia frowned at Alice. "She missed last week's bridge games."

"She said her arthritis was acting up, and it was hard to hold a hand of cards."

"It must have acted up quite badly, for her to miss a bridge session. She is absolutely the best, but she needs a stronger partner—and I don't mean me, I'm not in Florence's league at all." Georgia had stretched out her own fingers, thin and wrinkled, tipped with their red nail polish. She wore no jewelry except for a gold ring holding a huge hunk of jade, on her left ring finger. "She's really not old enough to be having arthritis. Tell her I hope she feels better, please."

"Thank you. I will." Alice lowered her fork onto her plate, a hunk of crumb cake still attached. "Speaking of my mother, you haven't asked me the typical mother-in-law question, now that Dan and I have been married for two years."

"What question is that? You do realize that I hope I would never ask a 'typical mother-in-law' question?" As Georgia leaned back slightly in her brocade chair, her spine remained ramrod-straight.

"Well. You know." Alice coughed. " 'When are you two planning to have children?' That question."

"I suppose that's your way of telling me? Congratulations, then."

"No. No! I—I'm not—"

Georgia was outright staring at Alice. "I am thoroughly confused. Why are you raising this topic, if you're not pregnant?"

"I just thought, you must have mentioned it to Dan? Over the years? How you want to, you know, be a grandmother?"

"Why would I? Isn't that up to him and you?"

"Of course. You're right. And we will. Decide." Alice wrapped her fingers together in her lap. "Don't tell Dan I mentioned this. It was so stupid of me."

•   •   •   •   •

From the second drawer of her desk at work, Alice pulled out an 8½-by-11 pad of blue-lined paper.

OPTIONS
1. *Keep trying to talk to Dan. Very rational, pros/cons.*
2. *Wait six months, ask him again.*
3. *Ask Roz for advice??*
4. *Marriage counseling??*
5. *Offer to baby-sit Jenny at our apartment, so Dan can see how much fun she is? For an hour? (Two hours?) (Why bother? He'll just go into another room)*

She picked up her pen and added:

6. *"Forget" to put my diaphragm in.*

Chapter Six

Google had a Robert Corning in Cincinnati getting a community service award from the Lion's Club, but he was way too old to be the Robert Corning who'd been arrested with Esme.

Googling Esme immediately after getting home from the Santa Barbara police, and again at midnight, and again at five A.M., all produced only the same black-and-white student newspaper photo as four and a half years ago: Esme and her sorority sisters cleaning the beach at El Capitan. Eight happy, healthy young women in jeans and wind-blown hair and T-shirts with the Delta Alpha Mu logo, arms around each other, one of them who wasn't Esme leaning on a tall shovel, another brandishing a big garbage bag. Laughing. Third name in the caption, Esme Wilson.

The old cellphone number had a new but equally useless message. Someone named Laura would return her call.

•   •   •   •   •

James walked his bike along the path next to Alice, weaving around palm trees and all the people sitting on bright green benches eating sandwiches and salads on their lunch breaks, his black helmet dangling from the handlebars.

"I spoke to that lawyer you suggested, this morning," Alice said, walking and talking fast. "And he told me that if Esme broke into a residence, that's considered first-degree burglary. A felony. She could go to prison for six years!"

"Shit."

"State prison! You've heard what happens in prisons. She could—She could be raped. Assaulted. Ki—"

"Allie, that's not gonna happen."

"And they could be setting a trial date any day! Depending on if it's a felony or misdemeanor, if they're doing a plea deal, how crowded the court calendar is, and the lawyer says that if she was arrested more than a month ago, the judge would have already held the preliminary hearing. I'm her mother. I have to be there!"

"Stop. Take a breath."

She couldn't. Her breath couldn't find its way out of her lungs.

Far below their path, at the base of the Palisades Park cliffs, cars were streaming along the curves of Pacific Coast Highway the same as any weekday lunchtime. Beyond the cliffs, the highway and the beach, a smattering of surfers in wetsuits made tiny black blotches in the grayish-white waves. Surfing in a storm would be safer than being in prison. Being in a car crash around the curve of a highway would be safer. Though Esme was out for now, on O.R., she could be sent straight back.

"Six years in prison!"

"She's gonna be okay, Allie."

"Plus a ten thousand-dollar fine. Plus the other—"

"Slow down. Stop." James had stopped himself and pushed out the kickstand for the bike. He began rubbing both of her upper arms, a little too roughly. "What if it wasn't a residence? Do you know what kind of building it was?"

"No."

"Do you know what the punishment is for breaking into a place that isn't a residence?"

If she swallowed deeply a few times, her throat would clear. A bell clanged, and then a red bike sped past, hugging the far edge of the path. The air smelled of French fries from somebody's lunch.

"The lawyer said—" Alice swallowed. "He said robbing a commercial building isn't as bad as a residence. It could be either a felony or a misdemeanor."

"That sounds more promising."

"They call it a 'wobbler.' Of all stupid things." As if this was merely about a toddler learning how to walk.

"So Esme might not go to prison at all."

"She could get sixteen months in county jail."

"That's a lot better than six years in state prison."

"She'd still be locked up! And there's all the other charges, too. Forcible entry. Trespassing. Vandalism. All of that. Those are going to add to the penalties, even if it's a misdemeanor. And if tools like crowbars were used. She already spent one night in jail, probably, when she was arrested. I don't want her another minute in any jail or prison!"

James resumed guiding the bike, silently, for a moment. "Did the lawyer say anything else?"

"You know how lawyers are, he said he can only speak in generalities, because I'm not his client, and he doesn't have all the details, what was taken in the robbery, blah blah. But he knows enough to know how serious it is."

Burglary. Forcible entry. Trespass. Vandalism. As if Alice and Esme were sprawled next to each other on the orange-and-red flowered couch in the living room, eating takeout chicken with cashew nuts and watching an episode of *Law & Order* on TV. Had Esme been making notes in her head, all those evenings? *Oh, this is how you break into a house.*

"How can I help?" James asked softly. "Do you need money for her legal fees?"

"James!" Stretching up on her toes, Alice lightly kissed him on the cheekbone below his right eye. "You're wonderful to offer, but you don't have any more money than I do. Especially if your newspaper does another round of layoffs."

"Hell, Andrea and I don't spend much. A pair of middle-aged married bookworms."

"Thank you, truly, but I couldn't take your money. Besides, I suppose Dan's paying for her lawyer, since he got her out of jail."

"At least he's good for something."

"We'd better head back to work, both of us. A major potential client is coming tomorrow, and Fred hasn't approved my proposal for them yet. And you need to eat more of your sandwich."

James wheeled the bike around so that now, in retreat, it was Alice who was on the side of the path nearer to the edge of the cliff, James nearer to Ocean Avenue. A jogger in a bright yellow T-shirt was running toward them. A skinny brown-and-white dog squatted on the grass too close to a bench where a woman was, obliviously, forking a salad and gazing out at the distant water. James took another bite of the salami sandwich she'd bought for him.

Alice kept talking. "I'm scouring my brain to think of anyone I could speak to, anyone who might be in contact with Esme. Even if they don't have information about the arrest, maybe there are other crumbs they can give me that could explain more about her. Maybe they know who this Robert Corning guy is. Is he her boyfriend? Where's she living? Does she have a job?"

"Those are solid questions."

"Should I try to find her friend Courtney, from cheerleading in high school? Her mom never returned my phone messages when I tried six years ago, so maybe she won't speak to me at all, ever, because of, you know, when Courtney came over to our apartment. Or I could go to the address the detective found in Santa Barbara. And the clothing shop where Esme used to work. She could still be working there. There's got to be something I can do! She's my daughter!"

"If you're planning to drive to Santa Barbara anyway, how about if you visit the crime scene? Let's see if we're dealing with a residence or a commercial business, first of all."

Oh. Alice pulled away from the bike a little, so that she could look James in the face. "That's a great idea."

"Good."

"Maybe after that, I'll stake out Dan's house until he shows up and force him to tell me where she's hiding."

"Sure. Should I get you a balaclava, as a disguise?"

"Why not?"

"Seriously." James pressed a hand on Alice's shoulder. "Just tell me how I can help."

"Come to Santa Barbara with me this weekend."

•   •   •   •   •

Hi, Georgia. This is, um, Alice. You know, your ex-daughter-in-law? I hope you're doing well. I'm just calling now because, um, you probably know about Esme's arrest, and of course I'm worried about her, so I was wondering if you might have any information. Do you know if she needs a lawyer or anything?

What if Dan hadn't, in fact, told his mother about the arrest? She would be almost eighty years old; getting this sort of phone message from Alice, out of nowhere, after two decades, would be a big shock, tough as she was.

It was too late to erase the message.

•   •   •   •   •

Hello. This is a message for Mrs. Michaels. My name is Alice Wilson. My daughter, Esme, was a close friend of your daughter Courtney's, in high school. In Calabasas. This must seem strange, after so many years, but, well, Esme is in a—a difficult situation, and so I was wondering if you could pass on a message to Courtney, to ask if she might call me or email me? Or if you want to call back or email yourself, I can explain more. I was just wondering if Esme and Courtney have kept in contact.

•   •   •   •   •

Penelope might know what was happening. She'd been married to Dan since Esme was six years old; Esme had lived with Penelope and Dan since she was fifteen and ran away from Alice. Penelope had taken Esme shopping, picked out the purple T-shirt with the smiling pineapple stenciled on the front. Made organic pasta together. All the things Alice was useless at. Maybe Esme had poured out her heart to Penelope on a shopping spree after the arrest.

And would Penelope talk to Alice any more than Dan would? There was no way to ask Penelope, because there was no way to reach her. She worked in PR somewhere. Name of the PR firm? Phone number? Email? None of Alice's business, Dan had said. Call her at the house in Calabasas? Nope. All contact was to go solely through Dan, per their divorce decree.

    •   •   •   •   •

A couple of the beaded necklaces Esme had made with Jenny in junior high were tangled together across the top of her bedroom dresser, alongside her line-up of worn-out stuffed animals. Brownie the Dog. Moosey. The ibex she and Alice had gotten at the San Diego Zoo. The *Titanic* movie poster was taped to one wall, although the two top corners had curled so far inward that they almost met in the center of the ship's prow. Eating ice cream with Alice after the movie, Esme and her friend Willow had calculated how they would have saved Leonardo DiCaprio, if they'd been Rose.

"Couldn't she have found another piece of wood for him?" Esme had demanded.

"She could've let her legs hang over the side, and then there'd be room on the wood for both of them," Willow added.

"She was selfish."

When Alice and Esme had first moved into this little apartment in Santa Monica, the bedroom walls had been a blinding, psychedelic green they both hated. Together, they went to the hardware store to scout out colors. Esme brought home sample strips of every shade of pink, purple, and orange that she saw on the store's display, then took the samples to her kindergarten to ask her classmates and teachers what they thought, passing the little strips of paper to person after person until the samples were totally wrinkled and bent. Alice had tried to suggest a gentle color, but it was Esme's room, after all, and Esme chose what the store called butterscotch orange, the same as in Jenny and Sharon's bedroom. Walt, James, Roz, and Alice had needed three coats to cover the green, while Jenny and Esme used white, orange, and bright blue to paint circle-like dogs and flowers along the bottom, and baby Sharon watched from her porta-playpen in the kitchen. And then they all colored each other's fingernails with Esme's paint set. The orange hadn't faded completely.

Of course, Esme had long ago thrown out the photos from her ballet classes. Pink tutu. Blue costume. Red-and-white costume. The little tiara jammed into her wild brown hair. Her ecstatic laugh. Yet on her night table she'd kept the picture of herself baking cookies with Grandma Florence. She would have been around six or seven then, perched on a stepstool in Florence's green kitchen, biting her lip as she wielded a wooden spoon to mix cookie batter in a stainless-steel bowl bigger than her head.

And the box. A square redwood box with white scalloping around the edges, brought back by Alice from the airport gift store in San Francisco when she'd gone up to the forests in Humboldt County. It was on the night table next to the photo from Florence's kitchen.

The room was not a hideaway for stolen goods. Not the necklaces. Not the stuffed animals. Not the black Ugg boots in the closet; weren't those the ones Alice had bought for Esme in eighth grade, the ones Esme wore every single day until all her friends abruptly stopped wearing Uggs? No crowbars were hidden in the underwear drawer, no skeleton keys mixed in with the necklaces.

It was the bedroom of a happy girl, wasn't it? A girl who went to movies and zoos and the Nutcracker ballet, who made jewelry and pottery. A girl with friends and a loving mother and grandmother.

Okay, a mother who pushed her when her grades slipped, but every mother did that, and their daughters didn't stop speaking to them.

Esme hadn't thrown out the redwood box.

But it was also a room that hadn't been used by that happy girl for six years.

•　　•　　•　　•　　•

In the fading orange of Thursday's dull sunset, Alice pulled her list out of the pocket of her linen slacks and handed it to Roz across the picnic table in Roz's backyard. The table was cluttered as usual, with crumpled plastic cups and greasy paper plates, sections of the *L.A. Times*, a purple sock, a powder-blue Barbie skirt and a half-eaten croissant sitting on a napkin. At the far corner of the yard, the swing set where Jenny, Esme, and Sharon used to play was sinking, off-balance, into the dirt, though Walt had supposedly reinforced the cement around its base. His empty easel leaned against the wall of the house.

For no reason at all, Alice fingered the purple sock. "James and I had a long talk yesterday. He said he'll come with me this weekend to Santa Barbara."

"And this is a list of the places where you two are going?"

"Yeah."

"The address where they were arrested?"

"And I was thinking about trying to meet with that sorority housemother, Mrs. Hanson, remember? But she was so clueless the time I visited her, so I don't know. What do you think? I didn't put it on the list."

Roz pulled off her eyeglasses, rubbed her forehead, then replaced the glasses. "Going to the scene of the crime seems awfully risky. What if the victims are there, and they get angry at you?"

"Why would they?"

"Well, you're the mother of the accused burglar. If somebody was hurt? I don't know."

"We don't have to speak to anyone. We can just look around."

"Or if the police say you're interfering with their investigation?"

"Huh? How would we be interfering?"

Roz broke off the croissant's tiny, curled end. "I guess I'm being silly. I don't want you or James getting arrested, too." She laughed.

Alice laughed in return. "Thank you for worrying about us, but I honestly don't expect there's much danger. I suppose the biggest danger is getting my hopes raised."

"This could be what encourages Esme to reach out to you," Roz said.

Gazing at Alice through her tortoise-shell glasses. As though what she'd said made any sense.

"Why would being arrested make Esme suddenly decide to confide in me? You think she stopped talking to me six years ago because she was law-abiding and didn't need a mother? And what's with the croissant? I thought you were on a new diet."

Roz dropped the piece of the croissant onto the cedar tabletop.

Alice shouldn't have said that, about the croissant.

During Roz's first attempt at Weight Watchers, about six months after she'd stopped nursing Jenny, she'd called Alice three or four times every day, in a panic. "Tell me something that will take my mind off of chocolate." "Tell me why I shouldn't go out right now and buy a KitKat bar." "Why should I stay on this diet? Who cares if I gain twenty-five pounds?" It hadn't mattered what Alice answered, just that she kept Roz on the phone long enough for the immediate craving to subside. Which had worked, for a few weeks.

"I'm sorry." Alice picked up the broken croissant and held it out to Roz. "I know being on a diet is hard. And you're worried about Jenny's morning sickness. I'm just on edge. I mean, look, I only learned about Esme being arrested four days ago, and then you dropped that bombshell about her phone call to you? I feel as if I'm in the middle of an earthquake. And if that's not enough, I met with an important prospective client today, and they want tons more information from me. And we have serious competition from a big bank. Shit."

Roz patted Alice's hand, although she didn't take the croissant. "It's a lot on you. I'm sorry you're going through so much. Plus." She paused. "Next month."

"Yeah. Esme's birthday."

How would a twenty-four-year-old Esme want to celebrate her birthday? Getting stoned with Robert Corning? Would she like a cake? Or, oh damn, would she be in jail for her birthday?

"And you won't be there," Roz added. "Again."

"Six birthdays."

The engine noise around the side of the house meant that Walt's old Saab was easing into the driveway. In a minute or so, Walt would limp across the flat grass to the picnic table. He would hug Roz, then Alice.

"Thanks for understanding," Alice said, squeezing Roz's hand. But if Roz truly understood, she wouldn't have kept Esme's phone call secret all those months.

•   •   •   •   •

"This is Georgia Wilson." The voicemail was businesslike and steady, quiet without being weak. *"Please don't call me back. I'm replying to your message because I don't want to be rude, and I certainly appreciate how concerned you must be about Esme's situation. I do believe that you have a right to have full information. As her mother. However, I'm sorry, Dan still requests that the family not communicate directly with you, that we go solely through him."*

•   •   •   •   •

TO: awilson@seshatadvisors.com

It has come to my attention that you directly contacted my elderly mother, Georgia Wilson, of Woodland Hills, California, without prior permission, causing her extreme distress. If this happens again, you will be subject to legal action, and if my mother or any of my family suffers any medical or other repercussions from your provocation, you will be held responsible. I WILL NOT ALLOW YOU TO UPSET MY FAMILY THE WAY YOU DID ESME, with such serious results. Dr. Daniel Wilson, DVM

CHAPTER SEVEN

James's scratched red Toyota cruised slowly along the quiet Santa Barbara street. Esme's street. Most of the houses were two or three floors, made of stucco or aluminum siding. A chunky, red-and-yellow kiddie car, the kind that Esme used to pretend to drive, rested on a patch of broken sidewalk in front of one house. A larger building at the corner was ringed by outside walkways on the second and third floors, for each unit. Autos with faded paint jobs parked in spurts along the curb.

"Here's the address," James said.

It was two stories high, beige stucco peeling in scattered spots, with a low stoop, a plain wooden front door, and a single palm tree standing sentinel. The whitish curtains on the ground-floor windows were tightly shut; on the floor above, no lights shone. A clean, blue welcome mat with the pattern of a cluster of daisies lay on the stoop in front of the door.

Had Esme chosen that mat?

Every day, Esme pushed open the wooden door, stepped onto the mat, and strode down the concrete path from the stoop to the street. Every day, she looked out one of the windows, past the palm tree, at the gray two-story house across the street with a red awning over a small patio, at the yellow aluminum-sided house next to it and its tiny yard of dull, short grass.

Of course, Esme might not live there anymore. It was more than a year since the detective had found the address. Alice should have made this trip right then, when the information was fresh. She should have come to this stoop and rung the doorbell right away, even if she was scared that it would backfire. Even if Esme shut the door in her face. Even if it wasn't definite that Esme lived there, no matter what the detective thought. Stupidly, she'd been waiting for a sign, a miracle. She'd figured she could always do it another time, next month, two months. She'd blown her chance. By now Esme might have flown away. Kids moved so much after college.

But what if Esme in fact was inside that house this very moment, behind one of the darkened windows, drinking black coffee and eating a bowl of Cheerios for breakfast? What if she answered the doorbell, coffee mug in hand, wearing a Delta Alpha Mu T-shirt like in the photo where she was cleaning up the beach, her brown hair in tangled waves and a laugh on her face—until she saw who it was at the door? What if Robert Corning was standing behind her?

"What if she slams the door on me?" Alice grabbed James's elbow.

With his free hand, James stroked her forearm.

"Or what if she's all warm and friendly?" Alice went on.

"Isn't that what you want?"

Was it possible? Esme, terrified about being arrested, and maybe Dan had reamed her out for it. *"Mom!" Sobbing and running toward Alice, with her arms outstretched.*

"I don't know what I want! For six years, I've dreamed about getting a phone call from her, or opening the door, and there she is. Esme. Her face. Hugging her, the two of us sitting some place, being mother and daughter again. Catching up on everything I've missed in her life. And seeing her again, the next day, and the next week, and … But could I? If she walked into my apartment, do I hug her and pretend that nothing happened, all this time? Do I ask her why she cut me off? Do I apologize? But I don't know what to apologize for. For pushing her on her history test?"

"Should we forget it and go home?"

And then what? Drive all the way here again another day? "No. We came this far. Let's just do it." Shaking off James's hand, Alice yanked open the car door.

The house had four numbered buzzers. Beside one was a strip of masking tape with an Asian name written on it in black marker. A second buzzer listed two last names, neither of them Wilson. The other buzzers, including the one with Esme's specific apartment number, were bare.

Alice pressed the buzzer for Esme's number.

Nothing happened. The building was quiet. Well, it was barely nine-thirty on a Saturday morning. Everyone could be asleep, or out of town. Or peering out through a sliver between closed curtains: *Shit, that's my mother! Don't answer!* Then the door opened.

A short, dark-haired young woman, blinking, leaned against the edge of the door, one hand clutching the thin wood. She was wearing a plain white T-shirt, a pair of red-and-white-striped men's boxers, and fuzzy yellow slippers with two tall bunny ears. She could be Esme's age, more or less the same height…Of course she wasn't Esme. Anyway, her face was too round, her nose too pug.

The first question on Alice's list: "Does, um, does Esme Wilson live here?"

Ponderously, the young woman shook her head. "Esme Wilson? No." Her voice dragged away.

"Or in any of the apartments?"

From inside the building, another young woman had stumbled toward them. She wasn't Esme, either.

"I'm sorry for waking you," Alice added.

The first woman shrugged, pushing some hair off her face.

The second woman hadn't heard of Esme.

They'd been renting their apartment since January, and they didn't know who'd lived there before them.

"Do you think the other tenants would know more?"

There were two guys in the unit next to them on the ground floor, but they'd only moved in a couple weeks ago. Upstairs, one apartment was empty, and a Japanese couple lived in the other.

It was getting easier to breathe, to ask the rest of the questions from her notepad. Alice's heart was beating at almost a steady tempo. "Do you ever get mail addressed to her?"

Frowning, the first young woman shook her head.

"Would the landlord know how to find her?"

At that, the roommate laughed. "Are you kidding? They don't even want to know if the toilet breaks. It's some big management company down in L.A. that owns a bunch of buildings around here. We just send them our checks every month."

"The person who lived in our apartment before us left behind a huge pot. Like, for cooking a big batch of spaghetti?" the first roommate added. "It could be hers."

Because Penelope and Dan had taught Esme how to make organic pasta?

Alice had finished her list.

Back in the Toyota, James slid the key into the ignition but didn't turn it. They both slumped a little in their bucket seats, and James began drumming on his thigh, reaching over to tap a few notes on Alice's thigh now and then. Inside Esme's maybe-former house, one light had gone on upstairs.

"Are you ready for the next stop?" James asked. "The store where she used to work?"

"Is it ten o'clock yet? That's when it opens."

"Twenty of."

"I guess we could head over. By the time we drive there …"

James turned the key.

Alice read the directions from her phone, while James hummed a tune vaguely similar to the Beatles' "Yesterday" but faster and bumpier.

"Did you write that? The music you're humming?"

For an instant, James glanced at her. Then he returned to the view ahead.

"You did, didn't you?"

"Not really. Bullshit."

"It's good, James."

"So what? Who's gonna hear it?"

"Your band is still together."

"Not really. Maybe. I'm too old to be a rock guitarist. And I'm too old to start fresh at a big newspaper. I'm old enough to be a grandfather, like Walt." There might have been a few strands of gray hiding in James's blond hair, where it fell over and behind his ears. A pair of faint wrinkles ran alongside his mouth.

"James, are you having your annual midlife crisis?"

"Not yet."

"Mick Jagger is older than we are."

"Well, that settles things. Thanks." James blew a breath out of the left side of his mouth. "I applied for a job at the *Union-Tribune* in San Diego."

"You're job-hunting?"

"I've been at the damn *Chronicle* for over twenty years. If I'm never gonna make it on my music, I sure as hell don't intend to spend whatever career I have at a bullshit local weekly with a total circulation of forty thousand that's laying off a quarter of the staff and probably'll go bankrupt in a month. I want to try something bigger."

Esme's clothes boutique would be on State Street. According to Google maps, a mere quarter-mile away.

"Andrea thinks I should focus on the journalism, too. Steady paycheck. She thinks I have talent as a writer."

"You do."

"Well, thanks."

"There'd be a lot more interesting news to write about in San Diego."

"Doubtful. This particular job is working the lobster shift. I'd finish at six in the morning, so I suppose the only news I'd see would be police blotter and hospitals. Fires. Car accidents. A murder, if I'm lucky."

A few more blocks. It would be the next left turn.

"But the main thing is," James continued, "it's a bigger paper, and I'd have my foot in the door. I could apply to move on to a better beat after a while. Hell, the way the newspaper industry is going, I'm lucky to find any job."

"Here," Alice said. "Turn left here."

All of a sudden, they were driving through what could have been the movie set for a bustling, historic Main Street. Red-brick sidewalks ran along both sides of the road, dotted with stone planters, wrought-iron benches, palm trees, and imitation gaslight lampposts. Gardens' worth of yellow, pink, and orange flowers exploded from the planters, along with rich shrubbery. Every store and office resembled a Spanish mission, adobe with a red-tile roof—Radio Shack, Staples, a bank, nail waxing, a bakery, CVS, Forever 21, a candy shop.

A shoe store. An optometrist. A body-piercing parlor.

A jewelry store. An Indian restaurant. A hairdresser. James stopped.

An empty stucco storefront, with a bench on the sidewalk and a sign in one dusty window. "For lease."

"Shit," James mumbled, easing rightward to double-park against a white car.

Two young women ambled past what should have been the Clothing Etc. shop, each holding a disposable coffee cup in her outside hand.

"It's the aftereffect of the recession," James said quietly. "A lot of downtowns were hard hit, and they never recovered."

"But I Googled it two days ago. It had great reviews on Yelp."

"Yeah, well, you can't believe everything you read online. Especially about things like stores that are still in business or not."

Do you know someone named Esme who used to work here? Alice could ask random people passing by. Or a clerk at the jewelry store. A manicurist at the hairdresser's studio.

Alice closed her notepad. "I'm sorry for dragging you here. I'll buy you a beer."

James didn't respond.

"But I don't suppose the bars are open yet."

"So what do you want to do?" James asked.

"What else is there to do?" Outside Alice's side window, the former Clothing Etc. was still shuttered. A twentyish woman was jogging past the sidewalk bench, wearing black bicycle shorts and a UCSB T-shirt. "The crime scene. Obviously."

•　　•　　•　　•　　•

It was an art supply store.

A boxy, low-slung, concrete building with a six-car parking lot in front, a half-mile away from the movie-set Main Street of downtown Santa Barbara, on a long block shared by a gas station, a liquor store, and a pizzeria. "Pacific Artists" declared the brilliant blue, green, and orange sign, outlined in seashells, that stretched above the front door and the plate-glass windows on either side.

An art supply store?

Had Esme and Robert Corning burst through the door wearing beautifully hand-painted bandanas as masks? Carrying woven Native bags for the loot? Did they shout, "Hand over the paintbrushes and no one gets hurt"?

Inside, the single room was crammed with metal racks stretching a foot taller than Alice's head. Little bottles of walnut oil and linseed oil, acetate and galkyd, whatever that was. It thinned colors and increased gloss, the label said. Acrylic paints in tubes and big round jars and small skinny jars; fluid acrylic in plastic bottles; enamel paint in paint guns. Brushes, sketch pads, painting knives, linoleum blocks, huge vats of glue, piles of colorful felt rectangles, long skeins of yarn. Books on how to draw animals, and 100 ways to draw with circles. Stick-on letters, masking tape, and beads for stringing, maybe for the type of beaded necklaces Esme used to make with Jenny. Had Esme run her hands along these shelves, searching for loot to steal? Fingered the bottles of galkyd? Toyed with the beads? Grabbed a painting knife?

"What the hell?" James whispered.

"Why would she rob this store?"

"Beats me. It's not a residence, anyway. That means it wasn't a felony." James grinned. "That's positive news, Allie."

"I suppose. But she's still a thief."

James lifted a squat jar shaped like a Vaseline container. "I bet they chose this place because it's in the middle of nowhere."

"Or she bought something here once and, I don't know, it was broken and they wouldn't give her a refund?"

"Allie, you're stretching."

"Fine, you're the newspaper reporter. You ask the questions."

"Didn't you write your own list?"

"Okay, okay."

The only other person in the store was a young woman with midnight-black hair that stuck straight up from her head in short spikes and a matching black T-shirt, sitting at the cash register and reading her phone, behind a semi-circular counter in the center of the room.

"Hey," she cheerfully greeted Alice and James. The silver lettering on the front of her shirt was scripted in an ornate thunderbolt motif, "Paint Power" or "Paint Forever," and she smelled vaguely of lemons. An assortment of trinkets surrounded her along the top of the counter: little rubber whales and penguins, flower-top pens, boxes of small plastic dinosaurs, sparkling bouncy balls.

"I was wondering," Alice began, "if you're acquainted with anyone named Esme Wilson?"

"I don't think so."

"Or Robert Corning?"

"Robert…What kind of art do Esme and Robert do?"

Would a burglar paint portraits or landscapes? Oil or water color? Esme used to make pottery and necklaces with Jenny.

"Oh, wait!" the clerk exclaimed. "Bobby?"

Bobby.

The clerk smiled. "Bobby? A big guy, with one of those little beards? The tie-dyer?" Then the smile slid away.

Behind Alice, James had put a hand on her shoulder.

"Why do you want to know about Bobby?" the clerk asked, her voice more careful. "Do you want to buy one of his shirts?"

No. Yes.

Bobby Corning. Who maybe wasn't fifty-one years old and active in the Lion's Club in Cincinnati.

"Stacey—she works here full-time—she knows him better than I do," the clerk was saying, a little more energetically now. "He buys a lot of dye powders. He makes T-shirts with all these color combinations that you'd expect would never work, you know, but they look great, actually. Deep purple and rust orange? And avocado and brown rose, which should be boring and dull, but the way he does it?"

From outside, the wail of a siren grew stronger. It hovered, then trailed away, followed by a brief series of car horns. A police car? Were Esme and Bobby Corning robbing another store?

"He's not allowed in here anymore," the clerk went on. "Felicia, the owner—Well, I don't know. Stacey would know more."

Alice grabbed the counter edge. "When does Stacey work? Can you tell me her phone number?"

"Oh no, I can't give out personal information."

"Sure. I understand. How about if I give you my phone number and email to give to her?"

The clerk frowned.

"This must sound a little strange," Alice added quickly, with a big smile. "I'm organizing a surprise birthday party for my daughter. It's her birthday next month. And so I'm trying to track down all her friends, or not exactly her friends, necessarily, but people she knows. Like Robert. Bobby. Without asking her directly for their phone numbers or anything, you know? For the surprise."

Holding a white flower-topped pen almost vertical, the clerk slowly wrote on a business card while Alice dictated.

"Nothing's going to come of this," Alice said to James, in the gravel parking lot.

"Worth a shot."

"What can Stacey know?"

"You can ask her if this Bobby character ever came in with a girl."

"If this salesclerk remembers to give my phone number to Stacey. If Stacey actually calls me."

"You can ask her if she knows how to get hold of Bobby."

Alice flicked James away. "She's never going to call. I'll have to come back here in person, a dozen trips before I find her. And take more time off work. And be late getting the revised report to the Cordwainers. And get fired."

"Stop being such a pessimist. You're going to meet the guy who knows why Esme got arrested."

James was grinning, and maybe she was, too. He wrapped his arms around her and pulled her close, bending his head to press his forehead against hers. She rubbed his back. Miracles could happen. Esme existed, after all.

CHAPTER EIGHT

ALICE AND DAN

November 1985
Westwood, CA

"I'm surprised we got so careless." Dan had shifted his seat on the dark leather couch at the same time that he muted the TV remote control, and now he was staring directly at Alice. He stayed there, next to her, spinning the remote in a tight circle on the steel coffee table, while Peter Jennings's mouth moved soundlessly on the screen across from them.

"I tried to calculate the weeks." Briefly, Alice stroked Dan's smooth-shaven cheek. "I think it was probably after we went to that French restaurant in Westwood. You remember, I had two glasses of chardonnay? I might have gotten sloppy putting in my diaphragm."

"Sure. That could explain it."

"Everyone has diaphragm-accident stories. It's only, you know, something like ninety-four percent effective."

An image of pieces of metal, a brown-paper package, and a stone-towered building appeared behind Peter Jennings's left shoulder.

"They can get worn out," Alice continued. Her voice was calm, wasn't it? "I try to check for holes, the way you're supposed to, every few days, but it can be hard to see. If it's a really tiny pinhole." Should she kiss Dan? A little peck, as if she was sympathizing with his surprise?

Dan patted her arm. "Anyway, it's early, so there should be no problem getting an abortion."

She shut her eyes. She clutched her knees. "No."

Her baby. Her blue-eyed son who was going to carry picket signs in front of Exxon headquarters with her someday. Her curly-haired daughter who would hunt for sea-glass diamonds on the beach.

Could the baby already be kicking inside her? No, it didn't have real feet yet, it was barely four or five weeks old. The kicking she was feeling was merely her stomach churning.

When she opened her eyes, Dan's were inches away.

"No," she repeated. A squeak.

"I thought we'd agreed." Dan's lips, usually so soft, barely moved as he spoke.

"I want to keep it."

Dan was breathing heavily, in curt puffs that hit her cheeks with a steady assault. Then he eased away from her, although he stayed on the couch. His stare wasn't, thankfully, boring into her face now. His head was turned toward the coffee table, and his fingers were spinning the remote again. "We've had our own private world, Alice. A good world. The two of us. That's all we've needed. We have our jobs, our independence, our home, each other, and we do the things we enjoy, together. If we feel like it, we can just get in the car and drive to Joshua Tree for a hike. Go out to dinner. Stay up for hours getting drunk on chardonnay. It's our schedule, our decisions. All that would be wiped out by—this. Our lives wouldn't be under our control anymore. Have you honestly thought about what it would mean?"

She nodded.

"Jumping up every moment it cried. Never getting enough sleep, constantly watching out for every dangerous little object it might grab. And you can forget about romantic dinners at French restaurants or any more vacations cleaning the beach in Spain."

"That's okay."

"How about those owls of yours? Will the logging companies wait for you to finish a maternity leave?"

"I'll figure it out. My mother would babysit."

"This wouldn't be as easy as you're pretending it would be."

Even before he finished speaking, Dan clicked the sound back on for the TV. Maybe that was a hopeful sign, that he needed the space of a neutral voice for a few minutes, to give himself time to get used to the idea of a child. Peter Jennings talked, and then a commercial followed, for something in a spray bottle.

"I realize this is kind of a head-spinner." Alice set a couple of gentle fingers on his thigh. "I love you, Dan. We can make this work."

"Do you also think it's okay to bring a child into the world when the parents haven't agreed on it? When only one of them wants it?"

Shaking her head "no" was the wrong answer. So was nodding.

Abruptly, Dan clamped his hand on the remote, so that its spinning halted. "Did you do this on purpose?" His voice was quiet, barely audible over the sound of Peter Jennings.

She shook her head rapidly. Of course, he couldn't see her, because he was facing the table. "These things happen. Sometimes."

He stood up. "This isn't a discussion I was expecting to have."

It was like the moment before a plane began racing down the runway, or more like the instant before someone jumped off the Golden Gate Bridge, a body poised between decisions. Would he hug her? Keep arguing? Laugh? Yell?

He didn't race, and he didn't jump. He didn't hug or argue. Instead, he walked out of the living room, and a minute later the front door opened and, gently, shut.

•   •   •   •   •

On TV, the news continued. Reagan was heading to Geneva this weekend for his summit meeting with the Soviet leader, Mikhail Gorbachev. A woman from Iceland was named Miss World. The 405 through the Sepulveda Pass had forty-minute tie-ups in both directions. It was seven o'clock at night. The calico cat had crawled onto her lap, though the black-and-white one was hiding. Dan's Camaro wasn't parked on the street in front of their apartment building.

By four o'clock in the morning, he still wasn't home.

He could have been driving around for the first hour or two. Random streets. Working out his thoughts. Furious at her. Maybe, when he'd gotten too tired to keep driving, he'd pulled into an empty parking lot and fallen asleep.

Dan would never sleep in his car in a parking lot.

So, he could have gone to his clinic to check on the animals, and stayed, dozing on the cot in the office. He could have taken a motel room. He wouldn't disappear forever, boom, in an instant. Whatever else he was, he was reliable. If he said he would be at a restaurant at seven o'clock, he'd be there at seven o'clock.

If he said he didn't want children, then he didn't want children.

What the hell had she done? Dan had been honest with her that he didn't intend to have children, period, flat, and she'd tried to trick him. Did she truly believe he was so clueless that he wouldn't see through "the torn diaphragm" excuse, especially after all the months that she'd been pushing him to have a baby? Did she honestly expect that he'd burst into a huge smile and exclaim: *What great news! Now that it's really happening, I've changed my mind completely.*

But it had been such a ridiculous long shot, to believe that her silly scheme would work. Take out the diaphragm after four hours instead of six. Use less cream then the instructions said. The human body wasn't a computer where all the coding had to be followed precisely. Who would ever foresee that she'd get pregnant on the first "accident"?

Even so, she shouldn't have. Tricked Dan. *Do you also think it's okay to bring a child into the world when the parents haven't agreed on it? When only one of them wants it?*

It was all wrong.

She had to confess. That it hadn't been an accident. Which he knew anyway.

And after that? She could try a little harder to change Dan's mind, but he'd made it clear that wasn't going to happen. The only ethical option was an abortion. Otherwise, she would still be tricking him into fatherhood.

But why was that ethical? Why was it more ethical to do what Dan wanted, instead of what she wanted? It was her baby as much as his. Her curly-haired daughter. Her blue-eyed son. It was her body.

Because she was the one who'd been dishonest. Therefore, it was her responsibility to come clean and take the consequences.

Six a.m. No Dan.

•   •   •   •   •

At eight-forty-five, the young receptionist with the annoying New Jersey accent and blond ringlets bouncing all over her head was at the front desk of Dan's clinic. "Hi, Mrs. Wilson. What brings you here today?"

"Is my husband, uh, is he available? I forgot something this morning. At home. You know, at breakfast. While we were having breakfast. Together."

"Oh, I'm sorry. He's in surgery at the moment." The receptionist's nose wrinkled, and her mouth turned dramatically downward, as though it was unbearable to disappoint Dr. Wilson's wife.

"Surgery."

"It's a poor kitty that was hit by a car."

"I'll wait for him."

The disappointment deepened into a frown. "I can't say how long he'll be tied up."

"That's all right."

Alice seated herself on a two-cushion bench that was around a corner from the reception desk, safely out of view. The cushions were made of a crinkly plastic and smelled of stale pee. So what? She could wait as long as she needed on these crinkly, smelly cushions. If Fred asked why she was late, she could always say she'd been working at home, which was in fact true if this waiting room counted as "home." She opened a red folder. It was nine o'clock. *Next year the U.S. Forest Service is expected to release its new Forest Management Plan, and it will undoubtedly forbid some amount of timber sales on public lands...* The clinic's doorbell buzzed, and the place abruptly smelled of old, slightly rancid dog food. Something blunt dropped on the floor. In the closed-off examination rooms beyond the reception area, a young woman spoke, a dog growled once, footsteps slapped the linoleum floor, and a door shut into silence. It was nine-thirty. What did the spotted owl mean for the stock market? Would veterinary clinics start taking care of owls?

Dan was in front of her.

His black hair was matted on his damp cheeks, and his blue surgical mask dangled around his neck. His feet, in light-blue paper booties over his Kenneth Cole loafers, were planted so near to hers that he was almost stepping on her toes.

"I'm sorry." *I'm sorry I tricked you. I'm sorry I lied.* Where should her apologies begin?

He was gazing straight at her face. Then he moved his eyes away, and he spread aside her hands and her folder, to rest his own right hand, splayed, on her belly. It was no bigger than a nonpregnant stomach might be. This was far too early for a baby to be puffing it out.

"I'll get an abortion. If you want." She was whispering. He probably didn't hear.

"All right," he said.

What was all right?

He kissed her mouth, hard and swiftly. "We'll have this baby."

She coughed, gulped more air, grabbed his free hand. "Really? Really?"

"If you want it that much. I don't want to lose you."

His blue eyes, as dark as the almost-night sky. His sweaty black hair. The tiny, nearly invisible oval-shaped scar on the edge of his jaw. His breaths blowing on her face, irregular, heavy.

Had anyone ever said anything so beautiful to her?

"You have to take care of that belly of yours now," he added.

Yes. Yes.

Now he was looking at her stomach again as he stroked it unhurriedly, clockwise. "You're going to have a great life, Baby. Your room will be full of toys and books. We'll go to the playground together every weekend, on the slide and the swings. And I'll show you all the animals in my clinic, so you won't be scared of dogs like your mother."

He was agreeing?

Suddenly Alice was giggling and gasping, and she pulled Dan closer.

"We'll see the Dodgers play," he went on, looking back and forth from her face to her stomach. "But you have to know that I only go when Valenzuela is pitching, and I always get top-notch seats at the third-base line."

Dan and their child could watch all the Dodgers games Dan's heart desired. Play with the animals in his clinic. Fill the house with Star Wars toys. Get a dog. They were going to have a baby.

CHAPTER NINE

ALICE, DAN, AND ESME

June 1986 to October 1989
Reseda and Santa Monica, CA

June 1986

The baby was a girl. She had all ten fingers and all ten toes, and thick eyelashes like Dan's on her sleeping eyelids, and a curly cap of pale blond hair, as she slept in Alice's arms.

Alice stroked one of the jellyroll fingers. Then she grinned at Dan, who was standing beside the hospital bed in his green visitor's scrubs, staring at the baby's head. "We did a good job."

Firmly, Dan lifted the little pink-blanketed body out of Alice's arms and pressed her against his chest. Alice's and Dan's fingers met when they toyed with the blond curls at the same minute.

"What should we name her?" Alice whispered. Dan could choose whatever he wanted, one of the names he'd mentioned over the last few months, or something entirely different. Anna, for his grandmother. Esme because he thought French names were classy. Leia from *Star Wars*. It was only fair, to let him make that important decision.

He didn't answer. She repeated the question.

"Esme," he murmured to the baby, as he ran a finger from her hair, down her silky cheek.

•   •   •   •   •

October 1987

A sweet hint of citrus drifted into their narrow backyard from the neighbor's clutch of orange trees. "See?" Alice pulled a tulip bulb out of the small pile on the ground next to her knees and showed it to Esme. "Let's pretend this tulip is a big, tall, fir tree we're planting, so the spotted owls will come visit us. Would that be fun?"

Nodding rapidly, Esme squatted and stretched out her fingers. Her legs were sturdy and smooth, almost shiny. Her hair had turned darker blond and wavier instead of curly over the past few months, and a definite dimple had developed on her left cheek, mirroring Dan's. She clutched the bulb.

"Thank you, honey. Can you put—"

Esme stuck the pointy end of the bulb into her mouth.

"No! Don't eat that!"

One by one, Alice pried Esme's fingers off the slimy bulb until she could yank it out. Esme's mouth was wide open, maybe ready to cry. Alice quickly kissed Esme's nose and tickled her chin, then plopped the bulb into the hole she'd made in the dirt. "Do you want to help me tuck in the tulip?"

Together, they gathered fistfuls of dirt from all around the hole and tossed the dirt on top of the bulb. Esme sucked on her pale pink lower lip as they smoothed the dirt into a firm covering. Looking at Alice, Esme beamed.

"How about a snack? Do you want some O's and raisins?"

Alice brushed off Esme's fingers just as Esme thrust them into the plastic bag of Cheerios and raisins.

"I used to help my mommy and daddy plant flowers, when I was a little girl," Alice continued. "Like when Grandma Florence came yesterday to help us."

"Dada!" Esme stretched up her chubby arms.

"Mama," Alice corrected.

"Dada," Esme repeated, and she pointed behind Alice, toward Dan in the kitchen doorway, a few steps away.

Alice waved. "Hi. We're planting tulips. Come join us."

Dan kissed Alice's forehead and swooped a giggling Esme off the ground, a small stream of Cheerios and raisins dribbling from her fingers. "Are you making a pretty garden?" he asked Esme.

"I'm hoping my mother will come again tomorrow with her green thumb—" Alice began.

"Her hands are filthy."

Alice rubbed her own hands against her gray Sierra Club T-shirt. "Well, yeah. A little. We're planting flowers."

"You let her eat food with those hands?"

"A few Cheerios."

"I'm a doctor. I know about hygiene, and I don't want my daughter getting sick." Dan lifted Esme up and down into the air, smiling at her as she shrieked and laughed. "Let's go inside and wash off the dirty germs while Mommy makes dinner."

Should she say something to Dan? He was doing what all the books warned against, that one parent shouldn't contradict the other in front of their children. It would upset and confuse the kids, so the books said. But Esme wasn't crying or upset. She was settled in her favorite traveling mode, riding horseback on Dan's shoulders as they headed to the kitchen door, clutching his collar, bouncing, and squealing.

"It's nice for Esme to learn about nature," Alice mumbled. Dan and Esme were too far away to hear.

Reheating last night's leftovers and setting the kitchen table took just ten minutes. When Alice peeked into the living room, Esme was cushioned on Dan's lap on the leather couch, her right thumb planted in her mouth. In her arms, crossed over her little torso, she hugged Brownie the Dog and also her tiny plush moose, and the calico cat was snuggled against Dan's thigh, purring like a refrigerator. Dan and Esme were both staring at the TV, at a scene of lions racing over a low, grassy field. "Roar. Roar," Dan sang, while he alternately stroked Esme's hair and the cat's fur.

Esme turned to Alice, pulling her thumb out of her mouth and flourishing it. "Dada! All clean!"

Smiling at Alice, Dan patted a spot next to him and Esme on the couch.

•   •   •   •   •

April 1988

With Dan inches behind her at their front door, Alice set her palms on James's shoulders, stretched high on her toes, and gave each of his rough-skinned cheeks a fast kiss. A bare brush of a kiss. "Congratulations! Come on in. Did you bring a copy of the newspaper?"

"Page ten? Yeah."

Alice stepped to the side while James and Dan shook hands, an appropriately polite shake, for an appropriate couple of seconds, for two men who occasionally met on social occasions. A husband and his wife's old high school buddy; a short veterinarian with curly black hair and a tall, lean musician-journalist with a blond ponytail. A perfectly cordial gesture. "Your first published newspaper article?" Dan asked, and James replied, "Sixth, but it's my longest," and Dan said, "Can I take your coat?" As James unbuttoned his Navy-surplus pea coat, Alice rubbed Dan's lower back.

"Would you like a beer?" Dan continued. "We made sure to buy two six-packs of Dos Equis just for you. Yes, by all means, let's see your long article on page ten. Congratulations."

"And belated congratulations to you two on this house. How does it feel to be suburban homeowners?"

"Alice and I love it here. After dinner we'll have to give you the Grand Tour. All five rooms."

"And you have a yard?"

"Absolutely. All we need is a dog, as soon as Alice gives the word."

"Dan, I told you it's fine."

Stretching out the newspaper on the living-room coffee table, Dan flipped to page ten. *Shouting Match at Zoning Meeting*, declared the headline above James's name.

At least two dozen residents from Encino, Tarzana and nearby neighborhoods pummeled the Zoning Board with questions Monday night, as a decision looms on a controversial proposal to rezone two blocks of White Oak Avenue for mixed-income housing.

" 'Pummeled,' " Dan commented. "That's very poetic, James."

"I guess I'm just a frustrated songwriter."

"But it's good to liven up a newspaper with a little poetry," Alice added quickly, patting James's forearm. "I like the way James phrased it."

"It's only the Valley *Chronicle*." James shrugged. "Not exactly a middle-8."

"Ah, middle-8. An important interlude in a song. Is your band still together, then?" Dan asked.

"Not right now."

"So this newspaper is a complete career change for you."

"Yeah."

"I'm sure you miss playing your guitar."

"Don't forget the freelance music reviews James is writing. He hasn't abandoned music or guitar at all," Alice put in.

Esme was kneeling on the tile floor near the kitchen, her purple-and-white sneakers tucked under her little butt, her curly-wavy dark-blond hair flopping in two short ponytails. She stretched forward to push Brownie the Dog along the floor, followed by her stuffed moose the exact same distance. When the two animals were aligned, she scooted herself closer to them and repeated the moves, as the calico cat padded over to her.

"She's so precise." Alice hooked an arm around Dan's elbow.

"Indefatigable." Dan kissed Alice's cheek. "She's been doing this little animal race for ten minutes. I clocked her."

"The way she concentrates and doesn't get bored."

"I'll have to take her to Santa Anita to see the real races."

"Do you think she'll jump on the seats and scream at the horses, like the scene in *My Fair Lady*?"

James had gone over to Esme and squatted beside her. "Hey, Secretariat." He scratched behind the ears of the stuffed dog. "Can I run one of 'em? We'll race 'em together?"

Esme nodded.

"What's this guy's name?"

"Brownie." She pulled him to her chest.

"And the other guy?"

"Moosey."

"Hi, Moosey. Hi, Brownie."

"Me first."

They slid the animals ahead, Esme with Brownie, followed by James with Moosey.

"Esme's hair gets darker every week," Dan said loudly. "It used to be far more blond. Almost as blond as yours, James. Which is unusual with two brunette parents."

"Stop that! It's not funny anymore," Alice hissed into his ear.

Hopefully, James didn't hear, down on the floor by the kitchen with Esme.

"What happened to your sense of humor?" Dan whispered.

•   •   •   •   •

June 1988

Resting against the back of the couch, Dan wrapped an arm around Alice. "If you want to, absolutely, we can have Esme's birthday party at the beach. Though it might be hot."

"We'll play in the water."

"Sure. But it'll be crowded, on a weekend."

"We'll go early and find a spot." Alice snuggled closer. "We'll dig for sea glass with her. We'll jump in the little waves at the shoreline. She'll love it."

"Getting sand in her birthday cake."

"It'll be fine."

"You can't wear your expensive high heels on the beach."

"Duh. Stop being such a party pooper."

"I apologize." Dan planted a prompt peck on Alice's cheek. "We'll give Esme the greatest party in the history of two-year-olds."

"Should we invite our mothers' bridge partners so they can have a game?"

"Why not? They'd love that."

"How about Roz and Walt and Jenny? And James?"

"Oh, let's keep it small. Just the two grandmothers."

By ten o'clock in the morning on Saturday, Santa Monica Beach was already fiercely hot, with sporadic, strong bursts of wind that repeatedly knocked over Florence's big turquoise beach umbrella. Georgia, her spine straight in a blue-and-yellow lawn chair, briskly fanned herself with her oversized straw hat. Perched on another chair, Esme giggled while Alice, kneeling, rubbed sunscreen on her smooth neck, her shoulders, then down her arms. "Like this?" Alice tickled the tissue-soft underside of Esme's upper arm, and Esme laughed. "And this?"

"More, Mommy!"

But Esme was giggling and squirming too boisterously, and the sunscreen was sticking more on her red-flowered bathing suit than on her skin. As Alice tried to spread it over her arm, Esme leaned forward and tugged at the tube.

"Esme, give it back." Alice pulled the tube.

Esme tumbled off the chair, face-first into the sand at Alice's feet.

She erupted into sobs, sputtering sand as Alice immediately pulled her on her lap. "It's okay, it's okay," Alice repeated, kissing Esme's hair and brushing harshly at the grit that insistently stuck to Esme's sunscreened face while Esme wailed harder. "Just spit it all out, honey." But the more Esme wailed, the more she swallowed. "Try to spit," Alice coaxed.

"Here." Florence had appeared next to them, stroking Esme's head with one hand while the other held a water bottle toward Alice. Esme stopped for a moment, taking little breaths.

"For crying out loud." Dan hoisted Esme, along with a clean towel from somewhere, and then he and Esme were gone, striding toward the ocean.

In the abrupt silence, Alice looked from one grandmother to the other. "I—She slipped."

"It's sand," Florence said. "Dan will rinse it off in the water."

"Yeah."

"When you were a little younger than Esme, you slid right off a chair at a restaurant one time with your father and me and fell smack on your face, on the floor. You screamed." Florence shrugged. "You were fine. A scratch."

Sounds had returned to the beach. Seagulls screeched, children shouted. Radios blared music. "Ice cream! Cold soda!" a vendor called out. The two huge towels Alice and Florence had laid out on the sand reeked of spilled sunscreen.

Alice stood. "I think I'll go find them. Dan and Esme."

"I'll walk with Alice partway there." Rising, Georgia tied her hat under her chin. "Do you mind, Florence? I'll be back in a quick minute."

Florence waved the hand that wasn't holding her umbrella steady. "You two have a nice walk."

"I don't know how it happened," Alice began, as soon as they'd gone a few steps. "I guess she slipped. She's so squirmy."

Georgia gripped Alice's elbow without answering while they stepped unsteadily on the soft sand, dodging sprawling blankets.

"It's so hard to take a little kid to the beach," Alice continued. "But she'll enjoy it more when she's older."

They were near enough by then to see Dan and Esme, sitting at the surf's edge. Esme was pawing into the sand, probably hunting for shells, and Dan was gently splashing her toes. She turned toward him, holding out something in her hand. A special shell? A crab's broken-off leg? In another year or two, she would be jumping into the waves like a fish in a pink bathing suit.

Georgia halted. "She's charming, isn't she?"

"Cutest little girl in the world."

"Now aren't you glad that you have her?"

"Of course. Why would you even question that?"

"Dan told me how you were reluctant at first."

What?

Georgia clamped her hat more firmly on her head. "Now I understand why you asked me that odd question when you came to my house that day. You remember, long before you were pregnant. You were trying to determine if I would mind if I never had grandchildren. And it's all worked out, hasn't it?"

"But I—" Alice exhaled fast. "I wanted kids. I wanted to get pregnant."

"Good, so you changed your mind."

"No! That's not what happened." Dammit, she was yelling at her own mother-in-law. Half the beach was undoubtedly eavesdropping. Swiftly, Alice smiled at Georgia. "Actually, I—"

What could she say? *Actually, I tricked your son into this pregnancy. And he lied to you.*

And then go home and ask Dan: *Why did you lie to your mother?*

What if he asked her, in return: *So why did you lie to me, Alice?*

If you want it that much, he'd said in the reception area of his clinic. What he hadn't said was: *So much that you'd cheat and lie to get a baby.*

Did it really matter, whether Georgia thought Dan or Alice had been the one who originally pushed to have a baby? Did Alice really need to open that buried can of worms with Dan? What good would that do? In fact, what Dan had told his mother might be seen as a positive sign, that he was ashamed about not wanting children at first. Besides, the important battle had been won: Esme, playing in the sand.

"Actually," Alice said, and she smiled again, even if her voice and her smile weren't as firm as they should be, "we both wanted to become parents. Very much. It was very mutual."

•   •   •   •   •

October 1989

"Alice, have you looked at Esme's preschool recently?"

"Of course. I bring her there and pick her up every day. Almost every day."

"Two girls were crying when I dropped Esme off this morning, and no one was paying attention to them. The floor was filthy. Total chaos."

"I've never noticed any filth, Dan."

"That's because you never pay attention to anything."

"That's not true. I'm always seeing her, you know, doing fun things." Half-turning away from Dan, Alice opened a door in the cabinet closest to her above the kitchen counter, as if she desperately needed to pull out a can of…something. Soup. Tuna. Tomato sauce. "Remember that little clay statue she made? All the pictures she draws? She has a great time there." The statue was pretty elaborate, especially for a little girl who wasn't three and a half yet. It was clearly meant to be a person waving, with a smaller ball on top of a larger ball and one arm-tube sticking out from the side of the bigger ball.

"A clay statue, Alice? Really? That's the most important criterion?"

"Roz sent Jenny there for two years, and she was very pleased with it."

"Oh, excuse me. Roz, the fount of all wisdom."

"She has more experience than either of us."

"I'm sure she does."

"So. You find a better place," Alice snapped.

That was the wrong thing to say.

A gradual smirk spread across Dan's tightly pinched lips as he pulled a piece of typing paper, folded into precise fourths, out of his shirt pocket. "I already have. I have the names and details of three excellent preschools, all within ten miles of our house, highly recommended by clients of mine." He thrust the paper at Alice. "You're not the only person who can make lists."

"Where did you—?" The paper dangled in the kitchen air and, stupidly, Alice took it. She even started to read it. "Why are you criticizing everything I do?"

"Really, Alice." Dan took his mug of coffee from the counter. "Why do you view this conversation as criticizing you? It's not about you. It's about our daughter's best interest."

Moving to another part of the counter, away from Dan, Alice toweled a couple of dishes from the drying rack. Of course she wasn't against her daughter's best interest. Why was Dan twisting her words?

"Isn't the most important issue her health and safety?" Dan asked blandly, from behind her back.

"And happiness. Friends."

"Very true."

"So. I mean…." She couldn't avoid turning fully around, face to face with him, any longer.

He was smiling. "I know you'll want to visit these three venues that I'm suggesting, before we make any decision. I've already been to them, and I was very impressed. Their staffing ratios. Their educational programs, too, which you didn't mention in your analysis. And yes, of course it should be a place where Esme will have fun." Walking over to Alice, he kissed her cheek.

It couldn't hurt to visit a couple of other preschools, before announcing her opinion.

CHAPTER TEN

Mrs. Hanson sat behind a wide desk in the sorority office, bright with an old-fashioned chandelier directly above her. Her short, curly hair was heavily speckled with gray now, and she was wearing eyeglasses with thin pink rims. Her lipstick, though, was the same deep-red as five years earlier. "We have so many wonderful girls here at Delta Alpha Mu. Friendly girls, smart girls. Caring girls. I like to think we become a family during our time together, and in fact many of them stay in touch with me after they leave. Of course, they're so active, they scatter all over the planet." She clasped her veined hands together on top of the desk. "You said in your telephone message that you had an important reason why you needed to see me about your daughter. When did she graduate?"

"Two years ago."

"Oh, yes!" Smiling widely, the sorority housemother sat up straighter in her wooden swivel chair. "The class of 2008. The ecology class. They were such a special group."

My daughter's so special, that I just learned last week that she's a criminal. "Thank you," Alice said.

Even James had told her that coming here was a wasted effort—James, the talk-to-every-potential-source journalist. And taking more time off work, barely a week after her dash to the Santa Barbara police, wasn't the greatest idea. Oh, James couldn't understand, no matter how much he cared about Esme. He and Andrea didn't have children. A mother had to try harder than a journalist did.

"As I explained on the phone," Mrs. Hanson was continuing, in her high-pitched, crisp voice, "I can't divulge personal details about one of our girls, not even to a close family member. They're legal adults at this age."

"I understand. But, well, this is difficult for me to speak about." From her uncushioned chair on the opposite side of the desk, Alice smiled weakly at the housemother. "I'm embarrassed to say that my daughter was recently arrested—Nothing violent. Not a felony! Gosh, no. Still, it's troubling, to think of an arrest record following her all her life. I'm sure this has never happened to your sorority before." Or maybe it had. A sorority sister arrested for DUI or drug dealing? Maybe Mrs. Hanson had broken the no-divulging rule before this, for the families of other Delta Alpha Mu's who'd been in trouble with the law. "So, I was wondering, perhaps, if there might be something in her file that could serve as a proof of her good character. An award? An example of community service? You mentioned the ecology class. Didn't she participate in a big beach cleanup at El Capitan?"

Mrs. Hanson was staring at Alice.

"Or something that might gain the judge's sympathy. If, I don't know, Esme had a serious illness? A bad accident? If there was anything that would possibly help keep her out of jail." Oh, James was right. It was a waste of time and effort. All those wonderful, smart, caring Delta Alpha Mu's who were supposedly like family, and why would Mrs. Hanson remember Esme Wilson out of the dozens from every past year?

The silence, after Alice dropped her balled-up fingers into her lap, was brief.

"Did you bring her birth certificate and your driver's license, as proof of your relationship with her, as we discussed?" Mrs. Hanson asked, with no change in her voice tone.

Alice handed the documents across the desk. "Whatever you could do, would help so much."

A four-drawer, old-fashioned steel filing cabinet filled one corner of the bright room. Mrs. Hanson took the birth certificate there, opened the second drawer from the top, and riffled through a series of folder tabs, licking her finger before every other one. Finally, she pulled out a sheaf of papers that were clipped together. "Oh," she said quietly.

She carried the folder back to the big desk.

"You came to visit once, didn't you?" the housemother said, her voice suddenly gentler. "You left a note for your daughter."

Damn. Mrs. Hanson remembered: This was the mother whose daughter refused to talk to her.

"Yes." Alice swallowed. "It's been…difficult. As I said. That's why it's so important now."

Mrs. Hanson didn't react. Instead, pressing her pink-framed eyeglasses higher on the bridge of her nose, she read aloud from the sheaf of papers. "The behavior began in approximately September of 2006, at the beginning of the student's sophomore year…"

The story that Mrs. Hanson told almost made sense. For someone else's daughter.

Night after night, for at least four months during the first half of her junior year at UC Santa Barbara, the student had sneaked into the sorority kitchen. And secretly stuffed herself with food. Ice cream and cookies and muffins and last night's leftover meat loaf and frozen French fries and raw English muffins and the lasagna that the Delta Alpha Mu sisters had planned to donate to the women's shelter where they volunteered. Then vomited it all up. For four months. Tiptoeing past Mrs. Hanson's room. Pawing through the cupboards, the pantry, the huge double-door refrigerator and the extra freezer, grabbing anything, and afterwards locking herself in whatever empty bathroom she could find. No one knew. Or they knew, but they ignored it. They undoubtedly smelled it on her hair, her skin, and her clothing, that sickly sweet odor of vomit. They heard her, while they pounded on the door to get into the bathroom. Her roommate would have noticed that she was missing for hours every night, and everyone must have seen how she barely picked at her plate during mealtimes. The sorority-house cook was confused about why so much food kept disappearing. Until finally, when her housemates couldn't stomach the stink and the sounds in the bathrooms any longer, they told Mrs. Hanson.

The student was over eighteen, technically an adult, so Mrs. Hanson didn't call her parents.

Prozac was prescribed, and the student went for counseling at the campus health center twice a week for the rest of the year, plus yoga once a week. Mrs. Hanson and the cook mapped out individualized meal plans. The whole house took turns staying with her in the evenings, holding her and telling her they loved her, telling her she could get past this thing, while she sobbed and rocked. She was never left alone, not for a minute. They made her join every Delta activity, cleaning the beach, tutoring the children in the women's shelter, painting eggs for the community Easter egg roll. Padlocks were installed on the refrigerator, the pantry, and both freezers. By spring break, there were no more smells or missing food. By her senior year, she'd terminated the counseling and the Prozac. By graduation, she seemed fine.

Noiselessly, Mrs. Hanson closed the folder. "You weren't aware that she was bulimic?" she asked, her voice a shade softer.

For four months Esme had been eating herself sick, and making herself throw up, and then eating again. Hiding. Stealing food. Lying to her sorority sisters. Trying to disguise the smells. Feeling sick to her guts and shoving more down her throat anyway. Over and over.

"No. I wasn't aware." Alice squeezed her mouth shut, breathing out through her nose.

"I thought, in high school, perhaps."

"Why did she do it?"

Mrs. Hanson shook her head and licked her bottom lip. "Unfortunately, it's not uncommon in a university environment today. All the pressures on ambitious young women. They want top grades. They're worried about finding a job. There are so many possible reasons. Many of the experts say it has to do with control." Mrs. Hanson pushed the sheaf of papers a little sideways on her desk. "Trying to control a part of their life or fill an emptiness in their life. A cry for attention, perhaps. And then the social pressure, the influence of the magazines and advertisements, all around them, the thin role models. I suppose they feel overwhelmed in a way, whatever the cause." The last sounds of her voice seemed to linger.

"Do you know if she had any, you know, side effects? Long-term?"

"Well, not every girl experiences significant side effects. If the situation didn't continue for too long, for instance. However, yes, there can be, ah, heart problems. Palpitations, arrhythmia. And other conditions. Anemia. Bowel issues. Inflammation of the esophagus, or possibly rupture. Those are all extremes, you understand."

Heart palpitations. Ruptured esophagus. Esme?

"Your daughter certainly didn't get to that stage," Mrs. Hanson added. "I'm confident that we caught it early enough."

"Did it really stop? Completely?"

"Well, some people compare it to alcoholism. They say that an alcoholic always remains an alcoholic, don't they? But certainly a person can significantly change their habits. Don't you think so? Especially if they can get to the root cause of the eating disorder. I can assure you that while your daughter stayed with us, for the rest of her college career, there was never a recurrence." Mrs. Hanson paused. "I'm sorry to have to tell all this."

A strong hum had started outside, probably a gardener trimming the bushes along the stucco walls, and a faint whiff of warm air blew in through the window screen. The slaps of several sets of sneakers padded rapidly along the hallway beyond the closed door of the office.

"Thank you," Alice whispered. "You and the whole sorority, you all saved her life."

"Of course. She was one of our girls." Mrs. Hanson pushed the papers toward herself, straightening them into a neat pile. She licked her lip again. "There was also a letter."

"A letter? From—whom?"

"It was a required part of her counseling at the end of the year, to write a letter to herself. A sort of self-analysis." Now Mrs. Hanson tapped the neat pile of papers against the desktop. "I don't really think I'm permitted to show you."

"Please."

Mrs. Hanson was no longer looking at Alice, but instead, down at the desk, then over toward the filing cabinet. The hum outside grew fainter.

"Please."

"If it might be relevant to a legal matter. Since she didn't specifically ask us to keep it confidential or destroy it." Mrs. Hanson's voice became crisper. "I'll have to request that you read it here. I can't let it leave this office."

It was a one-and-a-half-page computer printout, signed in Esme's elongated, slanted handwriting with the "e" at the end of Esme and the "n" at the end of Wilson both shooting a final stroke upward.

MY SELF-ANALYSIS

I look back on it, and I can't believe I did any of that stuff. I don't even want to think about it. As soon as I do, the smells smother me. Ucky-sweet and shit at the same time. Did everyone smell it, too? I want to smother my head in shampoo, but I feel like I'll never get rid of it.

I can't remember the food they say I ate. They said it was everything I could get my hands on. Even stuff I don't like. I mean, frozen English muffins? I feel like it was somebody else eating all that shit.

But I'm not going to totally stop eating ice cream now, just because I was disgusting back then and gorged on it. I'm not going to go to the other extreme.

I just never want to see anyone from this building ever again.

I honestly have tried to think and think, like the counselor asked me, and I don't know why I began doing it. I mean, yeah, Brian and I split up over the summer, but I'm not such a jerk to eat myself sick for that. We were only together a few months anyways, he wasn't that important. My classes were the same boring okay as always. I wasn't getting Fs. I wasn't feeling depressed. I wasn't imitating someone. I don't know anyone else who's done something like this. Or who admits it, anyway. All the dumb questions they ask me. No, I don't want to kill myself. I don't know if I hate my body. Was food a major issue when I was a kid? I don't know, what does "major issue" mean? Dad and Penelope are big on healthy organic food, cage-free eggs, all that stuff. They make their own pasta. Penelope makes all these sorts of weird veggie juices. I like a few of them, like cucumber-apple-celery. So how come that didn't give me healthy eating habits, right? Mom hates to cook, but she's always been honest about that, and if I wanted to buy organic stuff or cook my own recipes, she always let me.

The counselor says it's not necessarily about food anyway. I have to focus on my inner self, finding things inside myself to love. (How do you do that without being a conceited bitch?) I think I'm an okay person. Nothing special and nothing bad. I try to be nice to people. I do my homework and try to help my Delta sisters. I think I do a good job at Clothing Etc, being encouraging with customers without being pushy. I joined the art club this year, and that was fun. I think some of the jewelry I've made is pretty cool. I'm going to graduate, duh! I mean, I'm not flunking out, even if I'm not the smartest person in the world. No, I don't know what I want to do after I graduate or what I want as a career.

I'm supposed to answer, Do I think I'll ever do it again?

Here's what I think. If I'm ever ever tempted to do this shit again, I'll picture a toilet full of vomit.

•   •   •   •   •

Nearly every morning from the age of four and a half to fifteen, Esme ate breakfast with Alice at the round wooden table in the windowless kitchen of their small apartment in Santa Monica. Cheerios at first, then picking out the orange Trix in her orange-food stage, then a bowl of strawberry or peach yogurt as a teenager while she studied the super-thin models in *Elle* and *Seventeen* magazines, and the fake Tiffany dragonfly lampshade hanging from the kitchen ceiling washed the small room with pale streaks of yellow, green, and orange. Esme always started eating at the edge of her bowl or plate, moving inward to the center.

Was that meticulousness the first warning sign of a looming obsession with food? And then the insistence on organic fruit and crackers when Esme was thirteen? It had seemed such a healthy eating habit. Or did the problem begin earlier, with the orange-only food in kindergarten?

What did Esme say or do over the years that predicted this, that a good mother should have picked up on? Did she spend too long in the bathroom? (Well, yes, fixing her hair in the morning, when she was in junior high, because it was so wild, but that had nothing to do with eating. Did it?) Did the bathroom often smell of air freshener? (No, because they didn't keep air freshener in the apartment.) Did food mysteriously disappear from their refrigerator? Had Esme lost a huge amount of weight too rapidly? Did she move her food around on her plate without actually eating, the way Jenny did? No, no, and no.

Was the high school cheerleading part of the explanation, Courtney and all those other girls pushing themselves to exercise more and more? Look at how thin Courtney had been, the disastrous weekend she'd visited their apartment. Like the models in the magazines Mrs. Hanson had talked about.

What had Alice missed?

For that matter, why hadn't Dan and Penelope noticed anything? Esme had lived with them for most of high school, and she would have been staying with them during the college vacations smack in the heyday of her bulimia. *For at least four months during the first half of her junior year.* Dozens of meals, dozens of nights when she could have sneaked into their fancy kitchen to scarf down leftover homemade whole-wheat pasta. *Dad and Penelope are big on healthy, organic food. So how come that didn't give me healthy eating habits, right?* When Penelope took Esme shopping, didn't she see the actual girl who was trying on the purple T-shirt with the smiling pineapple, see her skeletal arms and her ribs poking through the cotton?

Sure, the bulimia might not really be about food. It was also about control, Mrs. Hanson had said; about filling an emptiness in a person's life. Maybe the motivation behind the bulimia was somehow related to Esme's arrest. Stealing food was the same as stealing art supplies? Filling an emptiness? Did that make sense? What was Esme crying out for?

Maybe that was what Esme had actually been asking Roz about, in the phone call last fall that Roz had kept secret. Not about Jenny's drug use. About Jenny's anorexia. Which wasn't exactly the same as Esme's bulimia, but similar enough.

It took Jenny nearly three years to recover. Was Esme recovered? Mrs. Hanson hadn't really answered.

Esme's self-analysis letter explained yet it didn't. She'd had a boyfriend for a short while. Brian, not Robert Corning. Was he an athlete, all muscle and vitamins and a tight six-pack, pressuring her to "look sexy"? Meaning, skinny. She was still getting mediocre grades in her classes, reading between the lines. Those could be causes of her bulimia. They also could apply to half the girls in her sorority. And honestly, why should anyone expect Esme to bare her soul in a "letter" that might go in her official university file? The poor girl would have barely emerged from an experience that was physically draining, if not terrifying; a trauma that had dragged everything out of her. She must have felt embarrassed, and as she wrote, she didn't want to think about it.

Would Esme have had a healthier attitude toward food and toward herself if she and her mother had cooked together? If Alice hadn't pressured her to study harder? To visit the historic mission in Santa Barbara? All the way up to that last history test before her high school graduation. *Even if I'm not the smartest person in the world.* Had Alice pressed so hard that she not only pushed her own daughter away until her daughter wouldn't speak to her, but she even pushed her into dangerous bulimia? Heart problems. Rupture of the esophagus. Was that possible?

No!

Esme didn't seem all that angry at Alice in the self-analysis letter. *Mom hates to cook, but she's always been honest about that, and if I wanted to buy organic stuff or make my own recipes, she always let me.*

There were times when they'd truly been happy together, weren't there? Esme had loved planting tulip bulbs, and painting pottery bowls at the children's workshops, and digging fishing pools in the sand. Making necklaces with Jenny. Taking ballet classes—at first. She'd felt proud, helping Mommy choose which high-heeled shoes to buy and being allowed to walk around the apartment wearing the Mommy shoes herself. There had been times when they'd been mother and daughter, together.

CHAPTER ELEVEN

ALICE, DAN, AND ESME

November 1989

West Hollywood, CA

James, on a bench seat next to his date, waved vigorously from a table at the far side of the crowded Indian restaurant. Alice and Dan waved back as they sidled around other tables, through semi-darkness and the keen smells of onion, mint, and mango.

"Why did we let him choose the restaurant?" Dan whispered to Alice. "The reviews of this place are pretty crappy."

Smiling, he pulled out a chair for Alice, across from the date, when they arrived at the table.

James gestured toward each of the three, in turn. "Alice. Dan. Andrea. Alice's my old high school friend I told you about," he said to Andrea.

A short, fat candle flickered inside a glass in the center of the white tablecloth. Andrea had dark-blond hair dangling below her ears in a mild flip, thick eyebrows like Esme, and a squat nose, and she was dressed a lot fancier than James's usual girlfriends, in a silky, rust-orange blouse that clung to her shoulders and a pendant necklace with a small ivory-doored locket. Then again, James had on a nicer-than-usual tan sweater. The two of them were seated with their backs almost pressed against the red-tapestried wallpaper, their arms not quite touching.

"How about you, Andrea?" Dan inquired, gently unfolding his linen napkin. "Where did you grow up?"

"I was born in London. My father was in the foreign service, in the State Department." Her voice was quiet, revealing the slightest upper-class British accent in occasional words. *Born. London.*

"That must have been an interesting childhood." Dan hadn't stopped smiling. "Did your family get invited to special diplomatic events? Dinner with the Queen?"

"No dinners at the Palace, but as a little girl, I admit, I was a tad obsessed with Princess Anne. I imagined myself as a princess in the Middle Ages."

James, dating a diplomat's daughter from England? Really? No wonder he was dressing better.

"A princess," Dan repeated. "England is certainly the place for that. Did you go to school there?"

"No. My father was re-posted shortly after I turned three years old. In the foreign service, one moves around quite a bit."

"Ah, so where did you move to, after London?"

"Amsterdam. Mexico City. Canberra. One of my brothers was born in Canberra, and the other one in Madrid, and my younger sister was born in Cairo."

James beamed while Andrea recited her family's geographical history, as if he'd personally escorted her to all those spots. "Isn't that an amazing childhood?"

"It certainly is. In which exotic foreign city did you two first meet?" Dan asked.

"Rabat," Andrea replied. "That's in Morocco."

"James, when were you in Morocco?" Alice asked. Had he ever mentioned meeting a woman in Morocco?

"Trying out the hashish in the casbah?" Dan patted the napkin on his lap.

"Do you guys remember," James said, "in late 'eighty-six and early 'eighty-seven, when I was hitching through Europe, trying to figure out whether I should give up on music? I ran into a drummer who offered me a gig with him for a couple months in Casablanca, and after that I decided to check out the scene in North Africa a little more. And Andrea was doing research in Morocco on French colonialism, for her PhD. So we were both just wandering around this cool place called Chellah, which is the ruins of a—well, a lot of ruins, in fact. Phoenician and Roman and Muslim. As a certain doctoral student of French colonialism informed me back then, over a lot of glasses of mint tea." He draped an arm around Andrea, ruffling the bottom of her hair. "And get this, people are talking about organizing a jazz festival there, at Chellah."

"But you've been in L.A. for a while now."

"Yeah, you know, I came back here to try freelancing for newspapers, like an asshole. Andrea went over to Paris. So we figured that was it. But." James grinned. "Andrea got offered a teaching job at USC. And luckily, she remembered me."

In the new silence, James fiddled with Andrea's hair again.

If only somebody would find a fresh topic of conversation. The spaniel with the broken leg in Dan's clinic? The little clay statue Esme had made? What did James think of Madonna's "Like a Prayer" music video?

Dan leaned toward Andrea, kitty-corner across the table. "You didn't mention Delhi or Bombay among all your destinations, but I'm sure you've been to India. Right?"

"Oh, yes."

"In that case, what dishes would you recommend for us tonight?"

Stretching one long, tasseled menu over their bare plates, Dan and Andrea took turns pointing at a flurry of food names.

"James loves lamb *vindaloo*."

"That's too spicy for Alice."

"Hey, James," Alice called to him. "Do you think they have Indian beer?"

James frowned. "Come on, I don't only drink beer."

Since when was James sensitive about drinking beer? Since when did he wear expensive-looking sweaters, for that matter, and date globe-trotting PhDs? What was next, hobnobbing at Davos?

At last, Dan and Andrea shifted back properly in their seats. Andrea glanced at James. He cupped his formerly callused, formerly guitar-playing fingers on top of her pale hand where it rested on the tablecloth.

"Of all those enticing cities that you mentioned, Andrea"—Dan laid his menu on his plate—"which was your favorite place to live?"

"I hope," James replied, "it's L.A."

"Really? Compared to Paris and Cairo?"

"We're getting married," James said.

He and Andrea smiled at each other.

"What joyous news. Long-lost love rediscovered. Congratulations!" Smiling broadly and dimpled, Dan raised his water glass. "We should certainly toast the happy couple. Is champagne in order?"

"We want to invite you two to the wedding," James went on, "except I don't think we're gonna have the big, traditional kind of thing."

"Don't worry about it," Dan said.

"We might just go to City Hall."

"Aren't you having music at your own wedding?"

"Yes." Andrea laughed, for the first time. "James has promised to serenade me if we can find a proper balcony."

Alice's hands were probably in her lap. Or maybe they were holding her menu, or on the sides of her water glass. Was anyone looking at her? Was she smiling appropriately?

Of course James was getting married. Why shouldn't he get married? And if he was happy with Andrea, even if they seemed completely mismatched, Bob Dylan marrying a PhD from London, well, as long as they were happy. James was old enough to decide for himself how to spend his own life.

"That was a heck of a punch line," Alice said, and certainly she was smiling now. Copying Dan, she raised her water glass. "Congratulations."

But her hand was shaking too much.

Dan pulled down her hand, keeping a strong grip on her fingers and on the glass.

Chapter Twelve

The short young woman folding white cardboard boxes on top of the bakery's glass display case was as thin as a breadstick, with piercings in her left eyebrow, her nose, the left side of her upper lip, and along the edges of both earlobes. Her cropped hair was a shade of green a leprechaun would love, except for a wide blue strip that ran diagonally from left to right, and she wore a pink T-shirt underneath a bright orange, full-length apron. Although the hair and piercings were new, Courtney Michaels, manager of MultiGrainery Bakery in a Silicon Valley mini-mall, looked the same as she had in high school when she'd come to Alice's apartment with Esme for the weekend, an excited sixteen-year-old pixie who never stopped moving.

Maybe Courtney didn't remember that visit?

The little shop was warm with the scents of chocolate, raspberry, and butter, like Florence's kitchen when she baked.

"I'm Alice Wilson." Carefully, Alice shut the glass door behind her. "Esme Wilson's mother from high school. Is this a good time for you? You said in your text that a Saturday in the late morning would be okay."

"Esme's mom! Hi!" Courtney beamed.

"Everything smells delicious."

"It's all organic."

"Nice. What's that?"

Alice gestured at different spots inside the huge display case, and Courtney answered. Berry-and-cream scones. Cranberry orange muffins. Chocolate pumpkin zucchini muffins. Zucchini mini-loaves. Banana bread mini-loaves. Seven-grain bread. A few clunky coffee mugs were stacked on the tile shelf in back of Courtney, alongside a shiny espresso machine.

"You mentioned that you've seen Esme a few times since high school." Alice smiled across the display case at Courtney. Was it the right kind of smile? The casual, friendly kind that said: *Oh, it's no big deal to see my daughter.*

"Yeah, a couple times when we were both in Calabasas visiting our families, we hung out a little. And she came in here once, last fall."

"Really? All the way here to Milpitas, to Silicon Valley? That's a long drive for an organic muffin."

Courtney had laughed a lot in high school, before the visit went bad, and now she burst out in a guffaw that continued for several "ha's."

"I mean, I'm sure your muffins are delicious," Alice added.

"You're funny. Yeah, her boyfriend and her were heading up north to visit some friends of theirs, so I guess they stopped here for a snack on the way."

"Her boyfriend?"

Was the boyfriend Robert Corning? Bobby. Did they attempt to rob MultiGrainery, too, before or after the art-supply store? No, no, Courtney sounded too cheerful about the encounter. Or it could have been Brian, the boyfriend Esme had split up with before she began having bulimia, and they'd gotten back together.

Shouldn't a mother know who her own daughter's boyfriend was?

But a post-college daughter? How many grown daughters told their mothers about their boyfriends?

Alice coughed. "Heading up north. So I guess she's still living near Santa Barbara?" Another stupid comment. California was a long state, and Milpitas was in the northern half, so Esme could be living in hundreds of places other than Santa Barbara that would be south of this bakery.

"She didn't really say."

"Yeah."

"They were on his motorcycle. So I suppose they couldn't go all that far."

Esme's boyfriend had a motorcycle.

The door behind Alice opened, and a man wearing faded jeans and clean Timberlands entered.

"Was the boyfriend's name Bobby?" Alice asked quickly.

The man was already at the rounded glass front of the display case, almost next to Alice. He glanced at her. "Are you finished?"

"No. Yes. Go ahead."

"What was that scone I had last week?" the man asked Courtney, as he bent to peer through the glass. "Not too sweet."

"I believe it was cinnamon, Mr. Joyce."

"More fruity than that."

"It could've been currant. Those are about the two unsweetest we have."

"That doesn't ring a bell. Well, you know what, I think I'll get a zucchini bread. Would that be good for breakfast?"

"I always say, you should have vegetables for breakfast, and zucchini is a vegetable."

The two of them laughed together, Courtney and Mr. Joyce, Courtney emitting another guffaw as she squatted and pulled out a small, dark, moist-looking loaf swaddled in plastic wrap. The man studied the offerings inside the display case for a few more moments, while Courtney slid the loaf into a white paper bag, then folded the open edges of the bag into a sharp line, then folded them again. "I might try one of the scones, too," the man added.

"Sure thing. Which kind?"

"I just don't like it too sweet."

"How about trying the currant?"

"Never mind."

Courtney rested her bony elbows on the display case's metal countertop after Mr. Joyce left. "Yeah. Bobby," she said.

The boyfriend. The criminal. Robert Corning. "What was he like?"

"I only met him that one time. A big guy, sort of. Quiet. He had like a little beard and a tiny hoop earring in one of his ears. I can't remember which ear."

A big guy, with one of those little beards? That was how the clerk at the art supply store had described him, a week ago, to Alice and James.

"Did he go to UC Santa Barbara, too?" Alice asked. Casually.

"I don't think so. He worked in a motorcycle place."

"Did he seem…nice?"

"I guess. Like I said, he didn't talk a lot."

"Did you notice anything else about him, in particular?" Dammit, Alice was starting to sound like Olivia in *Law & Order*, grilling poor Courtney. But Courtney had seen Esme within the past year, face to face, and met the criminal Bobby!

Courtney chewed the edge of a blue thumbnail. "He was wearing a tie-dyed shirt with this elaborate design, sort-of a spiral that explodes into a flower. Purple and orange. Actually, Esme had a matching shirt. She said he made them himself. She said he did a lot of tie-dying." Then she shivered.

Talking about Robert Corning made Courtney shiver? "Are you all right?"

"Yeah. It's the motorcycle, that's all. I can't be around motorcycles. They have that noise and smoke and the whole macho-big-pipe thing." Reaching with a large square of waxed paper into the display case, Courtney retrieved a muffin and held it out. "Want one? It's blueberry-walnut. It's a great source of antioxidants."

Esme had a quiet boyfriend with a little beard who made tie-dye shirts. His-and-her matching shirts.

And who broke into the store where he bought dye powder in shades of deep purple and rust orange to make those shirts.

"Did Bobby…did the two of them seem to be on any drugs?"

"Esme?" Courtney let out another one of her guffaws. "We were all so straight in high school. We were cheerleaders. Esme made the decorations for the school dances."

"I remember. Every Friday night."

The dark muffin was sitting in Courtney's outstretched palm, nestled in the waxed paper. Alice took it. "Thank you."

"Esme looked the same as high school," Courtney added.

"Really?" In her senior portrait in the Calabasas High School yearbook, Esme had a grin as wide as a laugh, her dimple a tiny dent in her cheek, her hair tousled and streaked with blonde highlights. She was also in the cheerleader group photo, at the left side of the row of five girls kneeling with their black-and-gold pompoms positioned against their chests, a second row of girls behind them, standing and holding pompoms high above their heads. They wore black-and-gold pleated skirts and long-sleeved gold tank tops, and their mouths were stretched open as if they were shouting out a cheer. Courtney must have been in that scene, too, among the shorter girls kneeling on the ground, alongside Esme.

Esme always seemed to be having fun at the Friday night games, shaking her pompoms, her hair controlled in a French braid.

"She enjoyed cheerleading a lot," Alice said. "Didn't she?"

"Oh wow, yeah. We were all totally into it. I mean, we never did the really advanced tosses and spins like they do in competitions, but we had fun. One year, a couple of the girls invented cheers for dumb things. Like, getting your period?"

"What cheer do you do for getting your period?"

Laughing, Courtney darted out from behind the display case, to the tiny spot of open space next to Alice. She pushed a wrought-iron chair against one of the two small tables in the store and began doing jumping jacks but with her hands alternately hitting her crotch instead of clapping above her head. She halted, hugging herself and still laughing, after four sets. "I know, it's gross. Like, you're slapping a Tampax on yourself?"

"Are you kidding? You didn't do it at actual games, did you?"

"God, no! Can you imagine?"

As Courtney walked back to the display case, she paused and rubbed her hands against the bib of her apron. "We had a health food club, too, if you can believe it. Esme, me, Jenna, Morgan. It basically consisted of baking muffins with organic raisins at my house."

"Esme always wanted me to buy organic fruits and things. And here you are, working in an organic bakery." Alice held up the muffin in her hand as a salute, then took a bite into the side. "This is delicious. It's almost a cupcake, it's so rich and juicy."

"Thanks."

"Are you certain it's not actually a cupcake?"

Courtney grinned. "Esme had on these cool earrings. When she and Bobby came here, I mean." Crossing her arms, Courtney leaned on top of the display case again. "They were like a string of glass beads in different colors, with silver half-moons dangling below them. She said she'd made them, that she was starting to design jewelry."

I think some of the jewelry I've made is pretty cool, Esme had written, in her bulimia self-analysis.

She'd liked making jewelry when she was younger. Now and then. Stringing the necklaces with Jenny. The idea of recycled jewelry that she'd mentioned once.

"Do you remember anything else from Esme's visit here?"

"I think they both got banana-carob muffins."

"Did Esme buy, um, just one muffin? Or a lot?"

"No, they each got one." Courtney straightened, frowning. "Is she okay? My mom said you were asking to talk with me, because Esme's having problems."

I'm kind of worried because she's been out of contact for a while.

And she had bulimia only a couple of years ago, and I don't know if she's really over it, and I'm scared she'll get heart problems or a ruptured esophagus.

I'm going out of my mind because she was arrested for burglary and trespass and a bunch of other charges, and her trial could start any day, and she could go to jail for sixteen months.

There was no script for asking her daughter's old cheerleading friend from six years ago if her daughter was still cramming food in her mouth and then vomiting. If her daughter had broken into a lot of stores, or only one. If her daughter's boyfriend was a nice tie-dying artist or a criminal.

"No, no, it's just that I—we—I haven't heard from her in a while. And I'd heard only a little about, um, Bobby. So, you know, we moms get worried." Damn, that was lame. "Do you possibly have a phone number for her?"

You don't have your own daughter's phone number?

Courtney, thankfully, didn't ask that. Instead, she said, "Gee, no, I'm sorry. We just connect on Facebook sometimes."

Facebook. Another dead end. "Could I check back with you?" Alice asked. "In a week or so?"

"Sure, but, like, I can't promise I'll hear anything from her by then."

"I apologize if I'm asking too many questions. I don't mean to be pushy."

"Nah, no problem."

One more question. Surely, Alice could be allowed one more. "Did you and your friends in high school ever, you know, talk about your mothers?"

For a moment, Courtney was strangely silent. "My mom was diagnosed with Parkinson's senior year."

Mrs. Michaels? The mother with the banana-colored hair, according to the high-school Courtney?

That was why she hadn't responded to the phone messages six years ago.

"I'm so sorry."

"She's holding her own, the doctors say. The tremors are only in her left arm and left hand, for now."

"I'm sorry," Alice repeated. "It must be tough on your family."

"Yeah, it's hard with my sister and me living up here, being a long drive away. My sister's the one who started this bakery, like six months before Mom got sick. So we take turns going back to Calabasas and spending a week or so with our parents. Still. We worry, like, if there's an emergency?" Then Courtney smiled. "Esme was really nice. She came over to visit a few times, even after she went off to college. She made these beautiful earrings for my mom, with silver wires shaped like long teardrops, and a little pearl in the center. My mom loves them."

Alice croaked, "I should get going."

"Here." Courtney held out a small paper bag, the kind she'd given Mr. Joyce. "You can put your muffin in this."

"Thanks. How much do I owe you?"

"For old times." Courtney waved aside Alice's wallet.

"Are you sure?"

"I'll text you," Courtney added, as Alice clutched the bag in both hands, "if Esme comes in. I'll ask for her phone number."

But by then, it could be too late! Theoretically, Esme's trial was supposed to start within forty-five days of her arraignment, which was more or less right now, though in fact it wasn't on the court calendar yet, and James's lawyer-friend said they never stuck strictly to the forty-five-day requirement. But they could. Any day.

A six-hour drive, at the fastest, from this mini-mall back home to Santa Monica. South and inland through the Central Valley, past Fresno, past Bakersfield. Perhaps Esme had ridden those same roads, on the backseat of Bobby Corning's motorcycle, to visit her old high school friend Courtney at her bakery. Or she and Bobby Corning could have taken the scenic coast route. Toured Hearst Castle and stopped for lunch at the Madonna Inn. As Alice and Esme had done, years ago when they were still mother and daughter.

Esme zoomed up the highway to Silicon Valley on her boyfriend's motorcycle.

Esme had a boyfriend who tie-dyed shirts and broke into stores.

Esme broke into at least one store with him.

Esme might go to jail for sixteen months because she broke into a store with him.

Was she in love with him?

If she broke up with him, would she get bulimia again?

Esme made beautiful earrings.

Esme made a pair of earrings especially for her friend's mother with Parkinson's disease and went to visit her. Yet she wouldn't speak to her own mother.

Who was this girl—no, this young woman, who would be twenty-four years old next month?

Flecks of blueberry muffin were wedged between Alice's teeth, and she sucked them deeper into her mouth. She should've insisted on paying for the muffin, instead of letting Courtney give it to her for free. Or bought something else at MultiGrainery. A dozen blueberry-walnut muffins. Two dozen. To thank Courtney. To help the bakery stay in business. Just one customer had appeared, the whole time Alice was in the shop; how could that little bakery survive? Especially with Courtney and her sister trying to run down to Calabasas every week to be with their mother, maybe closing the shop early, maybe having to hire extra help. In addition to how the recession must have hit them. Alice could buy muffins as presents for Roz, for James, even Fred. Roz was on another diet, so she'd need something low-fat. James would take whatever had strong, weird flavors. Chocolate-pumpkin. Cranberry-bran. Fred would pretend to roll his eyes and make a comment about adding organic bakeries to her green portfolio for the Cordwainer guys, but he'd gobble whatever pastry Alice gave him. She'd only gone a few miles. It wasn't too late.

Alice pulled off the highway and swung around, back north to MultiGrainery.

CHAPTER THIRTEEN

ALICE, DAN, AND ESME

January 1990
Reseda, CA

"Honey? It's Mommy." Still wearing her coat, Alice crouched beside Esme's bed and wriggled her fingers under the orange blanket to tickle Esme's toes. But Esme was lying rigidly face-down with her pillow clamped over her head, using her crossed arms to hold the pillow tightly in place, and her toes didn't react. She exhaled in spurts. It didn't sound like crying, though.

When Alice touched Esme's shoulder, the shoulder jerked away.

"It's hardly surprising that she feels abandoned," Dan said evenly, from the bedroom doorway. "She's not even four years old, and her mother's never here."

"Esme. Honey." Alice went on speaking to the prone body in the bed. "Honey, I'm so sorry I missed dinner and bath time with you again. I had to stay really late at work. You know, to save the trees? And the owls."

The body didn't move.

"To stop the bad men I told you about from chopping down all the trees."

"What do you expect me to say to her?" Dan added.

"Should I get some ice cream, and we'll eat it together?" Alice asked Esme.

Finally, from beneath the pillow, came Esme's muffled voice. "You love the owls more than me."

"Honey, no, that's not true!" Alice bent closer, to hug Esme's back. Esme's hair smelled like the thick citrus of Johnson's Baby Shampoo, and Alice stroked the chubby curves of her little shoulders. "You know I love you more than anything. But don't you want to save the owls, too?"

"No!"

It was impossible to remain where she was, awkwardly suspended above Esme, her arms bent like a grasshopper's legs. Alice straightened a little, keeping one hand lightly on Esme's shoulder. Could Esme be so upset about a couple of dinners? Three dinners. Four dinners, counting the evening Alice had stayed out with Roz last week. Plus the overnight trip to Humboldt County the week before that. But they'd had breakfast together almost every morning. Maybe it was something else. Something that had happened at the preschool? Alice laced a few fingertips through Esme's sprawling hair.

After a minute or so, Esme added from under the pillow, her voice sounding a little more as if it was asking instead of arguing, "You said you'll get ice cream."

"For sure. I'll be back in two seconds."

Dan followed Alice through the long hall and into the kitchen. "You can't keep doing this to her and me."

"I'm sorry I've been home late so much. It's only because we're under horrible pressure, you know, because the Fish and Wildlife Service is going to be issuing their decision on the spotted owls any month." Alice peered into the freezer. Chocolate or chocolate chip? Or both?

Dan slammed the freezer door shut so fast that Alice barely got her hands clear in time.

"I'm not going to keep covering up for you." His face was almost against hers. His spit slapped her check.

"Covering up? What?"

"Yesterday. And Monday. And two weeks ago. And at the end of October."

"You know it's been crazy at Seshat." She would need to reach around Dan to get to a paper towel. Or let his spit linger, heavy, on her skin. Alice rubbed at the spot with her palm.

"And the evening you went out for coffee with Roz. Supposedly."

"She's my friend. And she's having problems with Jenny, some trouble at her school."

"Precisely my point. Everything else is more important to you than I am. Or Esme. As I've had to explain to her."

"You've—? What have you been telling Esme?"

"By having a baby, you essentially made a promise to Esme. And now you aren't here when you're supposed to be."

"You're getting carried away." Never mind the spit, if Alice could simply retrieve the ice cream and go to Esme.

"And what about your promise to me?"

"What promise?"

"That we wouldn't have children."

His dark blue eyes, inches from hers. The tiny scar on the left edge of his jaw. His breath, hitting her mouth, smelling of coffee.

"But you agreed."

"When did I 'agree,' Alice?" Dan paused. "Was that before or after you lied to me about the so-called accident with your diaphragm?"

She couldn't get any air. She couldn't swallow.

"WHEN?" His palm hit the countertop right next to her.

Her husband. Her daughter's father.

"What else have you lied to me about, Alice? You're working late on the owls, huh? Helping your good friend Roz? I wonder if James is working late at some supposed zoning board meeting, too."

This couldn't be happening. She and Dan were middle-class professionals. Middle-class professionals didn't hit things. They didn't spit at each other.

Dan shrugged. He moved a step away, still staring straight at her. "You place your own career above Esme's needs. You endangered her safety by putting her in an inappropriate preschool that I had to investigate, not to mention dropping her on her head at the beach when she was two years old, because of your constant failure to pay adequate attention. You squander money on expensive shoes for yourself instead of clothing for her. You lie to me repeatedly. You can't even remember to feed two cats properly. And with your lack of basic sanitary protection--letting her play in dirt and then eat with filthy hands, for instance. It's fortunate that I'm a responsible person and I'm always available to take care of her in the mornings and evenings."

He'd made a checklist? Was Dan laying out charges against her? Like for a divorce? Unsanitary conditions. Child endangerment.

All of a sudden, he was unbuttoning his shirt. Button by button, his ordinary blue cotton shirt. "I'm not sure if it's safe leaving my daughter," he murmured, as the two sides of the shirt slid apart and he lowered the left side off his shoulder almost like a stripper, "alone with a mother who tried to stab me."

What?

On a pale patch of skin at the top of his arm, a gauze bandage maybe two inches square was held in place with first-aid tape.

"Fortunately, it was a superficial scratch," Dan continued. Keeping his arm straight out in the air toward Alice, he rotated it to one side, then the other. The bandage disappeared, then reappeared. He slouched against the counter.

Was there actually a wound under the bandage? Was Dan so crazy that he would cut himself, solely in order to blame her?

"Dan, what—?"

Slowly, he pulled the sleeve back over his shoulder and began to refasten the buttons.

There couldn't really be a wound. He was only trying to freak her out. She lunged for his sleeve.

He caught her with his right hand, just above her wrist. Gripping her tight, he yanked her against his chest, as if he was going to hug her. Of course, he wasn't going to hug.

She couldn't scream. Esme would hear.

He dropped her arm. With his shirt still mostly unbuttoned, he had veered away from her and was pulling at a drawer below the counter. He was taking out a knife.

No! No no no no this was too much.

Reaching above the counter, he opened a cabinet door and brought down two bowls and a plate. Next, he picked up a hunk of cheddar cheese that had been sitting on the counter all this time, set it on the plate, took the knife, and cut a couple of slices.

"Dan, what the hell is going on?"

He edged past her to the freezer, their arms not even grazing. He removed the half-gallon carton of chocolate ice cream.

That was her job, her apology to her daughter. Ice cream for Esme. "I'll—" Alice clutched the edge of the carton. Dan pulled it away. She hung on. "I'll do it!" They both tugged, and the bottom of the damn flimsy stupid carton started to rip, and then it ripped more, and goddam gooey chocolate slop slithered all over the floor and her legs and her hands and her new Jimmy Choo stilettos.

She tore off a fistful of paper towels and smeared the ice cream worse while she tried to wipe the goo from her hands.

This was impossible. Dan was a veterinarian; he saved animals. He owned a small business. He watched nature shows on TV with Esme. He was a Dodgers fan. He might be kind of inflexible occasionally. He might be absurdly jealous about James. He might get obsessive about cleanliness. He might even, maybe, be justifiably angry that she'd tricked him into having a baby. Still, he didn't do literally dangerous, crazy things like stabbing himself. This was not the man she'd married. This was not the man who cleaned up the beach in Spain with her, the man who'd been paralyzed at the thought of losing her. He'd gone mad. Out of control. Something had snapped. What if he truly had stabbed himself, under the bandage? And the way he'd grabbed her arm; he might do anything. Even to Esme! No! It wasn't safe with him. She and Esme had to get out. Immediately! Go to her mother's house. Hire a lawyer. Pack a suitcase. Do something.

But right now she had to get ice cream for Esme, as she'd promised, or Esme would never trust her again.

It was too late.

Dan was already at Esme's bedroom door, carrying two bowls, two spoons, and the other carton of ice cream.

Chapter Fourteen

The Cordwainer Foundation official with the shaggy brown hair and gray blazer—Martin—leaned across the oval table in the Seshat conference room, as if he hoped to gaze earnestly into Alice's face. "We love what you folks have created with your environmental portfolios."

"Thank you."

Next to Alice, Fred was rolling the end of his yellow tie up and down. Did Fred honestly think the Cordwainer folks would realize that the sunburst design was in honor of solar energy?

"Environmental issues are a new area for us, as you know, so we're feeling our way around at this point," Martin went on, with a smile.

"We totally understand," Alice agreed.

The table was too small for the six of them, the room too close-feeling without windows. Martin had brought three colleagues who hadn't been with him when they first met in this room, two weeks ago—a young guy with a buzz cut, a woman named Gina with her blonde hair in a ballet-style bun at her neck, and a balding man with round glasses and muscles that strained his dark suit jacket, who hadn't stopped staring at the blow-up of Muir Woods that dominated the wall opposite the door. Somebody was wearing an overdose of talcum-smelling deodorant. Each time Gina turned a page of Alice's report, the paper crackled like the snap of a teenager's bubble gum.

For all of Martin's smiles, everyone at the table had to be aware that this meeting would ultimately come down to the Cordwainers' definition of green energy versus Seshat's. Or versus Alice's. How green was green enough? Was nuclear power green? Was natural gas green? Were wages, jobs, and working conditions more important than being green? *The client is always right,* Fred might say. But that wasn't true. The science was always right.

"Our foundation has historically been zeroed-in on traditional workers' rights. Like a bull's-eye." Smiling, of course, Martin aimed his index finger at Fred, then at Alice. "Working conditions. Pay and benefits. Union organizing. That's where we prioritize our grantmaking, naturally, and we aim to invest according to the same principles. We've avoided investments in the garment industry, for instance, and I'm sure I don't have to tell you about the problems in that industry, that there's no way to guarantee the working conditions throughout the supply chain."

"Hence, our name," Gina added.

"You're named for the Federal Society of Cordwainers. Shoemakers. The first American union." There! Alice, and thus Seshat, would get Brownie points for knowing that bit of trivia.

"The Federal Society of Journeymen Cordwainers," Gina corrected her.

"But today everyone understands that labor issues can't be walled off from environmental issues." Martin spread his hands, palms up, one toward Fred and the other toward Alice. "Air quality in factories and mines, for instance. Toxic chemical emissions and accidents. And no doubt you both could name more examples. These sorts of problems directly affect our constituency."

"Not to mention that working people face the same overarching environmental issues as everyone else on Earth. Climate change, most importantly," Alice added.

"Exactly." Another smile from ever-earnest Martin. " 'No man is an island,' as the poet wrote. That's why we're aiming to carve out a portion of our portfolio that will be specifically targeted to environmentally responsible investments. Long-term, we might try to adopt a more encompassing green screen for the entire fund, but that's a bit of a stretch for now."

Fred sat back in his padded chair, stretching out his legs under the table and stroking his salt-and-pepper goatee; his pretend-relaxed pose. "Sounds like Alice's perfect cup of tea."

"Nevertheless," Gina said, staring straight at Alice. "We can't forget our roots."

And there it was: "Nevertheless." The inevitable excuse for saying No, after all the polite beginnings.

Martin wrapped his hands around each other, atop the table. Fred unrolled his tie.

It was the guy with the muscles and round eyeglasses who filled in the "nevertheless," in a voice that was surprisingly crusty. "Climate change and alternative energy are important, sure. But labor issues have to come first."

Alice nodded.

"There are a lot of jobs in the oil and gas industry and the nuclear industry. Our union allies support new drilling, new pipelines."

Really? The Cordwainers were falling back on that old "jobs" argument? "Over the long term, those oil and gas jobs will disappear," Alice promptly countered.

"Maybe. But that's a hell of a long term for our people to wait for."

"Alternative energy is already creating jobs," Alice said. Still calm.

"Nowhere near as many as traditional energy. They're all in China anyway. Solar panel manufacturing."

"And they're not union jobs," Gina added.

"They could be. I could see a lot of potential for the construction trades. The IBEW. The Operating Engineers." Was that true? Were any unions trying to organize solar-installation workers in California? Well, it might sound logical to the Cordwainers. "And what about the accidents with drilling?" Alice pushed on. "The Deepwater Horizon explosion in April killed almost a dozen oil workers and injured something like twenty more."

"Alice," Fred jumped in, "you've got those employment numbers for alternative energy, don't you? Let's pull them together and send them over to the Foundation tomorrow."

"That's fine," Gina said. "However, that doesn't respond to the basic issue. If we decide to dedicate part of our asset allocation to an environmental category, we can't throw natural gas and especially nuclear power plants overboard. After all, nuclear power has zero greenhouse gas emissions, so honestly, why wouldn't you include it in your green portfolio? We're happy to consider solar and other alternative investments, and we certainly want to avoid the worst players in the energy sector, but at the end of the day we need an environmental policy that encompasses nuclear and gas, which are important to our constituency. Your portfolio and screen omit those areas."

Fred actually kicked Alice's foot under the table. *Don't argue back that nuclear and gas aren't green. Just say you'll do it.*

"Bank of California's environmental portfolio, for example," Gina went on.

Not BofC again.

"… includes nuclear and gas companies, such as Westinghouse."

"What about the safety risk of nuclear? Chernobyl?" Alice demanded. Fred could kick her all he wanted.

"That was twenty-plus years ago, and wasn't it because of an outmoded reactor design? I'm confident that the technology and safety procedures have been thoroughly updated since then." Martin was still smiling at Alice.

"Chernobyl is only one example of the type of accident that can occur. There are earthquakes and other natural disasters. Human error. You can't design-out all risk, and when you're playing with something as powerful as radioactivity, you can't be lackadaisical."

Oops. She probably shouldn't have implied that the Cordwainers were lackadaisical.

"The co-founder of Greenpeace himself considers nuclear as green," the buzz-cut guy suddenly piled on.

"There's also the question of nuclear waste. We haven't figured out how or where—"

"Experts will never stop debating the fine points," Fred interrupted Alice. "But on the whole, we all here agree on the parameters." He was clutching hard at his tie now, even as he, too, smiled around the table. At everyone except Alice.

"I think our donors and our board," Gina said—and was she pronouncing each word more distinctly than before?—"would be more comfortable if we had a few well-known companies in the nuclear and natural gas spaces, such as Westinghouse, buttressing the inevitably less familiar names in solar and hydro."

How could Alice let the conversation end with their rival BofC as the role model? "We've been doing environmentally conscious investing a lot longer than Bank of California. I think we've got a pretty impressive track record."

The air in the room moved just a hint. People shifted in their seats, spewing quick breaths. As good as telling Alice that she should've quit arguing five sentences ago.

"Of course, we know that you've been the pioneers in this field," Martin said.

"Why don't we resume this again next week?" Fred leaned a little forward toward the table. "We'll customize a portfolio for you in the interim, show you some different asset allocation models that will all include nuclear and gas, you bet. Alice can pull together three or four excellent alternatives."

"Sure. We do it all the time for clients. Customized portfolios." Alice nodded more vehemently than before.

"I'll keep Alice to the grindstone. She won't get an afternoon off till this is done."

What about returning to the art store in Santa Barbara to find that clerk? What about Esme's looming trial?

People were pushing back chairs. Standing, nodding, murmuring. "Thanks." "Good talking with you." "Let's set a date." Martin shaking hands with Fred and Alice. "I like your tie." Fred not looking at Alice. Gina gathering papers, buzz-cut guy halfway out the door.

CHAPTER FIFTEEN

From the Bloomingdale's display table, Alice picked up a newborn-size sleeper, decorated with purple rocket ships and not much longer than a sheet of legal paper.

Roz stroked the tiny sleeve of a different sleeper that had blue and pink bears curled into half-circles. "Jenny said no blues or pinks. No boy-girl stereotyping. But if this has both colors, that should be okay, don't you think?"

"I'm sure it's fine. It's adorable."

"The pattern makes me imagine bears hibernating. I'm hoping it'll subconsciously help the baby sleep." Roz pushed the bears into her overstuffed shopping basket.

"How's Jenny feeling? Is her morning sickness still so awful?"

"It's finally easing up, thank God."

"Has she been doing anything for it? I don't know, eating saltines?"

"I've made her a lot of raspberry tea, and she said that helped."

"Good."

"She's totally the opposite from me. I popped out Sharon and her like bunny rabbits." Roz giggled.

"Oh yeah. One minute we were moseying along the Santa Monica Pier watching the crazy seagulls, and the next thing I knew, Walt and I were driving you to the hospital at a hundred miles an hour."

Esme had been as small as these doll clothes herself, twenty-three years ago. She'd had little dresses with rainbows and flowers, and miniature OshKosh B'gosh overalls in pastels and hearts, and sleepers as soft as the blue-and-pink bears in Roz's basket, as soft as Esme's cheeks had been. Her first cardigan sweater, orange with tulips. Her favorite orange corduroy overalls. The pink dress that Florence had sewed and then hand-embroidered a vine of flowers across the bodice, her novice attempt at embroidery, and it had come out astonishingly perfect. All the ballet costumes.

"I might take a drive to the bakery in Milpitas," Alice told Roz's profile, as Roz moved to another display table.

"Did Courtney hear from Esme already?"

"No. I mean, I could ask her. It's more because I really enjoyed talking with her, and I want to talk again. It made me feel closer to Esme, in a weird way. Hearing stories about her from high school that I never knew. Does that make sense to you?"

"It absolutely does." Leaning across the table, Roz squeezed Alice's arm. "Plus, you could get more of those delicious muffins."

"That's definitely an added incentive. It's not a pop-in visit, though. Six hours each way, at the fastest. James offered to come with me and share the driving."

"James has gone with you a lot on your trips, hasn't he?" Roz dropped Alice's arm and fingered a set of white infant towels. "You know, I'll be glad to drive to the bakery with you. I'm pretty free now that Jenny's feeling better. You don't have to always ask James."

"Thanks. That's a very tempting offer." Oh, who was Alice kidding? Fred had been unarguably clear that for the next couple of weeks, she had to be available, any day, any time, Monday Tuesday Wednesday Thursday Friday Saturday Sunday. "Forget it, Roz. I'm sorry, I can't take a whole day off work. I feel guilty just going shopping with you for an hour on a Saturday."

"Really?" Roz glanced up, a yellow-and-white polka-dot onesie in her hand. "I thought your boss was kind of more bark than bite."

"There's a big client we might lose—I suppose I should say, *I* might lose. So my boss is chaining me to the computer until we get a revised proposal back to them, which is due on Wednesday."

"Is it really that bad? You could lose a client?"

"I argued with the client at our meeting this week, pretty strongly. They know I disagree with their approach. Because what they're asking us to do is phony greenwashing! They'll hardly be making a dent in fossil fuel extraction—Oh, don't get me going."

"You know, sometimes people respect other people who stick up for their beliefs. These clients might—"

"This isn't a social work session, Roz. This is the business world. It doesn't work that way."

Gee, Roz, I might lose a major client, and my daughter is a criminal who doesn't speak to me, so do you think I might be feeling a little anxious? Do you think I might wish I could buy cute little pajamas for my own grandchild? Maybe I already am a grandmother, but no one told me. Maybe Esme and Bobby Corning broke into the art store to steal money for diapers.

. No, she couldn't say that to Roz, unless she wanted to be a complete bitch.

"I'm sorry for jumping on you, Roz. I guess it's all getting to me. The big client. Esme's arrest. I haven't even had a spare minute to call back another potential client, a family office up in San Francisco."

Roz spent the next few seconds folding the yellow-and-white polka-dot onesie in half and setting it precisely on top of a pile of other polka-dot onesies on a crowded display table. "I know it's been intense for you," she finally said. A red sweater and two sets of towels went into her basket, and Roz glanced toward the cashier's desk. "I'd better quit now."

"Do you want to get coffee?"

"Okay." Roz retrieved the polka-dot onesie.

"Jenny will love everything you bought."

The outdoor food court was so mobbed that Alice could barely tug her tiny metal chair far enough out from their table to squeeze herself into the seat. As the table tilted, she clutched her cardboard coffee cup, while Roz grabbed her own coffee and her package of Melba toast. A family carrying a large pizza box inched past them in the narrow space between Alice's chair and the table behind her, trailing the wonderful smells of tomatoes and melted cheese.

When Alice shifted in her seat to hook her right leg over her left, her knee banged the table's hard metal edge. "Shit."

"What's wrong?"

Her knee was throbbing with a painful thrill. "I hit my stupid knee."

"Do you need something? We could probably get a cup of ice to put on it from one of the food stands."

"It'll be fine in a minute. Don't worry. But thanks for offering." Oh, how could she be angry with social-work-caring Roz?

"If you're sure?" Roz picked up a slice of Melba toast and frowned at it, before dunking an edge into her coffee. "So, besides going to visit the Milpitas muffin-lady, do you have other ideas for finding out more about Esme's situation?"

"I don't know what to do! I haven't heard back from Courtney, or the clerk at the art store who's supposed to get us in touch with that Bobby person. Her case isn't on the court calendar so far, but it could pop up Monday. Tuesday. Any day, according to the lawyer. I can't begin to imagine what's going through her mind, Roz. A future of bare concrete walls. A cell that stinks of piss. Watching the calendar, checking the days off till her trial. She's not even twenty-four years old!"

"Oh, sweetie. There must be something." Roz took a bite of her mushy Melba toast. "What if you reached out to Dan's wife?"

"Penelope?"

"She'd be more approachable than Dan, wouldn't she?"

"I'm not so sure. And how would we find her? I still don't know her email, or where she works. You remember when we tried Googling her?"

"When we tried to invent careers for her? Porn star. Oil industry advertising." Roz grinned.

Alice grinned, too. "Tobacco company executive."

"She can't be worse to you than Dan is."

The people at the tables around them were near enough to eavesdrop. *A cell that stinks of piss. Porn star.*

"You don't suppose…" Roz's voice faltered. "If you emailed Dan?"

"No."

Roz nodded.

"I keep thinking about Esme's phone call to you last fall," Alice added.

"I wish I'd asked her more questions. I'm sorry."

"The more I think about it, I doubt she was asking about Jenny's anorexia because of her own bulimia. It might have been about Jenny's drug use, after all. Like I thought at first."

"We don't know."

"It's the only explanation that makes sense."

"What?"

"Think about it. Bulimia and anorexia might explain her phone call, but they don't explain the arrest. What's the most common reason people break into places? To steal a couple of jars of purple dye for Bobby Corning's tie-dying? I doubt it. They do it to steal money for drugs."

Roz's jaw moved rhythmically for a few seconds. Chewing? When she spoke, her deep voice came out slowly. "Alice, you're driving yourself crazy. I really don't believe she's on drugs. No one you spoke with ever mentioned drugs. Not Courtney. Not the sorority lady. Stop torturing yourself."

But what if she was? What if Esme was going through withdrawal right now? Or worse, drug withdrawal and bulimia together?

Or, on the other hand, what if Roz had told Alice about the phone call from Esme when it happened last fall? Roz hadn't thought of drugs at the time, but Alice would have. Maybe she could have whisked Esme straight to a clinic for treatment. Maybe they could have hugged. Talked. Maybe Esme would never have been desperate enough to break into the art store. Didn't Roz get it?

"You don't know she's not on drugs. I don't know. That's the whole problem, dammit, Roz, I don't know anything about my own daughter, and you can't help. She could be anyone." She could be Jenny. She could, God forbid, be Dan.

CHAPTER SIXTEEN

ALICE, DAN, AND ESME

November to December 1990

Santa Monica, CA

Everybody in her preschool was signing up for ballet classes at Madame Nadia's starting in January and getting pink tutus, according to Esme. Some of the girls already knew how to do first, second, and fourth positions and pliés. Esme stretched on tiptoes in her bedroom, with her chubby arms circled above her head.

"Am I a ballerina, Mommy?"

"Yes, you look exactly like a real ballerina."

"Please can I go to ballet class with everyone?"

Plopping onto her bed, Esme lifted Brownie the Dog by his front paws. His fur had become matted and rough by now, and his tan nose was worn down to dirty white. She tilted him from side to side on his hind legs as she sang the first two lines of Twinkle, Twinkle, Little Star in her high-pitched voice, amazingly almost in tune. "Look, Mommy. Brownie dances, too."

"Willow's going to see *The Nutcracker*," Esme announced the following day. "Can we see it?"

Madame Nadia's pre-ballet class for four-to-five-year-olds cost four hundred dollars for twelve weeks. And it was on Saturday mornings, in Westwood.

It was impossible.

"Esme has visitation with Dan every other weekend!" Alice wailed to Roz, almost like a four-year-old herself, as they sat at Roz's kitchen table. "She would have to miss half the classes."

Esme, Jenny, and Sharon came dancing into the kitchen from the living room, past the table, then out to the playroom, swinging their animals and Barbies and singing lyrics from *The Little Mermaid*. "You honestly think Dan would refuse to bring Esme to her ballet class on his visitation weekends? Even if she wants it so much?" Roz asked, when the girls were gone.

"Who can predict what he would or wouldn't do?"

"Why don't you ask him?"

"Roz! You know I can't talk to him like a normal person. You've seen how crazy he's being."

"I know he bosses you around, sweetie. But someone can be a bad husband and still be a good father."

"Not Dan. He cares more about making my life miserable than being a good father."

"That's only the part that's visible. You don't know what all this divorce and separation from Esme could be doing to him, underneath. Give him time. He'll ease off."

"He's thirty-five years old. He's never going to change."

Jenny skipped back into the kitchen and out again, singing.

Esme followed her, two words behind in the lyrics, but stopped at the table. "Roz, I took a napkin to make a tutu for Brownie. Is that okay?" A red-checked cloth napkin was tied around Brownie's belly.

"Hold on." Roz tapped Esme's arm. "I've got something better you can use." Two minutes later, she returned to the table with a large, wide triangle of black lace. Gently, Esme ran a finger along the edge.

"Roz, is that the mantilla you got in Mexico City?" Alice whispered.

"Yes."

"Thank you, Roz!" Esme ran after Jenny and Sharon.

"You can't let Esme play with that," Alice protested. "It's too special for you."

"She can have it for a few weeks. She'll lose interest in ballet soon, the way Jenny did, and then you can return it to me."

Roz had better not count on it. Though Jenny might be the one who dreamed up the ideas, it was Esme who stuck with them, through thick and thin.

On the three girls' next turn into the kitchen, the mantilla was tied around Brownie, and the red-checked napkin had become a skirt for Jenny's oldest Barbie. Esme stopped again at the table.

"Brownie looks beautiful." Alice patted the little dog.

"Could you make a tutu for me to wear, Mommy?"

How could Alice refuse this little dream? A frilly ballet costume, a sweet hobby with her friends. Esme's face, gazing up at her, was glowing in the kitchen light as though she was dancing under spotlights.

But to ask Dan for flexibility in the visitation schedule? After they'd fought World War Three for nine months over the divorce and custody? He demanded the house. He demanded that Esme live with him full-time. He refused to pay child support. He accused her of kidnapping when he knew that she and Esme were staying with Florence.

"I have already filed a complete report with the Los Angeles County Department of Children and Family Services spelling out the unsafe and unsanitary conditions in your dwelling-place," he wrote, in a notarized letter. "I will be insisting on weekly inspections if they regrettably permit her to reside with you."

Unsafe and unsanitary? Her mother's house?

"I'll hire the best lawyers in Southern California," he told her. "I'll fight you all the way to the Supreme Court."

"Don't worry," Alice's lawyer said. "The Supreme Court doesn't hear divorce cases."

Dan could threaten all he liked, the lawyer added, but mothers got custody ninety-nine percent of the time, especially when the child was a little girl, unless the father could prove something truly awful about the mother. The lawyer wonderfully laughed when Alice told her about letting Esme eat Cheerios with dirty fingers in the yard. She laughed again at Dan's fake bandage, and at his claim that Alice had failed to feed their cats. (Which wasn't true, anyway, because feeding them was supposed to be Dan's responsibility.) No, none of that proved that Alice was a violent, unfit mother.

"Dan thinks it does," Alice said.

"He'll learn soon enough."

"He won't learn," Alice corrected the lawyer. "He'll temporarily give in and re-strategize."

"The law is still the law. I've seen a lot crazier and angrier than him, believe me. Divorce brings out the worst in people."

However, according to the lawyer, the fake-bandage incident didn't help Alice's case or give her grounds to keep Dan away from Esme, either. As a judge would see it, this was merely Alice's word against Dan's, no witnesses, no evidence, no proof of physical harm to anyone, no proof of mental instability, and it had been a one-time, nonrepeated occurrence – if it had even happened.

"Dan never wanted a baby."

"So?" the lawyer asked.

"Couldn't that be some kind of, you know, evidence? To show he's an unfit father?"

The lawyer kept her pen suspended above her conference table. She didn't answer for a moment. "Alice, what does this have to do with anything? Many people have doubts about parenthood. Besides, it was years ago. He's been a devoted father since then, or so he'll claim. Drop it, Alice. Your case is fine without it."

And the lawyer was right; the custody agreement emerged as she'd foreseen and pretty much the same as every other custody agreement she had handled in her long career. Esme would live full-time with Alice, that was the most important part. She would spend every other weekend with Dan. He would pick her up at Alice's apartment at six o'clock on his Friday evenings and bring her back at six o'clock on Sunday, and Alice and Dan would confer as needed about particular issues for the weekend. Dan kept the house. So what? "You shouldn't give in so easily. You need to hold onto the house, for Esme's sake. For stability," the lawyer had urged. "I don't want it. It's full of bad memories," Alice retorted. Besides, where would she get the money to buy out Dan's fifty percent? Far better that he should buy her out, and with those proceeds she could rent a nice two-bedroom apartment in Santa Monica, hopefully within walking distance to the beach.

She did. And on Esme and Alice's first night in their new home, Roz and Walt brought them an orange-sherbet cake with orange slices on top, plus a rubber-tree plant in a red clay pot.

"Good riddance to Dan," Roz said quietly to Alice, while Esme and Jenny raced through the rooms. "Now you can enjoy your life with Esme. And let's see if we can find a nice boyfriend for you."

"Thanks for the offer, but Walt's track record in arranging blind dates for me isn't too great."

"And Walt feels terrible about it. But to be fair, sweetie, Walt didn't know Dan personally when he connected the two of you. Dan was a friend of his college roommate's. This time, I'll do the matchmaking."

"Can you find a boyfriend who wants kids?"

At six o'clock every other Friday evening, Dan's silver BMW arrived at Alice's building, and Dan waited, leaning against the passenger side of the car, until Alice and Esme emerged out the front door. He promptly squatted, his arms wide, as Esme ran to him. Without a word or a glance toward Alice, he opened the rear door, helped Esme inside, hooked her seatbelt, placed her little orange knapsack into the trunk, got into his own seat, and promptly drove away.

How was Alice supposed to confer with him about the Saturday ballet class, as the custody agreement required?

"Send him a letter, spelling out what you're seeking and suggesting a date to meet and talk," the lawyer advised.

"To talk—? This is Dan, remember?" Alice snapped back, over the phone. "The one who accused me of dirty Cheerios."

Fine, she would try it the lawyer's way. For Esme's sake. In case Roz was right, that Dan truly had Esme's best interests at heart. She mailed a letter to Dan, explaining the ballet situation. Of course he didn't reply. On the next Friday pickup, as Esme ran to Dan, Alice followed a few steps behind. "Esme wants to take a ballet class," she called out. "You know, with all of her friends."

Keeping his back to Alice, Dan opened the car door and murmured to Esme, who giggled.

"But most of the classes are on Saturdays."

Over his shoulder, Dan snapped, "You are interfering with my time with my daughter. I will therefore bring her to your apartment building as many minutes later on Sunday as you're wasting now."

In fact, he brought Esme home fifteen minutes late, although the conversation with Alice on Friday had lasted less than a minute. He roared away as soon as Esme was on the sidewalk.

"Daddy wants to see me dance ballet, too!"

"He does?" Dan was actually going to be reasonable about the class?

"He says I can go to ballet classes near his house every week, if I live with him."

"No!" Alice snapped.

Esme twitched backwards, dropping her knapsack.

Quickly, Alice crouched down and rubbed Esme's back. "Don't you want to go to Madame Nadia's with your friends? I—I already signed you up."

"You did?" Esme threw her arms around Alice. "I love you!"

Alice burrowed her nose in Esme's thick hair, as her racing heartbeat gradually eased. Esme's arms around her were soft and not very strong.

No more delays. Alice would enroll Esme in the ballet class. Immediately. Four hundred dollars. She and Madame Nadia would figure out a way to replace the missed Saturday classes, somehow, even if Alice had to learn ballet herself in order to teach Esme.

She hugged Esme tighter. "You don't have to move to Daddy's house just to take a ballet class."

"Can we go to *The Nutcracker*, too?"

Dinner was already laid out on the table, underneath the fake Tiffany lampshade: one bowl of orange rotini, one corn muffin, a few hunks of cantaloupe, and a glass of orange juice at Esme's place, and a salad, two chicken drumsticks, and an iced tea for Alice. "How about a little bit of chicken?" Alice asked, her fork ready above her plate.

Esme shook her head.

"It's sort-of orange."

"It's white inside the skin, Mommy."

Each morning heading out to preschool, as they set out down the sidewalk to their car, Esme practiced. She pointed the toes of one foot, raised the foot, lowered it a couple of inches in front of her body, then repeated the sequence with the other foot. She also had to twirl after every third step.

Each evening, Esme lined up her animals on the kitchen floor in front of Alice: Brownie the dog, Moosey, Junior Bunny, Big Bunny, and the dolphin from the aquarium in San Diego. One at a time, or sometimes two, Esme slid them forward, lifted a leg or an arm, twirled them, jumped them into the air, and moved them around each other, while she sang lines from *The Little Mermaid*. Afterwards, Alice, Esme, Brownie, and Moosey snuggled together on Esme's bed, and Alice read the book *A Very Young Dancer* to all of them. When Alice finished a page, Esme tugged her wrist and wouldn't let her turn to the next one—not yet. So Alice read all the pages twice, as Esme rested against her shoulder and traced an index finger around the photos of the beautiful ballerina girls.

They got tickets for the last performance of *The Nutcracker* at the community theater.

Through the entire first act, Esme perched all the way forward on the worn-plush seat between Alice and Grandma Florence, her navy-blue velvet dress scrunched underneath her thighs, her mouth half-open, her hair unwinding from the French braid Alice had tried to fashion, clutching both Moosey and Brownie against her chest. Girls in twirling pastel skirts and boys in bright jackets danced across the stage. Florence gasped along with Esme as the gigantic Christmas tree rose from under the floorboards. Huge toy soldiers marched menacingly toward Clara, the Nutcracker placed a crown on Clara's head, and snowflake dancers led Clara and the Nutcracker Prince offstage in their crystal sleigh. Esme's feet, dangling above the floor in black patent-leather pumps, pointed and flexed almost in rhythm with the music from the two loudspeakers.

CHAPTER SEVENTEEN

ALICE, DAN, AND ESME

March 1992

Van Nuys and Humboldt County, CA

"Mommy doesn't like dogs, but Daddy's giving me a puppy," Esme called out to Grandma Florence, who was waiting at the doorway of her green kitchen.

"That sounds lovely." Florence waylaid Esme long enough for a hug before Esme ran inside. Handing an old can opener to Alice, Florence nodded toward a can of Chef Boyardee raviolis in tomato sauce, on the counter next to the stove. "Could you open this for me?"

"A dog Daddy cured is having puppies, and Daddy and the dog's owner say I can have one," Esme continued, climbing onto her chair at the kitchen table. "Mommy, why don't you like dogs?"

"I like some dogs," Alice mumbled. "Daddy and I had a dog once."

"Are you going to teach your puppy tricks?" Florence asked, as she took the opened can from Alice. "How to shake hands? How to roll over and beg?"

"I'm going to teach him all the tricks. But Daddy says the puppy might forget everything I teach him, unless I see him more weekends."

"That's not—" Alice clamped her lips shut.

Don't put the child in the middle.

Don't contradict the other parent in front of the children.

That was easy for the parenting books to say. What was Alice supposed to do, when Dan played these games of his? *Mommy hates your adorable puppy. Your adorable puppy will hate you unless you spend less time with Mommy and more time with me and the puppy.* Carrying Esme's pink suitcase and her backpack with the ballerina decal, Alice sat down at the round table across from Esme. "Are you ready for your sleepover with Grandma? Which stuffed animals did you bring, honey?"

"Brownie, Moosey, Junior Bunny, and the new one from the zoo."

"The ibex? The one with the curvy horns?"

Esme nodded.

"Those all sound nice and cuddly."

Florence set Esme's Little Bo Peep bowl, filled with steaming, floppy raviolis, on the table. Esme dabbed her finger in the sauce and licked it, before sticking her fork into the ravioli highest up on the edge, where Little Bo Peep was guiding her sheep.

"And you'll help Grandma remember your toothbrushes? The red one in the morning and the purple one at night. Okay?"

Florence frowned, as she settled into the chair between Esme and Alice. "That's the opposite of the old saying."

"What saying?" Alice asked.

Esme had moved on carefully to the next-highest ravioli.

" 'Red sky at night, sailors' delight. Red sky in the morning, sailors take warning.' "

"What does that mean?"

"It's because of the way the sun—I think it has to do with water vapor. Or the light spectrum?" Florence's voice trailed off. "Well, in any case, a bright red sunrise means there's likely to be a thunderstorm that day."

"I don't want my toothbrush to make a thunderstorm!" Esme shouted.

"Your toothbrush isn't going—" Alice began.

"I don't want a red toothbrush! I want another toothbrush!" Esme had started crying.

"For Heaven's sake, Esme."

"Don't worry." Florence patted Esme's arm. "We'll go to the Walmart after school tomorrow and buy you a new toothbrush."

"Not Walmart!" Alice snapped.

"Why not?"

"We're supposed to boycott Walmart, because of all the lawsuits over working conditions."

Florence was shaking her head at Alice, and Esme had stopped in mid-cry and was staring at her.

Oh, what difference did Walmart make? Alice had less than an hour to spend here with Esme before she would need to go catch her flight to San Francisco and then the last connecting flight north to Humboldt County, to meet with the New York pension fund officials tomorrow. She wasn't going to waste her limited time today arguing about boycotts or about Dan and his stupid dog. Walking to Esme's chair, Alice smoothed her daughter's scalp between her two bushy ponytails. The hair was so soft, like the little cotton sleepers she'd worn as an infant, and the last bits of blond had completely darkened to brown over the winter. Esme's face, too, was changing, losing most of the baby puffiness in her cheeks and developing a lovely heart shape. Her eyebrows were as thin as pencil sketches. "I'm going to miss you a lot, honey, but you and Grandma will have fun. Do you think you'll bake raisin-chocolate chip cookies? And when I get home, you and I will do something special. Maybe we'll paint more bowls at the pottery place."

"And you're going to save the trees and the owls."

Alice stroked Esme's hair again.

"Aren't you going to save them?" Esme repeated.

"Yes. For sure."

"Will Grandma take me to ballet class?"

"I'll be back in time for that."

"I have a recital in June," Esme told Florence. "I'm a rose. My costume has a red top and a white lacy skirt. Will you come?"

"You bet."

"Like when we went to see *The Nutcracker*."

"That was beautiful, wasn't it?" Pressing her hands on the table, Florence stood up. "I'll get the ingredients to make the cookies now."

Alice followed as Florence moved slowly toward the green cupboards at the rear of the kitchen. "You don't know what a nightmare that whole ballet recital has been," Alice whispered, bending slightly down to her mother's ear, "because the recital is on one of Dan's visitation weekends."

"Why is that a nightmare?" Florence abruptly halted, holding onto the edge of the counter.

"Are you all right, Mom?"

"Yes, of course. Just the old arthritis. Why is the recital a nightmare?"

"You remember what I went through last year, trying to persuade Dan to let Esme go to the ballet classes on his weekends? Which I finally had to give up on. So it's happening all over again: Asking him to bring her for the recital on this one single Saturday afternoon. He doesn't call back if I leave phone messages. You know he never gets out of the car when he drives her home on Sundays, so I can't talk to him those times. I actually had to stand around outside his clinic for nearly an hour last Tuesday, to catch him for two seconds as he was leaving. And then he insisted that he would bring Esme to the recital only if he got three additional hours on his next visitation weekend to, quote, 'make up' for the time he'll be, quote, 'losing' due to the recital. As though watching his daughter dance with her friends is some kind of loss of quality time with her. But I had to say yes. What else could I do?"

"Maybe the two of you could have an arrangement to have coffee together every month, to share ideas about Esme."

"What?"

"I read about divorced parents doing that, in one of the magazines at the beauty parlor."

"You don't get it yet? He's a horrible—" Alice stopped. She kneaded the dull green countertop. "Mom, I realize you're trying to help, you and my lawyer and Roz with her rose-colored glasses and all the parenting books, but none of you understand. He's not normal."

"Shush, Alice. You don't want Esme to hear. I know he treats you badly, and that's not right. But he treats Esme fine, doesn't he? He takes her to the playground and movies and all those sorts of things?"

"Mom! What do you think? I wouldn't let her stay with him a minute if I thought there was any sort of danger."

"Well then, isn't that what matters?"

At the table, Esme was finishing her ravioli. She couldn't have heard their conversation, so far away. A dot of tomato sauce flecked the edge of her mouth, and Alice, sitting back down, leaned over and patted it with a napkin.

"Daddy got me a whole lot of clothes." Esme placed her fork inside the bowl. "I have a pink jacket with a hood that will keep me dry in the rain, and three pairs of slacks, one that's red, one that's pink, and one that's yellow. And four shirts, one with flowers, one with stripes, one with triangles and squares, and one with just colors."

"Really?" A gift from Dan? Alice pulled the backpack toward her chair.

"I didn't bring them. But there's a letter for you from Daddy. My new clothes have to stay at Daddy's house, so they'll stay clean. He says the clothes you give me are always dirty."

Alice threw the backpack on the floor.

"Alice!"

Esme was wearing pink overalls with a long-sleeved shirt decorated in a pattern of purple and pink hearts they'd bought together last fall. A little faded, perhaps. Were there any stains? They were Esme's favorite colors, along with red.

"Honey, your clothes at home are perfectly clean. Don't you like them? You picked them out yourself."

She ought to miss the damn flights to San Francisco and to Humboldt County with its stupid old-growth trees and owls. The hell with the New York pension fund officials and their investments in the lumber companies. The hell with the ten years she'd spent working to save a bunch of trees. She ought to stay and play with Esme and reinforce all the things Esme loved about her and do what she could to counter Dan's lies.

No. Canceling the trip would be worse. Esme would only be confused. Didn't Mommy need to go to the forests to save the trees and the owls? Why should Esme ever believe anything Alice said after that?

There was no winning strategy.

If Alice made certain Esme had her toothbrush when she went to Dan's house, he would criticize her clothes. If Alice bought an entire suitcase of new clothes, he'd accuse her of wasting the child support money he gave her. Hell, he'd probably mated his client's dog on purpose, just to produce a spare puppy for him to adopt so that Esme would want to spend more time at his house. After all those years when he'd claimed he wasn't emotionally ready for another dog yet?

Easy enough for the books to say crap like: *The child needs to be reassured that both Mommy and Daddy love her, and it's okay for her to love them both. Mommy and Daddy might have different rules about bedtime or TV watching, and both sets of rules are fine.*

How could Esme feel okay about loving both Mommy and Daddy equally, when Dan was constantly criticizing Alice? How much longer could a little girl who was not yet six years old avoid being torn apart or taking sides?

She couldn't.

Dan invented tales about Alice out of whole cloth, and somehow Esme always believed him. Alice couldn't stop Dan, and she couldn't go one-for-one with him. She couldn't dam up Esme's ears, and she couldn't keep Esme away from Dan. So how the hell was she supposed to protect her daughter from being caught in the middle?

All she could do was try her best at her two jobs – being Esme's mother and being Seshat Financial Advisors' environmental guru. Therefore, she would go to Humboldt County, and she would meet with the pension officials and Hugh from the Greenpeace office in Berkeley, and she would personally show the pension officials the landscape that the lumber companies would destroy, and she would buy Esme a souvenir from the gift shop at the San Francisco Airport, and she could return to Esme as the conquering hero who had saved a forest. And hopefully, the reality of seeing Alice as a loving mother, day after day, would weaken Dan's lies in Esme's mind.

When Esme went to the bathroom, Alice sneaked a glimpse inside her backpack. Right on top of the clothing Alice had packed, now jumbled, sat a note from Dan. *I was compelled to purchase an entire set of clothing for Esme, because the garments you "provide" for her are torn, stained, and inappropriate. I will be deducting the cost of these purchases from my next child support check.*

•   •   •   •   •

Hugh from Greenpeace piloted their rental car carefully around each curve of the narrow road as they climbed on and on uphill. On Alice's side, the ground just beyond the car plunged to a steep valley, and further beyond that stretched mountain after mountain crammed with dark green trees that soared to the clouds, taller than the skyline of downtown Santa Monica. On the driver's side, firs and hemlocks lined the edge where the road met the hill like the wall of a fortress, their rough, gray-brown trunks shooting up to thick clusters of needles, so tightly packed that they almost blacked out the sky. Abandoned green needles and occasional shoots of grass clustered here and there around the base of the trees. A tangy, fir-tinged breeze whistled irregularly through Alice's partially open window.

The New York pension officials were following too closely in their silver SUV. When Alice's car turned off the road into a graveled parking area, the SUV bounced directly behind. It parked, however, at the farthest reach of the small semicircle, and the two officials stayed inside for another few minutes.

Smiling, Alice signaled them over toward the gloomy-trunked tree where she was standing. "Like I told you, it's magnificent, isn't it?"

"Magnificent." The chief investments director slapped his palm against the furrowed trunk. In his polished loafers, he stepped around the ferns and the white and purple wildflowers that were sprinkled around the dirt. Why was he wearing business loafers and a pinstriped suit for a hike in a national forest?

The associate director strolled around the rim of the parking area, touching a few trees, bending once to scoop up something. He was shorter and huskier than his boss, and he wore more appropriate, dirt-grazed hiking boots.

"You realize," Alice continued, when the associate rejoined them, "that we're standing next to trees that were likely here in this spot already when the Pilgrims landed at Plymouth Rock? Or even Columbus?"

"Really?"

"It's a beautiful view." The associate nodded. "But this isn't the actual acreage that we've invested in, correct?"

"No, not on this specific spot. This is a national forest. Your area is on the other side of those mountains." Alice tilted her head vaguely toward the dark-green expanse beyond the valley. "We'll be going there next, as I mentioned at lunch. Or as much as we can, with the limited access roads. I thought I'd take you here first, so that you could get a sense of the context, the entire panorama that we're talking about." She swept her hand at the vista. The perfect blue sky was clear and wide above them. The only sound, besides their voices and shuffling feet, was the gentle puff of wind across a trunk.

The associate moved his head in short, jerky bumps, following the arc of a few of the nearest trees. "Are these, what kind? Douglas firs?"

"Yes," Alice agreed. "And hemlock, and I believe other firs. I need to refresh my memory on tree species."

Thankfully, Hugh picked up the cue, stepping toward her. "Mixed conifers. Douglas, grand fir, hemlock, yellow cedar, possibly some spruce. You won't find redwoods here, though." His Tennessee drawl was stronger with the pension officials than it had been in the car.

"Look, everybody loves birds and trees," the investment chief interrupted abruptly. "No one wants to kill endangered little owls. But you have to remember, we don't work for a lumber company. We're fiduciaries. If we did what you and Seshat are asking—if we voted in support of that proposal by that green group for a moratorium on harvesting, and the lumber company never harvested another tree— You're asking us to throw away two hundred and fifty million dollars that isn't ours. It's the employees' money, and we have a fiduciary responsibility, a hard-and-fast legal responsibility, as officials of their pension fund, to ensure that we invest their money such that it brings in a return sufficient to pay the pensions they've been promised."

Of course he would make the fiduciary argument. Alice nodded. "I completely understand. And I certainly would never ask you to violate your fiduciary duty. However, this is truly such a minuscule percentage of your portfolio; your entire basic-materials sector combined is less than five percent. No one's pension will be endangered."

"We still have to treat every penny in a responsible manner."

"And the shareholder proposal by the Green Fund wouldn't violate that," Alice answered promptly. "What it would do, is give us all some breathing room. While the moratorium is in place, everyone could have time to think of alternatives."

"What kinds of alternatives?" the associate asked. His tone was sharp.

"For example, you might do a more sustainable harvesting, instead of clear-cutting. Or possibly sell the land to the government for a state or national park," Hugh suggested.

"That's pennies. A public interest sale." The investment chief waved away Hugh's words.

"Our first duty is as fiduciaries, not our personal opinions about nature," the associate chimed in, glancing around again.

If only a couple of owls would swoop through the air and make Alice's point for her. If a tree would bend low and brush the men's hair with the smell of Christmas evergreen. What language would these two finance officials understand?

"Okay." Alice dug her hands into her pockets. "Let's talk about fiduciary responsibility. You really don't want to have two hundred and fifty million dollars sunk into a company that's seen as killing adorable, endangered owls and chopping down beloved redwoods, do you?"

"There are no redwoods in this tract!" the associate countered.

"That doesn't matter. It's the public image. People see a forest of tall, old trees, as old as Columbus, and they'll immediately picture redwoods. Giant, historic, ancient redwoods. And you know how powerful an environmental PR campaign can be. You remember what happened to Exxon's stock three years ago, after that oil spill in Alaska? Their reputation was as ruined as the coastline and the wildlife up there."

The two officials tilted their heads in unison, facing skyward toward the parasol of green needles high above them.

After a few seconds, the investment chief slid up the edge of his jacket cuff, barely revealing his Rolex. "I wish we had more time to discuss these forests, but we have to catch our flight to Frisco." He thrust out his hand toward Alice.

"But you haven't seen the real acreage."

"It's the only flight out of here. We have a dinner tonight and double-header meetings tomorrow." The investment chief smiled.

The associate also extended his hand. "Thank you for the tour."

"And lunch."

"We'll be in touch."

Three thousand miles the two men had flown from New York to San Francisco, and another hour-and-a-quarter flight from San Francisco to the Arcata-Eureka Airport, plus the winding, forty-five-minute drive up the mountain: To eat a hamburger and see a parking area? A little detour on their junket to San Francisco?

"The trees are dead," Alice muttered to Hugh, as the pension officials slid into their SUV and shut the doors behind them.

"I wouldn't be so ready to call it quits. You got their attention with that dang Exxon Valdez comparison."

Dang. No one in California said "dang."

"That's true," she admitted. "It seemed to shut them up, at least for a moment."

"Hell, they didn't just shut up. They ran away."

Hugh had a trim brown mustache, light blue eyes, and chestnut hair that flopped over his brow. His jeans rested loosely on his hips, encircled by a worn leather belt that ended in a huge bronze buckle shortly below his flat stomach. His lips were a little pale and dry, though that could be what happened when a nature advocate spent a lot of days outdoors with trees.

He touched her shoulder, then left his hand there.

"As long as we've driven this far, why don't we take a turn around and see what we're saving?" he continued. "I'm pretty sure there's a campground with some hiking trails and a stream, about a half-hour further on. There's nothing more we can do about these fellows just now."

He was right. Alice and Hugh had come all this way, and there was nothing more they could do at that moment to persuade the pension fund officials. They might as well take a nice hike. Have dinner together, maybe. A glass of chardonnay.

Her reservation back to San Francisco, unlike the New York officials' flight, wasn't until the morning.

•   •   •   •   •

Sheets of white typing paper, Scotch-taped end to end, were stretched across Florence's kitchen table in a long, super-wide ribbon when Alice pushed open the door Tuesday evening. "Hey, everyone! I'm here!"

Seated opposite each other, Florence and Esme were drawing with thick markers on different sections of the paper. Esme bit her lower lip as she bore down with her green marker. Florence, however, held her gray marker in an oddly vertical position, her thumb and middle and index fingers all clutching the top, instead of the usual way, with the marker resting on the side of her middle finger.

The first sheet, at Esme's far left, showed a row of stick-people wearing short red-and-white dresses, their stick legs flailing in various angles and directions. Next came a princess in a crown and a long white gown, side by side with a man also dressed in white. On the sheet directly in front of her, Florence was haltingly tracing a gray rectangle below a big yellow sun.

"We're making a mural." Esme waved her marker toward Alice. "Grandma says we could draw important things that happened this year or they're going to happen. There's me in my ballet costume, for my recital." She gestured at the stick figures in the red-and-white dresses. "And this is Daddy and me with my new puppy." The damn dog—a brown blob with four short legs, a head, and two ovals that jutted out from the head—was on the paper to Esme's right. "Now I'm doing your trees and owls." A pair of green-and-brown lollypops.

"That's beautiful." Alice leaned over Esme's head.

"How many trees should I draw? How many did you save?"

If her point about Exxon had hit home with the pension officials? "Hmm. It could be a whole section of the forest, so it's hard to count. Why don't you draw ten? Is that enough?" Lowering herself into a vacant chair, Alice stretched her legs full-length under the table and kicked off her navy pumps. A sharp little screw jutted out from the edge of the seat, and she shifted her leg away from it.

"Do my trees look right?" Esme asked.

"Perfect."

"What were the trees in your forest like?"

"They were really, really tall, and there were so many of them, jammed next to each other, so that while we were driving up the windy mountain roads, they were almost a wall on the side of the road to keep us out. And then, while I was looking out the window of the airplane, all I could see was mountain after mountain of trees. Like flocks of green wooly sheep huddled together."

Esme giggled.

"Can I draw a picture, too?" Alice asked.

"What do you want to draw?"

What was the most mural-worthy that had happened that year to Esme and her? They went to the zoos in San Diego, Santa Barbara, and L.A. They painted bowls at the new children's pottery center. They made necklaces with Roz and Jenny. They tried ice skating—no, Esme didn't like it, because she kept falling and getting wet and cold. "How about the pottery bowls we painted?"

"Okay. Do my bowl first."

Florence, meanwhile, had set down her marker and was massaging her right wrist.

"Is it your arthritis again, Mom?"

"It's nothing."

"Are you sure?" On a blank spot of the mural paper, Alice drew a big pink half-moon for Esme's bowl. "You know, Esme, honey, we need to go home soon."

"But I'm not done, Mommy."

"Grandma must be tired."

"I'll watch for a while, don't you two worry," Florence said.

"What did you draw over here?" Alice tapped the princess in the white gown.

"That's Penelope." Esme moved the green marker in a circle on top of a third brown lollypop stick. "Daddy's getting married to her in two more months, and I'm going to be the flower girl in a white dress."

●   ●   ●   ●   ●

Alice ripped her pantyhose on the screw at the edge of her chair, but she managed to stand, and to mouth *what the hell?* to her mother, and to declare fake-cheerfully to Esme, "Gee, that must be exciting. How come you didn't tell me before?"

"Daddy said it was a secret because you'd be mad at me, but he says I can tell you now."

"What the hell—"

"Alice!" Florence pulled at her arm.

"So. Esme, honey. What's her name? Have you met her a lot?"

"I told you. Penelope."

"Yes. Penelope. So, does she, you know, does she have dinner with you and Daddy?"

"Uh-huh."

"Has she been doing that for a long time?"

"Alice," Florence said firmly, "come in the living room."

"What does she look like? Does she have brown hair, like you and me?"

"Yeah, I think so."

"Or more yellowy, like James?"

"Mommy, can I just finish my trees?"

"Alice, come here. Now."

As soon as they were around the corner, in the living room, Alice faced Florence. "Did you know about this?"

"Esme told me yesterday."

"Why didn't you call me?"

"Why should I bother you all the way up there in the forests? You had your work to do."

Who was this Penelope person? How old was she? How long had she and Dan been dating? What was her career? Was she nice?

She had to be nice to Esme!

But a normal, nice person would never want to marry Dan Wilson.

(Once upon a time Alice had wanted to marry him. But that was thirteen years ago, when Alice was so young, straight out of college, terrified that she'd never get a job, feeling utterly lost in the world, too young and insecure to realize what a bully Dan was. Surely, Penelope wasn't that young and foolish?)

Esme seemed calm about the whole thing. Did that mean she liked this woman, she had fun with this woman?

Wicked stepmothers didn't make their stepdaughters clean the chimney cinders, not in real life.

What sorts of things did they do together? They would play with the puppy when it arrived. Throw sticks. Feed it treats. Read books in bed. Did they go shopping? Was Penelope the one who'd picked out the clothes that Esme wasn't allowed to bring to Alice's apartment, the three pairs of slacks and four pretty shirts, and the pink jacket to keep her dry in the rain? But would she let Esme eat her food according to Esme's strict pattern, starting from the top of the bowl? Would they hunt for sea glass on the beach, as Alice and Esme did? Make pottery? Bake raisin-chocolate chip cookies? Would they stroll down the sidewalk while Esme pointed her toes like a ballerina and twirled every third step?

Did this new wife hug and kiss Esme?

Did Esme like her? A lot?

What name would Esme call her?

Only one person could be Mommy.

CHAPTER EIGHTEEN

Bobby Corning was leaning over the gas tank and handlebars of a gleaming blue motorcycle that was parked at the curb, his back toward Alice.

Courtney was right. He was indeed big, probably more than six feet tall: muscled arms, wide thighs, broad back. His hair was as dark as Dan's—-what was the stereotype, that girls always marry men who resemble their father?—but Bobby's was a lot straighter and cut close to his ears. Hopefully, the hair color was the only trait he had in common with Dan.

"Ili," Alice began.

When Bobby turned around, the expression on his face was noncommittal. He was handsome in a skewed way, with a classically firm jaw line, pronounced cheekbones, dark-rimmed glasses, and a slightly beak nose. No beard. He must have shaved it off since the visit to MultiGrainery with Esme last fall. His short black boots were dusty but with shiny, new-looking heels. Tucked into faded jeans, he wore a T-shirt that was tie-dyed in a Venn diagram of green, purple and orange circles. One of the shirts he'd made himself?

For some reason, this was where Bobby's email had asked to meet, toward the edge of Santa Barbara's cute historic downtown, at eight AM on Monday or Tuesday. There was a small adobe bank behind Alice, and an old-fashioned black lamppost and a stucco planter at the curb a little past the motorcycle. Across the street, a few people were strolling out of an adobe Starbucks and an adobe CVS. Two blocks away was the building that used to be Esme's clothing shop.

"Thank you for emailing me." Alice smiled. Should she reach out her hand for a shake?

Pulling a red cloth from a rear pocket of his jeans, Bobby wiped his fingers, then screwed the cover onto a squat jar that had been resting on the bike's seat. Everything on the cycle sparkled, from the long, chrome exhaust pipes, to the blue fenders and even the tires. Its lean body was like an Olympic track star made of metal, tensed at the starting line, stretching forward, ready to take off.

"Stacey said you wanted to talk to me." Bobby's voice was reasonably deep, without any strong accent.

"Stacey from the art supply store?"

"Yeah."

"Oh. She told me she would give you my email and phone number, but I…" So, Stacey actually had, and Bobby had. A phone call from Stacey, when Alice got home from her Bloomingdale's shopping with Roz. An email from Bobby, a day later.

"I don't know why I sent you the email, to be honest." Bobby rubbed his right hand along his thigh, where the faded denim stretched snugly.

He was certainly direct. Not chatty, as Courtney had warned. Not rude, but not friendly, either.

So many questions to ask him, if he'd be willing to talk.

Where is Esme living?

What's she doing? Is she working? Is she in grad school?

Will she answer her phone if I call?

Why did you break into the art supply store?

Why does she hate me?

She had to sit down. She couldn't stand on the pavement in her Biviel ankle boots shooting questions at Bobby for an hour or however much time he would grant her, while the late-May morning sun grew stronger on her shoulders. A little farther along the cute brick sidewalk was one of the old-fashioned benches, with a polished wooden seat and wrought-iron legs and arm rests. Alice gestured toward it. "Do you mind if we sit?"

Bobby glanced at the motorcycle, then nodded and followed her. They each planted themselves at the farthest ends of the bench.

"So how is Esme? Is she working somewhere? Or, um, something else?"

"She's good."

Good. That meant nothing. It was because Alice's questions had been too direct, that was why Bobby wasn't saying anything meaningful. She had to start more gently.

"I was wondering, how did you two meet each other?"

Bobby sat forward a minuscule bit and wrapped his big palms around his knees, facing directly ahead at the street. A white car sped past, trailing Taylor Swift's voice. "She was sitting on a bench like this one. The kind of bench that looks like it's from New Orleans. A couple blocks from here."

Just a couple of blocks away.

Further down the street, a person called out a short burst of excited words.

"She was sitting on a bench," Alice prompted.

Bobby watched the street.

Esme was *good.* Well, that was information. It probably meant she wasn't in jail.

"She was on her break, from the clothing store across the street. Where she worked," Bobby said. "She was punching the keys on her phone over and over and swearing a mile high, like the phone wasn't working. So I sat down next to her. She was pretty, and I can fix things." A quick smile flitted across his face. He rubbed his knees. "She said she couldn't afford to buy a new phone, and she couldn't ask her dad for money."

"Why couldn't she ask her father?"

Crap. Wrong question again. Bobby exhaled through his nose, scowling.

"I'm sorry. Go on."

Bobby only hunched over further. A woman with a stroller emerged from the CVS.

"How long ago was it? When you met?"

"She was a junior at UC," Bobby finally continued, his voice almost as quiet as the neighborhood. "It was the spring. She thought I went to UC, too. I let her believe that for a while. I invented a fraternity I said I belonged to. Omega Alpha Alpha." Abruptly, he sat back against the bench and shoved his hands into his pockets, still facing the street, not Alice. "Yeah, I make my living fixing cars and bikes. I never went to college. I grew up in Ohio, and I moved here just to try a different place." He stopped.

Was he clamming up again? What topic of conversation wouldn't annoy him? What would break the thick block of ice all around him?

"That's a nice shirt." Alice gestured vaguely at Bobby's torso. "Did you do the design?"

"Yeah."

"The salesclerk at the art store said you use unusual color combinations. In an artistic way, I mean."

Bobby glanced at his chest.

"How do you choose your colors?"

With the toe of one black leather boot, Bobby kicked at the sidewalk. "I just experiment with things. Esme gives me ideas, too."

"Really? I know this sounds silly, but when she was little, she would only eat orange food. And now it's so funny that she combines colors—Oh, don't tell her I told you, please! She might hate that!"

He nodded.

"I'm sorry." Suddenly, Alice was rocking forward and back on the hard bench and hugging herself, like a crazy person. "This is kind of strange for me, okay? It's been six years, since I saw her, since she and I spoke. It's like I've been locked in a dark closet all this time, and now, out of nowhere, talking to you, I'm seeing a window way down the hall. Maybe a window. I've missed her so much, and I want to know everything. Even the littlest things. Do you have any photos? Does she still have long hair? I used to try to do her hair in French braids, which was hard, because she always had so many wild strands." Why was she blabbering on and on, to a guy who hated talking?

Alice eased her rocking, until it stopped.

Where does she live?

Does she have a job?

What did you mean that she's "good"?

Does she still have bulimia sometimes?

What has she told you about me?

"Yeah," Bobby said. "Her hair's pretty long. Below her shoulders."

He was gazing at the street as if he was itching to be out there with the cars, speeding away from her. Not yet!

"You said you're from Ohio?" Alice asked. "Do you still have family there?" But if he did, and they lived at the Cincinnati address the cops had given her, wouldn't somebody have replied to the letters she'd sent?

Bobby stood and nodded toward the motorcycle. "You want to go for a ride?"

"On your motorcycle?" That was a stupid question.

He stared at her as though "stupid" was exactly what he was thinking, too.

A motorcycle ride. That would mean squeezing close behind Bobby, on a seat that barely fit two people. Pressing against the back of the man that her daughter would have pressed against when they roared off to see Courtney. Wrapping her arms around the man that her daughter wrapped her own arms around. It was perverse. However, the offer was obviously a test, and to refuse would be to forever cut off any chance of reaching Esme through him.

"Sure," Alice said.

A white helmet was hanging by its straps on the motorcycle's handlebars. Bobby pulled out a second helmet from an orange nylon bag that lay on the ground near the bike, where they had stood, and held it toward Alice. "It's the law, that you have to wear it. But I'd insist, anyway. For safety." He slung himself on the seat, scooted all the way forward, and waited.

The helmet was a lot heavier than the one James wore on his bicycle. Her boots slipped a little against the footrest. She set her arms loosely around Bobby's waist, locking her hands atop the green-purple-orange T-shirt.

"Hold tighter," he demanded. "You'll fall off."

The engine burst into thunder. The motorcycle inched out of its parking spot, paused, wobbled a moment, and then it was rushing down the street, the wind pounding on her left side, metal vibrating against her shins, and she did, in fact, clutch Bobby tighter as the bike tilted, screeching, around a corner.

They were going to topple over. They were tilted too close to the asphalt. She was going to tumble off and break her arm. Did Bobby really know how to control this machine? They hurtled along an empty road, through a blink of green lights, past bare lots and occasional palm trees and long, low-slung, gray buildings that might have been warehouses or even the art supply store, too fast to tell. Her lungs grabbed for breath.

She should tell him to stop.

He wouldn't hear her if she shouted into the wind.

He would never speak to her again if she chickened out.

She dug her fingers into his T-shirt. It was too hard to keep holding onto him, her arms ached, and the helmet was too heavy on her head. How much longer was he planning on doing this ride? Her chest was desperately pumping in and out. But she was breathing. If she stretched her neck the smallest bit, she could see around Bobby's head, and the world was steadier.

Now they were passing small houses, one after another, scrawny lawns, a gas station, a small blocky structure. An orange sign. A Dunkin' Donuts? A few cars zoomed by in the other direction. They turned a corner, and the wind was too sharp in her face to see anything but flashes of white or brown. The entire world was the wind and the roar of the engine, the speeding breeze that slapped her helmet, the worn cotton of Bobby's shirt under her fingers and the strain in her legs, abnormally bent.

Maybe Esme loved it. Flying with the sky, and nothing could catch them; leaning into the turns as the motorcycle flirted with the asphalt of the road, clutching the softness of Bobby's shirt, the air whipping her face. Would she tie back her wild hair, or would the helmet restrain it from blowing everywhere? When the road curved, the bike swayed sideways along with it, as graceful as a dancer.

"Where're we going?" she shouted, although Bobby most likely didn't hear. That could have been the whole aim of the ride, an excuse for not talking.

Another turn, and they slowed. They were back where they'd started, at the squat little adobe bank, the Starbucks, the New Orleans bench. They braked. Keeping the motorcycle steady with his feet and one hand, Bobby held her arm with the other hand as she unhooked a leg from around the seat and staggered off the bike.

"You okay?"

Her legs must have been obviously quivering. Was her face green? She yanked off her hulking helmet. "I think this is maybe my second time ever on a motorcycle. I forgot how scary the turns can feel."

"Sorry. I thought you might like it."

"I did! It was amazing, to speed through the streets and look around at the world without any glass or metal separating me from the sky."

"That's a cool way to describe it." There was something a little more relaxed in Bobby's jaw now and in the way his arms dangled at his sides, something sweet, too, in the way his face lit up, even if it was for a short moment. It was as if he was personally happy that another person enjoyed his motorcycle. A young woman could fall in love with an almost-handsome, dark-haired man whose face could shine that way and who could also fix broken cellphones. But he was also a man who could break into a store.

"Honestly, the ride was great. Now I need to sit." She was panting too fast, catching her breath. Bobby nodded, and they returned to their same spots on the far ends of the same bench.

Were she and Bobby friends now?

"Can I ask you just a little more?"

Does Esme still eat organic stoneground crackers?
Or does she eat them and then vomit?
What kind of job does she have?
Why did you break into the art supply store?
Will she talk to me?

He nodded.

"What's she been doing since she graduated from college? Is she working?"

The air was getting busier, as stores began to open. The motorcycle jaunt must have lasted longer than it had felt. A woman in backless sandals strode past Alice and Bobby's bench, her heels clacking on the bricks. Two teenagers crossed the street toward them, sipping from Starbucks cups and shedding a trail of coffee-flavored steam.

"Please?"

Bobby rubbed the iron arm rest next to him. "When I met her, she said she was going to drop out of UC. She hated school, and she was going to work more hours at the clothing store, make more money. I told her she was crazy—Sorry. I called your daughter crazy."

"That's okay."

"I meant, she would be crazy to put in all those years of studying without anything to show for it, when she only had one more year left until she graduated. I never went to college myself, but I know how important a diploma is. She didn't have to go to grad school or that bullshit if she didn't want to, but I said she should get the B.A. under her belt, and then she could think about what to do with her life."

After six years of silence from Esme and words barely pried from Bobby, it was almost too much information to absorb, too fast. Had Esme seriously been planning to drop out of college? Were her grades terrible? Was she truly focused on making money? Did she hate school even when no mother was around to nag her?

"Did she graduate?" Alice whispered.

"Yeah. Then she kept working in the clothing store, till they went out of business a couple months ago. I was already laid off, from the garage where I was working. Because of the recession. So, well, she was already designing her own earrings and selling them on Etsy and—and places. So she kept doing more of that."

"What sorts of earrings?"

Bobby's mouth curved into a bigger smile than before. "She does a lot with beads. Sometimes she strings them on wire, and in-between the beads she'll shape the wire into patterns. Or hang something special from the bottom." He twisted his fingers, the tips against each other, as if he, too, was twisting a jewelry wire into a strange pattern.

"They sound beautiful."

"They are."

"Do you have any pictures? On your phone?"

He turned his head away, scratching at his neck. "I don't have that kind of phone."

Esme at her kitchen table, her jewelry supplies spread out before her, needle-nose pliers, coils of thin silver wire, a dozen little plastic boxes of blue, purple, orange, black, yellow, green, red, and pink glass beads, her wild hair—long hair, Bobby had said—long, wild hair falling in her face as she carefully threaded a length of wire through the holes at each end of a tiny bead. The same concentration, clutching her paintbrush, biting her lower lip, that she had while drawing the mural at Grandma Florence's house when she was six years old.

"Where is—?"

But Bobby, for once, was speaking before Alice could finish mouthing her thoughts. And he was looking at her straight-on, instead of at the street. "You've worked up north? In Humboldt County?" he asked.

"Well, sort of."

"Trying to save part of the forests up there, Esme said."

Saving forests was good, wasn't it? So did that mean Esme was proud of Alice's work? She'd sort-of bragged to Bobby about the good work her mother did, saving the forests, hadn't she?

"Does she know you're meeting with me today?"

Bobby frowned. "Yeah. I'm not sneaking behind her back."

"No, no, I didn't mean it that way. I just wondered, you know, what she thought about it. Did she, you know, not want you to talk with me?"

Lifting his helmet from the wooden seat, Bobby tapped it against his thigh. "We don't make rules for each other. She said I should come to my own opinion."

What will you tell her about me?

"I have to get going," Bobby was saying.

Not yet!

Please tell Esme—

Can I call her?

Can I see her?

"Do you guys, um, need money? For the lawyers?"

"What lawyers?" Bobby snapped. He'd stood up and was grabbing the second helmet from the bench.

But didn't they have lawyers to handle their legal case? Didn't they realize they needed legal advice? Hadn't they been arrested?

"Wait! Please."

She ought to stand, too, but her legs were shaky, as if all the muscles had been drained out of them. In their uneven positions, Bobby was looking down at Alice, but maybe that was no big deal. They didn't have to face each other like equals. As long as Bobby didn't walk away yet. "Will you ask her if she'll meet with me?"

"Okay."

Okay? It was that easy?

He shrugged. "I'm not her prison warden."

Damn. Oh damn. What if Esme said yes?

CHAPTER NINETEEN

ALICE, DAN, AND ESME

June 1992
Westwood, CA

Alice's thick bouquet of red and white roses was squished against her chest. Florence had brought a mass of purple and yellow irises from her garden, Jenny and Sharon each carried pink-and-yellow nosegays, and Roz had a camera. "Esme is going to drown in flower petals!" Alice laughed, trying to cheek-kiss Roz at the doorway of the high school auditorium, while dozens of other mothers, fathers, grandparents, aunts, uncles, and friends of Madame Nadia's aspiring ballerinas, along with more bouquets, shoved past them.

"Do you see Dan anywhere?" Roz asked, grabbing hold of Sharon's flowers just as they slipped from her fist. "I would think he'd have to get Esme here early."

"I guess so."

"Is he bringing his new bride? Are you finally going to meet her?"

"Who knows with Dan?"

"They've been married a month?"

"Uh-huh. Maybe she's already divorced him."

Roz giggled.

"Esme said she has brown hair," Alice added.

"What else? Is she tall? Short?"

"That's all I know."

"Does she have a career?"

"No idea."

"Dan really hasn't told you anything?" Roz said.

"I've asked him a zillion times, to tell me about her. Anything. Maybe she's an ax murderer."

"A porn star."

"Even worse: an oil company executive."

At the far side of the crowded room, in the center of a row of folding seats about three-quarters of the way from the stage, Walt waved vigorously. He was sprawled across four empty seats, with his suit jacket spread across another two in the row behind him.

"Did you invite Larry?" Roz asked.

"Nah, we've basically broken up. All he talks about is the restaurant he's opening in Malibu." And less than three hours ago, out of the blue, James said he wasn't coming, either. Andrea wasn't feeling well, supposedly. So, James could have come without her, if he truly wanted to see Esme do her little dance, as he'd claimed he did.

Where would Dan sit? Toward the front, to make sure Esme saw him? At the very rear, to spy on Alice? The room churned with dozens of men in golf shirts and button-downs, women in slacks and sundresses. It was impossible to pick out one short man with curly black hair. Wouldn't Alice feel a warning—a shiver, a premonition of evil—if she chanced to look in Dan's direction?

Jenny and Sharon clambered over people's legs to reach Walt, while Alice and Florence sidled into the two seats in the row directly behind. The house lights dimmed.

With a burst of cheerful piano trills, a dozen girls in lime-green tutus and golden tiaras darted onto the stage. The music sounded a little like a slow version of "Turkey in the Straw," and the dancers skipped, twirled, pointed their feet, rose on tiptoe. They waved their arms as the music speeded up. One little girl's tiara fell off. After a few minutes, the music ended, the girls bowed, and the audience applauded. As they ran off stage left, a line of blue costumes ran in stage right, while a woman darted among them to retrieve the tiara. This second group's score was more classical. The dancers swayed with arms outstretched, as if they were supposed to be flower stalks in the wind. Were Jenny and Sharon bored yet?

According to the program, there would be three more sets before Esme's class, Dancing Roses. Yellow tutus. Then taller girls in darker blue. Then purple skirts.

Finally, a flurry of red-and-white was on the stage, two lines of four dancers each. Beethoven's "Ode to Joy" boomed through the auditorium. Dah, dah, dah, dah, dah, dah, dah, dah, dah, dah, DAH dah-dah. Right legs extended sideways, almost in unison, toes pointed. Sliding in to first position, out again, in again. Repeat with left legs. Exactly as Esme had practiced. Arms curved in front of red bodices, fingertips meeting. Everyone's hair pulled back at the neck in a bun. But something was wrong. A grown-up figure—a woman—Esme's teacher—was in one of the red-and-white lines, doing all the leg movements along with the girls. That was strange. None of the teachers had danced with the other classes. Was Esme's group so incompetent that it needed the teacher on stage with them?

"Which one is Esme?" Roz whispered.

"I don't see her," Florence added.

She would be the one with wild, curly-wavy dark hair coming unwound from her bun.

Except there was no girl with wild, curly-wavy dark hair.

The teacher was dancing in her spot in line instead.

Seven little ballerinas in red bodices and white tutus and one tall teacher rose up on their toes, their arms forming a circle above each of their heads. Dah, dah, DAH. Seven girls and one teacher stretched their legs to the right, arms curved in front of their bodices.

"What the hell?" Alice whispered too loudly.

"Shh!"

"Where is she?" Alice leaned forward to Roz.

"I don't know."

"Do you think she got sick? Or they had a car accident?"

"I don't know."

"I have to get home. What if Dan calls?" A pile of red and white roses fell on the floor as Alice jumped up.

•　　•　　•　　•　　•

No message from Dan waited on Alice's answering machine at home.

None of the hospitals between Dan's house and the high school recorded any little girls nearly seven years old with wild, dark hair being brought to the emergency room.

Neither the Santa Monica nor Los Angeles police departments had any report of a traffic accident in the past five hours involving a silver BMW anywhere in the vicinity.

Walt called from the pay phone at the school. He'd found the ballet teacher backstage. Esme hadn't gotten sick or stage fright, the teacher told him. She hadn't been huddled in the wings. She simply had never appeared at the auditorium.

"Roz!" Alice screamed, grabbing Roz's shoulders. "Where is she?"

Roz wrapped both arms around her. "I'm sure it's nothing major. A stomachache. And wouldn't it be just like Dan, to make you worry and not tell you?"

Alice shook her head, side to side, like a stupid dog shaking off water.

"Should I call him?" Roz offered.

"Thanks. No, I'll do it. Esme might answer."

Hi. It was Esme's voice! Cheerful, giggly. A little tinny. Everything was fine.

Hi. This is Esme. We aren't home now.

Dan's goddam answering machine.

If something was really wrong—if there had been an accident, if Esme was seriously ill—Dan would have called. He wouldn't play games with Esme's health. Would he?

"Sweetie." Roz hugged her again. "I bet they just went out to get ice cream or something like that. To make her feel better. After, you know, after whatever happened to her."

Sure. If it was a stomachache, or a cold, for instance. At this precise moment when Alice had called, Dan was—He was watching TV with Esme. Reading in bed with her.

But it couldn't be something trivial. Esme wouldn't miss the recital for a mere stomachache. She would pretend that she was fine. She'd practiced so hard, for so many weeks, showing her dance to Alice every evening. All over her bedroom wall, she'd Scotch-taped the photos Alice took of her in the Dancing Roses costume. With her little leg stretched out to the left, her face turned upward. On her toes, arms spread wide to her side. Fingertips touching above her head.

These kinds of things were constantly happening to kids without turning into emergencies. Weren't they? When Alice was two years older than Esme, she'd once gone missing for hours and terrified her parents, too. It was when her classmate Cynthia had invited Alice to her house after school to play with her puppet set. At the house, Cynthia's mother asked Alice if she'd like to call home, but Alice didn't know her phone number. Why hadn't that mother instantly taken Alice back to her own house? But she didn't, and Alice and Cynthia had played for a couple of hours, at which point the mother drove her home, because at least Alice knew her own address.

Ridiculously, eight-year-old Alice had expected to stroll inside and sit down at the kitchen table, as if it was a normal dinnertime.

Her mother had hugged her tightly. Then she'd pulled Alice over to a lamp and inspected her face, her neck, her arms, her legs.

"Are you injured? Are you all right?" demanded her father.

They told her they'd called the school, the police, and all the hospitals in Los Angeles. Her father had raced out of work to tramp every block within a two-mile radius of their house, peering into yards and driveways, barging into stores. In the stretch that ran over the L.A. River, near the Sepulveda Dam…The water was so low, only a few inches. The police would have seen a body.

"How could you do something like that? We were worried to death," her father shouted.

"We're just glad you're safe," her mother added, hugging her again.

"Why didn't you call?"

Her father sat Alice in front of the kitchen telephone, which was brilliant green, while he yelled the phone number into her face, over and over. *758 0483 758 0483*

Alice had sobbed, though she'd learned the number, fast. All she wanted was for her parents to hug her.

That was what she would do now, as a mother, as soon as she saw Esme again: Hug her. No questions, no recriminations. *Why didn't you call? I was worried to death!* None of that!

Alice and Roz watched the six-thirty news, sitting on the orange-and-red flowered couch. A fire in a restaurant on Sunset Boulevard. A drive-by shooting that involved three teenage boys.

"Do you think Dan, maybe, he got into a fight?" Alice asked. "A driver tailgated him on the way to the recital. And he jumped out of the car and started beating up the guy. And so he's in jail?"

"Sweetie, if that happened, wouldn't the police call you to come get Esme?"

A minute later, Roz asked, "She had her recital costume with her, didn't she?"

"Of course she did. And what difference would that make? She could call and ask me to bring it."

"Okay."

"I think I should phone them again."

The answering machine clicked in.

"Hey, everyone," Alice told the machine. "It's Alice. We all missed Esme at the recital, you know, so I hope everything's all right." Then she had to call once more, to add that they could phone her at any hour, no matter how late.

"You need to eat," Roz said. "Should I order pizza?"

"You don't think he could—you know? Be abducting her?" Fathers did that. All the time. The newspapers were full of horror stories.

"It can't be abduction while it's within the hours of his visitation weekend. That's what they always told us at Social Services."

"Dan would do it."

Roz sighed. "You have to give him until whatever time the weekend officially ends. I know it's hard, sweetie. I'm sorry."

"Six. But he's always late."

"I don't think the courts would hold him to the minute."

"You go home," Alice told Roz, at ten o'clock.

"Are you sure? I can stay as long as you want. I'll call Walt to tell—"

"No! Don't tie up the phone!"

Sunday morning and Sunday at noon and Sunday afternoon, the police and the hospital still had no reports of injured little girls or BMWs in accidents. Alice started scrubbing the bathroom. What if the phone rang in the living room while the water was running, and she didn't hear it? She abandoned the dirty bathroom. She left seven more messages on Dan's answering machine.

At six o'clock there was still no call from Dan and no silver BMW in sight on the block. Six-oh-five. She stayed next to the phone and the living room window. Six-ten. A silver BMW rounded the corner and eased to a stop a few yards past Alice's building a little after six-fifteen.

Alice raced downstairs and outside. The passenger-side door was shut.

A heartbeat, and Esme got out. Climbed out, on both legs, like normal, no crutches, no plaster cast, her backpack on her shoulders, her ballet costume in a transparent plastic bag in one hand and a big stuffed elephant in the other. She waved the elephant toward the car, turned around, and ran to Alice.

Ran. On both legs. Smiling and waving the elephant.

"Hi Mommy. Can I have some apple juice?"

Alice pulled Esme against her chest and rested her cheek on the soft, tangled hair on top of her daughter's head. Esme's hair smelled flowery. But not like the roses in the bouquet Alice had brought to the recital, for Dancing Roses. She counted her own heartbeats until they ceased jumping.

Esme wriggled. "Mommy…"

So Alice eased off a little, though she kept holding onto Esme's upper arms. "I was—" she croaked. She started again. "What happened? You missed the ballet recital."

Esme frowned. "Daddy told you. He got tickets to the circus, and it's his only time he could go with me." She held out the elephant. "They had baby elephants, and ladies on the flying trapeze. And no one fell down! We stayed really late, until it ended."

"But…Grandma came. And Jenny and Sharon. And Roz and Walt."

"I can show Grandma my dance tomorrow. I have my costume. Can I have some apple juice?"

The BMW was gone.

CHAPTER TWENTY

A little boy eating a muffin, a smaller girl carrying a white paper bag, and a woman in a purple hoodie were all leaving MultiGrainery as James and Alice headed inside.

"Hi, Esme's mom! You're back!"

Courtney's hair was orange today, and her apron had a pattern of knives, forks, and spoons.

"Everyone loved your muffins so much, I had to get more."

"Wow, thank you. And you brought your husband."

Alice glanced at James. Then laughed a little. "He's just a friend. All my friends want to meet the person who makes those delicious muffins, but James asked first."

James reached his hand over the display case, and Courtney shook it.

Afternoon sunlight poured through the windows flanking the glass door like batter pouring into a baking pan. Three glossy posters had been mounted on one of the walls since Alice's last visit, portraying loaves of bread artistically laid out alongside different arrangements of wooden cutting boards, flowers, and fruit.

"You should've come earlier. I'll be closing in less than an hour, so there's not much left." Courtney waved a wrinkled square of waxed paper above the display case.

"Damn."

"I'll take whatever you got." James smiled.

"How's your mother doing?" Alice asked.

"Oh, that's nice of you to remember. She's been pretty stable my last few visits, luckily. But it's tough for her. Even trying to hold a cup of coffee? Her hand shakes, and she gets so frustrated."

"I can sort-of imagine."

"She's got some new physical therapy exercises."

"That sounds hopeful. Do you think it's helping?"

"It's a little funny, actually." Courtney gave one of her guffaws. "She walks around the block taking these huge, high steps and swinging her arms. She says she feels like a toy soldier."

"Not so much like a cheerleader." Alice grinned.

Courtney burst into another guffaw.

"Unless you had cheers like that in high school?"

"Nope. No toy-soldier-marching cheers. But I'll tell my mom your idea."

James had crouched down to eye level with the display case. Behind the glass, a meager scattering of unsliced bread loaves, smaller shiny-topped loaves, eight or so muffins of various shades of brown and tan, a couple of scones, and a few fat cookies was dispersed around the shelves.

"I was wondering," Alice began. "Has Esme been back here to visit?"

"No. I would've told you."

"I know. Anyway, I realize it's only been two weeks."

"But I remembered something she said from last time." Scratching one of her upper arms, Courtney leaned slightly against the top of the display case.

James was still staring at the goodies inside as if that was the main reason he'd come.

It couldn't be very important, the thing Esme had said. That Courtney had forgotten. And now remembered. It wouldn't be as if Esme had confessed: *I've been doing drugs. Bobby and I broke into the art store to steal money for drugs. I miss my mother.*

"I was meaning to text you," Courtney continued. "It wasn't all that big a deal, you know. Just that, when she was talking about making earrings, she said her father was pushing her to go to business school and get a corporate job, and that was the last thing in the world she wanted. Which I could totally understand. Other than my sister, I don't know anyone who ever wanted to work in an office."

"Yeah."

"So, it's probably nothing you didn't already know."

Bobby had said that Esme wanted to drop out of college. And that she couldn't ask Dan for money to fix her phone. But in her bulimia letter for the sorority, she wrote that she was graduating, that her grades weren't so bad. And it was Dan she'd turned to, who'd gotten her out of jail after the arrest. So who was the real Esme? Did she hate Dan or hug him? Was she the good daughter who listened to Daddy, and now she was a middle-manager at a jewelry company?

"Did she finally go to business school?" Crap, that was a ridiculous question. What mother wouldn't know whether her own daughter had gone to grad school after college? "I suppose she hasn't been here to see you," Alice added quickly, "because she moved further away."

"Sure. That could be."

"Because she's not living anymore in the apartment the detective found."

"Detective?"

Oh crap and crap again. Her big mouth. Why hadn't she prepared a script for this visit? She wouldn't fool anyone into believing she was a normal mother now. "Yes, I hired a detective, once, that's all, but it's not as creepy as it sounds. Really. It's just that I tried everything to find her. I wasn't spying on her, I honestly wasn't." *Not like that weekend in high school...* The only place to look, other than Courtney's face, was the metal top of the display case where Courtney's elbows rested.

"It's okay. It's not creepy," Courtney said.

The little bakery was quiet. The air had a wisp of a smell of butter, mixed with coffee. Why coffee? James was methodically rubbing her back. After a few seconds, something on the counter toward Alice's left made a fluttering-crackling sound.

"I envied Esme, in high school," Courtney added.

"You did?"

On top of the counter, Courtney was folding a fresh square of waxed paper, the source of the fluttering-crackling noise. "I think a lot of us on the cheerleading squad did. Because you came to the games sometimes, to see us doing our cheers."

"It was only a few games. In your senior year."

"But hardly any of our moms or dads ever came."

"I wasn't sure if Esme would be glad if I was there."

"Oh, you know teenagers. She'd roll her eyes and make a face and say, 'I can't believe my mother drove all the way from Santa Monica for something this dumb,' and it actually meant she was bragging."

Was that why Esme had stopped speaking to Alice, because Alice didn't attend enough football games? Or because she came to too many? Either reason was ridiculous.

"It sounds as though all you cheerleaders really bonded together. Did you spend a lot of time practicing the routines?"

"Every day after school. It was a lot of work. Not as much as the girls who entered the big contests, but a lot." Courtney shook her head while she laughed.

"All that jumping. You must have been exhausted."

"Oh yeah."

"Was Esme dating any football players?"

Courtney giggled. "I don't think so. That's what cheerleaders are supposed to do, on TV? It wasn't true of us."

"Esme once offered to teach me some cheers."

James's hand finally slipped off Alice's back. "Well," he said. The it's-time-to-leave hint.

Not yet! Courtney wasn't pushing them out.

"I suppose you remember—" If Alice looked at Courtney's face, she would see the immediate reaction "—the weekend you came to visit me with Esme, in high school."

"For sure!"

Of course Courtney did.

However, Courtney was still smiling, as broadly as ever, maybe more broadly, as though it was a happy memory. "You guys lived right next to the beach. Yeah?" Courtney asked.

"Um. Well, about a half-mile away." Three-quarters of a mile.

"And there was this long pier with little shops and ice cream places? It felt like being on vacation, like taking a stroll from your hotel to the beach at night? When Esme and I went out. I mean, there is literally no place to walk in Calabasas except to more houses."

"I—I guess so."

"We have a long drive home," James interrupted. "And Courtney said it was almost time for her to close the store."

"That's right. I'm sorry we're keeping you. Will you get to leave soon?" Alice asked.

"I wish! Nope, I've got to prep for my sister, for when she comes in tomorrow morning to bake."

"How long will that take?"

"A couple of hours, altogether." Courtney began counting out on the fingers of her extended left hand. "I have to pre-scale the flour and sugar, and cut the butter, and check that the bread dough is proofed. And there's cleanup and cashing out, too."

"When did you start today?"

Courtney smiled, locking her fingers together. "Six-thirty."

"Oh boy."

James ran a trill with his fingers along the countertop. "That's a long day."

"Oh, my sister was here at four."

"We'll leave right away!" Alice pulled her shoulder bag to the countertop. "But I need to buy some muffins before we go."

"What kinds did you get last time for your friends?" Courtney was suddenly efficient, squatting and sliding open a rear door in the display case, a piece of waxed paper already in her other hand.

Roz had loved the carrot-raisin, plus she could rationalize that carrots were vegetables and therefore she wasn't breaking her diet.

Anything chocolate would work for Fred. What had James liked? "I'll take one of everything you have left," Alice said.

"Alice?" James warned.

"Everything? Bread and cookies, too?" Courtney asked.

"Yes."

Courtney's squares of waxed paper dipped in and out of trays inside the display case, as she filled one white paper bag, then seven more, and placed each of those bags inside a plain plastic shopping bag. "I gave you doubles on the cookies and the cranberry scones, no charge," she said, handing all the bags across the countertop.

•   •   •   •   •

Outside MultiGrainery's door, the little strip mall formed a semi-circle surrounding a nearly empty parking lot: a pizza parlor, a nail salon, a UPS shipping outlet, a Laundromat, and a Subway. One woman emerged from the UPS store.

"What Courtney said in there, about me watching the cheerleading at the games? Do you think it's true?" Alice tugged at James's arm as soon as they were a storefront away. The bulging plastic bakery bags swung from her right hand, maybe slapping him lightly.

"Yeah. Esme was glad you came to see her."

"I don't know, James. It's hard to believe."

"Courtney doesn't seem the type to BS you, Allie. What you see with her is what you get."

"That's true. She seems like a good person."

"She works her butt off, doesn't she?"

They both glanced over at the bakery, its red-and-white *Open* sign swinging optimistically on the door.

"She's been here since six-thirty," James murmured.

"And I doubt that the store is doing that well. I've hardly seen any customers on either visit when I've been here."

"I wonder if she'd want a strolling troubadour wandering around the parking lot, to drum up more sales," James muttered.

"That's a great idea. I'll bring Roz and we'll applaud you."

James kicked at a wad of paper as they stepped off the curb, and he started striding across the asphalt toward his car. "I didn't get the job in San Diego."

"Oh James. I'm sorry." Alice caught up with him.

"Fuck it. It would've been a crappy commute, either for me if we stayed in L.A. or Andrea if we moved to San Diego. Or else we'd have to live in some armpit midway between the two, like Santa Ana."

"It would've been a wonderful career move for you."

He glanced at her, made a grimace that was also a half-smile, and continued walking.

"And San Diego is so beautiful. All those beaches."

"You and your beaches."

"What are you going to do now? Try for a promotion at the *Chronicle*? Apply to the *L.A. Times*?"

"They don't hire fifty-three-year-old reporters."

"You're not fifty-three until August."

"Journalism's a career for twenty-year-olds. I'm a has-been."

"That's not true, James. Look at your big series last year on earthquake preparedness in the Valley, and how little has changed since Northridge in 1994."

"So?"

"You're doing important work. Investigating sloppy government agencies. Writing stories that give people crucial information."

"Working at a pinhole suburban weekly no one reads, that's probably going to go bankrupt in a week." James paused, while a car drove past them. He surveyed a few directions around the parking lot. "Andrea says I've been kidding myself. Avoiding making a decision. If I'd been serious about music, I would've quit the *Chronicle* years ago and poured everything I've got into writing music, putting together a more professional band, sending demos to agents and labels. Or else I should've taken journalism seriously and applied to bigger papers before now, sell one of my guitars, how many do I need for a hobby? She doesn't—" He scratched the mass of blond hair at the back of his head. "She's always been confident of what she wants. That's one of her strengths, yeah. But she doesn't understand how a person might not be confident of their decisions all the time. Not really."

Alice shifted the bakery bags to her left hand, flexing the right-hand fingers.

"I know, I know. My annual midlife crisis again. Sorry." He brushed the air in front of his face.

"It's okay, James. You're allowed. This is a big setback, the San Diego job."

"If I focus a hundred percent seriously on journalism, we all know I'll be stuck forever at the bullshit *Chronicle,* or maybe I won't even have that job in five years because no one reads newspapers anymore. And if I focus totally on music, fine, great, and what kind of job would I ever get there? Giving guitar lessons to kids who're convinced they're the next Dylan, or whoever they want to be these days, three hours a week? Singing in front of Courtney's bakery for free pumpkin muffins? Let's face it, you and I know which one Andrea thinks I should choose. And it's not Dylan." They were at James's Toyota, and he unlocked the passenger-side door.

Alice stepped into the car. "I thought Andrea likes your music."

"She does."

"Isn't that how you first met? While you were touring with a band in Morocco?"

"Yeah. Basically." Moving around the hood of the car, James opened his own door and fell on his seat cushion. "Look, it makes sense, what Andrea says. A person can't have two first-priorities. Two simultaneous careers you love."

"Why can't you? Why do you have to choose between journalism and music?"

James drummed the steering wheel. "Not enough time, for one thing."

"That's a lousy excuse. You don't work at the *Chronicle* every minute, night and day."

"Attention span. Psychic energy. Heart."

"Really? You can only love one thing at a time?"

James grinned.

"You shouldn't be forced to make those sorts of choices." Alice gave James's arm one more squeeze, before he rolled down his window. He squeezed her hand in return. "It's like what Dan drilled into Esme her entire childhood," she said.

"What do you mean?"

"That she had to choose between him and me."

"It's not the same thing as me and Andrea at all."

"Sure it is. A false dichotomy. 'Mommy or me.' 'Music or a real job.' "

"No, Dan's bullshit is just another way that he's always criticizing you. My situation is a serious life choice."

"And you don't think that putting a child in the middle, making her choose between her parents, is serious?"

"Come on, Alice. I'm not belittling what Dan put you through. But it's not the same as a decision that will change my life."

"Never mind, you don't understand. You don't have kids."

"Right." James turned the key in the ignition. He backed out of the parking spot and swerved abruptly into the connecting lane. At the exit to the street, they waited while a few cars passed.

"Thanks for coming here with me today," Alice finally said. "I know I bought too much."

"I'm glad to help Courtney."

"How about this: If you lose your job with the *Chronicle*, and if the Cordwainers hate all of my sample portfolios and I also don't win this new client in San Francisco and lose my job at Seshat, and Courtney's bakery goes bust, then we can all camp out here and live on her muffins."

James nodded. "Doesn't sound too bad."

CHAPTER TWENTY-ONE

ALICE, DAN, AND ESME

November 1999
Santa Monica, CA

The way Monday evening was supposed to go was that they would sit at the kitchen table like a couple of girlfriends, digging their chopsticks into each other's takeout cartons of chicken with cashews or beef and broccoli, gabbing about maybe a movie they could rent on the weekend, or how Esme's friend Jasmine was learning to rollerblade, or a recipe for an organic something that Esme might like to make. Until finally, when the Chinese food was almost all gone, Alice would casually mention, "I got your report card in the mail yesterday…"

However, when Alice unlocked the door of their apartment at six o'clock, it was dark and empty. Esme had left a message on the answering machine. "Going to Thomas's house after school."

Thomas who? A boy. Was his mother there?

Did Esme know him from one of her classes? Had she ever mentioned a Thomas before? Where did he live? When would she be home?

A class list for Esme's eighth-grade homeroom was posted on the refrigerator door, but no Tom or Thomas was on it. Which meant nothing. He could be in one of her other classes. Or not from school at all. The lists that had been so reliable in elementary school, the year-by-year rosters of everyone in her class and their parents and their phone numbers, Willow and Masha and Ada and all the other girls who flew with Esme from birthday parties to musical puppet theater to pottery-making workshops over the years—those sorts of lists were totally out of date by junior high. Now Esme went to the mall with Pam one weekend, and the movies with "a bunch of people" two weeks later, and Alice never heard a word about Pam again. Or much else about Esme's friends.

And her schoolwork! The sweet little girl who used to produce all As and Bs was suddenly a thirteen-year-old bringing home Cs. She didn't read, except for gossip and fashion magazines. She'd become absolutely stupid the few times she agreed to play Scrabble, always picking the simplest three- and four-letter words. CAR. CARD. She wasn't even trying.

The divorce was no doubt a big reason for the problems. Esme went from one home to the other, not mentioning one parent to the other, to all appearances keeping the juggling balls in the air. Dan's fancy new house in Calabasas, with Esme's private bathroom and the swimming pool in the backyard, was a fortress barred to Alice. Still, living a split life had to be a horrible strain on Esme. How could she possibly focus on grades or friends, when she constantly had to remember what not to say to which parent.

According to the books, this was exactly when divorced parents should come together for the best interests of the child. On what planet? Alice sent Dan a careful letter, rewritten and rewritten and rewritten, spelling out her concerns: *Perhaps you could offer to do homework with Esme on her visitation weekends? I'd be glad to discuss this issue in more detail on the phone with you.*

Dan replied within twenty-four hours, by registered mail: *If you are incapable of fulfilling your responsibility concerning our daughter's educational or other needs, Esme can come live with me and my wife and attend our excellent local school.*

But inside his fortress, Dan must be lecturing Esme about her grades, too. Certainly this was one issue where Dan and Alice could agree, and Esme wouldn't be caught in the middle between two bickering parents. Dan wouldn't be pleased with Cs on the report cards that Alice was obligated to send to him, any more than he'd allow Esme to take a seat at their homemade-pasta-and-kale dinner with dirty fingernails. Did Penelope have a role in this, too? Or did she keep strictly to her and Dan's son and daughter? It would be nice if Alice and Penelope could chat, two women, two mothers. Alice should have pushed Dan harder for a way to contact Penelope when those two first got married. A phone number at work, an email address. Not that Dan would have agreed.

Maybe—hopefully—Roz knew what she was talking about when she said Esme was simply being a teenager, and it wasn't as drastic as it seemed. Teenage girls didn't talk to their mothers. Teenage girls didn't go shopping with their mothers. Roz knew from her social work experience. And from her own life, poor Roz. Jenny's grades were worse than Esme's, she wasn't eating, and she was always coming home way past whatever curfew Roz and Walt set. Roz wouldn't say it outright, but Jenny was probably smoking grass, like everyone in high school. Which Esme wasn't doing. Was she? Yet.

The best a parent could do, Roz said, was try to keep her kids as safe as possible through the teenage years,

And it certainly wasn't fair to expect Esme to be a straight-A nerd as Alice had been. Alice's great failure was when she missed being high school valedictorian because of one ridiculous half-semester B and had to settle for salutatorian. *A half-semester B in Health? Why does that even count?* Still, she would be delivering a speech at graduation, second-place though it was, and her mother had invited all of her colleagues from the accounting firm to the ceremony. "It falls to our generation to repair the damage your generation has bequeathed us, from the disasters of Vietnam and Watergate," salutatorian Alice wrote. James drove her to the beach with ice cream and a joint the night before, to cheer her up. He told her that she was brilliant and she would save the planet, whether or not she gave a bullshit speech or had straight-As. He didn't go to graduation himself; that was too bourgeois.

With a bang, the front door of their apartment was thrust open.

Esme was dressed in a deep purple V-neck sweater, low-cut jeans, and a torn pair of red Nikes, her backpack slung over one shoulder.

"Hi, honey. I'm glad you're home," Alice called out. Big smile, but no hug. Esme would hate a hug. "Where were you?"

"I left you a phone message. Like you always say I should."

"But who's Thomas?"

Shrugging and dragging the backpack by a strap, Esme moved toward the kitchen. "What's for dinner?"

"I thought we could order in Chinese food. Does that sound good?"

"Ugh. Chinese food has MSG. No one eats it."

Now Chinese food was bad? But Chinese restaurants didn't use MSG anymore. "How about if I make us cheese omelets?"

Alice breathed in and out before Esme mumbled, "Okay."

While Alice opened and shut cupboards and the refrigerator, Esme hovered silently in the kitchen doorway, somewhere between sitting down and walking out. Five eggs. Cheddar. Mozzarella. Two plates. Mixing bowl. Cheese grater. "So who's Thomas?" Alice asked, keeping her gaze on the bowl and the cheese grater.

"A boy."

"Umm. Is he in one of your classes?"

"What difference does it make?"

"I'm just wondering."

"He's not my *boyfriend*. It's no big deal. Can I put broccoli in my omelet?"

For at least a couple of minutes, Esme stood near Alice at the counter, silently washing and chopping a small crown of broccoli and stirring the pieces into the egg mix. She carried the plates to the table. "Did you ever get those organic stoneground crackers that Daddy buys?" she asked.

Dammit. No.

"What are your plans this weekend?" Alice said, after they were seated. "Would you like to rent a movie?"

"I don't know. Maybe. Can I invite some friends over?"

"Of course. Which friends?"

"Why do you always wear high heels?"

What? Alice wasn't wearing shoes at that moment.

"*Seventeen* says they're bad for your feet," Esme added.

"I know."

"Daddy says you're destroying your foot muscles. Or joints. Because of changing your natural balance."

"Well, I don't think it's a problem if I don't wear them too often. They make me feel good about myself."

"You should read magazines like *Seventeen* and *Elle*." Esme dug her fork into a hunk of her omelet. "All my friends read them. Daddy got me a subscription. They have serious articles, stuff about breast cancer and, um…food…That's how I learned about MSG."

"Really? What are some other topics they've written about? Anything about which shoes are healthy for you?"

"Well, like, whether vegetarians should wear wool. Because it's from sheep, and the whole process of raising and shearing them is so cruel. But the sheep would grow the wool anyways, so it has to be cut off or it would be too heavy for them to keep carrying on their bodies. And there could be a problem with parasites, I think. If they didn't shear the wool."

"Hmm. That's a tough choice."

"And I read a cool article about making recycled jewelry."

"Recycled? You mean from soda bottles?"

"No! That would be ugly." Esme put down her fork. "That's not the only way you can recycle. The idea is so you use scraps and stuff left over from making other jewelry, that you would normally throw out."

"That sounds great. What did the jewelry look like?"

"One pair of earrings was long with silver wire twisted together and broken pieces of, um, I think shells. They were really beautiful. The shells and these red beads alternated in a pattern. I think they'd come almost to my shoulders, if I wore them." A broad smile was actually spreading across Esme's mouth. For the first time, maybe, in years.

But wouldn't the rough edges of the earrings' broken shells cut a person's skin, if they dangled against her cheeks? Oh, never mind. "Do you want to go visit some jewelry stores together this weekend?" Alice asked. "I'll find out if there are places that sell recycled jewelry."

Shrug.

The moment she finished her omelet, Esme toed her chair away from the table.

"Are you going to do some homework now?" The words came out. Alice shouldn't have said them.

A pause. "I did it at Thomas's."

"So he's in one of your classes?"

Shrugging again, Esme stood.

"I hope he's not also a C student."

Esme moved her gaze to the crusted shreds of cheese on her plate.

"Honey." Alice's next words had to be softer. "We need to talk about your report card."

"I know, I know, okay? You don't have to keep pounding it into me. I'm not a genius superwoman like you."

Would a smile help? A self-deprecating smile? "Thanks for the compliment, but I'm not talking about being a genius. I'm only saying, you know you can do better."

"No, I can't."

"Yes, you can, honey. You've always gotten good grades in the past. You're smart."

"No. You just always pushed me. To make yourself look smart."

"Esme, don't be ridiculous. If I push you—if it seems as though I push you, it's because I know you're capable of doing better."

"You wish you had a smarter daughter. You wish you weren't my mother."

No, it's your father who wished he wasn't your father. Of course, Alice couldn't say that.

"Like with ballet," Esme added.

"What?"

Esme had shifted her stance, lowering her gaze further, as if she might be contemplating imaginary ballet slippers on her feet. She crossed her arms over her chest, hugging herself. "You pushed me to take ballet classes because you thought I should have—I don't know. Exercise. Culture. I don't know why you did it."

"What do you mean? All of your friends were signing up for ballet, and you desperately wanted to be with them. Don't you remember?"

"I was two years old."

"No, you were four and a half."

"Whatever. I was a baby. I didn't know anything. You forced me to do it."

"You know that's not true, Esme. I had to leave work early on Wednesdays, to get you from school and take you to the make-up sessions."

"I'm sorry I was so much *trouble* for you."

"Esme, come on, that's not what I meant."

"And you lied to me."

"How did I lie?"

"About the recital."

"What?"

"Daddy told you weeks and weeks in advance that he'd bought circus tickets. But you tricked me into believing I'd be dancing in it and got me all excited."

Esme couldn't be saying all this. Or believing it. She couldn't. Didn't she remember? She was goading Alice, that had to be it.

"Why didn't you tell me the truth?" Grabbing her backpack, Esme hefted it onto one shoulder and swung away.

"I told you the truth!"

Although Esme didn't turn around in Alice's direction, she also didn't take any further steps that would move her out of the kitchen.

Alice was panting, her lungs roped tight. "We were—all of us— Jenny and Sharon and Roz and Walt—and Grandma Florence—And I had flowers for you! We all had flowers. We were there, Esme. At the auditorium. We all went to see you." She panted into the silence, and there wasn't any other noise to give her company. No footsteps in the hallway outside their apartment. No dog barking. No dishwasher churning. "Would I have dragged Sharon and Jenny and Grandma to a recital if I knew you weren't going to be there?"

Alice should have explained her side of the story the minute Esme returned from the recital weekend, never mind her vow to herself back then just to hug and not make a fuss, never mind that the parenting books said not to criticize the other parent or put the child in the middle. She should never have let Dan's lie soak in all this time. But if she'd tried to explain, wouldn't she have made it worse? Whenever she'd criticized Dan, he'd always somehow turned it against her.

"I don't believe you," Esme mumbled.

"Esme."

"Daddy told me that he told you about the circus."

"DADDY LIED."

Esme ran out of the kitchen and slammed her bedroom door two seconds before Alice reached it.

•   •   •   •   •

"Esme?"

Silence inside Esme's bedroom.

"Honey? Can we talk?"

The closed wooden door was like a hand abruptly held up, ordering Alice to stay out.

"Forget what I said about Daddy." Alice had to speak the words with enough force to push them through the door. "I'm sorry I said that."

The door didn't move.

•   •   •   •   •

"Could I ask you a favor?" Alice said. "Would you call Esme?"

On the other end of the phone line, Florence's reply sounded exhausted. "Does it have to be right now?"

"Yes. I'm sorry. Just for a few minutes."

Florence inhaled and then exhaled loudly.

"Is something wrong, Mom?"

"I'm a little under the weather."

"Oh, then, never mind. You need to rest."

"Because Esme won't speak to you," Florence said.

"Yes."

"And you're trying to maintain contact somehow."

"Yes." Still no sound from Esme's room. Her door would squeak if she opened it. "And it has to be as if you called on your own initiative, not as if I'm asking you."

"Do you have any more requirements? Anything in particular I'm supposed to say?"

"Well," Alice suggested carefully, "you could see if she wants to go to the crafts show at the mall this weekend."

"At the mall?"

"Could you? I don't mean to push. If you're not feeling well."

When Florence spoke again, her voice was stronger. "I'm sure I'll be fine by the weekend. I'll call her in five minutes."

Five minutes later, in fact, the phone rang. A minute after that, Alice knocked on Esme's barrier door. "Esme, it's Grandma on the phone. Will you talk to her?"

The door opened forward, squeaking, into Alice's face. Without a word, Esme stalked swiftly past Alice and to the kitchen.

For a few minutes, sounds filtered from the kitchen into Alice's bedroom. A pleasant tone of voice from Esme. Some actual laughter. No clear words, however. After less than five minutes, the noises stopped, and Esme was in her room again, shutting the door.

●   ●   ●   ●   ●

Walt was guiding Jenny slowly around their small living room, holding her propped against his side, when Alice arrived at one-thirty in the morning. They inched along the braided rug, behind the green-flowered easy chair, into the center of the room, past the portrait of Jenny and Sharon that Walt had painted a couple of years earlier, next to the crowded bookshelves, back to the center of the room, and then repeated the figure-eight, foot after dragging foot. Jenny was exhaling rapidly and hugging herself, her eyes shut. Every few steps, as she started to slide, Walt pulled her up.

"Thank you, thank you!" Roz wrapped her arms around Alice. "I'll call you from the emergency room. As soon as we learn anything."

"Sure."

"Sharon's in her bedroom, sleeping. I hope she's sleeping."

"I'll bet she's out solid. Don't worry."

"I don't know how long—"

"I'll be here."

"Where's Esme?" Roz stepped back, panic on her face.

"It's her weekend at Dan's. It's fine. You go take care of Jenny."

Jenny's red hair was hanging down to her shoulders like the head of a string mop. Dulled silver rings stuck out of piercings in both nostrils and both lips. She halted abruptly and, bending over, clutched her left calf. Walt leaned over, too, alternately rubbing her shoulders and propping her up halfway to standing. She moaned.

"We have to go," Walt said quietly to Roz, over his shoulder. "Now."

"I need the car keys. I think. Maybe I have them."

Jenny slid closer to the floor and grabbed at her father's arm.

"Did she tell you what she took?" Alice asked.

"She admitted to vodka and Ecstasy," Roz replied tiredly. "At a party with a lot of older kids she didn't know. At someone's house she didn't know."

"There could be more," Walt added, his voice weirdly toneless, as he tugged Jenny straighter again.

"I don't know how—She just—She's never looked flushed or bloodshot, you know, none of the danger signs the pamphlets warn you about." Roz was pulling her red hair across her face. "Her room doesn't stink of smoke or incense. She hardly eats, but that's like every teenage girl. Like me, on a diet all the time."

"Yeah," Alice said.

"Her grades are okay. Well, mostly Cs, but grades can slip for a little while in high school. You know, kids stay out late, sleep during classes. Teenage girls never talk to their parents. I knew things weren't great with her, but I didn't …"

Alice squeezed Roz's hand.

"I was such a fool."

"No, you weren't." Alice gave another squeeze, then reached out to stroke Jenny's stringy hair. Jenny dropped her head onto Walt's shoulder. Her eyes were open, glazed. Her breathing was ragged.

Roz's hand, also reaching out, shook. She clutched her mouth. "It's my fault, with all my diets! She saw me, and so she took drugs to lose weight."

"Roz, stop that! It's nothing you did. It's the culture. The world." Alice pulled the car keys out of Roz's shoulder bag and shoved them into Roz's palm. "Now go!"

CHAPTER TWENTY-TWO

ALICE, DAN, AND ESME

April 2001

The California coastline, Santa Barbara to Carmel

The shoreline curved inward with an elegantly scalloped C, into a welcoming beach of white sand. It disappeared from highway view at the top of the C, but after a few minutes another curve arrived, guarded by palm trees along the rim of a solid rock wall.

"There's supposed to be some lovely beaches around here, or a little farther north," Alice told Esme, waving out the driver's side window. "Carpinteria. El Capitan. Refugio."

Esme was slumped in the shotgun seat, unmoving, her eyes shuttered, a cord trailing from her ears to the round, black, portable CD player in her lap. She breathed, at least.

"We'll be at the Santa Barbara mission building in about ten minutes. You studied it in elementary school. One of the missions that Father Junipero Serra established all around California in the seventeen-hundreds, to convert the Native Americans to Christianity. Or force them to convert, I guess that's more accurate, isn't it?"

Briefly, Esme opened her eyes. Without changing position, she blinked at the windshield.

"Isn't the view breath-taking?" Alice added.

It would be better once they were at an actual destination. Maybe. They would have specific things to show each other, all the various objects at the mission, like—like—Paintings. Old monastery kitchen tools. Seventeenth-century clothing; they could compare women's dresses from that era with the hoodie and skinny jeans Esme was wearing. In fact, it was really no surprise that Esme wasn't being very communicative at the moment. Stuck in a car with her mother, staring at the same ocean for an hour, would be deadly boring for any almost-fifteen-year-old, no matter how much she used to love playing in that ocean when she was little.

At the mission parking lot, Esme stayed in place, eyes shut.

"Hey!" Oops, Alice had said that a little sharply. "We're here. Shall we get out and take a look around?"

Far too slowly, Esme unclicked her seat belt. Her feet moved forward. She slid sideways toward her door, still holding the CD player and still attached to her earphones.

"Can you leave that thing in the car?" Alice tapped Esme's left shoulder and, as soon as Esme swiveled in her direction, pantomimed yanking a headset off of her own head.

Esme emitted a dramatic sigh. Nevertheless, she removed the earphones, and her footsteps echoed behind Alice's through the parking lot to the mission entrance and the cashier's desk inside.

The heavy blue door beyond the cashier's desk opened out to a square courtyard of utter quiet, enfolded by stucco walls. A three-tiered, circular fountain made of pink stucco sat in the center of the yard, with four dirt paths leading to it, one from each corner. Almost every spot was crowded with lush grass, cactuses, palm trees, and clumps of pink flowers.

"See how peaceful and beautiful this is?" Alice asked. "They call it the Sacred Garden. Can't you imagine a monk meditating here?"

Esme had already wandered away.

Which of Alice's clueless how-to-parent books had encouraged this insane trip? A mini-vacation during Esme's spring break, to get away from their everyday routine and stress. A little mother-daughter bonding. How about a drive up the Pacific Coast Highway to San Francisco? The route was beautiful, with so many spots Esme would surely love, and they would take their time, no fixed schedule, no hotel reservations, spontaneous, just the two of them, pulling over wherever they got the urge. Did Esme want to see the historic mission in Santa Barbara? Esme had shrugged. The flamboyant Madonna Inn, built by a zillionaire who threw away his money on every extravagance? Hearst Castle, a genuine mansion? A meaningless *okay* from Esme. After that, they could stop at the beach at Big Sur, the lighthouse at Pigeon Point, the artists' colony in Carmel. Was Esme still interested in pottery and necklaces? *Yeah. Sort-of.* And once they reached San Francisco, they would have all sorts of possibilities. Ride the cable cars! Find the sea lions at Fisherman's Wharf! Watch how chocolate was made and taste samples at the Ghirardelli factory! Was there any place in particular Esme wanted to visit? *Not really.* Would she rather go somewhere else, instead of driving along the coast? *Not really.* Did she expect a lot of homework during vacation? Esme didn't know.

Why had Esme agreed to this trip? She could simply spend her weekends at Dan's house, with his swimming pool and her own TV in her bedroom, which was probably more of a luxury vacation for her than this trek.

Esme materialized next to Alice.

"Hi." Alice smiled.

"I'm done."

"So soon? But we hardly—" Bonding! "So, do you want to see what's at the front of the building? Or go to the gift shop? Ten minutes? I'd just like to peek at a couple of the monks' rooms."

The first room had a red tile floor and wooden ceiling beams. So did the second room. Alice phone flashed with two messages from Fred, both asking about the status of the Forest Service's pending decision on clear-cutting. In less than five minutes, Alice was back in the car.

"What do you think?" She placed her hand gently on Esme's elbow, as Esme was about to plunk her headset atop her skull. "It'll probably be about two hours to get to the Madonna Inn, and another hour to

Hearst Castle after that. Would you like to have lunch at the Madonna Inn? Both of the places are supposed to have a lot of beautiful rooms to see. . ."

Esme shrugged.

Four and a half more days of this?

The highway had moved deeply inland, so instead of being able to watch waves and ocean, they were driving claustrophobically in a canyon between towering, boring mountains of dry dirt. Miles of it. Dirt, a tree, dirt, rolling scrub, dirt, more dirt, another tree, dirt. Esme slept, or disappeared into her music, or perhaps fantasized about jumping out of the car.

There had to be a way to make this vacation work. What might Esme enjoy talking about? The songs on her CDs. Who was popular with teenagers these days? Springsteen was always big. Did Esme still like Britney Spears? Alice could ask to borrow the headphones for a few minutes. Or they could discuss health food. Wheat germ; Esme now needed to have wheat germ in everything. They were almost at the Madonna Inn, and Esme hadn't moved. Would she care at all if they passed it and kept on driving?

In fact, Esme stirred, flitting open her eyes, when the car eased onto the highway exit ramp. And as they drove toward the sprawling, multi-turreted, pink-and-white-and-stone chalet, she sat up closer to the window.

"Wow," she said.

The curlicue-engraved front door opened into a lobby with a massive stone fireplace, a jungle of fake flowers hanging from the ceiling, and walls papered in red velvet. One set of marble banisters carved with cherubs went upstairs, and polished wooden banisters carved with clusters of grapes headed downward. "Wow," Esme repeated.

Ambling through the main dining room, she delicately petted the pink cushions of a nearby booth. "This is genuine leather. But it's really, really soft. Feel it! You can't get leather this soft except for, like, expensive clothes."

"How about for shoes?" Alice asked.

"Yeah. You should look at the leather skirts and jackets in *Vogue* and places like that."

They sat at a table by a window in the less-elegant café, further away from the lobby. Esme lifted her red water goblet and gently rocked it, catching the reflection of the window's etched glass from different directions. She studied the seashell design on her heavy silver knife. Giggling, she smoothed her palm along the pounded-copper tabletop. "Do you think the hamburgers here will taste like gold?"

"Let's find out."

The waitress brought their food on thick, oversized plates.

"Supposedly, the man who built this place was a zillionaire of some sort, and he was hoping to waste as much money as he could," Alice said. "So he included every silly extravagance he could dream up. Remember the stone wall in the ladies' room? I mean, who would put a stone wall in a bathroom?"

"It was kind of cool. But could bugs and stuff come in through the stones?"

"Good question. I don't know. And I've heard that there's one guestroom where the shower is a waterfall. Actually, it could be fun to use that shower."

"Like the place Daddy and Penelope took us on vacation last year. We got to swim behind a waterfall."

Where was this exotic, expensive, waterfall vacation that Dan and Penelope took Esme to? Never mind. Alice smiled, as she stabbed her seashell fork into a pile of spinach leaves in her salad. "Did all of you swim through the waterfall? What did it feel like?"

"Yeah. Like swimming in the rain?"

"I'll have to try it." Smiling.

"So why did the guy who built this place want to waste money?"

"To avoid paying taxes, believe it or not. It's called a tax write-off. He figured it would cost him so much to build, with all the marble and leather and stone walls and everything, that he would never make a profit. But it became famous, and so many people came to visit here out of curiosity, well, he ended up making money instead." Alice was jabbering too long about tax write-offs. Esme would be bored. "Or at least, that's the story I always heard," she finished.

"It's crazy." Esme shook her head. "This place is partly beautiful, and partly cheesy."

"What would you do if you needed to throw away a million dollars?"

"Are you kidding? I wouldn't know the first thing. I mean, how many CDs and jeans and earrings can you buy?" Esme rested her hamburger on her plate. "I saw some really cool earrings in a store a couple weeks ago, but I think I could make them instead of buying them. They had these tiny little tassels of blue thread tied onto a silver ring that was a half-circle. I want to try designing jewelry and stuff." Abruptly, leaning forward, she pushed back Alice's hair. "You ought to wear earrings more, Mom. You have nice ears."

"Really?" Esme thought Alice's ears were nice? What, specifically, were 'nice' ears?

Esme had already let go of Alice's hair and picked up her burger again. "I could take a fashion design class in Italy. My friend Caroline is doing that this summer."

"Who's Caroline?"

"A friend. So what would you do with a million dollars?"

"Whew. Save for your college, first of all. Get a big house on the beach?"

"Buy more shoes?"

"I'm not that obsessed, am I?"

"You're just funny. You have all kinds of shoes, but you don't know anything about clothing."

"That's what I need you for."

Around them, people were filling the tables. An elderly couple inspected their water goblets the way Esme had done. A little boy in a Dodgers cap banged his seashell knife against the copper tabletop until his mother snatched the knife away.

"Are we still spending our million dollars?" Esme asked. "Can we get dessert here?"

"Absolutely. Food on vacation has no MSG."

Esme laughed again.

If they could truly have fun together like this, then maybe there was a chance…A fresh beginning. If they could carry that spirit home with them, to their everyday life. To make meals funny. To find silly items in the news. To redecorate the apartment?

In the car, Esme strained sideways to watch out her window as the huge pink-and-stone chalet disappeared behind them. By the time they'd gone a half-mile on the highway, however, her headset was back in place, her eyes were shut, and she was slumped silently in the bucket seat again. Where she stayed, without moving, for the entire hour until they reached Hearst Castle.

"Look at this!" Alice pointed to the high door and stone carvings of the mansion's main entrance. "Doesn't it remind you of a cathedral? Like in Europe?"

Esme glanced at the door.

"The guidebook says that William Randolph Hearst deliberately tried to imitate a Spanish cathedral here in this part of the building, but the rest of the estate has some other styles, too."

"Mom, I'm on vacation. I do enough homework during school. Stop pushing me to be smart."

Bonding.

Esme fiddled with the volume on her CD player while their tour guide elaborated on the origins of the tapestries and the Persian rugs in the living room. She scratched her arms in the dining room. ("Look at all those silver pieces on the sideboard," Alice whispered to her. Esme glanced.) She was the first one out of the mansion and back on the shuttle bus for the return drive downhill to the parking lot. "Can we go to the motel yet?" she demanded.

But Big Sur? Dinner overlooking the ocean? Carmel? Monterey? "How about if we stop in Carmel a little first?" Alice asked. "It's a famous artists' colony. I'll bet they have pottery studios we could visit."

"I'm tired."

In their motel room, Esme instantly plopped onto one of the double beds and aimed the remote control at the television.

Alice retreated into the bathroom. She washed her face and redid her pink lipstick. She set up her toothbrush, toothpaste, floss, and mascara on the counter by the sink and placed the motel's little bottles of shampoo and conditioner into the shower stall. She checked her answering machine at her office. When she returned to the main room, Esme was lying on her bed, propped against the pillows and the headboard, a copy of *Elle* magazine in her lap and her thin legs in their jeans stretched out on top of the red blanket. She was about the same height as Alice now, though still little-girl awkward in the way that she pressed her elbows against the headboard, wriggling herself to a more sitting-up posture. Flung out against the pillow, her wavy hair seemed as soft as it had been the last time she'd let Alice touch it.

She didn't even flick her head in Alice's direction, as Alice sat down at the edge of her own bed and put her book on the night table. On the TV, a young woman with honey-blond hair that swooped to her shoulders was speaking energetically to a young man with a head of lush, sculpted, brown hair, sitting across from her at a restaurant. The pre-recorded audience laughed.

"So," Alice began. "It looks like they're eating dinner on your TV show. How about you, what do you want for dinner? I'll bet the seafood here is wonderful, being so nearby to Monterey."

Why did she bother? The two of them had no interests in common. Not the historic mission in Santa Barbara. Not the beach. Not fashion; Alice loved shoes, and Esme cared about everything she wore except shoes. Alice read novels by Toni Morrison and Edith Wharton; Esme watched inane TV shows. That was what this vacation was making clear, forcing them to be together every minute, without other people or school or work to distract them. If Alice dragged out this agony any longer, she would simply make their relationship worse.

"Do you want to just go home tomorrow?" Alice asked, staring at the TV.

"I thought we were going to San Francisco?" Esme's voice, which started out angry, squeaked as she finished.

"Well, it didn't seem..."

In the room next door, the guests were apparently watching an action movie or a detective show. Screeches and honking noises punched through the wall behind Alice's headboard, followed by a short rattle of gunfire.

"You didn't seem like you were having a good time," Alice finished, partly mumbling.

"It's okay."

"It seemed as though you've been bored a lot."

"It's fine."

"So you really want to keep going? With me?"

"Sure." Esme's magazine slid to the floor, and she leaned over to retrieve it, keeping her face toward the TV screen. She'd taken off her hoodie, and she was wearing a T-shirt that had never been in her dresser drawers before, purple, with an odd picture of a smiling pineapple.

"Okay. Good. Would you like to begin with—" Alice halted. She started over. "Is there something in particular you thought of doing in San Francisco?"

The TV was now showing a brown, shaggy type of dog with an older man. The man threw a ball. The dog refused to chase it. The man tried to shoo the dog away. "Could we," Esme finally said, "drive across the Golden Gate Bridge?"

Why would Esme focus on the Golden Gate Bridge, of all the possible sights around San Francisco? Because she could stay in the car with her headphones while they drove across, instead of talking? Because, maybe, she enjoyed gazing at the ocean as much as Alice did?

"I saw a photo." Esme glanced at Alice. "It looked pretty."

"Sure, I'll bet it's a gorgeous view."

"Yeah."

"Should we go to the chocolate factory afterwards?"

When they returned from dinner, they each sprawled in their own bed while Esme clicked the remote. A *Law & Order* rerun was starting, and an hour later, *Law & Order SVU* on another channel.

"It's the boyfriend," Esme declared, halfway through the second show.

"You think so? Don't you think he's too obvious?"

"Who else? It can't be the guy who found the body, because he's in the opening scene, and in *Law & Order* you never see the people from the opening scene ever again."

"True, but they usually have a kind of trick ending. Don't they?"

"Yeah. But it can't be someone super-unimportant, either, like a pizza delivery guy."

"Good point," Alice agreed.

During a commercial, Alice gave Esme five dollars for the vending machines in the lobby. Esme reappeared with a Nestle Crunch bar and a tiny bag of Doritos. Breaking the Crunch in half, Esme held out a piece to Alice, across the space between their beds.

CHAPTER TWENTY-THREE

ALICE, DAN, AND ESME

August 2001
Santa Monica and Calabasas, CA

A piece of college-ruled notebook paper, torn out of a three-ring binder and folded once, lay on the kitchen table when Alice got home from work.

I've gone to move in with Dad. It just makes more sense. I'll call you soon. Esme. With a flower drawn after her name.

Alice grabbed the phone. She also tried to grab the note, but she dropped it, and then she dropped the phone. Finally, somehow, she dialed Dan's house.

"Esme. Honey. What's going on? I don't understand." She needed time, to prepare a script. "Did anything happen at school? with your friends?"

"No."

"Or—What—?"

"Nothing *happened.*"

Was it a boyfriend who'd dumped Esme? Something Alice had said this morning? Yes, a constant underlayer of tension always stretched between the two of them; the last fun thing they'd done together was probably their drive up the coast to San Francisco, four months ago. But their tension was nothing new. Why, abruptly, today, was Esme just—gone?

The light filtering through the fake Tiffany shade darted yellow, green, and orange on the piece of notebook paper.

"Honey, can we talk about this? It's such a big step, a big change—you know, I—It's kind of a shock."

"I want a change."

"Sure, life gets boring. We all want variety. I understand."

Silence.

Except for the hip hop blaring from a car outside.

"But you know, honey," Alice stumbled on, "you don't have to go and move and totally uproot yourself to have a change. We could change a lot of things right here at home. Do you want to—do you want to redo your room? There's a ton of different clubs and activities at school you could join, I'll bet. I could check around. Do you want a—"

"We need to end this conversation." It was Dan's voice now, on the other end of the phone. His angry voice.

What the fuck was he—

"You've upset Esme," he continued, "and she can't talk to you anymore."

"Excuse me, you interrupted—"

"I suggest that we all discuss this in a more congenial setting, in person. Why don't you meet Esme and me at the Starbucks near my clinic? Is Thursday evening good for you?"

There were so many possible answers, and no time to decide.

Don't you tell me when and where to speak to my own daughter.

Please put my daughter back on the line.

I'll happily have coffee with Esme but I don't want to meet you anywhere.

That's fine.

"No," she said. "Wednesday."

•   •   •   •   •

It couldn't happen.

If Esme lived with Dan. If Alice didn't live with her own daughter.

To see her daughter only every other weekend, on "visits"? As if Esme were visiting a distant cousin. A fifteen-year-old girl doesn't "visit" her own mother.

To come home after work on Monday and Tuesday and Wednesday and Thursday, to darkness and silence, and just one plate at dinner. Not to know the highs and lows of Esme's week day by day. Not to hear about the two-tone nail polish her friend Mara wore yesterday, or the horrible history test she couldn't study for, or who she was going to the mall with on Saturday.

And how often did Esme actually sit down for dinner with Alice and chit-chat for more than two minutes about anything?

Nevertheless, they shared a daily life, mother and daughter. Alice bought the organic strawberries Esme asked for, and sometimes she remembered the stoneground crackers, too. She washed Esme's purple jeans. She heard the murmurs on the phone behind Esme's closed bedroom door in the evenings, and although she could rarely discern the words, she could tell if the murmurs were giggly-excited or draggy-miserable. She knew when Esme and her friends dyed their hair orange, and when Esme became vegetarian for a week. She saw the different pairs of earrings Esme wore each morning. They ate dinner together almost every night; a few words were exchanged. Even if Alice wasn't clear who Esme's friends were, exactly, she was the parent who answered the phone when they called, and it was her apartment where Mara or Caroline or Nina or Quinn might sleep over. She was the one who met with the math teacher when Esme failed the midterm. And if Esme was on the couch watching TV without her earphones on, maybe they might sit together for half an hour one evening, Maybe Esme would talk, maybe she wouldn't, maybe they'd just watch TV in silence, but they would be sharing a few moments exactly because they lived together. Maybe Esme would let Alice hug her. Maybe they'd eat some ice cream. Alice didn't have to make an appointment and drive an hour to Calabasas to eat ice cream with her daughter.

But if this Thing happened—if Esme left—there would be so much that Alice would miss. Alice wouldn't be the parent who pored over college brochures with Esme or who Esme turned to for help with her application essays, because the brochures wouldn't be mailed to Alice's address. She wouldn't have the chance to snap an embarrassed picture of Esme with her prom date. She wouldn't be the one taking Esme to get her driver's license, or the first person ever to be officially chauffeured by Esme, after Esme passed the test. Now it would be Dan doing all those things.

Brownie the Dog perched on top of Esme's little white dresser, next to a short pile of *Elle* and *YM* magazines, a tube of acne cover-up, a tangle of the beaded necklaces Esme had made with Jenny, the redwood box from the San Francisco airport, Moosey, the ibex, the little bunny, and Dan's damn elephant from the circus. The poster from *Titanic* was uncurling a little from its taping on the wall.

Why?

How? When? Where? It wasn't fair. She hadn't been such a terrible mother. She didn't hit Esme, or get drunk, or do drugs, or roll around having sex on the living room floor with a different boyfriend every night, none of the stuff that divorce lawyers warned about. So she hadn't been perfect. She got Chinese takeout too often instead of cooking a real dinner. She didn't make her own organic pasta. She bought Doritos and nonorganic bananas. Sometimes. But Esme liked Doritos. She'd dragged Esme on the drive to San Francisco. She nagged Esme when her grades stumbled. Pushed her, so Esme said. But who wouldn't? Was a mother supposed to let matters slide until her daughter flunked out of school? Was that enough reason for Esme to overturn everything?

Was the air in Calabasas so wonderfully cleaner than the sea breeze of Santa Monica? Esme had her private bathroom and the TV in her bedroom and the swimming pool in the backyard. (But she had a whole ocean in Santa Monica!) Was Esme so shallow that she'd abandon her mother and her world, for a TV and a bathroom? And the car Dan promised to buy for her next year, when she turned sixteen.

No, Esme wasn't that shallow.

She liked the life at Dan's house. She had good things there, of course she did. The brother and sister, the kids that Dan-who-never-wanted-children had suddenly decided he did want with Penelope. Graydon and Hadley, those were their names. They were, what, eight and six years old? Esme seemed to enjoy having younger siblings that she could be silly with. They played tag in the swimming pool, and she taught them gin rummy. More people around her, more choices to hang out with instead of being stuck with only her mother. Plus the damn dog. Esme had said she wanted a change. Their little apartment in Santa Monica could seem awfully cramped, after eleven years. The food at Dan's house was better. And healthier.

Maybe it was easier for Esme to just agree with Dan. After all these years, it was hard to keep juggling between parents who hated each other.

But Dan was too crazy to be in charge of raising a child! Even if he'd managed to control himself so far on Esme's weekend visitations, never nagging her about homework or criticizing her clothing or telling her to take off her headphones, he surely couldn't keep his true self under wraps twenty-four hours a day, seven days a week. Or worse. What if he cut his arm and claimed Esme did it? What if he cut her?

Alice had to fight this, for Esme's own good!

Esme didn't understand all the implications of what she was proposing. How about friends? She would be transferring high schools just as she started tenth grade, thrusting herself into an environment where she didn't know a soul, whereas most of the girls at Calabasas High School would've been together since first grade, or possibly going back to preschool. Teenage girls could be so cliquish and catty. The popular girls. The artsy crowd. The cheerleaders. The smart girls. How would Esme break in? Did she have a thick enough skin?

Or was that the point? Here in Santa Monica, she had friends, yes, but they were always disappearing. Nina had a birthday party, and then Esme didn't invite Nina to her own sleepover. She was going to go to Italy with Caroline, but she didn't. She never had one enduring, strong best friend to stick around for.

According to Roz and the parenting books, all teenage girls rebelled against their mothers. So perhaps the explanation was that simple: Penelope wasn't Esme's mother.

But sometimes mothers and teen daughters would be strolling along the sidewalk, giggling like girlfriends, arms around each other. How did they do it?

What were the magic words Alice could say at a table in Starbucks on Wednesday night, to bring her daughter back?

•   •   •   •   •

TOPICS TO DISCUSS ON WEDNESDAY

1. WHY????

<u>*Arguments against*</u>

1. What about your friends here in Santa Monica, at Pacific Coast High?

2. Transferring to a new High School/hassle

3. There's nothing to do in Calabasas. Here we have the beach and Santa Monica Pier, and you can take the bus to the mall and Westwood and UCLA

4. You're too young to drive. How would you get around the Valley? Will Dad chauffeur you everywhere? He's too busy. Here in SM you can be independent

5. Is #4 the same as #3?

<u>*Negotiating points*</u>

1. ESME WILL BE WITH ME EVERY WEEKEND!! (Dan will never agree but I can try)

2. I also get one weekday night per week with her for dinner. (But she'll have a lot of homework, 10th grade… and afterschool activities? clubs? no time? But she doesn't do afterschool activities now)

3. Specific visitation schedule with Grandma Florence, separate from my time

4. Do we need lawyers? Rewrite custody/divorce agreement?

5. Only a one-year experiment? (probably a lousy idea, she'd be transferring high schools two years in a row, but maybe?)

•　　　•　　　•　　　•　　　•

Not a booth, with Alice alone on one side and Dan and Esme next to each other on the other side, allied against her.

Alice arrived at the Starbucks ten minutes early and plunked her briefcase on a table far away from the counter, by a window fronting the parking lot: a square wooden table, four sides, four green-upholstered chairs, all equal. People walked out the restaurant's glass doors and toward cars in the parking lot, and other people walked in. Machines hissed, gurgled, made grinding sounds. A barista called out a name that had a long A. The room smelled briefly of hot milk, followed by cinnamon. Dan's new black BMW glided into the parking lot like an expensive knife slicing into Alice's gut, and Esme stepped out from the passenger-side door.

She was wearing cut-off jeans, brown gladiator sandals, and a pale-yellow T-shirt that said "Whatever," with her hair pulled to one side with a huge silver barrette. Was she squinting? Was she angry at being here?

As Dan and Esme entered the restaurant, Dan waved at Alice. Esme didn't. The two of them spent minutes at the counter, conferring, deciding, ordering, hovering close together, until finally Esme trudged to Alice's table, her face stoic, carrying a paper cup with the Starbucks mermaid. (A paper cup? Hadn't she learned anything from Alice about not using throwaway paper cups, because that meant destroying trees? Oh, what difference did it make?) She slouched into the chair opposite Alice.

"Why, honey?"

Dan had been right about one thing: Meeting in person was better than speaking on the phone. Sitting at their table, Alice could see any sign of annoyance that might whisk across Esme's face, any blink, any tightening of muscles around her mouth. Or perhaps her lips might flicker toward a smile?

With luck, Alice would have a few more seconds to make her case before Dan arrived at the table. "I understand, life gets boring. A break in routine can be nice. That's why people go on vacations. But you know, honey, this isn't a little vacation. This is a major life decision that you're talking about."

Esme edged her awful paper cup slightly toward the window, then moved her hand to the other side of the cup and edged it back toward herself. Chocolatey steam wafted from it.

Abruptly, dammit, Dan was sitting between them.

Never mind. Alice would simply keep going, as though his presence was of no import. "It probably is a good idea to shake up our routine a little bit. Let's think about possibilities. For instance, how about getting a part-time job? You could make some money to buy clothes and things. I bet one of the stores in the Santa Monica mall or Westwood would hire you."

"I just want a change," Esme mumbled, keeping her head bent over her cup. "Dad's house is bigger."

Another advantage of meeting in person was that Alice could pretend to drink her medium-roast coffee, so that she didn't have to find words every second.

"The high school is better," Esme added, her voice a little stronger. "Their SAT scores. *U.S. News* says it's one of the best public high schools on the West Coast."

"The SAT scores?"

"You're always complaining how bad my report card is. So I want a better school."

"I'm not sure if SAT—It's a lot of hassle, you know. Transferring school records. All that stuff."

Esme shrugged.

SAT scores? What teenager left her friends and her home because of a school's SAT scores?

"What kinds of changes were you thinking of, honey?" Alice asked. "What would you like to be doing?"

Another shrug. Another push of the paper cup.

No one had ever said that Esme particularly resembled Dan or Alice. Her eyes were bigger and her chin more pointed than Dan's, her nose straighter than Alice's. Now beige cover-up was crusted on the dots of acne sprinkled on her forehead. Her lips were pulled together. Her eyes were two opaque brown sheets of glass.

"There's a cooking club at Pacific Coast High. Do you want to try that?" Alice suggested.

Dan had still not spoken. He was undoubtedly enjoying their little performance, observing Alice with his cold, dark blue eyes and that nasty dimple.

"What about all your friends back home? Caroline? Nina? You'll just leave them?" Who were Esme's other friends?

"They can come visit."

"That's pretty far. To ask their parents to drive them."

Instead of answering, Esme began breaking off pieces from the rim of her cup, crumbling the shreds on the table.

A paper cup would have been helpful around now, or a muffin. Something that Alice, too, could pick at, to keep her hands and eyes busy. Something to delay finding the right words, while she breathed too loudly, and Esme also breathed loudly and crumbled the bits of her cup, and Dan undoubtedly watched.

Far behind Alice, the glass door of the restaurant opened and shut three times in succession, bringing in the energetic, high-pitched intonations of cheerful twentysomething girls. Esme would be their age in a few years. Were they so cheerful because they'd run away from their mothers?

"And also," and Esme was speaking rapidly, "it makes more sense, because Dad's house is really close to his clinic, and he always gets home by dinnertime. And there's Penelope, too, so I would have lots of adult supervision in emergencies. You know, at your apartment, I'm by myself too much, because you're always working late, and you travel a lot. Like, when you go to see the owls. And that's not safe for me. And they're teaching me to cook. Like we made sushi last week."

Sushi. Penelope. Emergencies. Esme was pumping out too many arguments. "Sure, you know, if you want more variety, you don't have to move out completely."

"I've spent all my life living with you. It's only fair. To live with Daddy now. He misses me."

"But I'd miss you if you leave!"

Crap, she'd blurted that out, too pleading, and her stupid left hand tipped her coffee cup, and the coffee was coursing over the smooth tabletop straight toward the lap of her linen slacks. Alice grabbed her shoulder bag, of all ridiculous things, to sop it up. As if leather was a paper towel. But how could she walk away from Esme at that moment to get napkins? The coffee rolled over the table edge. "If you lived with Daddy, you would need him to drive you whenever you wanted to do anything. You'd lose all the independence you have in Santa Monica. Going to the mall? The pier?" *Please don't leave me.*

Of course Esme wasn't listening. What arguments could Alice possibly offer against *I want a change. It's only fair.*

"Why can't you accept my decision?" Esme demanded.

"Esme's fifteen now." Dan's voice slid into the conversation, as silkily as his car had invaded the parking lot. "She's not a child anymore, and we need to respect her wishes." His words kept flowing, calmly and steadily and inexorably. "I'll make certain that Esme visits you every other weekend. Do you want to pick her up at eleven o'clock on your Saturday mornings, let's say, and drive her back here on Sunday evening? We don't need to pay a small fortune to a couple of overpriced lawyers to rewrite the divorce agreement. I'm confident we can arrange all this between ourselves as rational adults, don't you agree?"

Esme stared at the table, still toying with the crumbs from her paper cup. She'd picked off more than halfway down the sides of her cup.

It had been a done deal, every single clause, even before they entered the Starbucks.

•   •   •   •   •

"You have to give her space," Roz said softly. She pulled Alice's hands onto her own lap, thrusting aside the dishtowel and magazines beside her on the couch in her den.

Alice rocked back and forth.

"I know it sounds impossible, sweetie," Roz went on, "but it will be worse if you fight. Esme will hate you forever if you don't give her the space she's asking for."

"What do you mean? Space? I should sit around and do nothing? That's what she and Dan basically told me in Starbucks, an hour ago. Butt out and shut up."

"Listening to Esme isn't nothing."

"I can't do nothing!"

Roz cradled Alice's fingers tighter. "Can I tell you a story? Back when we didn't realize the whole truth about Jenny, before the trip to the ER, when she was around fourteen. There was a night that she supposedly went to a school dance, and she got home almost by the time she was supposed to, but she was barely able to stand upright, and she refused to utter a word. I couldn't get close enough to tell if she smelled of cigarettes or booze or whatever. Then she locked herself in the bathroom. Walt told me to leave her alone, but I couldn't. So I sat on the floor outside the bathroom for hours, waiting for sounds of—of anything. Vomiting. Coughing. Bumbling stuff around in the medicine cabinet. Breathing. I knocked a few times and tried to speak to her through the door, which she ignored, no surprise. I wanted Walt to get a screwdriver and take the door off the hinges, and he said he didn't know how to do it." Roz smiled a little. "I finally fell asleep, there on the hard wooden floor. Believe it or not, at some point Jenny must have come out of the bathroom and stepped straight over me, because when I finally woke up, the door was open, it was two-thirty in the morning, and Jenny was in her bedroom with that door shut. And she'd left a note on the kitchen table with a schedule of times that her parents were permitted to communicate with her." Dropping hold of Alice's hands,

Roz turned her head away, to face the woven rug on the floor. "Tuesdays and Thursdays from eight to nine."

"But I can't wait outside Esme's bathroom! She's twenty miles away from me!"

"I know that. That's not what I'm saying."

"I know you're not saying that. But it doesn't…"

They both took a few breaths, for another minute.

"You never told me about all that, with Jenny," Alice added.

Roz shook her head. "It was too… awful. Painful."

"Yeah."

"What I'm trying to say," Roz began again, "is that the most important thing you can do right now is to keep the lines of communication open with Esme, however you can. When you're with her on your weekends? Don't plan them out in advance. Just have fun with her, at her pace. I didn't learn that lesson soon enough. All my social work training was useless, and even quitting my diets so I wouldn't be a bad influence, and so was all my love for Jenny—Well, no, that wasn't useless. That was actually the only thing that mattered, but I had to love her differently. Do you see what I mean?"

"No."

"All I could do was let Jenny know that I was there and I loved her, whenever she was ready. Not to try to make things better. Just to listen to her. It was so hard, Alice. It was the hardest thing I've ever done. Harder than when she OD'd, actually."

"Why didn't Esme talk to me about this idea before now? This great need for a change in her life."

"Teenagers don't talk."

"There's got to be more of an explanation than those ridiculous excuses she threw at me at Starbucks. Come on, Roz. SAT scores? Adult supervision for emergencies?"

"Well." Roz was twisting her fingers around each other, in her lap. "Esme is kind of right, that she's been living with you all her life. She feels that it's kind of lopsided, and you can see her point—"

"No I can't! That's BS. Children in divorce always live with their mothers. Nobody counts minutes and days."

Roz picked up the blue-checked dishtowel from the sofa cushion, spread it out on her lap, pressed it flat, and folded it. Twice. "I've worked a lot with the family court system with my clients. When a child turns fourteen, the court will take their opinion more seriously. If they want to go live with the other parent, for instance." Next, she stacked the magazines.

Of course! Dan would have researched all the custody and divorce laws. He'd even waited an extra year, until Esme was fifteen, to make sure he'd win. "Dan's been working on this for years!" Alice almost shouted at Roz. "To make her want to live with him, like you said. Planting all the ideas in her mind, *U.S. News*, SAT scores. And don't forget the puppy and buying her a car and the supposedly dirty clothes I gave her and the circus tickets on the same day as her ballet recital."

"Alice, he's not a Svengali."

"Yes, he is! He's not normal. That's what you don't understand. The parenting books don't understand, my lawyer didn't, my mother doesn't, God doesn't—I'm sorry, I'm not knocking religion. But don't you see? No one understands. He even paralyzed himself. Remember when he said he was paralyzed, when we were engaged and I tried to break up?"

"That was strange, yeah." Roz nodded, one hand holding the stack of magazines.

"It was another way of him being in control. To make me feel guilty. Or he lied about being paralyzed. The point is, he's always in control somehow."

"Nobody is always in control."

"Now Esme's going to be living with him full-time. He'll have twenty-four hours a day to plant more lies about me."

"And you'll have your weekends with her—"

"Weekends! Two days out of fourteen?"

Roz pulled off her eyeglasses and ran a palm over her eyes, down her nose, to her mouth. Two-handed, she put the glasses back on.

"I should have fought harder." Alice punched her thigh, again and again. "All these years, I should have made up lies about him, the way he did about me."

"You couldn't do that to her."

"And she always believed him! Why? Why the hell did she choose him over me every time?"

"She didn't really."

"Yes, she did. She hates me. She's hated me for years." Alice shoved the neatly stacked magazines and the folded blue-checked towel to the floor. "Goddammit, sometimes I hate her, too." She pounded her thigh, and Roz was hugging her, and all of a sudden, from nowhere, the sobs took over her body. They were charging out of her mouth and rocking her, shaking her and shaking her, and big gobs of tears were pouring from her eyes and snot from her nose, and her breath was scraping raw out of her throat, until she slid down Roz's arms.

"Alice! Don't say that! You don't honestly hate her."

"I don't know. How can I love her when she treats me like dirt?"

"Because you're her mother."

But when she left Roz's house and went home, she would be a mother without a daughter.

CHAPTER TWENTY-FOUR

Esme had to know that Bobby was meeting Alice. Six o'clock this evening, downtown Santa Barbara, per Bobby's email, the same place where Alice and Bobby had met eight days ago. Bobby had said he wouldn't talk to Alice behind Esme's back, so she had to know. Still, that didn't necessarily mean she would come with him.

But she might.

What if Alice didn't recognize her, standing on the sidewalk across the street from the CVS? Alice's own daughter.

Esme looked the same as she had in high school, Courtney had said. The same wild hair? And Ugg boots? Would she smile? Hug? Would they cry together? Would they hug tightly and cry? Would she feel bony from bulimia, if they hugged? Would either of them say the magic words: *I'm sorry.* Or would Esme just stand there, almost dragged there by Bobby, hands in her pockets, stone-faced.

Alice didn't have time to write a script, dashing out of the Seshat office to her car, stop and go at every light on Santa Monica Boulevard, wriggling around rush-hour traffic on the Ventura Freeway, slowly out of the Valley, past Dan's horrible Calabasas, through the Conejo Pass, inch inch inch alongside green fields and housing clusters, north to Santa Barbara.

Hi. Thanks for coming. You look great. She had to begin with something noncommittal. Undemanding. Polite nothings.

What are you doing these days, now that you finished college? Definitely not. Alice couldn't mention college, because that would reek of Dan pressuring Esme to go to grad school.

If Esme had told Bobby that it was allowable for him to meet with Alice, whether or not she herself showed up, it had to mean that she had partway positive feelings toward her mother. Didn't it? She wouldn't send Bobby on an errand merely to spew insults at Alice.

•   •   •   •   •

Bobby was leaning against his motorcycle, parked in almost the same spot as their first meeting, across the street from Starbucks and CVS. This time he was wearing a green-and-pink T-shirt, his helmet dangling from one hand. Alone.

Alice shut her car door. Locked it. Put her key in her pocketbook. Her eyes weren't watering, and her hand wasn't shaking, but she was breathing too fast.

People were walking past Bobby, in both directions. Blabbing on their phones, or to each other, or moving silently straight ahead. No one else, however, was plain old standing around. No almost twenty-four-year-old young woman with wild brown hair.

She could be hiding. Inside the CVS. Drinking coffee in Starbucks.Watching.

Bobby lifted his helmet a couple of inches toward Alice, which might have been a greeting.

"Would you like to get coffee?" Alice asked. Six o'clock. She should offer dinner.

"I don't drink coffee."

He didn't? Esme had been drinking coffee in high school. Black coffee, at IHOP.

"There's a restaurant a block over," Bobby added, "if you want coffee. I could have a Coke. Thanks."

Is Esme coming?

The restaurant wasn't as adorable as the rest of downtown Santa Barbara. Inside, it had a red tile floor, a large but thankfully silent jukebox, and plain white walls decorated only with a smattering of framed black-and-white photos of beaches, and it smelled faintly of sweetness. A waitress in a white T-shirt and black jeans led Alice and Bobby to one of the wooden tables that lined the two side walls.

No, Bobby said, he wasn't hungry. A Coke was fine.

That meant he wasn't planning to stay long. That meant he didn't want to be obligated to her for the price of more than a Coke. He might even insist on paying himself. None of those little hints was promising.

But he was here.

He stared into his glass of Coke before he took it, removed the plastic straw, and slugged a long drink.

"I thought it'd be better to tell you in person," he said.

He put the straw back into the glass and stirred it with impossible slowness.

"Esme isn't coming." Did Alice actually get those words out?

"Esme doesn't want to … she doesn't want to meet with you. Right now," Bobby went on, not looking up from his glass.

Alice was stupidly clutching her coffee cup. She might burn her hands. No she wouldn't, restaurants wouldn't use cups that could burn their customers.

"I'm sorry," he added.

"Why doesn't she…want to?"

"She didn't really say." He paused. "I told her you seem nice."

Why had Alice ever thought Esme would agree to see her? To kiss and make up? Because so many years had passed, because Esme was older and more mature, therefore time must have healed her anger and hatred of Alice, whatever the reasons for the hatred and anger had been? Sure, but a lot had also gotten worse in Esme's life. She'd been arrested barely two months ago. She was facing a criminal trial, possibly as soon as next week. She still didn't know what was going to happen, whether she'd go to jail. She might not even have a lawyer. She had to be feeling horribly insecure and shaken, and she didn't need the complication of seeing Alice.

But why did seeing her own mother have to be a complication for Esme and not a comfort? Did she truly believe that Alice would hassle her about her grades at UC Santa Barbara? Was she hurt that Alice hadn't gone to her high school graduation? Or maybe, all these years, she remained angry about the debacle with Courtney, that Alice hadn't trusted her. Which was essentially true. But they'd been teenagers, Courtney and Esme.

"I wasn't a terrible mother!"

The waitress must be staring at her. Was Alice shouting? She lowered her voice. "I read to her all the time. We made pottery. I bought her organic crackers and fruit, and I let her eat nothing but orange food for years and years, did she ever tell you about going to the beach and digging fishing pools?"

"I don't think so. I'm sorry."

"Why?"

"She just said, it's a part of her life that's finished."

Finished? How could a mother ever be finished in her daughter's life?

"Why?"

"I tried to encourage her to see you. I really did." Bobby's deepish voice stumbled a little. "My mom died when I was ten, and I wish I could talk to her now, a lot of times."

I'm sorry about your mother. Alice needed to say that.

"But," Bobby continued, "Esme just doesn't want to. She told me to lay off."

"Could you try again?"

"No." Bobby ran his palms along both sides of his face, flattening the short ends of his black hair. "She got pissed at me." He bent his head low over the table. "I'm not going to fight with her like that."

The ice in Bobby's glass had mostly melted. Alice's coffee was no doubt as cold as his Coke by now.

That was it. Dead end. Bobby had already done more than most boyfriends would, standing up for the mother his girlfriend hated. Alice shouldn't have asked him to try again. Esme simply didn't want to meet with her.

At a booth on the far side of the café, newcomers were settling in, rustling and laughing. A shriller laugh in reply. The waitress was moving toward Alice and Bobby's table, their check in her fingers.

If only Alice could reach out, before Bobby left forever, and squeeze his hand, the way she could with James. But that was far too deep a chasm to bridge.

However, Bobby wasn't pushing back his chair or signaling to the waitress. He wasn't making any moves to go yet. So there was this tiny chance—one minute, five minutes—to pass along a message to Esme, through Bobby. *I love you. I'll always be your mother.* But it was also Alice's last chance to find out any answers. *What happened at the art supply store? What did I do as a mother, that was so wrong?* It was too much to say and to ask, for one minute.

"Could I have a refill?" Alice said quickly, as the waitress neared. "Would you like another Coke?" she asked Bobby. He shook his head.

"I'm sorry about your mother."

"Thank you."

"And thank you for doing what you could. For asking Esme."

Bobby nodded.

"Can I give you my phone number? Just, in case, you know."

He nodded again, and she scribbled the digits on a business card.

How many more minutes would he stay, while Alice dragged out sipping the coffee she didn't want? He had already spoken probably twice as much as the first time they'd met. Did he have any words left in him?

So, she might as well let loose with a biggie. What did she have to lose anymore? "Why did you two break into the art supply store?"

Bobby released a heavy breath that stirred the Coke-and-water pool in his glass.

"I saw the police report," Alice added.

"It's not the way it looks."

"Okay."

He scratched his nails against the wooden tabletop. He stared at the table, at the floor, at the windows on the opposite wall. He had a small bruise above his left cheekbone. A fast, pounding song burst out of the jukebox. James would have recognized the title and band.

"The art supply store?" Alice repeated.

Bobby formed a fist with his right hand, wrapping his left around it. Big hands. Hands that could fix a pretty girl's cellphone. Or hold tight a girlfriend who was crying about how awful her mother was. Or break a window at an art supply store. "I told you Esme makes earrings, yeah?"

"Yes."

"She was starting to kind of make a business out of it. She sold some at the store where she'd worked, but it shut down in March. And on Etsy. So, I asked Stacey at Pacific Artists if they could put a few pairs on display. Why not try? They sell the kind of beads and stuff you'd use to make earrings anyway."

"Sure."

Without looking at Alice, Bobby shifted in his seat, pulled out a thin leather wallet from a rear pocket of his jeans, and extracted three small, glossy photos. The kind that he might have taken with a disposable camera. "I brought you some pictures." He pushed them onto the table, toward Alice.

Each print showed a single pair of earrings, lying inside a cardboard jewelry box. A string of colored glass beads, the wire curled into a circle between the top two and bottom two beads. A long glass bead perched almost like a rider atop the saddle of a tiny silver horse. A crescent of silver wire with a row of beads along the bottom.

"She made these? They're beautiful."

"Yeah." Bobby smiled. It was a gentle smile, not a grin.

"Are they still on display at the store?" Had they been on a rack right in front of Alice's eyes when she and James had visited, and she had failed to see her own daughter's jewelry?

Bobby exhaled roughly. "I'm not sure they ever were."

"Why not?"

"I don't know. I mean, I know Felicia didn't like me. She owns the store. So I asked Stacey to say these were earrings from her own friend, not from me and Esme."

"Okay."

Another pause, while Bobby maneuvered his glass around the tabletop. How much more would he talk? Was he being nice so far only because he knew it was the last time he'd ever see Alice?

The waitress had arrived, bearing a carafe of coffee. She filled Alice's cup halfway.

"I'm not sure about everything that happened," Bobby went on, after the waitress stalked away. "I don't know if Felicia said no, or if Stacey never asked her. Anyway, I came in a couple times, and the earrings still weren't on the counter that I could tell. I asked one of the other clerks, but she didn't know anything. So meanwhile, Esme also had the earrings up on Etsy. And a lady saw them there and wanted to buy one of the pairs." At that, Bobby's jaw and cheekbones shifted slightly, into a little smile, as if he was seeing those earrings on Esme's ears. "It was one of my favorites. This one." He pointed to the crescent moons. "So if Pacific Artists wasn't going to put them on the counter and sell them, then we needed to get them back, and we were—" He stopped.

"You were what?"

Bobby sucked in his lower lip. "We were planning to move up north," he whispered.

They were moving away? Where? How far? Why? How would Alice ever find Esme? *Up north* could be any place. Could be Canada. Alaska. "Where? Why?"

"Like I said, we both lost our jobs. A friend of mine asked me to come work in his garage in—up north. And he knew a boutique that'd sell Esme's earrings on consignment. So we needed to get her earrings from Pacific Artists before we left town. Especially because of the Etsy buyer, who wasn't going to wait. We had to go. I had to start my job. I tried calling Felicia, and she wasn't calling me back. I mean it; I kept trying until the last minute." Bobby leaned forward across the table, finally facing Alice straight-on. "Stacey'd told me she'd put them in a drawer next to the cash register."

"So you decided to steal them."

"It wasn't stealing!" he snapped. "They were Esme's own property."

"I'm sorry. You're right." No, no, if Bobby got mad at her… Alice's lips made a little smile. "But why didn't you ask Stacey to return them to you?"

"They told me she was away for two weeks. We couldn't wait. Like I said."

"And you couldn't ask another clerk?"

"No one else knew about the earrings."

"And now you both might go to jail."

"I don't know," he mumbled.

"Or have to pay a huge fine, at the least. And you'll have an arrest record. This could be really bad for you two. I'm worried, Bobby."

"We have a lawyer."

"That's good. Do you have a trial date? Do you need help with paying the legal bills?" She could borrow against her 401(k), couldn't she? And Seshat occasionally arranged personal loans for employees, advances on their salaries.

"We have, um, help."

Dan was paying, of course. "What does the lawyer say, about your prospects?"

"I don't know."

"How serious are the charges?"

"We'll have to see, I guess."

"You didn't use a weapon, did you? Like a crowbar?"

"No."

"You didn't think the store might have security alarms before you did this? Cameras?"

Bobby stared at the table.

"How could you two be so stupid?"

I'm sorry. Alice needed to say that again.

CHAPTER TWENTY-FIVE

ALICE, DAN, AND ESME

November 2002 to February 2003
Calabasas and Santa Monica, CA

Esme was leaning into the shoulder of the girl next to her, laughing and talking, as they eased their way out the revolving glass doors of the mall. A few steps into the parking lot, they pulled apart, and Esme walked toward Alice's Honda.

Esme looked happy. Comfortable. An all-American, healthy, popular, normal sixteen-year-old California cheerleader. Her hair danced around her face in a mass of brown waves, not stringy as Jenny's had been in the worst days. She was wearing standard-issue adolescent garb: leg-hugging jeans, a red T-shirt cut above her midriff, beige Ugg boots, and an unbuttoned denim jacket. Big silver loops swung from her ears. She was thin in a fashionable way but not anorexic-skinny. She didn't slouch like a stoned-out druggie. She and the other girl moved with the confidence of teenagers who knew they could shop any time they wished.

Did she drink? smoke? do drugs? have sex? Nothing in Esme's clothing or gait hinted at delinquency. Dan claimed that her grades had soared. She was a cheerleader at all the football games. Did she have a lot of friends? Tight friends? Could she actually be as happy and normal as she looked? Those weren't the kinds of questions a mother could ask if she saw her daughter only every other weekend.

Which wasn't even a full weekend now. Hadn't been in more than a year. First, eleven o'clock Saturday morning became one o'clock in the afternoon, because Esme was sleeping, because she was up late every Friday night cheerleading at the football games. And when football season ended, there would be a school dance on Friday night where she was on the committee that made the decorations, or a friend's party. Then one o'clock inched forward to two or three, because she had an SAT prep class on Saturday morning or, like today, please, please, could she go shopping with her girlfriends for a couple of hours? And meanwhile, Sunday evening slipped backwards to afternoon, and dinner with Alice disappeared, because Esme needed to return to Calabasas to finish her homework.

"Can we get something to eat?" Tugging open the Honda's passenger-side door, Esme dropped into the seat and tossed two big plastic bags behind her. "I'll show you what I bought. It's for Erin's birthday party."

"Sure, honey. What would you like? How about pizza?"

Esme wrinkled her nose. "Mom, that's so greasy."

"Okay. Do you have a favorite organic café?"

"There's an IHOP on Ventura everyone goes to. I'll direct you."

So, not organic anymore. But not pizza, either. Esme's tastes had flipped again, in the last two weeks.

They sat opposite each other in a brown-and-blue booth. "How was the football game last night? Did Calabasas win?" Alice began.

"Nah. We always lose."

"Sorry to hear that. It must be hard to keep smiling and cheering when the team is losing."

Esme's hair waved like a wheat field as she shook her head. If Alice dared to touch it, would it feel as soft as it had when Esme was sitting in Grandma Florence's kitchen eating canned ravioli?

"Not really. The fun part is moving and dancing with my friends, whether we win or lose." Esme's lips smiled. Maybe.

"Dancing? Is cheerleading similar to dancing?"

"Kind of, yeah."

But Esme hated dancing. Or no, was it merely ballet that she hated? "Dancing," Alice repeated. "Well, not like a waltz, I suppose."

Esme laughed! An honest-to-goodness laugh. With Alice.

"Could I come watch a game sometime?" Alice pressed on.

"I guess. But the season's over till next fall."

"How many different cheers do you have?"

"A lot. Want me to teach you a couple?"

"Yes! Would you?"

Had she and Esme ever talked for this long, this easily, while they were living together?

Give her space, Roz had said. Was Roz right, that they had to separate in order to get along better? "Absence makes the heart grow fonder," and all those clichés. Maybe Esme missed Alice. Living every day with Dan, chafing under his rules. *Your skirt is too short. Your room is a mess. Just where do you think you're going?* Maybe Esme wished she had the independence of the apartment in Santa Monica, where she could walk and ride buses everywhere on her own, and was getting annoyed about always having to ask her father if she could borrow his car.

Or maybe it was the opposite. Maybe Dan was—if it was possible?—relaxed now, less demanding, less angry, because he'd "won." He was no longer pushing Esme to choose between her parents. And therefore, Esme could be more relaxed. She could enjoy being in Calabasas, cooking organic food with Penelope, playing with the two kids Graydon and Hadley and the dog, cheerleading at football games. And also enjoy hanging out with Alice.

"Is the school having a holiday dance? Are you making the decorations?" Alice asked.

"Ugh, the theme they're insisting on is so juvenile. Snowmen and snowflakes. I mean, like for starters, where do we live? Do you ever see snowflakes in the San Fernando Valley?"

They both laughed. Together.

"We're also in charge of refreshments for the dance. Do you think Grandma Florence would give me her recipe for raisin-chocolate chip cookies?"

"I'm sure she'd be very happy to do that."

"How is she, anyway?"

She'd love to see you. She hasn't been feeling well. No, that would be pushing Esme too far. "She's good."

When the waitress took their order, Esme said Caesar salad with chicken plus black coffee. She was drinking coffee? Since when?

"What are you doing nowadays at your job?" Esme queried, picking out a handful of pink Sweet'N Low packets from a bowl on the table and laying them in two parallel lines. "Whatever happened with the owls?"

"You mean the spotted owls in Humboldt County, that I was working on when you were little?"

"You stopped companies from chopping down the forest?"

"In a way. We persuaded the major stockholders—Do you really want to hear?"

Esme added two shorter, perpendicular lines of Sweet'n Lows to the original set, forming a square. "Yeah. Were the owls, like, endangered?"

"Almost. They were labeled 'threatened,' which is a step below 'endangered.' "

"So are people boycotting clothes made of owl feathers?"

"That's a good question. I can't recall anything that's made out of owl feathers nowadays. Have you seen owl-feather clothing in your magazines?"

Esme laughed as she picked up her coffee cup. "That would be funny. Like old-fashioned ladies' hats?"

"I'll have to start looking at what the fashion magazines are showing."

"It would be cool if I could do something like you do."

"Really?"

"To boycott something and save an endangered animal? I need a community service project for college applications."

"I'd be glad to help. Do you want to go to Humboldt County, to the owls' forests, one weekend with me?" A mother-daughter road trip. Stopping for an afternoon in San Francisco, if that evoked happy memories. Would Esme agree to so much togetherness?

"I'm volunteering at Dad's clinic two days a week after school," Esme went on, "so that counts for one project. But my counselor says I should try to do a second project, to make up for my grades."

"Your grades? I thought—"

"Forget it. I just need community service projects for college."

"Sure. What colleges are you considering? We could visit some of them." From her shoulder bag, Alice pulled out her small notepad and a pen. "Are there any colleges the counselor suggests? I suppose it depends on what major you go for."

"Mom! I don't know. Stop nagging me. It's way too early."

"But you brought up the topic of college."

Now Esme was her old, silent self again. Shrugging. Staring at the square of Sweet'n Lows. "You're always making those lists."

Give her space. Listening to her isn't nothing.

Alice restored her smile. "So, do you want to talk about boycotting? What clothing brands do you usually wear?"

"Dad says you won't pay your share of my college."

"What? Fifty-fifty, that's what he and I agreed."

"But he has two other kids to support."

"And he earns three times as—" Alice stopped. Kept smiling. "Honey, how we divide the college tuition is between your dad and me, and he shouldn't drag you into it."

"But he's right that he has more kids."

"We'll pay for your college wherever you go. Don't worry."

"Why are you always criticizing him?"

"I'm not—I am paying my full share. Look, do you want to discuss college or don't you?"

Esme blew at nonexistent steam on her coffee. The waitress brought her salad and Alice's bowl of French onion soup.

"Hollister," Esme announced. She dug her fork into her salad, spearing a hunk of chicken. "My friends all wear Hollister shirts. And H&M. Do you still buy those super-high-heel Jimmy Choo shoes?" and she sucked the chicken hunk off of her fork.

•   •   •   •   •

"I can't really talk, Mom," Esme said on the phone Wednesday evening. "I have a big history test tomorrow."

"Can you pick me up later on Saturday?" she asked the following week. "Like, four o'clock?"

"Four o'clock? Honey, that's almost the whole day gone."

"I know, Mom, but I'm on the planning committee for the Valentine's show, and we're meeting at one-thirty."

"Esme, I never see you." No, no, her voice was too shrill.

"Maybe," Alice suggested to Esme on Sunday, "you could send me a little email note when you have a free moment? To say hi? What's your email address?"

"I use Dad's. You can email me there."

What the hell? What sixteen-year-old used her father's email?

On the Thursday before her next visit, Esme phoned Alice. "Can my friend Courtney Michaels come with me this weekend?"

"With you? Sure."

"Thanks. She's a cheerleader, too. But Mom? Just so you know, things are kind of tough for her, because her dad was on one of those airplanes that crashed on September eleventh last year."

"How awful."

"I mean, don't say anything to her about it. Please!"

"Of course not."

"Because she's still not over it."

"I understand. And I'll be glad to meet any of your friends."

•   •   •   •   •

"See this hair!" Esme lifted a thick lock of Alice's light-brown hair, before letting the mass float down to Alice's shoulders. "What do you think, Courtney? Mom, can I blow-dry your hair and shape it a little? I saw some great ideas in *Cosmo*."

"My mom colors her hair such a fake blond. It looks like a bunch of bananas. It's so lame." Courtney was a pixie, thin and barely five feet tall, with a wide mouth, round face, and dark blonde hair cropped in a wedge cut. Even as she spoke, she sprang up from her seat at the kitchen table, skipped over to Alice, held out a few strands of Alice's hair, let go, sauntered to the deep steel sink, and danced back to the table, almost as if she was doing one of their cheerleading routines. "You have great hair, Mrs. Wilson," she continued, tapping her short, bright-turquoise fingernails on the wooden tabletop.

"Really? Thanks, both of you. Can you give me a whole new look? Make me look like, oh, who could I look like? Catherine Zeta-Jones?"

"I loved Catherine Zeta-Jones in *Chicago*! I want to be a dancer." Courtney sprang up again.

Esme crossed her arms as if she was pretending to be annoyed, but a moment later she leaned casually against the wooden chair with the peeling blue paint, and her pursed lips might have been tilting just slightly up. It was all right. She wasn't actually arguing. "Mom, no offense, but aren't you, like, ten years older than she is?"

"So? With a touch of makeup?"

"Do you have any makeup?"

"A few things. When you were little, you used to use my lipstick on your stuffed animals. Do you remember?"

"We'll manage. What color lipsticks?" As she spoke, Esme pulled a fat black hairbrush out of her jacket pocket and started drawing it through Alice's hair, firmly yet without tugging. On a patch of skin above her left wrist was a tiny brown sketch. "You'd be good, I think, in, umm… Dark pink!"

"What's that on your wrist?"

"Just a dumb tattoo. I don't remember why I did it."

It was a puppy face: the outline of a head, two short ears, a dark button nose, two button eyes.

It was cute. It didn't signify anything. Esme loved puppies. She loved endangered owls.

Alice relaxed into her chair, her hips sliding lower and her head lolling against the back, while Esme's brush pulled down and out, over and over. It was a long, easy, February Saturday afternoon, cold outside, but Alice was safely home with her daughter and her daughter's friend, and they had all afternoon and evening and night to hang out here in her warm kitchen, chatting, grooming, laughing. Like three friends. She could put on music. What did Esme listen to? Did she still adore Celine Dion, because of the song from the *Titanic* movie? Alice could introduce the girls to some classic folk singers, Joan Baez and Joni Mitchell, Woody Guthrie and Judy Collins. Eventually she'd bring in pizza, or Chinese food without MSG, or Caesar salad, whatever Esme and Courtney desired. The two girls would stay up until midnight or beyond, long after Alice went to bed, gossiping in Esme's room, fixing each other's hair the way they were playing with Alice's, painting their toenails—did teenagers do that these days?—perhaps calling friends in Calabasas. Normal teenagers sleeping over at each other's homes. Tomorrow morning, Alice could make French toast.

"Courtney, doesn't Mom need earrings? Long, dangling ones, I think." Esme half-swiveled toward Courtney, who had moved to the doorway. "Hey, did I tell you? Mom might help me with my community service project. She saved a lot of endangered owls in a forest up north, once."

"Cool." Courtney peered around the doorway into the living room. "Are you also a vet, Mrs. Wilson?"

"No, Esme's dad saves endangered poodles. I save endangered forests." Crap! How could Alice blurt out something so stupid?

But Esme was laughing. She wasn't annoyed? She twirled a clutch of Alice's hair. "That's cute, Mom."

"It wasn't very nice of me." Alice laughed, too, as she straightened up. "So, are you girls hungry?"

"Oh, yeah, Courtney, you want to go to the pier and see if anything's open? There's this whole long pier that stretches pretty far out into the water."

"Wait a second, girls."

Casually, Esme set her brush on the table, as if waiting with vague curiosity for an interesting suggestion from her mother. Courtney, at the refrigerator now, hopped from foot to foot.

Two weeks ago a young woman was attacked on the beach, very near the pier. Smashed in the face. Three broken ribs. Her purse stolen.

"I don't know if it's such a great idea for you two to wander around the beach at this hour," Alice said.

Esme was already moving toward the coatrack.

"It's winter," Alice added. "It's getting dark."

"So?"

"No one will be there."

"So what's the problem?"

"I mean, no one trustworthy. Like tourists. Police. In case something happens."

"Mom, we're not going to get into cars with strange men."

"I wasn't suggesting that you would, honey."

"We're not total jerks."

Alice had to take a breath. Courtney still hadn't spoken.

"I know that," Alice said. "But it's off-season anyway. None of the food stands will be open."

"We'll go for a walk and come back here to eat. I want to show Courtney around."

It's not safe!

But wasn't that one of Alice's big selling points, in trying to persuade Esme to spend more time with her? Here in Santa Monica, Esme could have so much freedom. She could go on her own to exciting, vibrant places without needing to ask an adult for a ride—including the pier, less than a mile from Alice's apartment. And now Esme wanted to show that wonderful Santa Monica life to one of her friends. Why in heaven's name was Alice arguing against her? The attack on the woman was horrible, but it was one occurrence, in all the years Alice had lived here. And it had happened a lot later at night, in a part of the beach more deserted than the pier.

But if anything happened to Esme!

Or what if, in a newspaper article or TV clip, Dan heard about the attack on the woman? Or if a client of his mentioned it? And he learned that Alice had let Esme go walking there. At night. Endangering Courtney, as well. He would have a police order the very next day, forbidding Esme from coming within ten miles of Santa Monica.

Unlikely. Of course. Nevertheless, not worth the risk.

"Let's go, Courtney," Esme declared. "Mom, we'll just be gone an hour. It won't be dark yet."

In fact, it would be dark long before that.

The two girls were pulling their puffy ski jackets from the wall hooks next to the door. One white, the other dark burgundy.

There was only one solution. Let Esme and Courtney go, and then follow them. Secretly. To make sure they were safe. Without, actually, *spying*.

"Which way are you walking?" Alice asked at the apartment doorway. "Why don't you go over to Santa Monica Boulevard, and you can turn left there, to Pacific Coast Highway, okay? Stay on major streets."

She spotted them a two-minute start before she grabbed her jacket and house keys, zipped on her brown suede Biviel boots, and ran down the stairs to the front door of the building and out to the already-dusky street. Two slim figures in ski jackets and knitted caps were well into the next block, a short figure and a medium-height one. The shorter one waved her outside arm in circles and said something. The other figure nodded.

The air tingled with cold. A few lights were sprinkled throughout windows in the two- and three-story apartment buildings lining the noiseless street, like the random squares on a board early in a Bingo game. B43 in the first house. N10 in the second. The buildings— beige, yellow, or white stucco in the daytime, most likely—were all twilight-tinged gray now, impossible to tell apart, if Alice needed to describe them to the police. Cars were parked fitfully along the curb.

A man in light-colored coat clip-clopped rapidly on the far sidewalk.

He probably wasn't dangerous. He was on the other side of the street, far enough away that Esme and Courtney would have advance warning if they needed to run.

The two girls had halted. Esme was glancing around the street, while Courtney bent over. To retrieve something? tie a shoelace? She abruptly unbent, and they resumed their route, cocking their heads toward each other, as if they were talking.

A dark minivan was cruising the block. Why was it moving so slowly? Searching for gullible teenagers to kidnap? Or simply seeking a parking spot? At the corner, it rushed through the yellow light. The two girls stopped at the same corner, Esme gestured rightward, and they turned. A few more blocks to go.

And what would happen once the girls reached the pier? If they went down one of the pier's empty lanes, past all the little wooden stalls that would be boarded up for winter, onto the small observation deck at the end, then what? They would have to turn around, to retrace their steps homeward. And they would see Alice. Full-on. Clearly illuminated in the moonlight and the light from the scattered lamp posts. Spying on them. No matter how far back she was following, there would be no way for her to duck into a shuttered stall, no parked cars to hide behind. Why hadn't she thought of that, in her stupid panic?

She had to quit now, before they got to the pier; to run into a different street, scurry home, go upstairs, and—and—and start baking cookies. Flick on the TV. As though she'd never left the apartment.

It was too late.

Esme had turned around, there on the sidewalk, without waiting for the pier. And looked at Alice.

What choice did she have? Alice waved and walked fast until she was standing in front of them.

"Mom, what are you doing?"

"I thought, maybe, we could all go out to eat? If you found someplace open?"

"You were spying on me?"

"No!"

The three of them stared at each other. Courtney, for once, stood still.

Esme was the first to speak. "You win. We'll go back."

Alice dragged a few yards behind, as they headed along busy Santa Monica Boulevard, to give Esme and Courtney privacy, but the girls didn't seem to be chatting now. They weren't turning their faces toward each other or gesturing at anything. They moved rapidly and silently, as cars sped past and streetlights flickered, and they filed into the apartment, blank-faced, after Alice opened the door.

"So," Alice declared, with a big smile. "What would—"

"Can you drive us back now?" Esme interrupted.

"But we are back."

"No. Back to Dad's."

The blood inside Alice's body was colder than the air outside.

Not again.

No. How much more could Esme run away?

"You just got here."

"Not really."

"But don't you want to sleep over? I hardly ever see you."

"Mom, can you just take us to Dad's?"

"Aren't you going to do my make-up? And earrings? I'll bake—"

"Mom!"

"My parents expect me home tonight," Courtney interjected. "I didn't tell them I was sleeping over."

"Oh."

So Esme had invited Courtney, knowing that—from the outset, never planning to stay for the weekend—without telling Alice?

But wait a minute. Courtney's parents?

Alice clutched the doorknob. "Your mother remarried already? That's nice."

"What do you mean? Remarried?" Courtney frowned.

"Because your father—"

"MOM!" Esme grabbed Alice's left arm. "Can you come with me a second?" she hissed, tugging Alice toward the stairs.

They hurried down the tiled staircase and around a bend to the next-floor landing before Esme's furious whisper resumed. "I told you not to say anything about Courtney's father."

"But she's the one who said. About her 'parents.' How can she have parents?"

Esme's face was turned away from Alice, aimed more at a corner of the landing where two faded-pink walls met. A small, framed watercolor of what might be a Parisian street was hanging, a little lopsided, on a nail on the higher wall.

"Esme? What's going on?"

"It—Okay, so—Her father wasn't on that airplane. On September eleventh. Okay? Now let's go."

"Why did you say that he was?"

"Just forget it."

"No!" Alice needed to breathe in fully and deeply. "Tell me what's going on."

Esme was already on the first step up the staircase toward their apartment. However, Courtney probably couldn't see or hear them, because of the bend in the stairwell. "I just wanted to make my life dramatic. It was a joke."

"You wanted more excitement?"

With her back to Alice, Esme shrugged.

"I can understand that. I guess Calabasas can be kind of boring."

"That's not what I said!" Esme had started climbing rapidly. "Stop criticizing everything I say. Can I just go home?"

Home.

CHAPTER TWENTY-SIX

ALICE, DAN, AND ESME

May to June 2004

San Fernando Valley, CA

The shoe-store window in the mall was showing a pair of ugly stilettos from Christian Louboutin, with black studs and a fur corsage-thing near the heel. "Who would ever wear this junk?" Alice asked, but Roz was already two windows away, pinned in front of a candy shop, where a dozen red, satiny boxes were displayed on easels at different heights.

"Tell me that chocolate in fancy, expensive boxes isn't fattening," Roz murmured.

"It isn't fattening, because you have to have to work so hard taking off all the wrappings."

"Thank you."

Alice followed Roz to the next window. "I guess I'll finally meet the famous Mrs. Penelope Wilson in a couple of weeks, at Esme's graduation."

"After all this time."

Did it matter now? In September, Esme would be off to college at Santa Barbara, and she wouldn't be living with Dan and Penelope and their kids anymore. It wouldn't matter what kind of organic dinners Penelope cooked. It wouldn't matter that Dan had refused to give Alice his or Penelope's cell numbers or email addresses, only the landline for the house. Esme would be choosing her own food and talking on her own cellphone, which even Dan knew he couldn't keep secret from Alice.

"Do you want to meet Penelope?" Roz asked.

"I sort-of do and sort-of don't. I'm curious, of course, but I think I'd rather pretend she doesn't exist."

A cluster of teenage girls, sandal heels clacking rapidly on the smooth floor, passed by so closely that Alice bumped into Roz. A mother dragging two little boys charged ahead in the opposite direction. The scent of French fries and ketchup wafted from the food court around the corner, while "My Favorite Things" from *The Sound of Music* blared from the mall's mezzanine.

"I thought Esme and I could go shopping together for her graduation dress." Alice paused. "Mother-daughter bonding. Should I offer to do that?"

"That's a sweet idea."

"Even though she thinks I know nothing about fashion except for shoes. Which is true."

"So she'll pick out the dress herself, and whatever she chooses, you tell her how beautiful she is. You will, won't you?"

"Even though no one will see it under her cap and gown."

"They'll see it at lunch afterwards."

"Which I'm not invited to."

Roz rubbed Alice's arm in her brief, soft way. "There's no correct answer with teenage daughters. What if you and your mother take her out to lunch another day? Meanwhile, you'll go to the graduation ceremony, and who knows? It might break the ice with Dan. A shared moment of pride. Your daughter graduating from high school. Maybe it could help?"

"Please. Dan? Shared moment?" Alice spit out a psst of air. "You should know better than that. But Esme has actually been excited about having my mother and me see her graduate. She asked me three times if I'd gotten the tickets yet."

"That's wonderful!"

"Yeah. It is. I tell you, Roz, the moment I'm really waiting for is September, when Esme is finally on her own, on campus at Santa Barbara and out of Dan's clutches. I guess I hope she and I can have a fresh start, without him always shoving his face in."

"She'll ignore the two of you equally."

"Fine. As long as it's equal."

With her elbow, Roz nudged Alice toward the mall's center aisle. "Beyond the Dan nonsense, you're letting her know you're proud of her, I hope."

"I guess so. I think she has a B average. Should I be proud of that?"

"Yes, Alice. Give her a break. She worked hard to bring her grades up, and she does all that cheerleading and everything. Now let's get some lunch for ourselves."

"Okay. I'm very proud that she's going to a state university, so I don't have to pay private-college rates. Especially since Dan manipulated me into paying sixty percent of the tuition instead of the fifty percent that's in our divorce settlement. Why did I let him do that? Because Esme got all snippy that I wasn't being fair to poor Daddy who has two other kids to pay for, that's why." As Roz was opening her mouth, Alice's phone trilled.

•   •   •   •   •

The receptionist at the emergency room said she had been transferred to intensive care, but the intensive care desk had no record of her name. The nurse there sent Alice and Roz to the admissions office, which sent them back to the emergency room.

Maybe fifteen minutes later, a man in green scrubs squatted in front of their plastic chairs in the emergency waiting area.

"How are you?" he asked gently. "I'm Dr. O'Neil."

"They said," Alice began. "She had a heart attack?"

"Yes. That's what we suspect. The people at the grocery store called 911 as soon as she fell. They were very concerned."

"She always takes her pills."

Dr. O'Neil patted Alice's hand. "I'm sure she did everything she was supposed to. But the heart is a very sensitive machine. And unfortunately, once it's been weakened, especially in an older person…She'd already had an incident? The records showed an event approximately a year ago."

"The pain in her arm. That we thought was arthritis at first."

"Yes. The symptoms in women can be obscure sometimes."

"And she's been more and more tired."

"No one can predict these things. Please don't second-guess yourself."

"Can we go see her? Is she awake?"

The doctor stared at her. "I thought you knew."

●   ●   ●   ●   ●

James and Roz sat beside her on Florence's bed, on Florence's crocheted granny-square afghan, on the bed where Florence should have been sleeping, and they held her hands, one on each side of her.

After a while, Roz went to the kitchen and returned with a cup of tea. In a drawer in the nightstand by the bed, James found a limp leather address book, while Walt sifted among the papers in the roll-top wooden desk in the living room.

"Didn't she have a brother in Connecticut?"

"Does anyone know the names of any of her friends?"

"That's a smart idea. We could start with her friends from the bridge club."

"Should we tell Georgia Wilson?"

"I have to call Esme," Alice said.

Roz sat down next to her. "Should we stay with you when you talk to her?"

No. She couldn't call yet.

On top of the pine dresser in the bedroom, three of Florence's bridge trophies were displayed in a line, the biggest one in the middle, the one from Bridge Week in 1981 when she and her partner had famously beaten Georgia Wilson and her partner, bidding six no-trump.

If Alice looked out the window, between the bed and the closet, she would see the four rows of lettuce Florence had planted, a parade of little green bouquets. Why did Florence go to the trouble of growing her own vegetables, yet she'd used canned ravioli and tomato sauce when Esme was little? What did it matter?

If she walked into the green kitchen, she could put on Florence's apron. She could tug open the heavy door of the avocado-green refrigerator. She could search through the brighter green cupboards. She could take flour, baking soda, salt, butter, sugar (white and brown), vanilla extract, eggs, chocolate chips, golden raisins, and three (greased) cookie sheets and bake raisin-chocolate chip cookies, except that they would never taste as delicious as Florence made them. Florence had also bought a cookie mold shaped like a tree and another in the shape of a bird, in order to make a forest of sugar cookies for Alice and Esme that would almost resemble a forest of trees and owls.

The Little Bo Peep bowl was in the kitchen cupboard. A box of organic stoneground crackers was in the pantry, opened, wrapped in a plastic bag.

I have some sad news, Esme, Alice wrote on a page from a small pad that Walt had found in the roll-top desk. *Grandma Florence died this morning.*

She had a heart attack. But it was very quick. She wouldn't have felt a lot of pain.

I'm so sorry she'll miss your graduation, but I know she was very proud of you. She loved you very much.

So I want to let you know that the funeral will be on Tuesday.

She sat on her mother's bed, after Roz, James, and Walt had left, and she lifted the receiver from the old-fashioned, yellow Princess phone on the nightstand. Calling from Florence's favorite phone, as though Florence herself were calling. It was far better than using Alice's cellphone. She kept her script on her lap.

"I have some sad news, honey. Grandma Florence died this morning. She had a heart attack."

"What do you mean? What happened to Grandma?" On the other end of the phone line, Esme sounded different than usual. Surprised? Sobered? "I just talked to her, like, a couple weeks ago."

"I know. It was very unexpected."

"She was excited about coming to my graduation."

"Yes. She was very proud of you. She loved you very much." Alice couldn't cry. Esme would probably hate crying.

"She didn't seem sick."

"It was quick. The doctor said."

"She was teaching me how to play bridge."

"I didn't know that." Florence must have loved it. Maybe dreamed of playing in tournaments with her granddaughter.

"She gave me a book about it," Esme added.

"You remember the raisin chocolate-chip cookies you used to make with her?"

"Sure. And I had a special bowl with—What was the picture?"

"Little Bo Peep."

"And her apron with pictures from a deck of cards."

"The four queens."

"Yeah. And they're each holding a cookie. Which is kind of weird, I guess." Esme's quiet sentence dangled.

Do you remember how we lived with Grandma for a while when we left Daddy? Uh, no, bad idea.

"So," Alice read instead. She had to stay with the script. "I wanted to tell you the information about the funeral. Of course I'll drive you there. It's Tuesday afternoon."

"I can't."

Alice glanced up from the pad in her lap, as if she were speaking to a version of Esme on the bed right beside her, eating canned ravioli from her Little Bo Peep bowl, instead of to a piece of yellow plastic. "Why not?"

"I can't. I have school."

"I know, honey. But the funeral's at two o'clock. I'm sure the principal would let you out a little early."

"I have a history test seventh period."

"Esme." Now Alice really had to keep her voice on track. That was the crucial thing. Steady. Reassuring. Motherly. Not shrill, as she usually sounded when Esme canceled her weekends. "The history teacher will let you make up the test another day."

"No, he won't. He's a total jerk."

"I'll write a note."

"That won't help."

"No teacher is that unfeeling."

"He is."

"You can miss one test."

"No I can't! Shit—You don't—You're just going to call me stupid."

What? No, not at all. Esme had been accepted at a state university. She wasn't stupid.

"I might fail history, okay?" Esme snapped. "Is that serious enough for you?"

"You're not going to fail."

"How do you know? You've been telling me all my life I don't work hard enough, my grades suck. For once I want to study, and that's not good enough for you, either?"

"Esme, this is not about your grades. This is about your grandmother, and the right thing to do."

"You wish I wasn't your daughter."

How could they be fighting with each other about her mother's funeral? This was all wrong. "Please, Esme. I'm asking you to come to Grandma's funeral. We'll deal with your history test later."

"And you'll say I'm dumb if I flunk history."

"YOUR GRANDMOTHER IS DEAD!" Alice was shouting, and then it was Dan on the phone.

"What did you say to Esme?" he demanded. "She's very upset."

"She's upset? Well, I'm upset. My mother is dead!"

"I'm sorry for your loss," Dan said, without a single instant's pause of surprise at the announcement, as though he'd been listening in on the phone call the whole time—which in fact he'd probably been doing during all of Alice's calls with Esme all these years, starting in kindergarten days, first on an extension on his landline, and maybe hovering outside the door after Esme got her cell, and why hadn't Alice figured that out before now? "I know my mother will also send her regrets," he continued, "but you can hardly expect a teenager to be broken-hearted when her elderly grandmother dies."

This wasn't the moment for a lecture about eavesdropping and privacy. Another day, Alice would have to do that. "Esme needs to come to the funeral."

"You may not realize it," Dan said sternly, "but this is a very stressful time for Esme."

"For Esme?"

"You don't seem to appreciate that she's about to graduate from high school. Her whole life is changing dramatically. She'll be moving away from home—"

"My mother is dead!"

"As always," Dan responded, with a sigh that he stretched out far too long, "you're putting yourself before Esme's needs. I can't let you upset her like this."

"What the fuck are you—"

"I really can't let you talk to her until you're calmer."

The phone, too, went dead.

How dare he? Interfere between her and her own daughter. He had no business. She had every right to speak with her own daughter.

Besides, she couldn't leave things this way, with Esme running away from her. At the least, she and Esme had to say a proper goodbye. Alice dialed.

"I'm sorry," Penelope answered. "Esme is too upset—"

"YOU LET ME SPEAK TO MY DAUGHTER!"

"Don't you dare yell at my wife!" Dan shouted. How were he and Penelope talking on Esme's phone?

"Don't you dare interfere—"

"If you keep upsetting my wife and daughter," Dan continued, lowering his voice, "I will change all of our numbers."

He couldn't.

Alice hurled the phone onto the wood-planked floor.

Her mother's phone on her mother's floor.

Her dead mother's phone on her dead mother's floor, and it hit with a heavy crack and an angry, final jingling.

Wasn't it illegal? Dan couldn't keep her from her own daughter.

Who would be eighteen in less than two weeks.

Who would then be a legal adult. Who could make her own decision not to see her own mother.

No!

The heavy ceramic lamp from the nightstand crashed to the floor next to the broken phone. She threw the Sue Grafton mystery after it, the library-hardcover's pages sprawling open, and then the useless pillows from the bed. No, no, no, no no. Alice ran to the closet and tore her mother's dresses from their hangers, her blouses, her skirts, her slacks, the pocketbooks on the shelf above, until streams of nylon sleeves were clinging to her shoulders and she was tripping on clothing wrapped around her ankles, red-and-blue-striped cotton, light green polyester, yellow flowers, pink chiffon. She ripped in half the pad of paper where she'd written her ridiculous, useless script. She shoved the bridge trophies off the top of the dresser, all fucking three of them. She pounded her fists against the wall.

No. No. No.

She yanked open the front door and she ran, past the pitted driveway where Florence's old green Subaru should have been parked, past the white house to her right, past the Newmans, the McDonalds, and the next and next and next houses, driveways, lawns, little picket fences, a fire hydrant, to a big thick tree. She grabbed the tree, and she leaned over, and she gasped out breath after breath. No. No! Dan wouldn't. He couldn't. Esme wouldn't. Her mother couldn't. Be. No!

Her mother's dresses, she couldn't leave her mother's dresses all tangled on the floor. Esme wouldn't. Esme had to—

The neighbors were no doubt watching the crazy daughter from their kitchen windows. She had to go back inside. Past all the houses again. It was too hard to move a single step now, and she needed to hold on to something, whatever her hand could grab—little white picket fences, hedges, trees, anything to keep her legs from collapsing, one block, and the one after that, finally Florence's block, and oh shit luckily, luckily, there had been no wind to blow the front door shut and locked. She tumbled onto the living room carpet.

•   •   •   •   •

In ones and twos and threes, the mourners lingered at Florence's front door. "She was such a nice lady." "The best bridge player." "We're so sorry." "If there's anything we can do."

Florence's brother and his wife from Connecticut, their son who lived in Arizona, cousin Kim from San Diego. Roz's parents. Florence's former co-workers at the accounting firm and her friends from her bridge club (but not Georgia Wilson). Fred and a few others from Seshat. The neighbors who might have seen Alice running and screaming down the street. They hugged Alice. She hugged them. Jenny and Sharon, wearing black skirts and black T-shirts, collected the dirty cups and plates, rinsed off the cookie crumbs and the shreds of layer cake and the mushed-up chocolate icing, and switched on the dishwasher. Did Roz tell them to do all that, or did they volunteer on their own? They were sweet girls. Alice gave Jenny, Sharon, Roz, and Walt bigger hugs than she gave the rest of the guests and told them to go home, they'd already done so much. She could pack up the leftovers herself. James said he couldn't stay long, he had to get back to Andrea, who was sick. He wrapped Alice in his sinewy arms and kissed her on the cheek and promised to call in the morning.

Esme didn't come.

Alice picked up her cell. No. She put it down and instead lifted the receiver from Florence's green wall phone in the kitchen and stretched the cord to the table.

If she didn't call Esme today... Each hour she procrastinated would make the conversation more and more difficult. She'd already let two days go by since their last, disastrous call. Today, the day of the funeral, was the time to do it. A day of peace. Reconciliation. Space. Giving Esme space, like Roz always said. No recriminations. Besides, Esme ought to be feeling less stressed now, with her big history test out of the way.

"Hello?" Esme's voice was cheerful as she answered her cellphone.

"Hi Esme. It's Mom." She couldn't pause for air. She couldn't give Esme the chance to hang up. "I wanted to find out how your history test went."

"Oh."

For a second, there was silence.

Okay, it was a good first step, to open with a topic that mattered to Esme—her history exam, not the funeral—

Then, barely audible, two clicks.

*   *   *   *   *

Hey, it's Esme. Do your thing and I'll do mine.

"Hi, Esme, it's Mom. I think we got cut off. Call me, okay?"

*   *   *   *   *

Hello, this is the home of Penelope, Dan, Esme, Graydon, and Hadley. We're sorry no one can come to the phone just now. Please leave a message, and we'll call you back as soon as we can.

"Esme? It's Mom. Are you there? I think we got cut off."

*   *   *   *   *

This phone number is no longer accepting calls.

*   *   *   *   *

Hello, this is the home of Penelope, Dan, Esme, Graydon, and Hadley. We're sorry no one can come to the phone just now. Please leave a message, and we'll call you back as soon as we can.

"Hi. It's Alice. Is Esme there?"

•   •   •   •   •

"It's Alice again. Hi. I'm just trying to finish Esme's and my conversation from a couple of hours ago."

•   •   •   •   •

"Hey, Esme, if you're there? It's Mom. I wanted to hear about your history test. Call me back when you get a chance?"

•   •   •   •   •

"It's Alice, if Esme is there … Esme, honey, um, I'm just wondering, you know, if everything's all right. Would you like to get an ice cream or something together? Or coffee? I'm still planning to see you at graduation, of course."

•   •   •   •   •

This phone number is no longer accepting calls.

•   •   •   •   •

Hello, this is the home of Penelope, Dan, Esme, Graydon, and Hadley. We're sorry no one can come to the phone just now. Please leave a message, and we'll call you back as soon as we can.

"Esme? When you get this message, it's Mom. Um, gee, it's been more than a week, and I haven't heard from you. I guess I'm a little worried. I hope everything's all right. I'd love to talk with you sometime."

•   •   •   •   •

"Hi. It's Alice, again. Esme, um, is it okay if I come to your graduation? I'd really like to. It's such a special day. I'm proud of you."

•   •   •   •   •

"It's Alice. Esme, um, let me know if you…

•   •   •   •   •

She had a ticket. She could sit at the rear of the auditorium, where Dan and Penelope and their kids wouldn't see her. Afterwards, before Esme joined Dan and Penelope, while all the new graduates were throwing their mortarboards into the air and hugging each other, she'd find Esme. Make sure Esme saw her. Wave. Step toward her, if Esme seemed welcoming. Mouth the word: *Congratulations!*

How would she find Esme?

What if Esme turned away?

What if the only empty seat was next to Dan?

•   •   •   •   •

"Hi, this message is for Esme. It's Mom. I'm sorry I wasn't at your graduation, but I didn't want to force anything… Maybe, you know, we can celebrate your birthday and your graduation together? Is everything all right? It's been almost a month. Please call me. Okay? Please."

•   •   •   •   •

The following four times she called, voice mail didn't pick up.

CHAPTER TWENTY-SEVEN

On the dais at the front of the meeting room, an assistant in khakis and a navy sweater unplugged the microphones at each seat around the environmental commission's vacated, semicircular table and stacked the metal nameplates into an uneven pile. A handful of remaining audience members, clutching folders and whispering, lingered by the left-side door where the janitor waited with his vacuum cleaner. James was speaking with the commission chairman, scrawling rapidly in his old-fashioned spiral notebook, his phone sticking out of a rear pocket in his dark-brown slacks. Finally, the chairman shook his head and picked up his briefcase. James continued writing as he walked toward Alice.

"How do you think it went?" she asked when he reached her at the rear wall. Across the room, the vacuum cleaner had already started roaring. "Do you think the commission will vote to ban plastic bags next month?"

"Who knows? I'll get a dipshit two-inch story on page twenty-six in any case. But I'll quote your Green friends, don't worry. They were very passionate in their speeches."

"They're not exactly my friends. I've heard impressive things about their organization and their work, that's partly why I came tonight."

James was moving so sluggishly, the way he shoved his notebook and a pile of handouts into his worn-out backpack. The skin near his brown eyes sagged. His pat on Alice's shoulder was as weak as the plop of a leaf.

"You look exhausted," she told him. "Do you need to go to the office now to write up your story?"

"You kidding? The bullshit *Chronicle* shuts down at six. News can wait till Friday."

"So should we get some food? It looks like the janitor wants to finish up."

"Sure. Lemme call Andrea." He fumbled his phone out of his pocket. "I should tell her I'll be later than I thought." Ambling a few steps away from Alice, James hunched his bony shoulders as he spoke into the phone, his voice too low to hear. His white shirt was coming untucked from his waistband. "Okay." He swiveled around toward Alice. "What's available at this shit-eating hour? Dunkin' Donuts? Nah"—he glanced at the phone screen—"They close at nine."

"Pacific Coast Diner?"

"The *Chronicle*'s arts reporter got food-poisoning there last week."

"Ugh."

"Pancho's Bar? It's open for another hour, and they'll give us pretzels, at least."

He walked her to her car in the parking lot, then got in his Toyota and followed her the mile or so to Pancho's.

"I called them stupid. Right to Bobby's face yesterday." Sitting across from James, Alice exhaled toward the room's bare ceiling, gray in the dim light. "I mean, I told him I was sorry the minute after I said it. I told him it was because I was so worried. I said I'd help however I could. I asked him not to tell Esme—Can you believe I did that? He didn't say anything back to me. But he never talks. He crumpled a dollar bill next to his glass and nodded and then he just left." She slapped the smooth wooden table. "I want to be a good mother, James! I want to see her, I want to talk with her, and I blew it again."

"You are a good mother, Allie."

"Yeah. So good that my own daughter has refused to have anything to do with me for six years?"

James put a hand on top of hers, where it rested flat. His fingers were warm, callused from all those past years with his ever-changing bands.

"You remember that birthday party, I think when Esme was seven?" he said quietly. "When you asked me to come and teach the kids how to play guitar?"

"You were wonderful! You were so patient, and all the girls adored you."

"And I had fun with them. But my point is, did you watch Esme there?"

Esme's seventh birthday. A flower garden of little girls in pastel party dresses and ballet-recital costumes running around the living room and kitchen in their apartment in Santa Monica. Florence had baked a chocolate cake with a vanilla cream icing, in addition to her raisin-chocolate chip cookies. The girls had hovered around James, squealing when he let them strum his guitar. He sang songs from *Beauty and the Beast* with an exaggerated French accent. At unexpected lines, he let go of the guitar and held out his hand to Esme, twirling her around.

"After we finished our last little duet, and I put down the guitar and gave her another twirl, she ran over to you and hugged you," James continued. "It was like she'd never let go of you."

Did she? Was there ever a time when Esme had wanted to hug Alice? Had loved Alice?

They'd dug fishing holes in the sand together. They'd made bowls out of clay at the pottery center. They'd curled up in bed, Esme's soft wild hair nestling against Alice's shoulder, while Alice read *A Very Young Dancer*. But that was all so long ago.

"I'm going to call Bobby back. I'm going to ask him—I'm going to demand!--He has to ask Esme again if she'll speak with me, even if she slams the door on him. It's my only shot." Alice shook her head, as though shaking would send her tears scooting back into her eyes.

Bobby could have told Esme to forget about the earrings. He could have hopped on his motorcycle without her and zoomed up north to the job that was waiting for him. Esme could have found a new boyfriend in a dozen different places. Hung out in Santa Barbara, gone to fraternity parties, sold her earrings online from wherever she desired. Enrolled in business school, as Dan was pressuring her to do.

"No," Alice said. She had to force her voice through her constricted throat. "I'm the stupid one."

"What do you mean?"

Under James's hand, her fingers curled into a fist against the table, and his hold tightened. Massaged her fist. "I thought they were trying to steal money for drugs. I thought Bobby was just a dropout and Esme was a lousy C student, that's what I really thought, in my heart. Ever since she was in junior high, I've thought she's not smart enough or not trying hard enough, and she called me on it. Over and over. She knew I was disappointed in her grades. She knew I was disappointed that she didn't watch *Meet the Press* or whatever egghead TV shows I watched. And I've been wrong about everything. They love each other, don't they? Esme wears shirts that Bobby tie-dyes. They're moving up north together. He risked getting arrested for her."

With his free hand, James took his mug and downed a long swallow of beer.

"I can't ask Bobby to push her again. What am I saying? They love each other. What do I know about love?"

"Allie."

Yanking her hand away from James, she crammed her palms and fingers flat against her face. "And if that doesn't prove I'm stupid enough? I wrote a letter to Dan, asking what's happening with her trial. Of course he didn't reply. What the hell was I thinking?" The skin of her palms and fingers was clammy against her cheeks and eyelids. "I've screwed up so badly that I'm never going to see my daughter again."

James's palm was cupped over her left hand. He was gently lowering her hand to the table, and he kept his fingers wrapped around hers. "Why'd you stay with him, all those years?"

Was anyone else in the room, other than the bartender, yards away? The air held no clinks of glasses, no waves of movement. The football game on the wide-screen overhead TV had been on mute ever since they came in. The whole room could have been listening to Alice and James, or merely empty.

The chardonnay in Alice's glass was sour. "With Dan? I ask myself that constantly. It seems ridiculous to say this, but he was funny and smart and—and less crazy at the beginning. Or the crazy stuff seemed sort of normal, if you considered it from a different viewpoint. I told you how romantic he was, proposing to me on the beach. Nice to the dogs and cats in his clinic. We both loved to go hiking. And after Esme was born, it was the usual excuse, I guess: I stayed because I thought it would be better for her to have a stable family. Honestly, I was clueless about what to expect from a boyfriend or a husband. You know I didn't date much in high school. You never asked me out." She jabbed James's arm with her elbow.

"I was an asshole. Sorry."

In the dim light, his hair seemed more gray than blond, lapping against his ears. He breathed out the faint aroma of beer toward her lips.

"It's my turn to ask a personal question." If she took a sip of the crappy chardonnay, she could pretend she was too drunk to be aware of what she was doing. "Why didn't you ever tell me what you honestly thought of Dan? Until after I was divorced?"

James half-turned his face away, as if he was staring at the silent football game on the TV.

"Because you thought you'd be butting in? That was Roz's excuse."

"Because you stayed with him." James turned back around. "So I figured you must've been happy. And like you said, Esme had a stable family. I thought he was a self-satisfied asshole, sure, but I didn't realize how lousy he treated you." James must have been holding a breath, because the one he finally released was strangely long. "If I'd known, Allie, I would've—I don't know what, but I would've done more to help you. Carried you off on a white horse. I swear."

James was looking down now, maybe at their entwined fingers. Ten fingers, middle-aged skin, the veins already showing.

The bartender called a five-minute warning.

"I need coffee," Alice declared. "Come on, I'll make us both some strong stuff at my place."

•   •   •   •   •

Her living room was dark, except for a weak yellowish glow from the tall lamp with the tasseled shade. "Umm." Alice sighed, falling onto the couch at the farthest end from the lamp and cradling a mug. "I love the smell of coffee steam. More than actually drinking coffee."

James sprawled beside her, perhaps an inch away from touching her body, his head against the orange-and-red flowered cushions, his eyes closed.

She put the mug on the floor and also leaned her head back, parallel to his.

She ought to get up, put on music. The old songs from high school she and James had loved. Joni Mitchell. Dylan. Especially the "Nashville Skyline" album. Too bad James had never recorded the song he'd written for her in twelfth grade. *Allie,* he'd named it, and he sang it to her just that once, sitting on a lawn chair by the little vegetable garden her father had planted years earlier, before he died in the freak accident clearing their roof gutters. *She gives me chills, Allie. She's all the thrills I need, Allie.* Just practicing his songwriting, he'd said. It didn't mean anything.

"How come we never dated in high school?" he murmured. As if he was reading her mind.

"You were always dating some other girl."

With his eyes still shut, James snaked his arm around her back and pulled her nearer.

She nestled her head against his shoulder.

Just sitting.

He stroked her hair.

Even though his shoulder was bony, it was comfortable, too. The soft cotton of his shirt, the dip of his armpit. The heat of his wiry arm behind her, protecting her. Some flesh and muscle to rest against, that was all.

"We're too old for this," he mumbled, as he cinched his arm tighter. He kissed the top of her head.

Had he ever kissed her hair before?

He'd already pulled off his necktie, in Pancho's, and unfastened the top two buttons of his shirt. She unbuttoned the next one.

His chest tightened.

When she wriggled her hand underneath the cotton, his torso was firm and warm and not too hairy. No middle-age flab, not even with all the beer he drank; she should reassure him. *We're not so old, James.* Gently, she pulled at a few of his chest hairs. His heart thumped fast under her fingers.

What the hell were they doing? They were friends. In high school she went to all the dances where his band Wolf played, with or without a boyfriend to dance with. They marched together at Earth Day protests. They took a lot of hikes on the beach, talking about Big Issues. About his music, and how the beat invaded his body and took over his muscles when he was playing his guitar, and it was as if the music, not his heart, was pumping his blood, even when he wasn't stoned. About the kinds of songs he wanted to write. They would be like Dylan and also like the Stones and Pete Seeger a little, but his own unique vision, his own beat. Songs you could dance to but you'd love the words, too, just as passionately. Did that sound completely asinine? Could he ever be good enough that people would want to listen to his stuff? Did Dylan have those kinds of doubts when he was unknown? And they talked about how scared Alice was, because she had no idea what job or major in college she wanted, her only hobbies were weeding her father's garden, reading historical novels, and walking on the beach, and how could she earn a living from any of those? He told her it was terrific that she was so open to life, not confining herself to a rigid career path. They hugged a lot.

He took Sally Carter to the senior prom.

Then he headed off to college at Santa Cruz, and Alice stayed behind and went to UCLA and dated a little and met Walt and Roz, who introduced her to Dan.

She couldn't remain in this position, her body twisted, her neck straining to keep her head resting on his shoulder, while she stretched her hand to fumble under his shirt.

His fingers flitted against her earlobe.

Oh damn. Oh damn. His thigh was pressed directly against hers. His khaki against her linen. His lips on her hair. He was breathing against her naked neck.

His body shifted.

His lips were at the edge of her mouth. An instant. A pause. A kiss, at the tender curve of her skin, and her mouth opened, and she moaned, and his tongue was inside. She grabbed his shoulders. He rolled halfway onto her, pushing his hips against her, pumping his hips, darting his tongue all around her mouth as if he was desperately searching through every crevice of her gums. She locked her arms tighter around him.

But where were the tingles? Where were the hot and cold chills racing each other in her veins? The clamp in her chest, the scream, the catch an instant before her body burst apart? Or even the shivers she used to feel with Dan, dammit?

She pushed at his chest. She twisted her head to the side, until his tongue slipped out of her mouth.

Before she could wriggle away, he'd fallen off of her, back to his former spot on the couch.

"I'll make more coffee," she mumbled, clambering up.

His breathing, from his seat, was loud and fast in the quiet, dimly lit room.

"Because we had too much to drink. We got silly," she added.

"Yeah."

She leaned over to switch the tall lamp to a stronger level of brightness.

"No," James said. "We weren't drunk."

Air went into Alice's mouth, and her lungs expanded, and then her lungs contracted, and other air came out.

"We weren't drunk," James repeated, spitting out a breath. He looked at the floor, not at Alice.

"It doesn't matter. It's over."

"Oh yes, it does matter. In case you forgot, I'm married, and I love my wife."

"I know. I'm sorry."

"We made a commitment to each other, Andrea and me. We made promises."

"I know."

"And one of those promises was honesty. That was what we promised to each other. Love and commitment and honesty. Yeah, we've had disagreements and shit, about my career, all that, but we always told each other the truth. And now what? Now I've almost cheated on her." James was speaking to the floor. "I've never cheated on her. Never. Never lied to her. Not in almost nineteen years of marriage." Slowly, he stood. "I gotta go."

"Are—" Alice's voice was coming out too scratchy. "Are you going to tell her about this?"

James snapped up his head so that they were face to face, and he emitted a brief, angry laugh. "Are you fucking kidding?" His lip was actually curled, and his eyes narrowed, so that he looked like a cartoon of someone being furious. "She almost left me five years ago. Had a bag half-packed in the hall. She was sure you and I'd been having an affair for years. Ironic, huh? It took everything I had, crying, pleading, God-fuck knows why she listened to me, but she stayed. She stuck with me. I don't know if she believed me, when I said there was nothing between you and me. But she stayed."

"Well, there wasn't."

"Oh?" One syllable. Two letters. He threw them at her like a flaming log.

"What?"

"Fuck there was."

"What are you talking about? We never did—anything."

"Cut the bullshit, Alice. Touchy here, flirty there, come on, who're you fucking kidding?"

"You're right. We've been kind of, a little, over-friendly. Pushing the boundaries. Maybe leading up to this. We had to, you know, get this out of our system. So, it's finished. It's okay. We go back to being friends. Your marriage doesn't change."

"No, it's not okay, Alice." His shoulders rose and fell, twice. "Now you put me in a situation where I have to lie to my wife."

"I put *you*? What's that supposed to mean, did I have a gun to your—"

"Okay, okay—"

"You're the one who kissed me!"

"Okay!"

"And if you think we were flirting all these years—"

"If?"

"Well, why did you go along with it?" She had to hold on to something. But she couldn't hold James. She grabbed an edge of the couch's armrest. "Yes, I've been squeezing your hand, and hugging you, and—and whatever you want to accuse me of. Too much of it. Pretending it didn't matter. I knew better. But you were doing all that stuff, too."

Or had he in fact done very much? Had she misread too many signs? He rubbed her back, true. A lot? He hugged her, occasionally. Often. He complained about Andrea not understanding what his music meant to him, how he shouldn't have to choose between music and a job. And had she built all those actions into more than he intended? After all, she must have totally misread Dan somewhere along the line, missing when he became more controlling than loving. She'd obviously misinterpreted whatever was going on with Esme. She'd undoubtedly misread the Cordwainer people during their meeting, too, pushing so hard against nuclear energy that they would now refuse to consider her four model investment portfolios. She'd been blindly stupid, seeing only what she hoped to see, everywhere, with everyone. How could she have ever believed that James would jeopardize his marriage by flirting with her?

But he had! James had truly hugged her. Dan had truly lied. What else could she have seen, that she didn't see?

James was taking a lot of short breaths, his fists clenched against his thighs. "Yeah, thank you for rubbing it in, I've been a piece of shit all these years, you think I don't realize that?"

"I'm not saying that."

"Yeah, sure, I kept telling myself, Alice and I are just being friends. Close friends. It's normal for close friends to hug each other. I know the difference between a friend and a wife. Yeah, yeah. Bullshit. You want me to tell you that you turn me on? You want me to tell you I've been imagining making love to you, ever since high school?"

"No! Damn it!"

Now? When it was too late?

"We both lied, Alice. We both lied to ourselves. That's the truth. But I'm the only one who's cheating on their spouse."

"You're not cheating."

"Bullshit. Technicality."

"So go back to Andrea and fix things. Tell her what happened, or don't tell her. You haven't lost your marriage."

He glanced over toward the apartment door.

"I know you feel like crap. But James, she loves you, and she'll listen to you. You know she will," Alice went on, leaning forward, clutching the armrest and rushing out her words. "You can talk to her, make things right with. Tell her you were stupid. Tell her we never had sex. Do you realize how lucky you are? You have a wife you can talk to."

"Maybe."

"I don't have that chance with Esme."

"What?"

"You don't know what it's like to have a daughter who won't speak to you."

"It's not about Esme right now!" James shouted. "Why the fuck do you—" Swiveling, he began striding away from the couch. "Forget it. I gotta go. I'm too tired for a heavy conversation."

"Wait!"

He waited.

A friendship of nearly thirty-eight years didn't simply walk out the door. Did it? Her daughter of eighteen years had, once upon a time.

Would the words that hadn't worked with Esme possibly work with James? Any words? What did Alice know about keeping the people she loved in her life?

"I'm sorry," she whispered. "No more hugging. But we can have coffee now and then, can't we? You'll tell Andrea whenever we do, no secrets."

With a sharp outtake of air, James took two more strides and grabbed the doorknob. "I think we need to stay away from each other for a while," and he wrenched open the door.

Chapter Twenty-Eight

ALICE, DAN, AND ESME

September 2004 to March 2005

Santa Monica and Santa Barbara, CA

Email addresses for staff and students at the University of California at Santa Barbara might be first and last names, or first initial plus last name, or two initials plus last name; with dots between names, without dots…And what if Esme chose, for instance, "EWilson," and the school had more than one EWilson? In that case, would Esme be EWilson1 or EWilson2 or EWilson15? She might even use a private nickname, something she and Dan had invented years ago.

So, instead of emailing, Alice could write an old-fashioned, U.S. mail letter. However, for that she'd need a street address, a dormitory name, a student ID number.

How about phoning?

This phone number is no longer accepting calls.

Alice Wilson was not included as a person authorized to have access to Esme Wilson's school or residence information, the clerk at the student records office said.

What classes was Esme Wilson taking? Was Esme Wilson, in fact, enrolled? The university records office couldn't confirm that.

How could someone contact Esme Wilson?

Only if Esme Wilson wished to be contacted.

•   •   •   •   •

All of a sudden, in early October, Google had a photo. A black-and-white photo from the UC Santa Barbara student newspaper, showing eight members of the Delta Alpha Mu sorority cleaning up debris from the beach at El Capitan. The third name in the caption was Esme Wilson.

The third girl from the right? That girl was far too tall. And the way she slouched, hunching her shoulders, Esme had never stood that way. Whereas the third one on the left side seemed closer to the appropriate height, five-foot-three-ish, and her hair had the appropriate amount of curly-waviness. (Was her hair too dark? Esme could have been experimenting with colors. Were her eyebrows thick enough? The photo was too blurry and small to tell.)

The girls were all smiling, arms wrapped around each other, wearing jeans and T-shirts with identical logos. Their sorority letters? Triangle, A, M. A girl who wasn't Esme leaned against a propped-up shovel. Another brandished a big, dark garbage bag, lumpy and bulging.

Smiling. Healthy-looking. So, Esme was happy and healthy? She had a friend that she hugged. She had time and energy for extracurricular activities like the beach cleanup. She'd joined a sorority. Sororities used to be elitist and frivolous, but this sorority was obviously doing valuable community service, which wasn't elitist. Did Esme enjoy cleaning the beach? Maybe she'd thought about Alice while she was collecting discarded plastic bags and crumpled straw wrappers from the damp autumn sand. *My mom protects the environment, too.*

Roz came straight over to the apartment, as soon as Alice called. "You see, sweetie? She's a good person. She's cleaning up the beach."

"Maybe she's doing other community service, too."

"Sure."

"I wonder why she chose a beach project. Do you think she remembered all the times we played on the Santa Monica beach, when she was little?"

"Maybe. Sure."

Alice couldn't enlarge the image on the screen any further. "Do you think she might major in environmental studies?"

"Sweetie, we probably shouldn't overanalyze this one photo."

"Okay, but it gives me an excuse to try to email her and congratulate her about it."

For a moment, Roz pressed a hand on Alice's shoulder. "Now that she's away at college, away from Dan as well as you, maybe things will loosen up, if you—you know. Let go, for a while." She smiled at the computer screen. "Don't contact her yet. Give her a little space."

But it was the perfect opportunity! If Alice got lucky and guessed the correct email address, she could say: *Hi Esme. I saw the sorority photo where you're cleaning up the beach. Congratulations.*

Was "congratulations" too patronizing?

Hey, Esme, that's really cool that you're cleaning up the beach. Was there a ton of litter?

Oh please. "Really cool." That made Alice sound as if she was pretending to be eighteen years old.

Hi Esme, I just wanted to tell you I think it's great that your sorority is cleaning up El Capitan.

Hi Esme, Thanks for making the Pacific shore a little cleaner.

After almost four months of silence, an email would have to hit precisely the perfect note. Not too lengthy. No demands, no criticisms, no pleas, no questions. Nothing to remind Esme of their last fight, or of anything Alice might have said or done that could have made Esme so angry at her. Nothing about Esme missing Florence's funeral, or Alice missing Esme's graduation. Whatever Alice had or hadn't done, Esme was carrying on her teenage snit ridiculously long, but never mind, this first outreach had to ignore all of that baggage. It should simply be a few casual words, as though it was one of a hundred emails that a normal mother and daughter would dash off to each other during a normal week. There would be time later, after they reconnected, to sit down with Esme and talk about what had happened between them.

TO: emwilson@ucsb.edu

SUBJECT: El Capitan Cleanup

Hi Esme

What a great photo of you and your sorority cleaning up El Capitan Beach. I'd love to come see the beautiful results.

Mom

Oh no. Had Alice just invited herself to visit Esme?

Too late now. The email was sent.

•   •   •   •   •

"Do you have children?" Clarke asked, forking a small hunk of his salmon filet.

The restaurant on Sunset Boulevard was so crowded that Alice and Clarke's table was smack-up against another two-seater where a man and woman were arguing about the movie *Final Cut*. The woman loved it; the man hated it. A waiter in a black shirt and tight black jeans raised his tray above their heads as he gracefully twisted right, then left, to glide between Alice and the table on her other side.

"I have a daughter. At UC Santa Barbara. I think Walt said you're an engineer with the Department of Water and Power?" Alice said quickly.

"You're close. Southern California Edison."

"So you keep my lights on? When I remember to change the light bulbs."

Clarke laughed. It was a nice laugh, neither too shrill nor not too strong. His eyes were a calm shade of hazel. "I guess I should urge our customers to turn off their lights, not on? To save the planet. Isn't that what you tell your clients?"

"We'll allow one electric outlet per house."

"Ah, Walt told me I shouldn't ask you out if I didn't either bike to work or have solar panels installed." With his glass of cabernet sauvignon, Clarke toasted Alice's chardonnay.

"And?" Alice held her glass a half-inch away from clinking his.

"I'm getting steadier on my ten-speed." Clarke grinned.

Alice clinked, laughing. "Actually, if you can get around this car-addicted city regularly on a bike, that's pretty admirable."

"I enjoy biking, but you've got a point, it's a challenge in terms of everyday life and most of the streets near me. I try to get in one long ride every week. That's my real escape."

"Where do you go?"

"Sometimes the trail along the coast, from Will Rogers down to Santa Monica Beach and Venice. You know the area?"

Santa Monica Beach. The Pier. Venice. Clarke biked. Alice hiked. Esme dug in the sand. Once upon a time. "Kind of," Alice said. "I have a thing about the waves, how they never give up. An obvious metaphor. Where else do you bike?"

"There are some paths along the L.A. River. Problem is, they stop and start a lot."

"So you have to zigzag to side streets and back?"

"I manage. My son is the real cyclist. He does these trips called century rides, where they bike for a hundred miles. Have you heard of them? My legs buckle at the idea of it."

"No. I haven't."

"He does them as fund-raisers sometimes," Clarke added.

"Fund-raisers?"

"The idea is that people sponsor the riders, a dollar a mile, for instance. For various good causes. He did one for the library a couple months ago."

"He sounds, um, like a great kid."

"He is. He's a sophomore at UCLA. Majoring in biology." Smiling, Clarke leaned into his elbows, which were crossed on the table. "How about your daughter. What's she studying at Santa Barbara?"

She couldn't do this. She couldn't go out to dinner and meet new people and chit-chat about her daughter, no matter how interesting they were, or how nicely they laughed. Walt and Roz had meant well, setting up this date with their neighbor, but it was impossible.

"She belongs to a sorority. Delta Alpha Mu."

"No kidding? What kind of sorority is that? Is it more academically oriented, or focusing on social services kinds of projects? Or purely social?" Clarke laughed.

"Um. I—They clean up the beach."

"So she takes after you. An environmental crusader. Does she live in the sorority house?"

The—?

Of course! A sorority would have a building, a house, a location with an address that would be posted on the Internet, where it held keg parties with other sororities and fraternities. An address that a mother could write to.

If the daughter would open an envelope with her mother's name on the return address.

But also an address a mother could visit.

·   ·   ·   ·   ·

emwilson@ucsb had replied.

Oh God. Oh God.

Dear Alice Wilson,

Did you send me this email by mistake? I don't know anything about a cleanup at the beach, and I don't belong to a sorority. But good luck in your efforts.

Ellen Wilson

·   ·   ·   ·   ·

On a Thursday afternoon, Esme would most likely be in class, if Alice happened to drop by the Delta Alpha Mu sorority house.

It was a two-story, pale-pink stucco building surrounded by a matching stucco wall half as tall, on the corner of a busy boulevard a few blocks from the university. On the side of the building that faced the boulevard, bushes and thick clusters of pink, coral, and purple flowers flanked a dark-green set of double doors, shiny with fresh paint. On the second floor, every window was filled by Venetian blinds from sill to top, like a woman who'd buttoned her blouse up to her chin. The building displayed no big Greek letters, no indication that this was anything other than a middle-class house.

This was what would greet Esme, every time she came to this building.

From the green door, a flagstone path curved leftward around the far side of the building, away from the street. At that point the lush garden ended, leaving a few short bushes. Halfway down that side of the building was a second, narrower green door. Esme could walk out that door, at that exact moment.

Of course the door handle was locked. Of course the windows laid out across the stucco wall were Venetianed tight. No way to get in or look in.

Except that one second-floor window above the door was open to the world. No blinds, no curtains, no shutters. Pure, transparent glass.

It was too high above ground level to see inside. Alice jumped. Crouching for more liftoff, she jumped again, but her sightline remained below the windowsill. If only she had a ladder, or a tree, even a table to climb on, anything to gain a couple more feet of altitude.

Spying through a window? What was she thinking? She'd come here to get a glimpse at the sorority house from the outside, a taste of Esme's world, that was all. What if someone caught her climbing a ladder? Someone looking out a window in the sorority? someone passing by on the sidewalk?

But inside that building were rooms where Esme sat, studied, ate meals, planned beach cleanups with her sorority colleagues. Maybe she slept in one of those rooms. Was the furniture modern or old? Did the rooms have twin beds, or were they singles? This bare window might be the only view into that life.

Around the corner of the building, the sorority's small rear yard was empty except for a set of palm stalks embedded in a huge, round, concrete planter, and then the flagstone path ended at a wall.

The planter was, perhaps, as tall as the glass coffee table in the Seshat waiting area. That might give Alice sixteen or eighteen inches of elevation, if she could drag it around the corner to the naked window and balance herself on the rim. Too bad she was wearing ankle boots instead of her black Jimmy Choo stilettos. The stilettos' heels would have added another three and a half inches.

Alice gripped the rim and tugged backwards. The planter didn't move. She leaned over, she bent her knees, she curled her fingers around the rim, she poured every muscle's worth of power into her fingers and tugged—It didn't budge.

She would have to reduce the weight of the planter. Cupping her hands, she dug in and scooped a handful of dirt from around the palm stalks, then tossed the scoop into the narrow strip of lawn next to her. And another. And again. The planter remained thick with the stuff. Scoop after scoop, she piled dirt in pyramids that slid onto the vivid green grass like dry sand on the beach. Dirt splattered all over her black sweater, her jeans, her Biviel boots and into her mouth. She spat. The level of dirt in the planter was definitely sinking now, two-thirds full, half-full, and she was scooping and scooping, until the poor palm stalks were tilting steeply, their fronds drooping like empty green gloves, without enough dirt to support them. Georgia Wilson would be appalled. Well, she could restore the dirt later. The main thing was that the monstrosity might finally be light enough to move. She grabbed the rim again. She tugged. She wiggled the box from left to right. Scratching sharply on the concrete path, the planter shifted forward a toe's worth.

This was nonsense. It could take her an hour to drag the stupid thing over to the window.

But it was working. Alice wiggle-tugged the planter left and right and toward her, took a step back, and yanked again. The planter creaked forward. Step and tug. Step and drag. Inch by inch. Her hands stung in a half-dozen places where they'd scraped against the rough concrete. She was inhaling dirt, and every muscle in her arms screamed. Now around the corner. Step and drag. She panted, pulling in air with short, fast breaths. A few steps further until the window.

"Hello?" a girl's voice queried.

Oh no. Oh no.

But it wasn't Esme. It was a tall teenage girl with two thick braids and a coal-gray puffy vest, shutting the narrow green door behind her. "What're you doing?" The voice was short of hostile.

Alice stood on the path, crumbs of dirt sticking to her jeans and her sweater, her hair tangled and sweaty, her legs wavering, clutching the rim of a humongous concrete planter with a bunch of drooping palm stalks.

"My daughter… I need to bring her…"

"You're bringing her that plant-thing?"

"No, no. No. I'll just see if she's in."

"Who's your daughter?"

Alice rubbed her gritty palms against her jeans. Pinpoints of blood dotted a few of the scratches. "Esme Wilson."

No sounds came from inside the house. No one opened a window to peer out and ask what was happening down there by the rear door; no one else popped up on the path in front of them.

"Oh, Esme. But why're you moving that plant-thing?" the girl asked.

"Yes. The plant. Because it, uh, needs water. Do you know Esme?"

The girl looked at the planter, then at Alice, then shifted a half-turn to survey around the yard. The traffic light must have changed on the boulevard beyond the stucco wall, because the rumble of car engines was suddenly louder.

"Well," the girl said, "everyone's supposed to go in through the front. I'll show you."

Abandoning the planter, Alice and the girl walked side by side along the flagstone path to the front of the house. As they walked, Alice alternately slapped her dirty, scraped palms against her thighs, and tried to dig out the dirt caked under her nails. At the shiny green double-doors, she hastily swiped at the dust on her cheeks.

"Mrs. Hanson?" the girl spoke into the intercom beside the door, her tone neither friendly nor harsh. "Esme Wilson's mom is here?"

The door buzzed open.

•   •   •   •   •

It opened into a small foyer, the perfect size for a set of parents to hug their daughter goodbye. A purple-and-green coleus plant hung from the ceiling, and a huge, framed display of the Delta Alpha Mu letters in royal blue all-but-filled one shockingly white wall. Water was running directly above, presumably from a sorority sister taking a shower.

That could be Esme, in the shower. Washing her hair with shampoo that smelled of apricot.

A large woman in crisply ironed jeans, red pumps, and a long-sleeved beige blouse was already striding down an empty hallway toward the foyer. She wore lipstick that matched her shoes and had short, curly brown hair, interrupted with occasional strands of gray. Mrs. Hanson, presumably. Alice had about three seconds before this Mrs. Hanson-woman would be in front of her, inquiring as to how could she help Alice? And Alice would answer…?

Alice was here to bring Esme a big, heavy planter with dead palm leaves?

Alice was here because she and Esme had made plans to meet for lunch today—Yes, that was the explanation! A lovely mother-daughter lunch. Wasn't today Thursday? Oh, it was Wednesday? How silly of her.

Alice was here because, after nearly a full year of phone messages to Dan's house during school breaks that stayed glued in voicemail, and emails to maybe-possible addresses for EWilson that bounced back, and letters to this very sorority that apparently fell into a black hole, a one-second glimpse of this sorority house might be the sole way she could learn even the smallest bit about her daughter's life. Was there any way she could tell this woman in red pumps and lipstick that truth?

Why hadn't she prepared a script in case something like this happened?

"I'm Irene Hanson, the housemother for the girls here. How can I help you?" The woman's voice was jarringly high-pitched.

"I'm Alice Wilson. Esme Wilson's mother? She's a new member, I guess."

"Esme! Oh yes, what a sweet girl." Although Mrs. Hanson shook the hand that Alice offered, she let go too soon, leaving Alice's dirty fingers fluttering. "Did you say that you're Esme's mother?"

"Yes."

Mrs. Hanson clasped her hands in front of her stomach. "I beg your pardon, but, ah, I've met Esme's parents several times."

Oh.

Alice moved her lips into a smile. "You've probably met Esme's stepmother, Penelope Wilson. My ex-husband's wife. With their two children? A boy and a girl?"

"Certainly."

"So, I'm her real mother."

They smiled at each other.

"What can I do for you, Mrs. Wilson?" Smiling.

Alice clasped her own hands, grinding the dirt into her palms.

She'd already given Mrs. Hanson too many reasons to be suspicious, what with her gritty fingers and sweaty face, the dirt clinging to her hair and clothing, and possibly trying to impersonate the woman Mrs. Hanson believed was actually Esme's mother. The housemother's body was poised, as if it was a rubber band that would spring loose in exactly one minute. The fake lunch-date excuse was not going to work. It would have to be the straight truth.

"This will no doubt sound a little odd. Esme and I are somewhat, um, estranged, which is why you haven't met me before, and I'm sure you can appreciate how painful that is. For a mother. Of course I don't want to put you in an uncomfortable situation, in any way."

Mrs. Hanson's head was tilted slightly to the left, as she gazed at Alice.

. "I'm just so curious about this sorority. Which is obviously an important part of Esme's life." Alice's voice had stayed calm, thankfully. Not whining or squeaky or too fast. "How many members are there?"

"We have thirty-six girls at the moment."

"Do they all live in this building?"

"My goodness, no. We can only fit twelve residents."

"Is Esme one of them? The girls who live here?"

"I'm not really at liberty to discuss our individual girls."

"I understand." So, what could Alice ask? Blasé generalities? "In general, what sorts of activities do you do, as a sorority? I know that Esme participated in the cleanup on the beach."

"Our girls have many different interests, as you might expect. Each fall, they vote on a special project for the year, so El Capitan is our current project. Have you been to the beach there? It's becoming quite beautiful."

"And are there other projects that you do?"

"Certainly. I think, as a sorority, we're particularly respected for our volunteer work with our local women's shelter here in Santa Barbara."

"A women's shelter. That sounds so, um, important. Helpful." Alice had to keep smiling. Smiling was a signal to Mrs. Hanson that Alice was a friend, no danger, no harm intended, even if she was shedding dirt on the sorority's clean floor with every twitch, even if Esme had inexplicably never mentioned her existence. "Is Esme very active in your work at the shelter?"

"As I said, I can't talk about individual girls."

"Of course. I understand. But can you tell me if Esme volunteers a lot at the shelter? Or on environmental projects?"

"As I said, I can't discuss our individual girls." Mrs. Hanson's voice still showed no emotion. She could have been an elevator recording.

"I'm her mother!"

Mrs. Hanson smiled.

The water upstairs was no longer running. There were a couple of footsteps, a door shutting. The single ring of a phone. Silence.

That was it? Was Alice supposed to leave now? To be so close to Esme, and just quit? Wasn't there any crumb that Mrs. Hanson could offer her? The sorority's weekly schedule. Its social calendar. Could Alice see Esme's room? The housemother's name was "Mrs." Hanson, after all, and thus she must be married or, even better, divorced. Old enough, with her spots of gray hair, to have a college-age daughter herself. How much would Mrs. Hanson empathize, and how much could Alice ask, before Mrs. Hanson kicked her out?

Alice hitched the strap of her leather bag higher on her left shoulder. "Would it be possible for me to leave a little note for her? I'm just, you know, trying every method of communication I can think of. After this, I guess my next step would be carrier pigeon."

Maybe Mrs. Hanson in fact had a daughter. Or maybe it was simply that the house rules allowed visitors to leave notes. "You may sit in the library to write," she said.

Despite the name, the room that Mrs. Hanson took Alice to held only a few books scattered on shelves built deep into a long white wall. From a drawer beneath one of the shelves, Mrs. Hanson retrieved a small pad of unlined paper, a pen, and a notecard-size envelope, placing them on a round table beside a green-and-yellow striped armchair. "I'll be in my office when you're finished. It's the second room on the left." A few steps from the table, the housemother stopped. "Esme's a sweet girl," she repeated. "She's so reliable about helping tidy up in the kitchen. She remembers where to put everything."

Alice should have asked Mrs. Hanson if she could use the bathroom to wash her hands. It would be awful if she smeared blood or dirt on this letter, the one letter from Alice that Esme was certain to receive. Alice spat into her palms and rubbed them together, the best she could do.

Nearly a year of straining to guess what words would reach her own daughter, and she still didn't know what to say, because she didn't know what Esme cared about, other than cleaning a beach with friends. And tidying up the sorority kitchen. Should the words be matter-of-fact? Nostalgic? Ask about Esme's life? Tell about Alice's?

The table was too low for the chair, probably meant originally for holding teacups. Scooting to the edge of the slippery seat cushion, Alice bent over the table and picked up the pen. It produced delicate blue lines, which weaved across the bare white paper.

What a lovely sorority house

I hope you're enjoying

I was so impressed to read about your work cleaning on the beach

I miss you. Could we have lunch sometime?

What did I do wrong

On the other hand, did it really matter what Alice wrote? One glance at the signature, and Esme would either read the note or throw it in the trash.

Dear Esme, This is a lovely sorority house, and it looks like you all do great community projects here. I miss you

CHAPTER TWENTY-NINE

ALICE, DAN, AND ESME

February 2007
Santa Barbara, CA

Walt helped her upload photos to her pristine Facebook page. She gathered snapshots of a couple of the pottery bowls Esme had made, Esme's room with a tip of the Titanic poster showing at one side, generic pictures of kids playing on the Santa Monica beach, and then Roz and James sent her more. Jenny plaiting Esme's hair in French braids. Jenny and Sharon posing and making faces in front of Walt while he painted at his brand-new easel. Roz with all three girls, cutting a long stretch of shiny purple fabric into … something. Doll clothes? James showing a three- or four-year-old Esme how to pluck the strings on his guitar.

What did people put on their Facebook pages? It was so new. Sure, college students had been doing stuff on it for a few years, but adults hadn't been allowed to become members until last fall, and so far almost no one older than thirty used it. Roz didn't, Walt didn't, James did it only because the online visibility might help him get a job at the *LA Times* or another big paper. Still, they all insisted it was the best method for communicating with a college student. Anyway, nothing else had worked for Alice in the nearly three years since Esme had graduated from high school—not letters addressed to the sorority, not random email names, not even swallowing her pride and writing to Esme at Dan's house during school breaks. Might as well try this as much as anything else.

"Should I include pictures of me and Esme when she was little, to remind her of the fun times we had?" Alice asked Roz. "Or more photos of my current life, to make me seem interesting? There's a sweet one of us making a tower out of her stuffed animals."

Roz asked Jenny and Sharon.

"Way too embarrassing," Jenny replied immediately.

"It would be okay if Esme was really little," Sharon said. "Like two years old?"

"If she's genuinely cute."

Photos from the Internet that would evoke happy memories for Esme, Walt suggested. A zoo. Tall forests. The Madonna Inn in San Luis Obispo, where Alice and Esme had their fancy lunch together. Imelda Marcos's roomful of shoes? Although Esme had probably never heard the name Imelda Marcos, she might smile if it reminded her of going shoe-shopping together. No pictures of ballet performances or school graduation ceremonies, obviously. Happy memories only.

Next, Alice's Facebook status: Single. Divorced. Schools: UCLA, BA in environmental studies. What did Alice "like"? Of course she loved Esme, but that didn't count for Facebook. She liked the Wildlife Conservation Society. She liked Greenpeace. She liked UC Santa Barbara. (Not particularly. More accurately, she neither liked nor disliked it.) She liked Joni Mitchell and the Village People and Springsteen and Dylan. She liked solid, serious novels about American history, from almost any era—*Beloved, The Age of Innocence, Ragtime*—and yeah, she also liked Stephen King, for fun. She liked good hiking boots, and she particularly liked the state park in Humboldt County. She would like to climb the Inca Trail up to Machu Picchu and also see the barrier reef in Australia. Did would-like-to's count?

Late on Saturday, Jenny and Sharon gave her page a final check. "You need an update," Jenny advised. "Something exciting you're doing."

"I'll Friend you," Sharon promised.

Finally. Alice had an official Facebook personality. She went to "Find friends." She typed "Esme Wilson."

And—oh God—It was like—It was a treasure trove. Like reading Esme's mind. Like being right next to her! It was Esme at last, after all this time, the real Esme, the actual living Esme of today, who was almost twenty and a half and went to UC Santa Barbara. She liked Delta Alpha Mu. She liked Calabasas High School. She liked shopping at Zara and H&M. She liked a restaurant in Santa Barbara called The Organic Onion and a store called Clothing Etc. and jewelry made by Princess Philippa that she found on Etsy. (Nothing in Santa Monica, where she'd lived with Alice for eleven years?) She liked the ASPCA; well, yes, because of Dan and his clinic. Maybe also a little because of Alice's spotted owls? She liked *Vogue* and *Elle* magazines, and Johnny Depp and Leonardo DiCaprio (sure, the Titanic poster) and Shakira and Christina Aguilera. (The silly bubblegum singer that all the teenagers adored? Honestly?)

(Didn't Esme like any books? Never mind. No nagging.)

She liked the movie *The Da Vinci Code*. So did Alice!

And the photos. There she was. Her dark brown eyes. Her long, wavy hair; she hadn't dyed it oddball colors. The same beautiful eyes and hair and thick eyebrows and small chin as the messy-haired kindergarten Esme who'd practiced her ballet steps with her stuffed animals lined up alongside her and the teenage Esme that Alice had last seen three years ago. The face might be a bit thinner than it used to be, but it was hard to tell. What a big, wonderful, full-mouthed smile she had! She seemed to be doing various sorts of arts and crafts in several of the pictures. Five or six young women, including Esme, were bent over a wooden table on a lawn, surrounded by paint cans and strips of canvas and jars with brushes sticking out of them. Another cluster of shots was apparently from a bake sale or picnic, possibly a fund-raiser for one of the sorority's projects, with kids holding up paper plates full of cake and cookies. Then there were a couple of images of long earrings laid out on a table, for some reason. Three pictures with Dan and a tiny woman with a blonde shag haircut who must have been Penelope, and a little boy and girl—Graydon and Hadley, their kids—everyone wearing swimsuits, hanging out at a lake. In one of the photos, the boy was pitching a red Frisbee. A perfect family vacation… Well, yeah, that was what people posted on Facebook. Vacations. Family. Their moms.

What mattered was that Esme was having a good life! These pictures, the beach cleanup on Google, friends and outdoor activities and smiles as wide as the ocean. How about the guy Esme was pretending to throw a whole pie at? Was that her boyfriend? What was his name? He looked like a younger, brunette version of James, lanky and tall, hair tumbling over his ears, a touch of fashionable stubble, a green T-shirt. What was the drawing on the shirt? A tiger? A flag? A fraternity logo? He was laughing along with Esme. Glad to be with her. Like everyone in all the pictures. They were young and healthy, hugging in groups, mugging for the camera, painting on the wooden table, eating cookies, sitting cross-legged on grass, waving, holding hands.

Esme's face. Laughing straight at Alice. Happy.

But the images were getting too blurred, no matter how often Alice wiped her eyes. She would have to take a break and return tomorrow. And the day after. Every day, she could explore more pieces of Esme's Facebook self. Every day, she would see Esme.

She sent a Friend request.

Would Esme reply?

"I found her!" she told Roz.

•   •   •   •   •

"Can you come on a class trip with me, Mom?" Esme asked on the phone. "We're going to see *Annie* at the L.A. Music Center."

Esme wanted Alice to come on a class trip? Esme had called her.

"Yes! Yes! I'd love to come."

"It's tomorrow. We have to be there at eight."

"Tomorrow? That's kind of short—" No! No complaining, not when Esme was actually reaching out. "Sure," Alice corrected herself. "Where should I meet you?"

"So, we're going to the Northridge Mall first." Esme's voice sounded a little nervous. Of course it would be. They hadn't spoken in so long. Maybe she was worried that Alice would be angry at her. Never!

"And can you bring baking soda and vinegar?" Esme went on. "We're doing a science experiment."

"At the Music Center?"

"Yeah. It's for Graydon."

Graydon? Oh, sure, that was Esme's younger brother, Dan and Penelope's son. "Is Graydon coming, too?" Alice asked. That would be awkward.

"His whole class."

"Your class and Graydon's class? Both of them?" But Esme was in college. Did college classes do field trips? With parent chaperones?

"And you need to bake a pie," Esme added.

"A pie."

"Raisin-chocolate-chip pie. For the bake sale."

Esme had to know that Alice had never baked a pie in her life.

"Everyone's mom is baking a pie."

"I—"

"Look, do you want to come or not?"

"Yes! Of course I do."

"Never mind. The bus is leaving."

"No! I want to come! Don't go—" Alice jerked upright. She grabbed for the phone. But it wasn't against her ear anymore. Or fallen on the bed. It was sitting on her night table, as always. Silent. The room was dark, it was two in the morning, and there had never been a call from Esme.

•   •   •   •   •

What the heck, as long as Alice was awake, why not check Esme's Facebook page for a couple of minutes? Esme hadn't yet replied to Alice's Friend request from yesterday, but that wasn't surprising. The request must have been a shock to Esme. She would need time to think about it.

Esme's page had been wiped almost blank.

It showed a formal eleventh-grade photo from her school yearbook. A picture of puppies. She still liked Calabasas High School and UC Santa Barbara.

If Alice clicked on any topic—"photos," "friends," "more," "about" —the identical message appeared: *To see what he shares with friends, send him a friend request.*

•   •   •   •   •

"Esme raised her privacy setting," James said. Sitting at Alice's desk, four impossible hours later, he hit a few more keys on her laptop. "She's only making her posts visible to people she Friends."

"But there was a lot more yesterday. All kinds of pictures," Alice protested.

"She switched it fast. And raised it really high."

"Why would she do that?"

"She doesn't want strangers to see anything about her."

"I'm not a—"

James laid his hand on hers.

Alice stared over his shoulder at the useless screen. "Aren't there all kinds of codes, to retrieve things? Isn't that how the FBI does it, and they find, you know, evidence?"

"I'm not the FBI, Allie."

"Or if I tried from your computer?"

"The same thing would happen."

"So the only way for me to … is if she lets me Friend her."

"Pretty much. Yeah."

"I could try Friending again."

"You could. But I'd wait on that." James clicked over to her photos folder. "I don't suppose you took a screen shot of some of her pages yesterday? Or a printout?"

"I didn't even take notes with pen and paper, James! I thought I'd be able to see her page any time I wanted. Forever."

•   •   •   •   •

She held out for a week before she tried again.

Chapter Thirty

Fred hadn't shut the blinds in the wide window across from his desk as tightly as usual. The horizontal shadow lines from the slats flickered over his face as the blinds swayed gently, like the swing set in Roz's yard before it broke, and the sunlight shifted in and out. Light/dark. Clear/shadowed. Readable/opaque. He was sitting behind his steel desk, his arms crossed on the desktop. Not fiddling with his tie or a pen. An abstract-style painting, bright splotches of primary red, blue, yellow, and green in a frame that matched the desk, was propped on the carpet, against the bare wall to his left.

"The Cordwainers hired Bank of California," he said, his face aimed at the window behind Alice, his voice oddly businesslike. Toneless.

So that was that.

Should she bother asking why, or what the Cordwainers had said? They wouldn't have said anything, except platitudes and appreciation for Seshat's hard work. Alice's four model portfolios. With nuclear energy included. She ought to defend herself, a little.

"We knew we were at a major disadvantage, going against a bank that's far larger—"

"We do it all the time. Successfully," Fred interrupted, his voice tone unchanged. "As you like to point out, we have the advantage of longer experience in ESG investing."

His face was shadowed for a moment, as the blinds moved, and then a touch of sunlight briefly flickered on him. His pink mouth was a straight line above his goatee. His eyes were still aimed in the indiscernible distance.

He wasn't going to explain more, was he? Not yet.

She went on: "I realize that I shouldn't have disagreed with the Cordwainer people so much in our meeting. But you saw my proposal, Fred. You know I had four strong, solid strategies that did specifically what they asked for."

He wouldn't fire her, after twenty-seven years, for losing one client. Deals and bids fell through all the time in the financial world. Even if the Cordwainers would have been the biggest single investment in any of Alice's green portfolios, with a six-figure management fee, Fred wouldn't fire her. She didn't always screw up. Look at how she'd persuaded the New York pension officials regarding the trees in Humboldt County, all those years ago!

However, her bonus would be slashed, that was all but guaranteed. The air around her would be tense. No more eye-rolling jokes from Fred about green money and organic bakeries. And forget about taking a day off to go to Esme's trial—which could be happening this week, next week. All the muffins in the world from MultiGrainery couldn't conciliate Fred, or anyone else at Seshat, for that matter. Word was probably circulating in the office already: *Alice lost a big client. Alice's big mouth lost a big client.*

At last, Fred moved his hands. Negligibly. With his right middle fingernail, he snapped a ballpoint pen forward until it hit the edge of his computer keyboard. "So what's your plan?" Finally facing her.

What did that mean? Her career plan? Was she supposed to offer her resignation? "My plan?"

"Seshat's years of experience in ESG investing. How do you plan to leverage that next?"

Of course! The Cordwainers weren't the only investors in the world who wanted an environmental guru these days. And Seshat wasn't the only firm that might be interested in having a guru on staff.

Alice didn't need a written script for this. All she needed was enough breath. "A family office in San Francisco contacted me, and we're supposed to follow up on Thursday. It's not as big as the Cordwainers, but the younger generation is quite gung ho on environmental issues. So they'd be allocating a relatively large percentage of their assets to the ESG space. Also, I'm aiming to put together a proposal for a panel at the II conference on sustainable investing next winter in Florida. I'll be attending the conference in any case, but you know that the way to really have visibility is to be on a panel."

Fred rolled his pen back toward himself. "How big is that family office?"

"I'm not definite about the full portfolio size, but they're saying ten to fifteen percent in ESG. That's one of the things I'm hoping to pin down on Thursday."

"And the kids you're talking to, they have investment authority? Or do they have to get approval from Mommy and Daddy?"

"For up to ten percent, yes, they do." Breathing was becoming easier.

"All right. Keep me posted. And send me a writeup about your panel idea." Now Fred spun the pen around, flat, in a circle. "And this time, listen to what the clients want, huh? They call the shots."

•   •   •   •   •

The twilight sky outside Alice's living room window was fading from pale yellow and orange, to gray, over the apartment rooftops, the palm trees, and her tiny, tiny edge of the Pacific. If she got into a boat and kept going out in that ocean, sooner or later she would reach Bali. She could take severance pay from Seshat, whether she was being fired or not, and go clean up the Bali beach, as she and Dan had never gotten around to doing. Live on fresh fish and chardonnay. Throw out all her shoes, even her Jimmy Choo heels. Have a truly natural, eco-lifestyle. Forget about clawing to sign new clients. Forget about Esme's trial; well, fat chance of forgetting that.

Her phone trilled.

She would have no cell service out on Bali, would she?

So what? Who would ever call her? Not James. He wanted to "stay away from each other for a while," and he was right. Obviously, not Esme. Ever. A potential client? Fat chance of that, too.

"Esme wanted me to tell you," Bobby began in his deepish voice at the other end of the line, pleasantly but unemotionally, as though they'd just spoken yesterday instead of a week ago, "that she's willing to see you."

The seconds hand on the round white kitchen clock clacked steadily as it jumped from one dot to another. Far away outside her window, the Pacific waves were flowing on toward Bali.

"A week from today," Bobby continued. "From six to seven p.m., on the beach, at the bottom of the pedestrian bridge from Arizona Boulevard. At the staircase."

Esme.

The pedestrian bridge to the beach.

"Do you know the place she means?" Bobby added.

Esme was going to talk to her. She was going to see Esme. On the beach. The route they used to stroll to the beach together. "Yes."

"Okay. So you're set."

"No! I mean—Don't hang up!"

Why? Why was Esme suddenly saying yes? After Alice had called her and Bobby stupid, on top of whatever other reasons Esme had for refusing contact for six years. Unless Alice had misunderstood what Bobby was saying. "Six o'clock?" she stammered.

"Yeah. From six to seven."

One hour.

Face to face. Hugging?

"Will I recognize her?"

A different kind of noise came from Bobby's side of the conversation, verging on a laugh. "Yeah, I think you will. I can ask her to wear one of my tie-dyed shirts."

Esme would be the girl with wild brown hair and a tie-dyed T-shirt and a little tattoo of a dog on her wrist.

"Is—Can I—Can you give me her phone number? If it's changed. Or email?"

Bobby's voice was still calm and kind. "No."

No?

"She said you can just contact me," he went on, "if you need to cancel or anything."

As if Alice would ever cancel!

Was Esme in jail? And that was why she couldn't be reached by phone or email? Yet she would be released in time to meet with Alice next week? It was possible. The trial should have started last month. No, that wasn't the reason for the lack of contact!

"Why is she… talking to me?"

The phone didn't answer.

"Is there anything else you can tell me?"

"She'll see you next week," Bobby said.

How could Alice say everything she needed to say, in one mere hour? What would Esme be willing to hear? Or answer?

Seven days away.

CHAPTER THIRTY-ONE

Roz was panting heavily. She draped her arm over the handlebar of a stationary bike, her sweaty red hair clinging to her forehead, her cheeks, her neck, and the shoulders of her baggy T-shirt, which had a sketch of a lion from the L.A. Zoo. Alice bent forward to take deep breaths.

A cluster of young women who could have been Esme's age—their sleek blonde hair bolted in taut ponytails, their thighs tucked firmly into their Spandex shorts—pushed past Alice and Roz toward the door leading out from the gym.

"Okay," Roz said finally, with a brief smile in Alice's direction. "The first time is always the hardest. Right?"

"Yeah." Alice let out another breath.

"I just have to get used to the routine. Lifting ten pounds is a lot heavier than I realized."

"I'm wiped, too. Do you want to rest a little more?"

"No, I'm good now. I think. I really appreciate that you came with me."

"That's what friends are for."

"I would've chickened out, without you."

Two more Esme-age classmates, in bright tank tops, Spandex, and high-top Converse sneakers, squeezed by, clutching water bottles.

"I need to ignore how gorgeous everyone else is," Roz continued, her voice growing more cheerful. "If I keep coming here and working out, twice a week, someday I'll look like them." She took a few steps away from the bike. "Well, not totally like them. Let's go."

"You'd have to be thirty years younger, I think."

"And thirty pounds skinnier. But if I don't do this now…"

As soon as they were outside on the sidewalk, Roz leaned against the gym's stucco wall, lowered her head, and emitted one heavy breath after another. Pulling off her glasses, she wiped the lenses and rims on the hem of her T-shirt.

The walkway was bare, without even a rusty chair to bring over for Roz to collapse into. Nothing a friend could do, except maybe stroke Roz's sticky hair. "Should we get some coffee?" Alice asked.

"Or." Roz panted. "A doughnut?"

"If you really want."

"I shouldn't."

The teacher was locking the gym door. As trim and blonde as the students who'd preceded her, she paused near Roz and Alice. "Are you ladies all right?"

"Yeah. We're good." Roz smiled again.

"Good. See you on Wednesday!"

Alice stuck out her tongue, behind the teacher's departing back.

"Alice!" Roz giggled feebly.

Of course they ought to head home now. Roz was so obviously exhausted from her forty minutes of impossible weightlifting and treadmill-striding. They could talk another day. But the words leaped out of Alice's mouth: "I'm going to see Esme."

"What?"

"Next week. For one hour. Bobby called me yesterday."

"Esme wants to see you?"

"I guess so."

Suddenly, Roz was laughing and hugging Alice, squeezing Alice with strength she sure hadn't had a minute ago. "I'm so happy for you!"

"Don't make too much of it, please. I could blow it. She could cancel."

Roz was going overboard with her celebration. Still, her arms felt so steady and loving. Her hair smelled only faintly of dried sweat.

"You're going to see Esme!" Roz actually shouted. "Yay!"

"It's the first time in six years. What do I talk about? What do I say to her?"

"You have to hug her."

"How can I do that? What if she rejects me?"

"She won't reject you. She loves you."

"She's already rejected me."

"You're her mother. She won't reject you."

"You don't get it, you and your goddam social work and baby clothes and God!" Alice snapped. "This is my one chance, and I'm terrified!"

Roz stepped away.

In the fading summer daylight, she almost melted into the beige wall, her hair limp, her arms dangling at her sides, her T-shirt hanging listlessly over a pair of Walt's washed-out blue basketball shorts. Her smile was gone. The gym's windows were dark, although a few figures moved around inside the nail salon two doors away.

Somewhere in the gray parking lot behind Alice, a car roared to life.

From a bulky canvas bag slung over her shoulder, Roz pulled out a water bottle, decorated with a sketch of a green-and-red Christmas tree. Her face was trained on the bottle as she unscrewed the top and took a short drink. "I need to go home."

"Okay."

Roz screwed the cap back on, returned the bottle to her bag, and pulled out her car keys. For a moment, she shifted the keys in her hand. Finally, she looked straight at Alice. Her voice was tired, of course. "There's no reason to yell at me." She turned away.

"I'm not yelling."

But Roz was right.

"I'm sorry," Alice said. "I shouldn't have yelled at you. You were trying to help, the way you always are."

"Yeah. Well. My help is never what you want." Roz started trudging toward the mostly empty parking rows.

"You did great tonight. In class," Alice called after her.

This was all wrong. This wasn't the way to leave things. This was the same point where James had walked out the door of Alice's apartment, wasn't it? And where Esme had walked out, on the Saturday that she and Courtney came to visit Alice in Santa Monica back in high school.

"Please," Alice called, louder. She couldn't shout across the whole damn parking lot. In her black-and-white Nikes, which thankfully she was wearing sneakers and not heels, she ran the few paces after Roz, until she was at Roz's side. "I appreciate that you want to help."

No, those were still the wrong words. Too bland, too Hallmark Card. The two of them were striding steadily toward Roz's green Volvo, alone in its aisle. A baby carrier was already strapped into the back seat, awaiting the grandchild who wasn't due until November. From a few parking spots away, Roz hit the beeper to unlock the door.

"I seem to mess up with everyone who matters to me." Alice kept talking to Roz's silence. "Even people who don't matter all that much, like my clients. I don't want to hurt you, or Esme, or Bobby, or James, but I don't seem to know how not to do it. Please—Please don't walk out on me, too."

They went another few steps.

"I need a doughnut," Roz said.

•   •   •   •   •

"Do you have a pen?"

In response, Roz pulled a blue Bic pen, missing its cover, out of her canvas bag and handed it to Alice on the other side of their booth in the coffee shop. A short line had been gouged diagonally across the middle of the Formica tabletop, already blackened with a few years' worth of food, as if a customer had started carving his name while he waited for his meal. "Do you honestly want my advice?" Roz asked. "Or only my face as an audience, while you vent?"

"Your advice. And your pen."

"Then listen to me. You can't script out every conversation in your life in advance. You know that, don't you?"

With Roz's pen, Alice wrote a capital E on her notepad. To see if the pen worked. "If I don't have a script, I'll say something I shouldn't. Like calling Bobby stupid."

"You're always telling me how you forget to follow your script, anyway."

"Sometimes."

"Alice, you've got to let the conversation go where it wants to go. Where Esme wants it to go."

"Just help me with a few sentences, to get me started, okay? This is too important to mess up. And I can't simply stare at her, waiting for her to begin. We could spend the whole hour staring at each other."

"You won't."

"You can't be sure of that."

Roz raised her eyebrows. Unlike her hair, they had no strands of gray among the red. "Do you want to argue with everything I say?"

The air conditioning in the coffee shop was blasting too strong. Instead of sweat, goose bumps were dotting Alice's neck.

"What if I started by saying happy birthday and asking how she celebrated?"

"Hmm. Why start that way?"

"Why not? It's light-hearted. And it's an obvious opening. We both know that she just had her birthday. But the birthday already happened, so it's not as though I'm inviting myself to her party."

Roz put a hunk of chocolate doughnut in her mouth. "I guess that makes sense."

"And then, whatever she answers, I'll say, 'Oh wow, that must have been fun!' "

"That doesn't sound at all like you."

"But it's a friendly thing to say, isn't it?"

"And she'll see straight through you. She won't trust this phony Mom for a minute."

Damn. Roz had a point. "What if I bring her a birthday present?" Alice suggested, as she dug her index finger into the custard in the center of her Boston cream doughnut, the sole part worth eating. "But I don't know what she might like. I don't know who she is."

"You can try to put yourself in her shoes."

What sort of shoes was Esme wearing these days? Sandals, no doubt, for summer, but would she go for the sturdy Teva type or a quirky Dr. Scholl's? Or something leather and sleek?

"She's caught between her parents," Roz was saying. "Juggling Dan's control-freakness and—well, no offense, but you know, her memories of your criticisms? Think about how that might be affecting her."

Of course, they weren't speaking about Esme's actual shoes.

"I suppose she's relieved that she's finally finished with school," Alice said slowly. "And excited that she and Bobby are embarking on a new life 'up north.' Wherever that is. At the same time, she could also be a little scared?"

"Sure."

"She doesn't have a steady job. I don't know if she has any friends in the 'up north' place they're moving to. And Dan's probably making her feel like a failure, for not getting an MBA."

"She might still do bulimia binges on occasion. It's not so easy to cure by snapping your fingers."

"Damn, you're right. Plus there's the trial! It could be starting now. Tomorrow. Or it could already be over, and I missed it on the court calendar. Roz, it's too much for her!"

Roz sighed. "And on top of all that, she's about to be talking to her mother for the first time in six years. The same way you're feeling."

Was Esme, too, worrying about their upcoming meeting? What was she picturing? A mother who always pushed her, who never thought she was smart enough. Who focused on Esme's grades, instead of Esme the person. Who asked: *Why aren't you trying harder in history class?*

When she should have been asking: *What would make history class more interesting for you? How would you run the class if you were the teacher?* A mother and father who both pushed her, in their own ways.

But Esme was the one in control. Wasn't she? She was the one who'd rejected Alice.

"So how do I begin?" Alice demanded. "What does she want to hear most of all from me? That's the most important sentence of the whole hour!"

A trickle of milky coffee sloshed over the lip of Roz's cup, as she set it on its saucer. "You could say something about Bobby."

"Such as?"

"Something you especially liked about him, when you met him?"

Sure, what daughter wouldn't be glad that her mother liked her boyfriend? "I could tell Esme I really enjoyed riding on his motorcycle with him. Which is true, in fact."

"Perfect!"

Tell Esme I loved riding on the motorcycle with Bobby, Alice wrote on a fresh page of her notepad. "Or what if I start with the beach? It's a positive sign, isn't it, that she wants to meet me on the beach? She knows I love the beach."

"That works, too."

Alice used her free hand to wipe each of her cheeks, although her gym sweat had long ago dried off.

Tell Esme thank you for choosing the beach as our meeting-place. Ask if she remembers digging fishing pools in the sand.

"I can't do this." Alice shoved the pen aside, though not too hard, so it wouldn't roll off the table. It hit the heavy glass saltshaker. "What if I say the wrong thing and she clams up? What if she only agreed to see me in order to dump on me? Or she just repeats more of Dan's BS, the way she's been doing all her life, and I lose it and get mad at her? What if Dan comes with her?"

"He won't. I mean, I don't think he will."

"What if she's only doing this because Bobby is pressuring her, and she's worried he'll break up with her if she doesn't?"

"Sweetie," Roz said, leaning forward, "please don't invent all these horrible scenarios that make you feel worse."

"What if she doesn't come?"

"She will."

"Why did I keep insisting on this meeting? I wish I could send her a letter instead. If I did a letter, I could revise it a hundred times over and over, until I got it right. Maybe I can cancel our date."

"Do you honestly want to cancel seeing Esme?"

"I don't know! I mean, I don't want to cancel, I want to see her, but I also don't want to see her!" Alice banged Roz's pen on the Formica. "I'm not fighting with you, Roz. I'm fighting with myself, because this is too important and I don't want to blow it. I want to understand why she had bulimia and what's happening with her trial and if I can dare offer to help. I want to know where she and Bobby are moving to and what she hopes for in her life. Who she is. Why she shut me out. Why she agreed to see me now. Whether she misses me. If she'll see me again."

"And whether she loves you?"

Alice shut her eyes. Yes. That question, too. "I suppose," she said, with her eyes curtained, "if I'm really going to face all the facts, I should talk to Dan."

"What?"

When Alice opened her eyes, Roz had removed her tortoise shell-framed glasses and was staring at her, as if a statement that absurd could be understood only with lousy eyesight.

"I mean," Alice added, "if there's anything factually in Esme's life that I ought to be aware of before I see her. I don't mean some kind of kiss-and-make-up with Dan, hell no! But this conversation with Esme is too important for me to screw up. Is there something in addition to the arrest? Has she been arrested before? Does she still have bulimia? What has Dan been telling her about me? There could be more stuff happening with her! I need to know these things before I see her, and there's no one else who can tell me. So I should be a big girl and ask him."

"Sweetie. Don't go overboard on being Pollyanna, okay? That's my job." Roz restored her eyeglasses to their place on her nose. "We'll work on the script for seeing Esme. You have a few more days."

"You'll help me?"

"You know I will."

"Maybe it's not so bad having a friend who's a social worker with rose-colored glasses who has faith in me." Now it was Alice who was smiling.

Taking the knife from her place setting, Roz sawed off a corner of the remainder of her doughnut. "I know there are no guarantees, about Esme welcoming you."

Alice wiped her fingers on a thin paper napkin.

"I thought, all these years, as things got worse with Esme and Dan," Roz continued, staring at her knife as she cut off more doughnut pieces, leaving them on her plate, "that the best way I could help was to be an optimistic friend that you could lean on. You're always bringing yourself down, so I thought you needed more encouragement in the other direction. It wasn't naive optimism, Alice. It wasn't rose-colored glasses. I never told you anything I thought was way out in left field. Just a little push toward the rosy side. That was what I figured. But why should you or I trust anything I said? Look at how I blinded myself to what was going on with Jenny and the drugs in high school, and what a horrible influence I was, always obsessing about my diets. And even tonight, pretending that I'll come back to this gym class another time, let alone lose thirty pounds. I'll never do any of that. I couldn't last two minutes at the lowest speed on that elliptical thing. Every muscle in my legs and arms is screaming at me."

"Don't give up on the class!" Alice reached for Roz's wrist. "I mean, of course, give up if you want, don't force yourself to do something that makes you miserable. But don't give up on yourself, Roz."

"I should get a new pair of glasses and drop the rose-colored ones."

"No." With both hands, Alice nudged Roz's eyeglasses a touch higher on her nose. "I love the Roz I've always known. The one who brews gallons of herbal tea when her daughter has morning sickness and buys every sleeper-pajama set in Bloomingdale's. The one who's so proud of her husband that she hangs all of his oil paintings in the living room. Please keep helping me see the world more optimistically."

"Are you sure?"

"Someone has to be the optimist. Someone has to balance me out."

Lifting her cup two-handed, Roz finally smiled again.

A lingering dub of custard was buried inside Alice's doughnut, and she dug it out. "Lousy doughnut. I should go to Courtney's bakery and get her good stuff."

"Do me a favor. Please don't bring me a treat. It's all too delicious and too fattening."

"Okay, I won't."

"But you could buy a muffin for Esme."

"As a birthday present? That could be nice. But I won't have a chance to get to Milpitas before I see her."

"For your next time."

Next time?

•   •   •   •   •

A letter sat in Alice's mailbox. More accurately, a heavy notecard in a matching, cream-colored envelope, with Georgia Wilson's name and address engraved on the flap.

You're Esme's mother, and you have as much right to know as Dan does. He hasn't given me many details, but apparently, Esme was arrested along with a boyfriend on some minor, silly theft charge a few months ago. She's not in jail now. I gather that Dan paid her bail fine, or whatever the term is. I don't know if the legal process is ongoing or if that's all been settled. I will keep you informed if I learn anything further.

CHAPTER THIRTY-TWO

ALICE, DAN, AND ESME

June 2008
Santa Barbara, CA

Dozens of rows of blue chairs were set out in four big sections on the UC Santa Barbara Faculty Club lawn, which sloped down to the meandering, dark-green campus lagoon. People streamed onto the grass from the road that curved around the lagoon and from another road to the side of the lawn, around a small copse of trees and past a large white tent. Mothers, fathers, brothers, sisters, grandparents, friends, boyfriends, girlfriends. They hugged and laughed. Kids chased other kids, and parents called out to kids. They waved. Babies cried. They made a mad painting of colors, vivid dresses and multi-hued skirts and pastel shirts and hair of every shade, the people that the about-to-be-graduates of the College of Humanities and Arts of the University of California at Santa Barbara loved best of all in the world.

Dan would be in the mob, with Penelope and their son and daughter. Was his black hair going gray yet?

Esme, sequestered with the other cap-and-gowned seniors, could have sighted Dan and Penelope and given them a wave.

Or not. In that shifting, rustling crowd, and with the hubbub of frantically waving relatives, Esme wouldn't be able to distinguish Dan and Penelope. Or Alice. Or if she did? Surely today, of all days, Esme would be so happy, so relieved, so busy hugging, so caught up in the excitement, that she would forget that she hated her mother.

What's your plan? Sneak into her graduation and not tell her? James had asked.

Yes, exactly! Today was Alice's last chance, the one and only time in the past four years that she could be close-to-confident about where to find her daughter. No need to wheedle college records-office clerks or tiptoe around sorority windows. She would, finally, see Esme. She would make up for missing Esme's high school graduation. That was all. There didn't have to be a teary-eyed reunion, though that would be nice, maybe, on such a joyful day. . . Or just to shake hands. "I'm proud of you, Esme." And the university made it so easy, no ticket required to attend. What mother wouldn't do the same thing? James didn't understand, as usual.

"Pomp and Circumstance" burst through the shouts and laughter. Lines of black robes immediately began step-marching down the three center aisles, and the lawn rocked with applause.

A set of parents with a teenage boy sat on Alice's right, in the last row of the audience, as a middle-aged couple sidled in from the left, smelling faintly of bananas. "Chrissy made plans for us all to have lunch afterwards with her roommate and her family," the mother said to the father and the boy, who was texting on his phone. The hundreds of black robes moved toward the front of the lawn, halting abruptly before reaching the lectern to pivot around and into a series of empty rows that had been roped off. They were too far away to distinguish any details as they marched. Tall, short, fat, thin, brown, white. Hair flopping to the shoulders. Cropped hair. They swayed slightly, flowers in a breeze, in rhythm with the steady, endless loop of the music: *DAH, dah de dah DAH DAH. DAH, dah de dah DAH.*

Esme was there. In a black robe, medium height, with wild brown hair, somewhere in those rows of black. The official program listed the names of all the Humanities and Arts graduating seniors, in alphabetical order, and Esme's name was on page forty. The program didn't reveal much else. It didn't mention each student's major, and it cited only a few honors, the departmental awards, the summa cum laudes and magna cum laudes. None of which were alongside Esme's name. Still, it was solid written evidence. Esme Wilson existed, and she must have studied and worked hard, even while also finding time to volunteer for her sorority's beach cleanup. After all those years getting Cs on her report cards and worried that she'd fail a history test in high school. she'd found the strength to push herself onward. She was graduating from the University of California at Santa Barbara in June 2008.

Two women and two men clambered through Alice's aisle, almost tripping over her Jimmy Choos and banging her knees.

The Grand Marshall officially opened the ceremony. Everyone sang "The Star-Spangled Banner." The university chancellor spoke. Graduation was a beginning, not an end, which indeed was why it was called "commencement." After the chancellor came the dean of the college, the student speaker, and the guest speaker, an alumnus who'd made big money in investment banking. The world was open to these graduates, literally, as they sat here on the shore of the mighty Pacific, they could aim westward toward Asia or eastward toward—chuckle— Wall Street.

"Chrissy suggested a Mexican place downtown," the mother next to Alice told her husband and son.

Presentation of candidates for baccalaureate degrees. Major by major. Student by student. They stepped up to the chancellor, they shook his hand, then they shook the dean's hand, then another person's hand, and finally they received their diplomas.

Art. Could Esme be an art major? She'd loved making the pottery bowls and the beaded necklaces with Jenny. Perhaps she was heading to Italy with her friend Caroline to design clothing, as she'd envisioned during their lunch at the Madonna Inn.

A girl about Esme's height, but with satin-straight blond hair, got an art diploma. An Asian girl. A boy with a ponytail like James used to have. Whistles. Applause.

Dance? Esme had once said that cheerleading was similar to dancing, and she'd spent all those years as a cheerleader at Calabasas High School with Courtney Michaels.

English?

Environmental Studies? Never! That would be copying Alice's career. But Esme seemed so happy in the photo of the beach cleanup at El Capitan, with her sorority friends.

Japanese? Linguistics?

A very tall boy with a monstrous beard and mustache. A heavy girl; Esme wouldn't have put on so much weight, would she?

Hundreds of names, one black robe after another. They didn't seem to be arranged in alphabetical order or even height order, so it was impossible to predict who was coming when, or whether Alice had missed her one chance. Esme could march right by Alice's row, never turn to look at her, and disappear forever. A short black gown. A tall black gown. A hijab. A huge Afro. Lots of beards. John Doe. Jane Smith. Jane Gomez. John Chang. George Washington. Esme Wilson.

Was it?

Was that really the name they read out?

Long brown hair sliding shoulder-length below a black mortarboard.

Half of the girls in black gowns had long brown hair sliding shoulder-length below a black mortarboard.

The next student was already shaking the chancellor's hand.

Mathematics. Medieval Studies.

Applause.

"You go, Zack!"

The almost-noon sun coated Alice's shoulders in heat.

Was Esme's moment gone already?

"There he is!" screamed the middle-aged woman next to Alice, grabbing her husband. "Do you see him? Joey!"

The names all sounded the same. Emma Nelson. Esther Winston. Ismail Nelson. Ellen Wilson. Or not.

Too tall. Too short. Male. Male. Asian. Blond frizzy. A black robe shook hands with a man also in a robe, and moved aside, and another black robe took its place.

Philosophy. Religious Studies.

Whistles. Applause.

Esme could have cut her hair. Or dyed it, or permed it, or straightened it. She could be any of the bodies in a black robe.

It was too late. The dean hereby presented the Class of 2008. Wild cheering. The graduates rose and flipped the tassels of their caps. A few mortarboards flew limply into the air. The graduates pivoted toward the aisles, the recessional music blared, and all at once the littlest children were zig-zagging around the chairs toward the black gowns, and the rest of the audience was elbowing their way forward, too, Joey's parents from the seats next to Alice, Chrissy's family, hugging their graduates, laughing, crying, clicking cameras, and somewhere among all that joy Esme was hugging Dan and Penelope and Graydon and Hadley. Waving her diploma. Giggling for groupings of photos. They would give her a huge bouquet, as big as a window. She would set her mortarboard on each kid's head—no, they were too old for that. More likely, she would embarrass Graydon by hugging him, and she would tease him, "Your turn, soon." "You looked beautiful up there," Penelope would say.

No one else, besides Alice, was running in the opposite direction, stumbling in her usually reliable stilettos, away from the celebrating graduates and toward the parking lot.

CHAPTER THIRTY-THREE

"James," she said.

He wasn't smiling. Not rubbing her shoulder or squeezing her hand, the way he would have done less than two weeks earlier. But he was there, as she'd asked, standing at the bike path atop the Palisades Park cliffs, overlooking the Arizona Boulevard walkway to the beach where Alice would, supposedly, be meeting Esme in just four more days.

His dark jeans looked new. So was the gray-blond stubble around his jaw and upper lip.

She sat down on a bench alongside the hard dirt path, but James didn't. "We've been friends for a long time," she continued. She had to tilt her neck and head to see his face. "And I know I haven't been enough of a friend. Always dismissing your worries as midlife crises. Flirting so stupidly, pretending I didn't what I was really doing."

"Half the blame for that's on me," he mumbled.

"I've screwed up with Roz, too. I kept accusing her of seeing things through rose-colored glasses, when she was trying to help. But I truly do appreciate both of you. Being there for me, all these years. I do. I will."

He nodded, as he drummed a short trill on a nearby tree trunk.

"I'll get better about it," she added. She couldn't keep straining her head, but the only other option was to stare at his stomach.

"You'll get better with practice?" he asked. "Like playing guitar?"

Was he offering a joke? An ice-breaker?

He'd finally sat, though he perched as far away as the bench would let him and faced the horizon, not her.

On the sand a few yards from the walkway staircase, a group of four lithe people in bathing suits was keeping a long volleyball rally going with bursts of shouting. The gray-green waves were sluggish as they rolled onto the shore. High above Alice and James, seagulls squawked hoarsely, like flying Dylans.

"We've been friends since we were fifteen." If only Alice could crawl her fingers across the green slats toward James, the way she used to do without thinking twice. Well, those days were over. All she could do was spew out words. "That means a lot to me. That's more important than whether or not you can understand exactly what it's like when my own daughter isn't in my life. Or how scared—"

"Would you the fuck stop saying that?"

"Sure, you know, I don't expect someone who hasn't—"

"No!"

Damn, he was loud. A brown-and-white dog raced in front of their bench. Had its owner heard James's shout? "Shoo!" Alice flapped her hand toward the dog, though it was already gone.

James was gripping his thighs, through his new jeans. "Yes, I do."

"You do what?"

"Understand."

"No, you don't."

"Yes. I do."

"What do you mean? When did your daughter run away from you?"

"She died," James said.

"What? You never had a daughter."

"And he died. And they died. And it died." James enunciated each phrase carefully and tonelessly, pausing between each one. "Andrea had four miscarriages."

"When…?"

"So we tried IVF. With donor eggs. Twice." He scratched the bench slat next to his thigh. "Those failed, too. We investigated adoption, but

Andrea was forty-three and I was forty-six, and we were way the fuck too old for most agencies. We'd have to do it privately. Probably international. Which costs a fortune. And after the IVFs, and neither of us earning all that much, me at my crappy newspaper and she was only an adjunct, we didn't have the money."

It was amazing how thunderous simple breathing could sound when the air was still. The volleyball players, the seagulls, the brown-and-white dog, the cars steadily rushing along Pacific Coast Highway, and the smell of salt water, were all far away.

Her mouth opened. Her eyes were blinking too fast. The only thing to hold onto was her own fingers.

"I'm sorry," she whispered.

Four miscarriages. Two IVFs. Six bouts of morning sickness, maybe. Months of hormones and taking temperature, all the months when Andrea's period was late and they started daring to calculate when the due date might be. Over the course of eleven or twelve years, between when James and Andrea got married, and James turned forty-six. "How far along were the—if I can ask?"

"The longest was the third one. Eleven and a half weeks. We really thought we were going to make it, that try."

"Why didn't you tell me, before now?"

"When?" His voice wasn't angry, merely neutral. "Think about it. Dan was giving you shit, and then Esme left you to go to live with him, and your mother died, and Esme wouldn't talk to you …. You were, uh, kind of preoccupied."

"I would have been there for you."

"Oh?"

She …

James continued, "When Esme went to live with Dan? We'd just had the first IVF failure. Great timing, huh?"

Her fingers were twisting around each other in her lap. Her feet in her old Birkenstock sandals were crossing and uncrossing.

"And when your mother died," he went on, "and Andrea couldn't come to the funeral, and I had to rush away? That was when we were rejected by the second adoption agency."

"Did Roz know?"

"Yeah."

Four miscarriages. Two IVFs. At least two rejected adoption efforts. And James had kept his mouth shut, and he'd stayed with Alice at Florence's house when Florence died, and he'd hugged her after the funeral, and again when Esme ghosted her on Facebook. While his own adoption hopes were dying. But he never cried about his own pain. And Alice all but called him a crybaby for his midlife crises. She cried on him, again and again, and he was always there to hug her.

And he never told her. His supposed close friend since high school. Because she was never there for him.

"So I kinda understand," James said, far more softly than he usually spoke, "what it's like to lose your kid. Though it's not the same, what happened to you, and what Andrea and I went through. I get that."

"Oh James, let's not start comparing pain. We've both lost children, in a way. There's nothing worse than that."

Now it was a pair of bicycles invading their conversation, first a teenager on a black bike who sped along the hard dirt path almost at their toes, then a slower red bike.

Andrea and James had begun reaching out to adoption agencies when James was forty-six, nearly seven years ago. Which meant that in the four or five years before that, even while Andrea suspected that he was sleeping with Alice and cheating on their marriage, she was trying to become pregnant with their child.

James had pushed himself up from the bench. "I gotta get going."

Why would Andrea do that? Why not dump the supposedly cheating husband? Because they loved each other, of course, but that wasn't the entire answer.

Because, in the end, they knew they could count on one another. Like Bobby and Esme. Andrea knew James would break into an art store and risk getting arrested for her, if he had to, and he knew she would do the same for him. If their dreams collapsed, and their pregnancies failed over and over, they would still be there, together.

"Listen," James was saying, "it's nothing personal, but I gotta go. I, uh, I've got a rehearsal."

"What? James!"

"It's just a couple bullshit things," he added quickly. "I ran into Ced, my old drummer, remember him? A few months ago. He's been teaching music at a high school in the Valley, and we decided to get together and jam a little. With a bass player Ced knows."

"So you and Ced are forming a new band?"

"Don't make a big deal of it, okay? We've got a thirtieth wedding anniversary gig. And we're doing a midnight thing at a club in Highland Park in a couple weeks."

"Can I come watch you?"

"You want to?" A half-smile crept across James's lips. "I guess you could come to Highland Park. Don't worry, I'm not a complete idiot. I'm keeping my day job at the *Chronicle*."

"That sounds like a wise idea."

"The club owner's promoting us as playing oldies. Shit. Should we bring canes?"

"Never mind that, James. This is exciting."

"You've always been my biggest fan."

"Because I've always loved your music."

With one Teva-sandaled foot, James stabbed at the faded green grass. "You and Andrea, you've both got me on stage at the Grammys."

"Andrea's good with this?"

"Yeah. She kinda changed her mind. And I was overreacting, too. She says what the hell, it's what I love, so go for it. So what if I never make a penny? Go for them both, journalism and music. I don't need to choose."

"I'm glad, James."

"Yeah. Well, people'll probably be listening to oldies long after newspapers disappear."

"Maybe Andrea and I can go to Highland Park together?"

James let out a brief laugh. "I don't know." He added, "First, Ced and I need more practice, anyway."

Alice stood up, facing him. "About what happened. At my apartment, last time."

"It didn't happen."

"I know we didn't totally—"

"Nothing happened. I wasn't there." James had shoved his hands into the front pockets of his jeans. His smile had fled, and his tongue was circling around his lips.

They both stood, unmoving, staring at each other, while the June sun fell hot and heavy on her shoulders.

"You're right," she said.

James reached out his arm, in handshake position, so Alice extended hers. They shook.

CHAPTER THIRTY-FOUR

ALICE, DAN, AND ESME

January 2009
Santa Monica, CA
NEXT STEPS TO REACH ESME
   (now that she's graduated)

1.   *The alumni office at UC Santa Barbara*
2.   *Does the sorority do any alumni tracking? (What help would that be? Mrs. Hanson would just keep repeating that she couldn't discuss individual girls)*
3.   *Ask Roz to Friend Esme on Facebook? Again*
4.   *Call Courtney Michaels's mother again*
5.   *Check Esme's LinkedIn profile again*

The profile hadn't changed since October, and even that was skimpy. B.A. from UC Santa Barbara. Delta Alpha Mu. A generic sketch of a woman's silhouette, no actual photo. The part-time job at Clothing Etc., the shop that she'd "liked" on her Facebook page, before she shut it from view. It must have been ideal for her, getting paid to keep up with the fashion magazines.

6.   *Hire a detective*

In books, people hired private detectives. Skulking around the shrubbery, finding cheating husbands and missing heiresses. Did they still exist? The Internet probably put that whole industry out of business.

And if one last detective agency had survived, hidden behind a wooden door with a frosted window in the dank hallway of an old office building—and if the detective actually located an address for Esme—what could Alice do with that information? Arrive on Esme's doorstep, unannounced? As if Esme would rush into her arms, after ignoring her letters and phone messages for four years?

•   •   •   •   •

"Easy," promised the first detective Alice called. "You've got her Social Security number and DOB? She graduated from UC Santa Barbara last June? You're pretty sure she's in the U.S., likely California? Piece of cake."

He didn't question why a mother needed to hire a detective to talk to her own daughter. Two hundred dollars.

Within a week, she had an address for an apartment in east Santa Barbara, although the phone number was Dan's landline in Calabasas.

Dear Esme

It's hard to believe that it's been a year and a half since you graduated from college. How does it feel, not to be a student, after 16 years? Or are you still at the books, in grad school? Have you found an interesting job? Maybe you're enjoying a well-deserved break year.

Whatever you're doing, congratulations on your achievements.

Now that so much time has gone by, would you be willing to get together for a cup of coffee? (Or wine? After all, you're over 21 now!) I'd love to see you.

Love, Mom

The letter was back in Alice's mailbox ten days later, with four crisp words neatly written on the envelope in black ink and highlighted in psychedelic yellow: *Refused. Return to sender.* Plus a sunshine-yellow sticker from the post office: *Return to sender. Refused. Unable to forward.*

"You got the wrong address!" Alice yelled over the phone.

The detective said he would double-check, and he would also search again for another phone number. He called her one day later. "It's the correct address and phone. It's what's on every search engine, either that or the house in Calabasas that you said is where your ex lives. Esme N. Wilson. Born June 17, 1986. Her driver's license is Calabasas, for example, but she's registered to vote at that Santa Barbara address. I'll send you all the printouts."

"Well, she could've moved and didn't switch her voter registration."

"Yes. But wouldn't she forward her mail?"

And what if she was in fact living at that address, and she'd seen Alice Wilson's name on the return address, and she didn't want to be found by the sender?

•   •   •   •   •

She was almost fifty-two years old. She was a grown woman. She was Esme's mother. Dan was Esme's father. Normal parents spoke with each other. Even divorced normal parents who hated each other managed to communicate courteously about the basics. Such as: Where is our daughter living? What's her phone number? Does she have a job? Is she happy?

She should stop running around, badgering the sorority housemother, trying to find a four-year-past high school friend's parents, sending emails to random UC Santa Barbara addresses. She should do it already. She'd made Dan into a big bad bogeyman, and it was time to puncture that myth. She would prepare a script. If she followed that, and prevented him from controlling the conversation too much, and kept herself from reacting when he pushed her buttons, then she could focus on the goal of this call: information about Esme. Without begging. She had a right to know at least a few things about her own daughter.

Penelope answered the phone.

Although she put Dan on fairly promptly, the delay had already blown Alice's surprise.

"Hello." It was his too-calm voice.

"Hello, Dan. How are you?"

"I'm fine, thank you. And how are you, Alice?"

"Fine, thank you. How are Penelope, Graydon, and Hadley?"

"Very well, thank you."

So far, all according to Alice's script. Banal pleasantries, setting the stage. Most important, her voice was calm and not squeaky. "I know it's been a while." Small laugh. "But I figured, what the heck, we're grown-ups, and we should be able to talk to each other about our own daughter, don't you agree?"

"Absolutely," Dan said.

"I'm sure we're both very proud of Esme."

"Oh, Penelope and I certainly are."

Fuck him. Who said Penelope had any part in this?

Never mind. Back to the script. "Graduating from Santa Barbara. It's not an easy school."

"No, it's not," Dan said.

"Esme worked very hard."

"Yes, she did."

"Now she's out in the big wide world. Job hunting." Alice paused, but Dan didn't step in. "It's a bad time to be job-hunting, with this economic mess," she added.

"Yes. It's a very tough job market."

So he wasn't going to volunteer information. Therefore Alice would have to ask, but that was fine. It would be the same as any business conversation. "What sorts of jobs is she looking for? Did she find something yet?"

"You should ask her directly."

What did that mean? Would Esme speak to her now? Alice didn't need Dan's permission to talk to her own daughter, only a working phone number or email address.

"Of course," Alice agreed. "I just don't happen to have her current phone number. What, uh, what's her phone number these days?"

"Oh, I can't disclose her personal information without her permission."

"Come on, Dan. Don't be ridiculous."

"I don't think honoring my daughter's wishes is ridiculous."

"Keeping me from talking to her is." Her voice was rising too high. It should be as butter-smooth as his.

"That's up to her."

"Well then, you tell me. Where's she living?"

"Again, I can't disclose—"

"I'm her mother!"

"I'm sure you are," Dan said.

"So I have the right to know." Her voice again. She had to tame it, as if this was a business conversation. "Is she safe? Is she working? Is she happy?"

"You'll have to—"

"What was her major? Does she have a boyfriend?"

Was Dan hesitating? He never hesitated. But there was the barest delay before he answered, in his usual patronizing voice, "You have to calm down, Alice."

"Don't you tell me what to do!"

"If you don't calm down, I'm going to have to hang up."

"When did you last see her?"

"I'm sure she'll contact you if she wants to."

"What kind of bullshit is that?"

"She's an adult. I don't speak for her."

"Then give me her phone number, so she and I can speak directly."

"Again, that's her decision."

"Are you blocking me from my own daughter?"

"She'll make that decision herself if she wants."

"What lies have you been telling her to make her hate me?"

"I'm going to have to hang up if you keep shouting."

But he didn't hang up. Alice was the one who jabbed the End icon and slammed her phone on the kitchen table and screamed.

CHAPTER THIRTY-FIVE

A shiny black BMW swung rapidly into the driveway, braking a few yards before reaching the wide front door of the sprawling, stucco-and-wood house. Seconds later, a short man in a light blue, button-down shirt and khakis was out of the driver's side and striding around the hood of the car.

"Dan!"

Was it? Really? Damn, he was getting old. He had a big bald circle high on the back of his head, and the ridge of curly hair below it had some gray mixed in with the black.

The man stopped. He didn't turn toward Alice's voice.

She moved, only a little wobbly in her good old black Jimmy Choo's that she never wobbled in, a couple of steps toward him from the sidewalk hedge that had hidden her. "Why did you lie?"

No, that wasn't how she'd meant to begin. She was supposed to calmly say: *I realize that it's strange to see me here, but Esme might be in trouble. Isn't it time we talked like grown-ups?* Not that Dan would ever give her a chance to say all those words, but still, maybe the very surprise of seeing Alice would rattle him enough to listen for a few seconds. Or maybe he'd let slip a tidbit of information that might give her a small insight before her meeting with Esme on Tuesday. Anything.

Now he swerved around. He wore steel-rimmed glasses over his blue eyes, and when he spoke, he sounded tired. "Why can't you leave us the fuck alone? You think I'm playing games?"

"You've been playing games with Esme and me since she was born."

He shook his head briefly, as if brushing off an annoying teenager.

Once upon a time she and this man hiked to the Wonderland of Rocks in Joshua Tree National Park, and he arched his neck at the top of a boulder to howl like a coyote, and he picked the spines out of her arm bit by bit when she got pricked by a cactus. Once upon a time this man held out a little velvet box with an engagement ring in the middle of a picnic on the Santa Monica beach. Once upon a time she and this man went to see *Return of the Jedi* with Walt and Roz, and he bought them all light sabers, red for Walt and Roz, blue for her and him—because they were a team, he said. The two of them against the world.

And once upon a time this man said yes, he was willing to be a father. He said he would take their child to Dodgers games and *Star Wars* movies and show the child the dogs in his clinic. What he didn't say was that he'd steal that child away from her.

"Why did she stop talking to me?"

"Lower your voice. I don't care to put on a show for my neighbors, thank you."

Of course the neighbors couldn't hear. Rambling lawns, thick-branched trees, and rich clumps of bushes cloistered the houses on this expensive street in Calabasas, and besides, their windows would be firmly sealed to hold in the central air conditioning. Even the dog probably couldn't hear anything, unless it was dead by now, or wouldn't it be barking to welcome Dan home? More Dan BS. He might be losing his curly hair, but he hadn't changed his personality.

"What were you telling her all those years? Why did you lie about her ballet recital? Why wouldn't she answer my emails or phone messages? Why did you try to steal her away from me? How often do you see her? Do she and Bobby come over to your house a lot?"

"That useless motorcycle bum?" Dan blew out his lower lip. "I bet you like him, don't you? Just your type. Did you know he robbed a store?"

"He didn't rob a store."

"Check the police report."

"He didn't actually take anything."

"Bullshit. The report says 'burglary,' clear as day."

"They only took her own earrings."

"I suppose you'd rather have her hanging out with a criminal instead of getting her MBA, that would be just like you."

"Just because you're paying her legal bills, that doesn't give you the right to keep information from me."

Two long strides of his dark-brown Dockers, and Dan was so close that his nose was almost hitting hers. She jerked backwards as his words kept attacking. "You want to know why she came to live with me in high school? I didn't have to 'steal' her, as you put it. She wanted nothing to do with you. Every weekend and vacation she stayed with me, from the very first, she was always sobbing about the way you treated her. How you nagged her, and you criticized her grades in school, and—"

"All teenage girls—"

"And you never bought her the clothes she needed, and you forced her to take ballet, and you even criticized her for trying to eat healthy."

"You're lying again."

"You refuse to hear the truth."

"No. I know you're lying, because she and I had great times eating all kinds of food together." Dan didn't argue, so Alice added, "Ice cream. Omelets." She waited some more. "Doritos."

In the newly quiet air, a car drove past the house, its engine roaring up the tree-lined street and around a curve, higher into the Santa Monica Mountains. The view of the San Fernando Valley from Dan's windows would be the sort of scene a photographer would put on a picture postcard, especially the panorama at night, with the streetlights and house lights tossed over the landscape far below like little crystals.

The people living in these multi-bedroomed houses would wake up and go to sleep breathing in the constant scent of oranges and roses from their thick gardens.

"Some of it's true," Dan muttered, kicking at the asphalt like a little boy. Then he straightened, and it was as if he'd gotten a hit of adrenaline directly into his spine. "She was happy with me and Penelope. We made a life. A family, which you wouldn't know what it is. Stability. Cooking together. School activities. A better life than you ever gave her. She had a brother and sister and a dog."

The damn dog.

"Why would she want to speak with you," he added, suddenly calm, "when you didn't want her to begin with?"

WHAT?

Smiling now, Dan took a step back and leaned his spine against the BMW, his forearms resting on the hood behind him. "I told her all about it. How the pregnancy was an accident. How you complained that it was so inconvenient, because you had an important project protecting a bunch of birds and forests. How you were planning to get an abortion." He crossed one foot over the other. "Have you forgotten that? You came to my clinic to insist on getting an abortion, and I had to talk you out of it."

There was nothing to hold onto, except the weak leaves at the top of the hedge. "It's a lie," she whispered.

"She certainly could see for herself, how you never had time for her. From the minute we got divorced, you were always leaving her with your mother, so that you could go off on your business trips. Or jaunts with your boyfriends, or whatever your trips really were. You never cooked real meals for her. And you didn't bother to show up for her high school graduation." He shrugged. "I told her the whole story a couple of weeks before the graduation. She was about to turn eighteen, you might remember. She was an adult, and she certainly had a right to know."

The graduation. Their last phone call. Their fight. *You criticize everything I do. You wish I wasn't your daughter.* Sometime between that call and the next time Alice had tried to phone, that was when Dan had done it.

But what about all the messages she'd left for Esme on Dan's answering machine, asking to talk, pleading to talk, asking if Esme still wanted her to come to the graduation? Had Dan erased them before Esme could hear them? And Esme's cellphone that wasn't taking calls anymore, had he blocked Alice's number? He couldn't have. He couldn't be that desperate to—to win? Nobody was that cruel.

Sure, he could. He'd done a trial run once before, with his mother: *Now aren't you glad that you have her? Dan told me how you were reluctant at first.*

Stupid her, she'd thought she'd figured out what Dan was up to when he constantly badmouthed her to Esme. And she'd recognized that it was hopeless to try to fight back on his terms. How could she refute his criticisms if she didn't know what he was saying? If Daddy told Esme that Mommy had been aware all along that he'd bought circus tickets for the same day as her ballet recital, and Mommy never said that wasn't true because Mommy didn't realize he was saying it, of course Esme would believe Daddy. By the time Mommy learned, it was too late. Daddy's message had sunk in.

Still, even knowing all that, she'd believed that if she was a good mother, if she showed interest in Esme's fashion magazines and respected her desire for organic food and mostly let Esme have enough "space," that eventually Esme would recognize that her mother wasn't as horrible as her father described. If she acted like a normal mother. If he acted like a halfway-normal father.

She'd misjudged Dan as badly as she'd misjudged Roz and James and Bobby and Esme herself. Whatever she never could have imagined that he would do, he would.

A phone rang faintly from the direction of Dan's house.

"You're the one"—Alice's voice croaked—"who didn't want a baby."

He pushed himself off from the car hood. Any second, he would start walking to his house, and once he reached the door, he could lock her out.

Oh no, he wasn't getting away that easily.

"You had Thanksgivings and summers and birthdays with her all those years, after you lied to her and stole her from me," she shouted, stepping closer. "You hugged her when she graduated. Twice! High school and college. You got to take pictures of her in her cap and gown. You're the first one who rode in a car when she drove, as soon as she got her license. You met her sorority sisters; did she show you the beach where they did their cleanup? Did you help her move into the dorm, or the sorority, wherever she lived in college? You celebrated Mother's Day with her, didn't you? You and Penelope."

Still standing by the car, Dan folded his arms over the front of his blue shirt, blue like his stupid eyes. Silent.

"Tell me! All the things I missed. What color was her prom gown? What was her roommate's name at Santa Barbara? What was her major?"

Dan unfolded and refolded his arms.

"Is she still having bulimia? Is she seeing a doctor about it? Is there going to be a trial for the break-in?" Alice ought to be quiet and give Dan a chance to answer. But she had so many questions to ask.

"Lower your—"

"Does she have a job? Are she and Bobby—"

"I don't fucking know!"

"Don't know what?"

Dan's voice began speeding, as if he were a sports car racing down the freeway. "She stopped speaking to us about six months after she took up with that motorcycle idiot and I told her to break it off with him if she wanted to keep getting her nice fat checks from me. She didn't invite us to her college graduation. She blocked us on Facebook. We haven't had any Mother's Days or Father's Days in three years. Yeah, same as you, I called her, I left messages, week after week, until she changed the damn cell number. I emailed. Fuck you. We wouldn't have known about her arrest except that her driver's license had this address, and she needed money for bail, but she sneaked away after one night here and I don't know any more than you do about where she's been living since then or what's happening with her case, and no, I haven't been paying her legal fees." Dan slapped the hood, and the ping of the metal reverberated in the quiet driveway. "She hates me, too. Are you satisfied now?"

For some reason, he was still standing by the BMW, breathing heavily, instead of walking away.

"Back in high school, she already started fucking off, and I kept my mouth shut," he went on. "All her football games, her cheerleading every Friday night. Fine. Her little 'planning committee' for every school dance. Fine. I was the supportive dad she could count on. We cooked family dinners together, healthy dinners, with organic food. I bought her a car. I took her to visit all the colleges she was considering, even if she had no chance in hell, fine, she wanted to apply to Berkeley, to Santa Cruz, to Pomona, I backed her up, as long as she kept to the goal we discussed, college, grad school, career. I wrote the checks for the application fees. I paid the tuition, even if you wouldn't pay the fair share you should. I didn't criticize her like you did. I never asked her where she was going, when she went out on the weekends."

Alice's breath stopped somewhere between her lungs and her mouth. Esme wouldn't have told her father about the way Alice had followed her and Courtney to the Santa Monica pier the weekend when they'd visited. Or she might have.

"Then she zooms off to Santa Barbara and meets that biker and flushes everything I told her down the toilet. Making earrings, for Chrissake. Threatening to drop out of school." Dan spat onto the driveway.

Since when did Dan Wilson do anything as unsanitary and demeaning as deliberately spit in public?

He was looking at his tasseled loafers, not at Alice. The wide front door of his house opened.

"I only wrote to you about her arrest," Dan snapped, "because Penelope said I should."

"Dad!" a voice yelled from the gaping doorway. An angry teenage boy's voice.

Dan swiveled in an abrupt half-circle, toward the door and away from Alice.

"I told you," the teenager shouted across the distance. "You have to sign my permission slip for lacrosse. The tryouts are at five, and I'm going to be fucking late because of you!"

From the back, it could have been a different man. The fringe of graying-black hair below the bald circle, the shirt loose against the torso. Dan's body had gotten skinny with age. Perhaps he no longer had the muscles to slam a freezer door in Alice's face, or to carry a daughter horseback on his shoulders. Anyway, that daughter wouldn't answer his phone calls now or let him see her happy photos on Facebook, no more than she'd let Alice into her life. They were both, equally, parents without a daughter.

"DAD!"

"Well," Alice said loudly to Dan's skinny back, "it looks like you've got your hands full."

"I'll sign right away." Without glancing around at Alice, Dan strode toward the doorway, to his other family.

Chapter Thirty-Six

She was walking slowly along the busy highway edge of the beach toward the concrete staircase where Alice waited, as instructed: *at the bottom of the pedestrian bridge from Arizona Boulevard. At the staircase.*

Her hands were shoved into the front pockets of a set of denim cutoffs, her head bent down. Her hair, tumbling around her cheeks and shoulders, was as brown and wavy as always. Her bare arms might have been slightly tanned. In addition to the cutoffs, she wore Roman-strapped sandals and a dark blue T-shirt that didn't look tie-dyed in Bobby's style; it had a horizontal blotch of a picture or design instead, too far away to see the details. A big, lumpy leather bag hung off her right shoulder. She seemed thin but not too skinny, not like Jenny when she'd been anorexic, just typical twenty-four-year-old thin. She could have been the young woman in the Facebook photos of Esme, picking her way in the uneven sand toward a picnic.

It was truly Esme?

She hadn't sent a substitute, to tell Alice that she wouldn't be coming after all?

Pockets of beachgoers flowed past, hauling their towels, their huge canvas carryalls, their kids, their folding chairs, and their reek of sunscreen. People whistled for dogs or called out to stragglers. Occasional seagulls cawed overhead. From an iPod or a radio came metallic singing. Waves hit the shore with languid regularity, and the sky, even at six o'clock, was soft blue and beaming with sunlight.

The maybe-Esme was only a few yards away. She finally raised her head.

A closer view: Her eyebrows were still thick, her face still heart-shaped. Her pale lips were clamped together. Her shoulders were thrust a little backwards, with her elbows bent out at the sides as her hands remained locked in the pockets of her shorts. The horizontal blotch on her shirt was a series of parallel lines in different shades of blue, with a sketch of a dolphin leaping in front of a sunset and the words "Santa Barbara, CA" in delicate script. Flashes of turquoise and gold darted through her waves of hair.

And what was Esme seeing as she stared at Alice? A middle-aged woman with short, wind-tossed, mouse-brown hair and a weak smile. Khaki slacks that came to mid-calf, canvas espadrilles, a pale-green T-shirt with a cluster of flowers painted in the top left corner. Did she look frumpy? Striving too hard to appear cool? Was her anxiety written all over her face? Did she look like a mother?

Esme was almost near enough, that if Alice took a step forward and reached out her hand…What if Esme jerked away?

You have to give her space, Roz said.

When would Esme stop needing space?

"Hi." A breath emerged, along with Alice's hoarse voice.

"Hi." Esme's voice was matter-of-fact. A little lower, surprisingly, than it had been in high school.

You look great.

Happy belated birthday.

What's the picture on your T-shirt?

Alice said, "Thanks for, um, meeting me here. Today."

"Sure." Esme switched her bag to her left shoulder.

If Alice reached out, and stroked Esme's hair, would it feel soft? Rough? Would it smell of apricot shampoo?

"The earrings you're wearing. Did you make them?"

Esme's hand jerked up to her right ear. A smile darted across her mouth like a wink. "Yeah."

"Can I see them?"

After an instant's pause, Esme unfastened something from the ear she'd just touched and held it out toward Alice. It was a chandelier earring with a string of three teardrop-shaped sterling-silver wires, the teardrops growing progressively bigger. Inside each teardrop dangled a bead of a different color, blazing yellow, then cobalt, then Kelly green.

"It's beautiful." Alice reached out her index finger.

"Thanks."

"How did you make it?"

"Well, I buy the beads. And then, so, the beads come with two holes next to each other, okay? So I thread wire through those holes and twist the ends together, to make a little hook. Then I attach the hook to the top of the teardrop."

"And you attach all the teardrops to each other?"

"Yeah."

The earring sat in Esme's upturned palm. Alice tapped the three beads, one by one, smooth and cool, with her finger, and Esme didn't shut her hand. "Do you go to a studio to make your jewelry?" *Like the studio where you took the pottery class with Jenny, when you were six years old and you lived with me?*

"Just at home. That's why my stuff is mostly wire and beads. Because I only need basic tools for that."

"What else might you do, that would be more elaborate?"

A shrug. "I'm learning how to cut out shapes from these really thin sheets of silver. You need a special jeweler's saw."

"Where do you get your ideas?"

"Different ways." Esme refastened the earring onto her earlobe. "If I see an interesting flower or something. Or a song. Different things."

"Bobby told me you sell them. Online."

"I try."

"You know I met him? He took me for a ride, on his motorcycle." Esme nodded.

"It was fun, though I have to admit I was a little scared. Especially going around corners, I almost thought we were going to fall over. I mean, I knew Bobby wouldn't actually lose control and let the motorcycle fall, but it was, well, as I said. A little scary, how the bike tilted so close to the ground." Alice pulled air into her lungs.

"Yeah. I was scared at first, too."

"Not anymore?"

"I'm used to it."

"Mainly I had a great time," Alice added. "It was like flying."

Esme laughed, and for an instant her dimple split her cheek, the way it used to happen when little-girl Esme smiled. The blueish skin below her dark brown eyes crinkled. "It is like flying, yeah. That's why Bobby and I love it."

A clatter of voices passed behind Alice, moving in the direction of the staircase to the pedestrian bridge. Something scraped on the sand, maybe a kid's boogie board. Engine noises from the highway were growing stronger and more frequent.

"Do you want to sit down," Alice asked, "while we talk? Or get coffee?"

Simultaneously, they both swiveled their necks, toward the beach still dotted with a few people and the tumbling ocean stretching westward, then toward the noisy road and the jutting-edged cliffs eastward. They could sink onto the sand where they stood, or move somewhat so they didn't block the staircase. They could perch on the low curb that barely separated the sidewalk from the rushing highway. They could climb the shit-stinking concrete stairs, cross over the highway, and head up the brick staircase on the cliffs, to the benches along Ocean Avenue. Neither of them took a step in any direction.

Would it break the spell if they moved—the very, very beginning of a spell that had briefly summoned Esme's dimple and let Alice touch an earring in her hand?

But how much longer could they stand in their spot, balancing on lumpy sand, dodging crowds?

"Maybe we could…" Alice inched one foot forward. "Should we get out of people's way?"

Esme started walking, her feet alternately sinking and lifting in the soft sand.

So that was acceptable, Alice's suggestion to move elsewhere. With two rocky steps, she caught up to Esme.

Not far ahead, an abandoned volleyball net sagged between a pair of poles. Esme flopped onto a spot beside one of the poles, facing the water and folding her arms on her thighs. Alice eased down a few inches away. Underneath her, the sand was like a waterbed, firm beneath one part of her butt, a gap next to that. She and Esme weren't touching, but they could, without a lot of effort. If they wanted. So close by, Esme sent out a bare scent of sunscreen and…cinnamon? Why cinnamon? From a doughnut? Or a latte? If she'd switched to drinking lattes instead of black coffee.

A boy was chasing a small white dog along the final trickle of Pacific Ocean that dribbled onto the wet beach.

Did that remind Esme of Dan's puppy? Not a puppy by now, of course.

What was the most important question to ask Esme? What was a safe question to ask?

"You and Bobby are planning to move up north?"

Esme opened her mouth, shut it, and opened it a second time as she spoke. "Bobby told you that?"

"Yes."

Scraping her right foot forward and back, Esme dug a shallow trench in the sand. "He got a job at a friend's motorcycle shop, and you know, I can make jewelry anywhere."

"Do you like it there?"

"I do, actually. It's pretty, you know? Different from any place I've ever lived. No loud traffic, no tall buildings. Zillions of kinds of trees. Maybe the beautiful scenery will inspire me."

"Sure. Nature is an inspiration for a lot of artists."

"We're hoping to move there in the fall. If we can."

"Where up north are you moving to?"

Esme shook her head.

Her hair flopped around her face and neck.

The waves lapped quietly. The beachgoers' noises were far away, over at the highway. The boy and the dog were long gone.

"Didn't you save a whole stretch of old trees, years ago?" Esme asked abruptly. "Near Mendocino? Or Arcata?"

"Yes. Near Arcata, in Humboldt County."

"Because of the endangered owls?"

"You remember all those details about my job? You were pretty little."

"Sure. Little kids, cute little animals and birds, you know."

"Yeah."

"What big project are you working on these days?"

Esme truly wanted to hear about her life?

But what answer could Alice give? *I screwed up and lost an important client.* "I'm hoping to persuade a super-wealthy family to hire us to invest their money in more environmental and socially conscious ways. I think the younger generation is supportive, but they need to persuade their old fogey parents."

"Like, investing in companies that make solar panels?"

"Yes. Exactly."

Though the sky was blue, the sun had inched noticeably downward. Twenty minutes could have passed since Alice and Esme had met at the staircase, or maybe fifteen, or even thirty. Thirty? Half of her allowed hour? A few figures remained in the graying water, probably surfers half-bent atop their boards.

Why did you stop speaking to me after high school?

No, no, no! Not yet. What was a safer but not insignificant topic, if Alice had less than half an hour remaining? "Roz mentioned that you called her? Six months ago."

Releasing a long hiss of air from her nose, Esme looked at her sandals.

"It's okay that you called her," Alice added quickly. "I'm glad you did. Roz was glad to hear from you." Damn. From Esme's point of view, it must seem as if Alice had been running around interrogating anyone who'd ever spoken with Esme in the past six years and was now parroting gossip from Bobby, from Roz.

"I don't know if you knew," Esme finally said. Mumbled. "I had bulimia when I was in college. Sometimes I still—The clinic at school was pretty useless. So I thought it might help to talk to someone who's been through it, and the only person I could think of who had any kind of eating disorder was Jenny. Roz's daughter."

"You're still having —?"

"I'm fine."

For a set of long breaths, Alice Veed her hands around her mouth and nose.

Well, bulimia was better than drugs, wasn't it?

Dropping her hands to her thighs, Alice smiled at Esme. "Did you get to talk with Jenny?"

"A couple of times."

"You know she's having a baby?"

"Yeah. I'm glad for her. She seems really happy."

A hint of salty wind blew in from the Pacific, sprinkling sand on Alice's neck. *Why did you stop speaking to me after high school?* When was the right moment to ask? How could she sneak a look at her phone to see what time it was?

"I've been wanting to apologize," Alice said. "About Grandma Florence's funeral. I pushed you. I'm sorry."

Esme shook her head again. "I was a dumb teenager."

"You were worried about your history test. I understand."

"Actually, there wasn't a test."

"There wasn't?"

Esme was staring straight ahead, at the horizon. Her fingers had begun kneading the skin above her elbows. A few dark grains of sand were stuck to her cheek, like the grains on Alice's neck. "I didn't want to see Grandma dead. In a box."

Then … their big fight? Esme hanging up on her? Alice missing her graduation? And the silent years since?

"But I also was honestly close to getting a D in history," Esme added. "I honestly was worried."

"I see."

"I really hauled butt, you know? To pull up my grades and graduate. I dropped out of the planning committee for school events. I studied every weekend."

Alice shut her eyes. She dug her fingernails into her knotted palms. "That's—very loving of you. To feel so bad about Grandma. But why didn't you tell me the truth? About not going to the funeral?"

"I don't know. You just made me feel dumb. So I thought you'd rather hear that I was studying." Esme hunched her shoulders, huddling into a C over her lap.

This thin young woman with the mass of brown hair covering her face, folding into her own body—this person who had pushed Alice away, cut her off, lied to her, hurt her, maybe hated her—this was Alice's daughter. Who had never felt smart enough to satisfy her own mother. Whose father told her that her boyfriend wasn't good enough. Who was now facing the possibility of a jail sentence for burglary and trespass. Who had been so miserable a few short years ago that she'd wracked her body with bulimia that she was still apparently not cured of. If Alice and Dan were parents without a daughter, Esme was a daughter without parents.

Yet, for all her struggles, this young woman had built a strong, loving relationship with a good young man who clearly cared about her. She'd been willing to stand up against her father, in defense of that relationship. And if she'd never been a star in school, this young woman had a talent and passion for creating beautiful jewelry that had already attracted customers.

She loved flying on Bobby's motorcycle. She loved the zillions of trees "up north," wherever "up north" was. Maybe she still loved organic crackers.

Whether they ever spoke again or not, this magical person was Alice's daughter.

Very lightly, Alice set her fingertips on Esme's nearest shoulder.

The shoulder twitched.

The T-shirt was rough, and the shoulder was bony beneath it.

"I've missed you," Alice said, as gently as her fingers had landed on Esme. "It's been a long time."

Esme sprang up and began striding, or stumbling, more or less toward the water.

The sun must have been sinking faster, because the air was suddenly splattered with chills that clawed through Alice's T-shirt. She stood, waited another beat, then hurried after Esme until they were more or less aligned, and they picked their way wordlessly up and down the ruts and bumps in the sand toward the shoreline, keeping a foot apart. Esme's arms swung by her sides, while Alice stumbled occasionally, one arm or another extended for balance. The ocean dribbled closer.

"Why did you agree to see me now?" Alice asked.

Esme continued walking.

"I'm glad you did," Alice added.

"It was Bobby's idea."

"Oh. That was very nice of him."

"He said you were a good person." Esme shrugged. "His mom died when he was a kid, so he's kind of sentimental about mothers. He said that you deserve a second chance. That you and I deserve a second chance." They'd arrived at the beginning of the wetter sand, where the wavelets darted forward erratically, and Esme swerved back to the drier sand, so that she was now going roughly parallel to the water.

"Thank you," Alice said.

"And he appreciated that you were honest."

"Honest?"

Esme let out a breath. "You said we were stupid to try to get my earrings the way we did." Another breath. "And you were right."

Alice had to look straight ahead, copying what Esme was doing.

"So, I was arrested, which is why Bobby and I can't move away from Santa Barbara for a while—And I'm not going to talk about that." Before Alice could agree or argue, Esme went on. "I just want to explain about Dad getting me out of jail, so you don't start getting all—whatever. When the cops who arrested us asked us who to contact, they had Dad's address because I was a jerk, I never bothered to change my driver's license, you know, most college kids do the same thing, they keep their parents' address on their license. So when the cops asked, I wasn't going to call him. But Bobby told me I should take advantage of Dad being a quote 'responsible adult' who had stable local ties, who could vouch for me, all that BS, and get myself released on Dad's money or his O.R., whichever. That the important thing was both of us shouldn't be rotting in a jail cell. That if Dad got me freed, I could get together the money to bail out Bobby. So that's what I did. I got out, and I went straight back to Santa Barbara. Bobby has a cousin there, and his friend at the garage where he worked, and I asked the manager of the store where I used to work, and from everyone plus our savings, which wasn't much, but with all of that I pulled together enough money. And I bailed Bobby out. And that's all I'm going to say about Dad."

They could have been the last people left on the beach. The sole noises were the ever-stronger splash of the waves, the muted whistle of the cold wind, and the coarse cries of seagulls.

"What your dad said to you in high school," Alice began, "that I didn't want—"

"I'm not going to talk about any of it. I told you, I don't want to get involved in your fights with Dad."

"Please, Esme. I need you to know this. Just this one thing, even if we never speak to each other again. Please hear me. I always wanted you, Esme. I always wanted a baby."

At least Esme didn't run away. She continued walking at the same speed, pacing the slapping waves, a foot or so from Alice's left side.

"I think I knew that all the time," Esme finally said.

Alice nodded. She needed to pull up words.

"You wouldn't have kept pestering me with letters if you didn't." In profile, there might have been a little smile on Esme's face, though it was hard to be sure because it wasn't the side with the dimple. "I have to go," she said.

An hour couldn't have passed already! The sky was still bluish-white. No sunset streaks of yellow or orange hovered anywhere along the horizon.

"Can I see you again?" So what if Alice was begging, if her voice was too desperate. They were out of time.

"I don't know."

"Or text you? The first Sunday of each month? I'll put it on my to-do list."

Now a faint smile had definitely flashed across Esme's face, although she didn't answer.

"Is there any way I can help you? With the legal fees, for instance?"

"We're okay. Bobby's dad is helping."

"Those lawyers. The charges can really shoot up. I could send you guys some money, to take part of the load off Bobby's dad. If that would help?"

"No."

"Oh."

"The lawyer is pretty sure we can plea-bargain," Esme continued. "You know, first offense. And that I was only taking my own property. So it could be all settled soon. But we'd probably be on a kind of probation."

The ocean splashed. A voice called, from not too far down the beach. Cars whooshed on the highway. The air rustled, and salt hit Alice's lips.

"If you want to text Bobby," Esme mumbled. "Sometimes. That would be nice."

"Sure."

Esme was scrabbling inside her lumpy pocketbook with one hand. When her hand emerged, it was holding a plastic sandwich bag that in turn held a small packet, enclosed in white tissue paper. "I made this for you." Esme's fingers were wrapping around Alice's hand, the packet was inside Alice's palm, and then Esme was running clumsily through the sand, toward the highway.

"Wait! Esme! What is this?"

For a second, Esme turned her head. She gave a little wave of her hand.

Alice started to run, too. But she stumbled in her espadrilles after just a few steps. Her ankle buckled. A dull pain shot up her calf. The sand dipped, the little plastic package almost slid out of her hand, she grabbed it, she had to wipe her eyes, and Esme was a far-away dot of blue and brown, racing toward the concrete staircase to the bridge over the highway.

The package was lightweight, with sharp edges. The tissue paper had been wrapped three times around it. Inside was a pair of long earrings, each one made of a thin, flat piece of silver cut in the shape of a little fir tree.

ACKNOWLEDGEMENTS

I've been working on this book off and on since 2016 (also writing and publishing two other novels during that time). It's taken the help and patience of so many friends, strangers, family members, acquaintances, and experts: People who've given advice about bakery operations, jewelry-making, police procedures in Southern California, parental alienation, Parkinson's disease, bridge tournaments, veterinary training and practice, child development, car "personalities," expensive shoes, Facebook quirks, life in a rock band, Joshua Tree National Park. Fellow writers in workshops, developmental editors, and friends who offered to read bits and pieces. People I barely knew, who bravely shared their own painful stories of being cut off from their children. My family, who put up with the emotions this story has summoned.

I can only begin to name some of you, in alphabetical order:

Jerry Aylward, Amy Baker, Julia Ballerini, Claire Berger, Susan Breen, Robert Calem, Elaine Cobb, Ellen Alexander Conley, Elizabeth Crowens, David Freedland, Susan Friedman, Karen Gamer, Sophie Gamer, Rachel Gertzog, Richelle Gist, Sharon Goldzweig, Judy Graeff, Linda Gunsberg, Masha Hamilton, Jamie Holloway, Joan Kloth-Zanard, Cheryl Krauss, Pam Laskin, Carolyn Levin, Lilja Lundquist, Sandra Newman, Cynthia Payne, Linda Peckel, Norma Rollins, Theresa Seabaugh, Alexandra Shelley, Len Silverman, Nechi Sirota, Kate Spota, Will Suarez, Ted Thompson, Jessie Vanamee, Murray Weiss, Kate Wheeler, Joyce Yaeger.

And special thanks to Reagan Rothe and the staff at Black Rose Writing, for your faith in this book.

I thank and cherish all of you.

About the Author

As an award-winning nonfiction author, journalist, and fiction writer, Fran has traveled from Switzerland to Washington DC, from Maine to California, investigating the pharmaceutical industry, hanging out in high school classrooms, and exploring second-generation Holocaust guilt (among other topics). When she's not seeking the right words, Fran runs seven miles a day, volunteers at a 200-year-old New York history museum, studies French and Hebrew, and helps clear trash at her local park.

In her research for *Her Daughter*, Fran drove through the winding mountain roads of a national forest while dictating scenic descriptions into her tape recorder—finally speeding back downhill to catch the last flight out of Arcata-Eureka Airport. (See Chapter Seventeen)

OTHER BOOKS BY FRAN HAWTHORNE

FICTION

I Meant to Tell You

The Heirs

NONFICTION

Ethical Chic

The Overloaded Liberal

Pension Dumping

Inside the FDA

The Merck Druggernaut

NOTE FROM FRAN HAWTHORNE

Word-of-mouth is crucial for any author to succeed. If you enjoyed *Her Daughter*, please leave a review online—anywhere you are able. Even if it's just a sentence or two. It would make all the difference and would be very much appreciated.

Thanks!
Fran Hawthorne

We hope you enjoyed reading this title from:

www.blackrosewriting.com

Subscribe to our mailing list – *The Rosevine* – and receive **FREE** books, daily
deals, and stay current with news about
upcoming releases and our hottest authors.
Scan the QR code below to sign up.

Already a subscriber? Please accept a sincere thank you for being a fan of
Black Rose Writing authors.

View other Black Rose Writing titles at
www.blackrosewriting.com/books and use promo code
PRINT to receive a **20% discount** when purchasing.

9 781685 136994